ChangelingPress.com

Dagger/Steel Duet

Harley Wylde

Dagger/Steel Duet
Harley Wylde

All rights reserved.
Copyright ©2021 Harley Wylde

ISBN: 9798590174300

Publisher:
Changeling Press LLC
315 N. Centre St.
Martinsburg, WV 25404
ChangelingPress.com

Printed in the U.S.A.

Editor: Crystal Esau
Cover Artist: Bryan Keller

The individual stories in this anthology have been previously released in E-Book format.

No part of this publication may be reproduced or shared by any electronic or mechanical means, including but not limited to reprinting, photocopying, or digital reproduction, without prior written permission from Changeling Press LLC.

This book contains sexually explicit scenes and adult language which some may find offensive and which is not appropriate for a young audience. Changeling Press books are for sale to adults, only, as defined by the laws of the country in which you made your purchase.

Table of Contents

Dagger (Devil's Fury MC 4) 4
   Chapter One 5
   Chapter Two 16
   Chapter Three 33
   Chapter Four 44
   Chapter Five 55
   Chapter Six 68
   Chapter Seven 81
   Chapter Eight 94
   Chapter Nine 108
   Chapter Ten 122
   Chapter Eleven 134
   Chapter Twelve 144
   Chapter Thirteen 157
   Epilogue 172
Steel (Devil's Fury MC 5) 179
   Prologue 180
   Chapter One 187
   Chapter Two 197
   Chapter Three 215
   Chapter Four 225
   Chapter Five 237
   Chapter Six 253
   Chapter Seven 264
   Chapter Eight 275
   Chapter Nine 287
   Chapter Ten 297
   Chapter Eleven 307
   Chapter Twelve 319
   Chapter Thirteen 329
   Epilogue 339
Harley Wylde 346
Changeling Press E-Books 347

Dagger (Devil's Fury MC 4)
Harley Wylde

Zoe -- I would give my life to protect my son, and it nearly ripped my heart out when I learned the person I'd trusted had turned on us. Luis is in trouble, held captive by the cartel, and there's only one way I know to save him. Marry Dagger. He's an outlaw, a biker, and hasn't made it a secret that I'm not his first choice. But Dagger and Jared have shown me what it means to love someone, and I only hope they'll have enough love for me and Luis as well.

Dagger -- Being bisexual in a club full of alpha bikers means walking a fine line. The only way I could ever have an acceptable relationship with another man is if there's a woman between us. I didn't count on that woman being a sexy señorita with a little boy. It doesn't take long for Zoe and Luis to wrap me around their fingers, and I can tell Jared is falling for them too. I have the family I've always wanted, and I'll do anything to keep them safe. Even wage war with the Mexican cartel if that's what it takes.

Jared -- The Devil's Fury are my family, the only place I've felt like I had a home. That's the only thing holding me back from telling Dagger how I really feel. When I find out he's married, it never occurres to me he'd want to share Zoe, or that the three of us could be together permanently. But first we have to get Luis, her son, back, and end the threat that could take our family from us.

Chapter One

Dagger

I couldn't believe the Pres had actually done it. He'd asked Shella to leave, even if it was temporary. He'd sent her to the Devil's Boneyard to visit her half-sister, but I'd seen how loaded her car was when she drove out of here. The anger in her eyes had been a clear indication she wasn't coming back anytime soon. If ever. I'd had my eye on her since she turned eighteen, even though I mostly wanted to put her over my knee and spank her every time she acted up.

It was bullshit. There was no reason she couldn't stay here, even though we'd recently had a bunch of women dropped at our doorstep. So what if some of them were moving into the Pres' house? If Shella didn't want to stay there, she'd had other options. I'd have gladly taken her into my house. And into my bed. I knew she wasn't as innocent as most thought, but I didn't think she'd gone all the way yet either. The thought of taking her innocence, making her mine, had heated the blood in my veins.

I punched the wall in my kitchen, pissed that I'd had no control over whether she stayed or left, all because I'd never manned up and claimed her. The Pres hadn't balked when Badger paired off with Adalia, or when Dragon kept Lilian. What was the difference in me keeping Shella? Besides the age difference. There were a lot more years between me and Shella than the others and their ol' ladies. Didn't matter to me, but I knew it would to others.

A hand gripped the back of my neck and squeezed. "Easy, Dagger. You put holes in all the walls and you'll either have to buy a shit ton of pictures to hang, or you'll be patching drywall for the next week."

I looked over my shoulder at Jared, a Prospect who'd become more to me. I didn't flaunt the fact I was bisexual in front of the club, but what we did behind closed doors was no one's business but our own. He was younger than me, but he'd seen too much of the ugliness in the world and it had aged him. I sighed and tried to release the tension in my body. Being pissed over Shella leaving, when I hadn't flat out said I wanted her to stay, wasn't going to solve anything.

Jared gripped my beard and pulled me down, pressing his lips to mine. I let him have his way, kissing him back. I knew he cared, and I had feelings for him too, even though we'd never put a label on what we had. It wasn't like I'd moved him into my house, even if he did come over nearly every night. We weren't exclusive, or out in the open about our relationship. I still put in my appearance at the clubhouse, and I enjoyed the club pussy as much as anyone else there, but I knew having only a woman in my bed night after night would never keep me satisfied, or happy.

Jared released me and grinned. "See? Now that you're calmer, let's discuss this Shella issue. Yeah, she was hot. And I know you got off on the idea of taming her sassy mouth, but how pissed are you because she got away and how much is because you really wanted forever with her?"

I knew he was right. Didn't like it. I shook my head and leaned back against the kitchen counter. Reaching for him, I pulled him closer. Jared wrapped his arms around my waist, our lower bodies pressed together, as he assessed me.

"I'm right, aren't I?" he asked. "We both wouldn't have minded having her between us, or under, whichever, but I know she wasn't the woman who was going to be with you forever. You know it too on some level. She didn't have the right temperament."

"Yeah, yeah," I muttered.

"Look. We have fun. We've even had some fun with the club whores, apart and together. I know damn well the club will never accept the two of us as a couple on a permanent basis. Not out in the open at any rate. Other clubs might not care, but Devil's Fury? Can you imagine the look on Demon's face if you tried to claim me as property?"

I snorted, knowing he wasn't wrong. My brothers might turn a blind eye for the moment, but if I wanted a forever that included another man and only another man, there could be problems. Only way it could work is if there were a woman between us, and even then it might be dicey on them accepting the relationship.

"I say we enjoy this for however long it can last. You're happy, right? Or happy-ish?"

"Of course, I'm happy," I said. "I hate having to hide that we're together, but I wouldn't give up my time with you."

Jared kissed me again, his hand tightening on my shirt as his tongue thrust between my lips. I worked his tee loose from his jeans and slipped my fingers underneath, feeling the heat of his skin and needing more contact. Breaking the kiss, I tugged on the belt in his jeans. "Clothes off," I said.

He glanced around. "In the kitchen? Dagger... you have two windows in here and neither of them have anything covering them. Kissing you was risky enough. Anyone could walk past and see us."

I gripped his shirt and yanked it over his head before removing my own. Placing my hand against his back, I pulled him tight against me. "If the fuckers around here have nothing better to do than peep in my windows, then they get what they get. I'll deal with the fallout. Now, are you going to get naked?"

Jared shook his head and tried to pull back, but I wasn't going to budge on this. I put my hand on his shoulder and pushed him to his knees, before I started unfastening my belt. I saw his chest rise and fall rapidly and his eyes grew darker as he watched me unzip my jeans and pull out my cock. Yeah, he might fight me on this, but I knew he wanted me every bit as much as I wanted him. "Open."

He started to part his lips, then shook his head.

"No? Do you remember what happens when you disobey?" His eyes slid shut and a shiver raked him. I gripped his hair and pulled his head back, painting his lips with my pre-cum. I dropped my voice so that it was harsher, darker. "Open your fucking mouth, Jared. You know damn well you want to. Gonna fuck your throat until you gag, then do it some more. You want my cock. My cum. Want me to bend you over and fuck you. Ride your ass until you're begging me to come."

"Jesus, Dagger," he muttered. His gaze focused on mine and I saw the heat and longing. "You fucking know I want you, but I can't get tossed out of here. If one of the officers sees me…"

I sighed, knowing he was right. I started to put my dick away, but he placed his hand over mine, and slowly leaned forward to lick the length of my shaft before swirling his tongue around the head. I groaned and rocked my hips forward. The heat of his mouth closed over me, then I felt his tongue lash the underside of my cock as he swallowed me, taking every fucking inch.

I ran my fingers through his hair, savoring the moment. I knew what it cost him to give in, to show

how much he needed this. I fucked his mouth with slow, deep strokes. He sucked me so hard his cheeks hollowed and it damn near made me come. I tightened my hold on him and fucked his mouth harder, driving deep until I emptied my balls, coming down his throat.

Jared licked me clean, then looked up at me with a smirk on his lips. I jerked him to his feet and crashed my mouth against his, kissing him so hard I knew our lips would be bruised. Fuck but he drove me mad. Even now, my dick twitched and wanted more, wanting to be buried in his ass, giving him a proper fucking. And I knew he'd scream and beg for more. He liked it rough, pleasure with a mix of pain.

I pulled back and traced his lower lip with my thumb. If things were different, I could easily love him. We'd been playing this game for months now, without anyone the wiser, as far as I knew. We were careful, really fucking careful, when we were around the club. If anyone noticed him hanging out at my house a lot, they kept their mouths shut. If anyone speculated we were more than just friends or brothers, they hadn't said anything or come right out and asked.

Jared glanced toward the bay window that faced the front yard and his body stiffened. I heard his inhalation and I looked to see what had him so freaked. One of the little Mexican ladies was outside, staring straight into my kitchen. I couldn't read her expression from here, but I knew I needed to do some damage control, and quick. I zipped up and went outside to see if she was going to be a problem.

When I stepped out onto the front stoop, she jerked like she'd been shot, but she didn't run. I couldn't remember her name, or even her fucking age. For all I knew this was one of the teens, but I sure the fuck hoped not since my dick was pulsing behind my zipper, and it wasn't the aftereffects of Jared's mouth. Little señorita had curves in all the right places, and then some. More than a handful. Fucking perfection.

"Why are you in my yard?" I asked. I knew my tone was harsh when she flinched, but I didn't do soft. Not for anyone. She stared at the ground at her feet, refusing to look at me. Fuck. The sunlight filtered through her dress making the damn thing transparent and I got even harder. I was a sick fucking bastard. "I asked you a question."

I felt a hand on my shoulder and the heat of Jared's body against my back. "You're scaring her, Dagger. Ease up."

"When I ask a question, I expect a fucking answer," I said. "Disrespectful little shits get their asses paddled."

I heard her gasp and noticed she still wouldn't look up, but there was a flush spreading across her chest and up what I could see of her neck. Interesting. I stepped off the stoop and moved closer to her. She tensed, but didn't run. Her fingers clenched on the skirt of her dress, fisting the material. It only served to pull it tighter across her body, accenting her curves. She was tiny, barely reaching my chest, but damn, was the woman stacked. Ass and tits for days, and a slightly rounded belly I'd be willing to bet was soft as hell. She had the perfect hips for holding onto during a good, hard fuck.

"Why are you here?" I asked again. "And fucking look at me when I'm talking to you."

She lifted her gaze. Her skin was sun-kissed, and her eyes were a brilliant blue. The blonde of her hair hung in thick heavy waves down her back, and I knew from previous sightings of the sexy señorita that it went all the way to her ass. When people thought of

Mexican señoritas, they thought of dark hair and eyes, but this little honey didn't fit the typical stereotype. I saw her lower lip tremble and hoped like fuck she wasn't about to start crying. I hated it when women cried. Manipulative little bitches. They might have been dropped on our doorstep for safekeeping, but I wasn't about to let her blab about what she'd seen.

That was it. I was done with this shit. I stepped closer, grabbed her waist, and threw her over my shoulder before turning to carry her into the house. It didn't escape my notice her nice, round ass was right by my face. Perfect range for taking a bite. She didn't squirm or fight. Just hung there, accepting her fate. Made me wonder if I did paddle her ass, would she let me? Even like it?

I carried her inside, with Jared trailing after me. I heard him shut the front door. A sane man might have dumped her ass on the couch, or in a kitchen chair. But I was a crazy bastard. I carried her down the hall to my room, tossed her onto the bed and before she could escape, I clicked one of the handcuffs on my headboard around her wrist. Her eyes went wide as she looked at it, then glanced at me.

"Dagger, what the hell are you doing?" Jared asked. "Grizzly is going to have your ass for this, and not in a fun way."

The woman looked from me to Jared and back.

"Let's try this again. Why the fuck were you standing in my yard, watching us through my window?"

She shifted on the bed. "I saw you."

"I fucking know that. Peeping Thomasina."

"No, not just now. I meant..." Her cheeks warmed. "I know we aren't allowed near the clubhouse, but I was curious about the music. I thought if I stayed in the shadows at the back, maybe I wouldn't get caught but I could still listen."

The back of the clubhouse. I shot a glance over to Jared and knew he was thinking the same thing I was. Last night, we'd gone back there in the dark, where we'd thought no one was watching. I'd kissed the hell out of him, and we'd ended up jerking each other off. Still, even if she'd seen us last night, it didn't explain why she was here today. Unless she'd planned to blackmail me?

"What do you want?" I asked.

"To stay here," she said, glancing at both of us. "You like each other so I'd be safe here. You wouldn't try to touch me. Even when you picked me up, I knew you wouldn't force yourself on me, even if you did bring me to your bedroom."

I snorted and shook my head. I waved a hand at my crotch where my dick was still hard. "Honey, this isn't all because of him. Seeing you out there with the light shining through your dress got me hard as fuck."

"We like men and women," Jared said.

She looked completely crestfallen as her shoulders slumped and her chin dropped to her chest. "Oh. I'm sorry. I didn't know."

Something wasn't adding up. Why was it so important to her that we not like women? She'd said she'd be safe. What had happened to make her feel like she *wasn't* safe at the compound?

I hunkered down in front of her, gripping her chin and forcing her to hold my gaze. What I saw pissed me off. *Fear.* Someone had terrified the shit out of her and I wanted a damn name. Even worse, now that she knew I wasn't gay, she seemed afraid of me too. "Who tried to touch you?"

"I don't know. It was dark and I couldn't see

their name on their…" She waved a hand at my chest. Even though I wasn't wearing my cut I knew what she meant. "They were drunk, I think. But I got scared."

I stroked her cheek with my fingers, noting how soft she was. I didn't like that someone had frightened her, bad enough she came here thinking I was gay and wouldn't touch her. I wanted to know who the fuck had gone after her. Everyone knew we were supposed to give these ladies a wide berth for now. Grizzly hadn't decided what to do with them yet. The chunk of cash Ramirez had given the club meant they were here for the long haul, but we didn't exactly have a good setup for a lot of single women, unless they were spreading their legs.

"How did you get away from him?" Jared asked. "Or did he stop when you said no?"

She paled and dropped her gaze, pulling free of my grasp. I looked over my shoulder at Jared and knew what he was thinking. Reaching for her, I ran my hands down her sides, then up the insides of her legs. She didn't push me away, but I felt her shaking. I didn't feel a weapon.

"Were you armed then and not now?" I asked.

Her gaze jerked to mine again. "What? No! I just… I kneed him between the legs when he didn't want to let go. He kept telling me I'd like it and trying to pull up my dress. I didn't like his attention."

The way her cheeks burned it was almost as if… *Whoa.* I stood so fast I got dizzy, and took a few steps back. Was she a fucking virgin? I knew Griz said the women had worked in a sweatshop and not a brothel, but I'd figured there were guards of some sort sampling them on the side. Just thinking she was untouched both excited and fucking terrified me. I'd never been with an innocent before. The thought of being the first to touch her made my cock swell behind my zipper.

I couldn't be here. Not right now. I tried to shake it off as I headed out of the bedroom, leaving her with Jared. He wouldn't hurt her. Hell, he'd probably set her free and escort her back to the apartment where she was staying. Sweet thing like her had no business being around a guy like me. It was like offering a pure soul to the Devil.

I braced my hands on the kitchen counter, staring out the window over the sink. I didn't think she'd tell anyone about what she'd seen, either time. Even if she did, I couldn't imagine trying to scare her into keeping her mouth shut, not after hearing one of my brothers had already tried to hurt her. I couldn't think of a single one who would force themselves on a woman, but if she was right and he'd been drunk, then he might honestly have thought she was playing hard to get. Might have even mistaken her for a club whore if he was sloshed enough.

Still, we needed to make sure those women stayed far the fuck away from the clubhouse once the sun went down. It wasn't safe. I also didn't trust the bitches who came here to spread their legs. If they caught wind of women living here, unclaimed ones, they'd raise hell and cause trouble. Just like that bitch Cheri had done with Dragon and Lilian. Demon had made an example of her, but we had some fresh blood coming through the doors these days.

Might be time for a refresher on what happened if you fucked with someone, or any of the women under our protection. Wouldn't matter that we were only offering those ladies a safe place to stay, the whores wouldn't see it that way and would feel threatened or jealous.

Sometimes I had to wonder if things wouldn't be simpler if I did just like men.

Chapter Two

Zoe

"Did I say something wrong?" I asked the other man after Dagger fled the room.

He smirked. "No. He doesn't trust himself around a virgin. Guy like Dagger? You dangled forbidden fruit in front of him. He knows he's too rough and hard for someone like you, but thinking of being your first? Yeah, it's going to fuck with his head for a while. I'm Jared."

"Zoe," I said. Damn it. I wasn't a virgin, but if I told them, would it make me fair game for anyone here?

His gaze caressed me, paying close attention to my hair. I sighed, knowing he wondered why I had blonde hair and blue eyes if I was from Mexico. A lot of people didn't know my people weren't all dark haired and dark eyed. It had been offensive at first, but now I was just tired of trying to explain why I looked different from what they expected. "Zoe Lopez," I said. "Yes, I'm really Mexican."

"I should get the keys to those cuffs and get you out of here."

I eyed the cuff on my wrist and followed it to the headboard. "Why does he have these on his bed?"

Jared coughed and his cheeks turned a little pink. "Uh, yeah. So I'm just going to find the keys and you can be on your way. Start praying he doesn't remember you're cuffed to his bed."

I eyed the cuffs again. I'd read books, watched movies. I just hadn't realized people actually did things like tie up their partners. Why would they want to? I didn't understand even a little. I yanked at the cuff. I might not be a virgin, but I was still innocent when it came to men. My first, and only, time hadn't been with my consent. The result of that incident was why I'd escaped Mexico and taken this opportunity.

Jared rummaged in the bedside table, then stood with his hands on his hips. "So, there's no key in here, which means Dagger must have it. I need to go get it. Promise I'll be right back."

He ran from the room. I'd really thought they were together. Twice now I'd seen them kissing and doing other things. My cheeks warmed as I recalled the way Jared had taken Dagger's cock. No, the way Dagger had forced him to take it. I'd seen the look of pure bliss on Jared's face. Did he really like it when Dagger took control?

I eyed the cuffs again. Did Dagger shackle Jared to the bed and do other things? It was clear they liked each other, trusted one another. At nineteen, I knew I had plenty of time to find someone like that, a man who would love me, care for me, give me pleasure and passion. But I didn't think I'd find it anytime soon, and if I hadn't managed to get away from that guy last night, I'd have lost my faith in men completely. Being violated once was bad enough, but twice? Did these guys see women as fair game if they were unattached?

It wasn't Jared who returned, but Dagger, with the key in his hand. He knelt next to the bed and unlocked the cuffs. His hands were gentle as he rubbed my wrist, a stark contrast with the large man who had been so demanding earlier.

"I want a name," he said, his tone gruff. "I don't believe for a second you don't know who grabbed you."

I shook my head. There was no way I was telling him anything. If I did and the guy got angry, things would be much worse. I'd not seen his name, but I did see something. A title. He held a position of rank here, and I wasn't about to rat out someone in a position of power. He could hurt me, make my life hell, or worse... toss me out of here. I didn't have a penny to my name or a way to provide for myself. I'd end up on the street.

"Little girl, I can't protect you if I don't know who tried to go too far."

"I'm not a child," I said, lifting my chin.

A smile flirted along his lips, but he stifled it. "Not a kid, huh? You're what? All of eighteen?"

"Nineteen," I mumbled. He didn't have to poke fun at me just because I was young.

He did smile that time, a quick lifting of his lips on one corner. He reached out, took my chin between his fingers and held my gaze. "Still can't protect you if I don't know who it's from."

"It doesn't matter. You're not gay and I can't stay here."

Jared appeared in the doorway behind him. "Dagger, why don't you let her stay at least through dinner?"

Neither of them had hurt me, or tried to touch me inappropriately. Even if they weren't gay, I still felt safe with Jared and Dagger. Being here even a little while was better than returning to the apartment I shared with one of the other women. It wasn't that any of them were cruel, but they weren't my friends either.

"I'm grilling steaks," Dagger said. "We have plenty if you'd like to stay."

"Stay here with both of you?" I asked, wanting to clarify Jared would be here too. Dagger on his own was a force I wasn't ready to tackle.

He nodded. "Yeah, it's movie night. Every Wednesday we grill out and binge-watch a few movies. Unless the club has something going on."

I wanted to. More than anything, but I'd looked forward to staying in for the night. Hiding in my room wasn't much fun, but I didn't like being around a lot of people. At night, I could pretend I was at least going to sleep and avoid everyone. I'd been eager to change into the only comfortable thing I owned, a pajama set. It was the one purchase I'd permitted myself when we got here. The other women had bought new clothes, shoes, and other things they wanted with the money Grizzly had given us. Even though they'd been trying to buy a way for their families to come here, none of them had something as precious as I did back in Mexico. Every cent I got needed to go back home, if I could manage it. I'd asked one of the men wearing a leather vest with *Prospect* on it to help me mail the package.

"Sugar, why are you wearing this rag when I know damn well our Pres gave you cash to buy new stuff?" Dagger asked.

I stiffened, dropping my gaze and releasing the hem of my dress. I hadn't even realized I was toying with it as I'd thought about wanting to change. "I needed the money for something else."

"Who do you have back home? You were working in that hellhole to bring someone here. You got a boyfriend back home? Fiancé?"

I shook my head. Not even close. "Nothing like that."

"Then who?" Dagger asked.

"My… little brother," I said. "I'm all he has left. He's staying with a friend, and I send money back to help pay for his clothes and food. If I don't, they might throw him out. He's only three."

Please believe me. If they called my bluff and I had

to tell them Luis was my son, I didn't know what would happen. Right now, they believed I'd never been with a man. I wanted to trust them, but part of me held back, regardless of how safe they made me feel. They were still strangers, and I'd learned the hard way never to trust a man.

"Brother." Dagger's gaze held mine. "Your brother who is sixteen years younger than you? How many other siblings do you have? Why are you only taking care of one?"

I hadn't thought my lie through very well, but I'd hoped he'd take my answer and leave me be. It didn't seem that was going to happen. Jared moved in closer and I felt pinned in by the two of them. Oddly, it didn't scare me, but there was a flutter in my stomach I couldn't label.

"Angel, I'm pretty sure we all know he's not your brother. So, who is he to you?" Jared asked.

I twisted my hands in my lap, wishing I could get up and make a run for it, but it wasn't like I could go far. What would they do if I told the truth? Would Dagger cuff me to the bed again? Or worse, would he tell Grizzly? The older man seemed nice, but I didn't know what his plans were for me and the others. Just because he seemed like a good guy didn't mean anything.

Dagger gripped my hair and forced me to focus on him. "Who's the boy, *princesa*?"

"*Mi hijo*."

"Was that so difficult?" His gaze held mine. "So, not a virgin, but probably close to it. If your boy is three, you were only sixteen when he was born. Was it your choice?"

I licked my lips. "Are you asking if it was my choice to have him, or my choice to get pregnant in the first place?"

"He's asking if you were raped," Jared said softly.

"*Sí.*" It had brought shame on my parents when I'd become pregnant, and they hadn't cared how it happened. I'd been tossed from the house. It had been hard to keep a roof over my head and food in my belly, even harder to take care of my son after he'd been born. Luis had been two months old when the opportunity presented itself to come to this country and earn passage for my son. Except no amount of work I did ever seemed to earn his passage.

"Who has him?" Dagger asked.

"A woman I met while I was pregnant. She has a family of her own, but agreed to keep Luis for me if I sent money to cover his expenses. I didn't get much cash before coming here, but I sent her what I had."

"Tell me who she is and where she is," Dagger said. "I'm getting your boy here one way or another. No more money goes to that bitch. You never should have been forced to leave your kid behind."

"Dagger, how the fuck are you going to…" Jared clamped his lips shut at a glare from the man in front of me. "Right. So, this is Devil's Fury Dagger and not the man who had his cock in my mouth. I'm just the lowly Prospect right now. I get it."

Jared stormed off and I heard a door slam. Had he left me here? Alone with Dagger? I clutched at the bedding on either side of me and fought the urge to bolt from the room. Dagger pulled a phone from his pocket and made a call.

"I need papers for…" I told him my name. "Zoe Lopez, and her son Luis. I also need someone to bring the kid here," he said. "Somewhere in Mexico. I'll get more details and send them over." I didn't hear what was said on the other end of the call, but it made Dagger scowl. "What the fuck does that mean? Outlaw, if you can't handle it, get Wire to do it."

He growled at whatever was said next, then ended the call. His gaze locked on mine and the fury I saw was enough to make me put more space between us. I didn't know what the other person had said, but it wasn't good. I trembled as I scooted farther across the bed. He reached out and grabbed my ankle, but he didn't hurt me, or try to yank me back toward him. Just held on. "I can get your boy here, but you won't like how it's done," he said.

With men, it generally meant one thing. They always seemed to want something in return. The previous deal I'd made had been to sew clothing. I knew a man like Dagger wouldn't have use of that skill, nor would his club. "Would I have to whore myself out?" I asked.

He gave a dark chuckle, making my hair stand up. "Only to me."

My heart slammed against my ribs. "What? I don't understand."

"Outlaw said making you and your boy legal citizens is not as easy as it seems. I know other clubs must have handled this shit before, but he's refusing to reach out to anyone. The only way he'll make you and your son legal citizens is if you're my wife. How the fuck is that red tape any easier to get through? I honestly think he's fucking with me."

"*La esposa?*"

He nodded. "I know he has to be full of shit. He can damn well work his magic without us getting married. If he can't, Wire can do it. There's no way Saint's woman was a legit citizen before he claimed her, or without some illegal help. Maybe I should call someone else. Ever since Outlaw took a woman, he's been different. Softer."

"If he doesn't need us to actually be married, then why ask?"

"Because he knows if you're mine I'll stop at nothing to keep you safe. And same goes for your son." He sighed and ran a hand through his hair. I'd noticed he did that when he seemed agitated. "If that's what you want, I'll do it, but it won't be in name only. There are men out there who wouldn't give a shit they had a spouse at home, but I'm not one of them. If I'm married to you, I won't be fucking around with the girls at the clubhouse."

Not the girls, but with Dagger, there were other options. Even if he didn't partake in what was freely given by the women who came to party, what about the men? One in particular came to mind. "What about Jared?" I asked.

He shook his head, released me, and stood up. "I'll end it. You're not that kind of woman."

What did that mean? Did he think I wouldn't let him be with Jared? It wasn't conventional by any means, but maybe we could be together in name only and he could keep his relationship with the other man. Except he'd said he wasn't gay and liked women too. Would he want to have both of us? Was that what he'd meant by his comment? I wasn't sure how I felt about it, especially since I didn't know if Jared would only be with Dagger or would be with other people. I didn't want to risk him giving something to the two of us.

"I wouldn't care if you wanted to keep seeing Jared, but if you're going to be with me too, would he be offended if you used condoms?" I asked. "Just for safety reasons."

He tipped his head back and stared at the ceiling,

muttering under his breath. "*Princesa*, that's not what I meant. The kind of relationship I want, the kind I need, means I'd have you both. In my bed. At the same fucking time. It wouldn't just be me and him, or me and you. It would be the three of us."

"The three of us." I still didn't know what he meant. How would something like that even work?

"We'd both fuck you, *princesa*. And each other. When we went to bed at night, you'd be between the two of us. I can tell by the innocence in your eyes, that's not for you. The only experience you have with men is your rapist, and it doesn't count because it wasn't sex. It was an act of violence."

Could I be with two men? I'd thought that sort of thing only happened in books, movies, or maybe at wild parties. But as an everyday thing? I had a hard time imagining myself with a man as large and... *alpha* as Dagger. Add Jared to the mix, and I didn't think I could handle it. Although, the other man seemed more laid back and sweet. They seemed to be opposites, which is probably what made their relationship work. Jared softened Dagger's hard edges, and Dagger... I didn't know what he did for Jared, other than apparently give him pleasure.

"Tell me what you want me to do," he said, his voice lower but far from gentle. I didn't think he *had* a tender side, despite the way he'd rubbed my wrist earlier.

"You'd give up Jared, or your chance to have the type of relationship you want, just to bring my son here?" I asked.

"Boy doesn't need to be with strangers. He should be with his *madre*."

I studied Dagger, noting his tanned skin and dark hair. His eyes were a warm chocolate. Ink covered what I could see of his skin from neck to waist, including a rosary and the Virgin Mary. I'd seen those types of tattoos back home. Then he had others I didn't recognize. He sounded American, but he wasn't as white as Jared. I wondered about his heritage. The way he spoke...

"You toss in Spanish words as if it's no effort on your part," I said.

He rubbed the back of his neck. "My mother was half Hispanic and half white. My grandmother immigrated here from Mexico City when she was young, and fell in love with my grandfather. She taught me a little. My dad was Samoan, and some of my ink is in honor of his family heritage."

I wanted to say yes, to bring Luis here, but I wasn't sure I could handle belonging to Dagger. He moved closer and sat on the edge of the bed, facing away from me. His shoulders hunched, and it was the first time he'd appeared uncertain, or perhaps burdened was a better word. "Before you say yes, there's something you need to know. It's not something anyone at the club knows, not even Jared. I'm clean. Get tested every fucking month."

Wouldn't he have shared that with the man he was with? Or any other person for that matter. I didn't understand why it would be a secret. "Okay. You make that sound bad."

He made a sound, part laugh and part derision. "I get tested because of my past. Going to the clinic every month isn't the secret. It's the why. I'm always worried the last test was wrong and something will pop up on the next one. Most of the guys don't go as often as I do, but I can't take any chances."

"So, you were with a lot of women. I'd thought that was common for men," I said.

He stared straight ahead, not looking at me. I crept a little closer, but kept my distance, not because I was afraid, but because I felt as if he needed some space. Whatever he was trying to say, it obviously weighed on him. What was so horrible about his past?

"My family is gone. My grandparents died in a car crash when I was thirteen. Two years later, I lost my parents to a fire. The system wasn't kind to a kid like me. I ran before my sixteenth birthday and lived on the streets. Only one way to stay safe out there and that was to pay for protection. Except I didn't have anything to offer."

My heart ached for him. I knew what he'd offered. Himself. It's why I'd fought so hard to make a better life for my son, to get us both out of Mexico. I didn't want that life for either of us, and with no job skills other than being able to sew, I knew it wouldn't have been long before I ended up on my back. I didn't look down on anyone who'd been forced into that life, or chosen it, but I'd known it wasn't something I was willing to do. It sounded like Dagger still struggled with his decision.

"Started out just being the one guy who said he'd keep me safe, but things changed. A guy offered him money to have an hour with me, and he took it. After that, my protector became my pimp, whoring me out. I could have left, but I had nowhere to go. At least if I stayed with Rick, I knew he'd watch out for me, make sure no one went too far. Out on my own, I'd have probably ended up raped. And yes, I know what happened to me is essentially the same thing, but it was still safer. I didn't bulk up until I was closer to twenty. Scrawny kid on the streets didn't stand a chance."

I couldn't stop the tears from falling down my

cheeks, and I reached out, placing my hand on his back. He tensed, but didn't pull away. I wondered how long he'd kept this bottled up. He said no one here knew about his past, yet he was sharing it with me. Even though we were strangers, he had to trust me at least a little to keep his secret. If he'd not wanted the club to know, surely he wouldn't have told me if he didn't believe I'd hold his confidence. Or maybe it's because of what I'd been through that he felt a connection of some sort?

"I eventually ran when I was eighteen. Didn't have a single fucking life skill except sucking cock and taking it up the ass. Grizzly found me. Offered me a spot here as a Prospect. Worked my ass off doing shit jobs, but I had a roof over my head and food in my stomach, and I didn't have to bend over or hit my knees to get it. I eventually earned my patch and my name. Never did tell him where I'd come from or what I'd been. He never asked."

"I won't tell anyone," I said, pressing myself closer to him. If anyone ever needed comfort, it was this man. I wrapped my arm around him and laid my cheek against his shoulder. "If you thought it would make me see you as less, you're wrong."

He sighed, but I felt a little of the tension leave him. Maybe telling me about his past had lifted some of the burden. I knew keeping secrets could weigh you down.

"I always knew if I settled down I'd have to tell my partner, whether they were female, male, or I got lucky and had one of each. It's why I've always kept things casual, never made any commitments. As long as we were just having fun, then it wasn't their business. I was clean and that was all that mattered."

"Jared doesn't know," I said. "Were you going to

tell him?"

"Someday. Maybe. Depends on whether he sticks around for the long haul. We've just been having fun, no commitment."

He reached up and wrapped his hand around my wrist. I'd thought he meant to pry me loose, but he held on. Was his rough side, that dark edge, because of what he'd been through? I would imagine for a big guy like him, not having control had been difficult. It would explain his need to be so dominant now. I could respect that, and everything he'd survived.

"Can I stay here while I think about it?" I asked. "Get used to being around you, and see if we're even compatible?"

He nodded. "There's a guest room. You can stay there. No fucking clue why I have one because I didn't need the room for anything. Used to be a club whore here who liked to decorate homes and shit. When Grizzly had these houses put in, he let her put basic furnishings in a few. Some of the guys wanted to pick their own shit, but I picked a furnished house. If it had been up to me, that room would be empty like the others."

"Others?" I asked.

"House has four bedrooms. This one, the guest room, and then two others. Never use more than this bedroom. I don't even go in the other three. If you decide to stay, decide to be mine, we can set up one of the other bedrooms for your son." He cracked his neck. "Our son, I guess. If you want me to marry you."

And that right there was the main reason I was even going to consider this insanity. If I married Dagger, he not only offered to be faithful, but my son would have a father. I just had to decide if I could handle being with Dagger and another man, or if it would mean asking him to give up Jared, or any other man he'd want to settle down with. There was a chance Jared wouldn't want any part of this and would walk. I didn't know how Dagger would react if that happened.

"Looks like it's just us for dinner," Dagger said. "I'll go start the grill."

I released him as he stood, but he turned to face me. There was still a haunted look in his eyes, and I wished I knew how to chase it away. He was offering me so much, and I had nothing to give him in return.

"You don't have to make the steaks. I know you wanted to have them with Jared." And then I'd come here and wrecked their plans, and possibly more. What if my being here tore the two of them apart?

"Not sure that's going to happen anytime soon." He glanced around the room before turning his gaze to me. "You need more than things like that dress. You up for going out to eat? We can make a quick stop at the superstore, get you some shorts or something."

"You don't have to buy me clothes."

He smiled a little. "Yeah, *princesa*. I do. Can't have you in things like that. The sunlight let me see straight through it, and while I enjoyed the view, I don't like the idea of you running around here with all these men being able to see what's under your dress."

If I were going to consider marrying him, even if it were only for the sake of getting my son here, then I needed to learn to let someone help take care of me. I could tell Dagger wasn't the type to let his woman do things on her own. He might be bossy, but I had no doubt he'd protect and provide for any woman he claimed. "All right. But only a few things," I agreed. "I don't need much."

"We'll see, *princesa*. We'll see." He eyed me

again. "Can't have you riding on my bike in that, though. We'll have to go up to the clubhouse and get the keys to a club truck or SUV. Need the space for your new things anyway. Just need to find something to cover you up before we leave."

I wasn't going to argue. For now. But if he tried to buy too much, I wouldn't accept. I didn't need anyone spending a bunch of money on me, not when it could be used for something better... like bringing my son here. A few changes of clothes were more than enough. I could always wash them. It wasn't like I needed a new outfit for every day of the week. That might be important to some women, but not to me.

He pulled a button-down shirt from his closet and helped me put it on. I only fastened it partway, and Dagger had to roll the sleeves. It hung on me, nearly as long as my dress, but I supposed that's the way he wanted it. Part of me liked the thought of someone caring whether or not another man could see through my clothes. It had been a long time since anyone took an interest in my wardrobe or well-being. The only other kindness I'd been extended was being left here, because it seemed this man would help me get my son back, one way or another.

* * *

Jared

Any other time, I'd use one of the club whores to work out my frustrations, but it felt wrong. Yeah, I'd fucked a few, or let them suck me off, since I'd been with Dagger, but I'd thought we actually had something. I might just be a Prospect as far as the club was concerned, but I'd thought I meant more to him. The look he'd shot my way when I'd questioned him had proven that to be false.

So why wasn't I balls-deep in club pussy right now?

Because I was a fucking moron, that's why. Even though Dagger had made me feel like shit, like I wasn't worthy to be included in the conversation, I still wanted him. It wasn't even just that. He wasn't the only one who had gotten hard over seeing Zoe out in the yard. The woman had some serious curves, and her skin felt like satin. I had to wonder if Dagger had even considered the possibility Shella had never been the one for us, and little Zoe dropped into our laps for a reason.

She seemed sweet and innocent. Maybe too much so. Could she even handle being with two men? My dick got harder thinking about it. Picturing her lips wrapped around my cock while Dagger fucked her from behind. I didn't know if that was something Dagger even wanted, or if Zoe would agree to it. And since I'd stormed off, I wouldn't be finding out anytime soon.

I knew I needed time to cool down and think things over, and Dagger was probably pissed as hell at me. I'd try to see him tomorrow. That should give both of us enough time to clear our heads, and maybe we could have a conversation so I could figure out exactly where I stood with him. If he was going to help Zoe get her kid back, I wanted to be part of it too. I'd seen the look in her eyes and knew she was hurting. I didn't know how Dagger would pull it off, but if he gave her his word, I knew he'd come through one way or another. I shouldn't have questioned him, not in front of Zoe. If it had just been the two of us, then he wouldn't have thought anything of it.

"Way to go, asshole. You let your emotions get

the better of you again," I muttered to myself.

Having twenty-twenty hindsight was a bitch.

Chapter Three

Dagger

Telling Zoe about my past hadn't been easy, but it had been the right thing to do. Not just because she might be my wife, but it had changed things between us. She wasn't afraid of me, and had relaxed more. I'd even seen her smile a few times since we'd left the compound. To say my brothers were shocked when I grabbed the keys to an SUV, then left with Zoe was an understatement. I had no doubt I'd be getting a call from the Pres, asking me what the fuck I was doing with her. He'd made it clear they weren't here for our amusement, even though it seemed at least one of my brothers didn't listen. It still pissed me off that someone had tried to touch her.

One way or another, I was going to find out who had done it, and kick his fucking ass. I just had to get her to trust me enough to open up. She was silent on the drive to the store. I had a feeling she was going to be difficult when it came time to buy the things she needed. I wondered how long it had been since someone took care of Zoe. I looked at her, really looked. I could see the circles under her eyes, and the stress lines bracketing her mouth.

"There's usually a pen and small pad somewhere in the club vehicles. See if you can find them. I want you to write down the name and address of the woman who has your son," I said. I wanted to make sure the bitch still had the boy and wasn't taking Zoe's money, but I wasn't about to tell her that and make her worry even more.

She dug around until she found them in the passenger door. She started writing, then ripped off the page and handed it to me. I folded it and shoved it into my pocket. While she shopped, I'd text the info to Outlaw and get him to check on the boy by whatever means necessary. I couldn't imagine leaving my kid behind, but I understood why she had. There probably hadn't been a lot of opportunities for her back home, and I knew the assholes who had brought her here wouldn't have let her bring the kid. Not unless they had a reason. Just sucked she got caught up with some bad men who were taking advantage. I had no doubt she'd have worked herself to the bone for years before they'd killed her and dumped the body. She'd have never seen her boy again.

I parked as close to the door as I could. After I shut off the engine, she reached for the door, but I placed a hand on her arm, stopping her. "You wait right there."

She released the door handle and nodded. I got out and walked around to the passenger side to open her door and help her out. I made sure the vehicle was locked, then placed a hand at her waist and led her inside the store. She stared at everything with wide eyes and I wondered if she'd never been shopping at a place like this. Since she'd been sending her money back home, she'd probably shopped at the dollar-type stores for her essentials. This place wasn't on the same level as the mall shops, but it was definitely better quality than those cheaper spots.

"Let's start with the bathroom items, and we'll work our way around to the clothes and shoes," I said. She opened her mouth, no doubt to say she didn't need all that, but I silenced her with a look.

I let her push the cart, thinking it might keep her hands occupied when I started grabbing stuff I knew she'd need. I could already tell she was going to argue with me. Or try. There was no fucking way I was walking out of here without making sure she had everything she needed. Didn't matter if it came from my account or the club's money. The fact no one had made sure she had the basics made me want to punch something. Yeah, Beau had said he'd prep the apartments for the women, but it was obvious Zoe had needed clothing and shoes as well. The Pres might have given her cash for those things, but not a damn brother or Prospect had ensured she actually got them. And I was no fucking better. I hadn't given a second thought to those women.

"*Princesa*, anyone else sending money home? Are you the only one who didn't buy clothes and shit when Griz gave you that cash?"

"I think everyone else went shopping," she said. Then her brow furrowed. "Except maybe Franny. She went with them, but she only came back with one bag. The others bought more."

So Franny probably sent her money elsewhere too, unless she was saving it for something else, like a way out of the compound. Griz wouldn't let them loose unless he knew they could take care of themselves. I filed that info away for later. I knew Wolf had been keeping an eye on Franny, or had been trying to without being obvious. I'd let him know she might need some shit.

While Zoe eyed the shelves, I pulled out the slip of paper she'd given me, snapped a picture, and sent it off to Outlaw. *Check on the boy.*

I'd get the kid here, whatever it took, but I'd have to come up with a plan. The border patrol wasn't going to let me waltz back into the US with a little boy in the back seat who didn't have the proper documentation. Sneaking across wasn't as easy as some people seemed to think, and I wasn't about to use a fucking coyote to get the boy here. Didn't trust them for a second. Little kid would fetch more money than they'd make getting him here. I could easily see them selling the boy before I got him to his mother.

We made it all the way down three aisles of girly shit without Zoe reaching for a single item. She was going to piss me off. I didn't have a clue what sorts of scents she liked, or know the damn difference between the brands lining the shelves. The only dresses I'd ever seen her wear had flowers on them. I didn't know if that was due to a lack of options or because she liked floral stuff. It was a gamble, but I grabbed some soap and lavender-scented lotion. I added one of those poofy things women washed with, and a pack of razors with some shaving cream. If she didn't like it, she could damn well pick out her own stuff.

Zoe narrowed her eyes at the items in the cart, but was a smart girl and didn't say a damn thing about any of them. Her hair was long and beautiful, but I knew damn well to keep it shiny and soft she needed something better than the basic shit those apartments had stocked. I'd gone with Outlaw once when he'd picked up a few things for Elena. I remembered the brand of shampoo she'd gotten, but there were about six different kinds. I grabbed one that had a matching conditioner available and tossed them into the cart. Then I grabbed a brush, a comb, and a few different hair things. I didn't know what any of them were called, but I'd seen Meiling, Elena, and some of the club whores wearing this sort of stuff. Not that I would dare compare Zoe to a club whore, but she had long hair and most of them did too.

"Dagger, it's too much. I don't need all this," she said, reaching into the cart.

"*Princesa*, you take so much as one item out of

there and I will spank your ass right here and now."

She gasped and yanked her hand back, but I noticed her cheeks were flushed and I didn't think it was entirely from embarrassment. She might not be experienced, but with the right man, I'd be willing to bet she'd try just about anything once. Not that I'd be finding out, unless she decided she wanted me to marry her so we could bring her boy here. It wouldn't surprise me if she accepted. Not because I thought I was such an awesome catch, but because it was clear she'd do whatever it took to keep her son safe and have him in her arms again. I wanted nothing more than to go after the kid and bring him home to her, but I wasn't stupid enough to try it on my own. I'd need some help, and if Outlaw wasn't going to lend a hand, I didn't know if my club would back me up on this one or not.

We left the bathroom shit and I led her over to the clothes. From the stubborn set of her jaw, I knew this was going to be fun. If she didn't tell me her sizes, I'd have to get creative. I held up a shirt that seemed feminine yet thick enough no one would be looking through it. "You either tell me a size, or we'll head into the fitting room while I pull this over your head to see if it fits."

"You wouldn't."

I arched an eyebrow. Oh yeah, I certainly would. And I'd gladly pull that dress off her first. Except I'd be tempted to shred the fucking thing so she'd never wear it again. She must have seen all that in my expression because she answered quickly enough. I was a little disappointed. Part of me had hoped for a bit more of a fight, and maybe getting to take a peek under her dress. It hadn't been a lie about taking her to the fitting room. I'd have done it whether the staff in the store liked it or not. What were they going to do? Ask me to leave? Right, because that was terrifying.

"I wear an extra-large in shirts, but I need an eighteen or 2X in pants. Sometimes a little bigger if they're cut slim."

I eyed her up and down, wondering how the hell she needed something that big with as little as she looked. Yeah, she was curvy as shit, but the height of a pixie. Personally, I liked the extra padding, but I knew some men wouldn't. Never did understand men who liked skinny women. Then again, I was a big guy and didn't want to worry I might break the woman I was fucking. To each their own. I could admire the beauty of a woman regardless of her size, skin color, or even her damn hair. Didn't mean I wanted them in my bed.

I found her size in the shirt and grabbed a pair of shorts hanging on the same rack. Figured it meant they went together like a matching set or something. Getting her to pick out anything was a damn nightmare. I hoped she liked the shit going into the cart because I planned to get rid of all the rags she'd been wearing. Starting with the one on her body right now. I made sure she had at least ten different outfits, and tossed in a few nightgowns. I stood staring at a rack of bras.

"Don't even think of asking me what size I wear," she muttered.

"I suggest you pick some things out before I do it for you. Unless you just like my taste in women's fashion."

She huffed at me. "If I let you pick my underwear, you'll end up getting the ones that go up your butt. I'll pass."

I snickered as she went through the racks, selecting two bras and a package of cotton panties.

Nope. No. There was no fucking way I was letting her put that boring shit on her hot body. Even if I wouldn't be the one looking at it, she deserved something better. I took note of the sizes of the items she'd added, then found her four more bras and a half dozen pair of sexy panties.

"Dagger, you can't pick out my underthings," she said in a loud whisper. "What are people going to think?"

"That I'm making sure my woman has everything she needs?"

She opened and shut her mouth, then nodded. She might not be my woman, but no one here would know that. I started to lead her back to the shoes, but as we passed the baby department, I hesitated. I was bringing her son here, and I had a feeling he'd need things too. Although... my chest hurt at the thought that the people she'd trusted might not have him anymore.

I checked my phone and saw a message from a number I didn't have programmed into my phone. Alabama area code. I opened it and saw a picture of a dark-haired boy with blue eyes. My throat grew tight when I realized it was Zoe's son, and he was alive. I scanned the message that came with it and wanted to beat the hell out of someone.

Boy is alive but in trouble. Bitch who had him sold him to the cartel.

I tried to take a calming breath, then returned the text. *I'm getting him back.*

My phone rang a second later with the same number popping up. I answered, having no doubt it was Wire. He was the only man I knew in Alabama who could get this shit to me, especially as fast as he had. "What did you find?"

"It's bad, man. So far, they haven't hurt him, but there's no good reason for those fuckers to buy a kid. You know he's on borrowed time. Luis Lopez is three years old, and too fucking cute, if you ask me. Outlaw says you might be claiming his mom."

"Yeah, well... Ball's in her court on that one. It was Outlaw's suggestion."

Wire growled and I heard something slam. "Are you fucking shitting me? He backed you into a corner, didn't he? Refused to help if you didn't keep the mom?"

"Something like that."

"Why the hell would he do that?"

"I think it's so she'll have someone in her corner." I eyed Zoe, but she was too busy looking at the baby clothes with longing to pay any attention to my conversation. Some of the stuff she was checking out would be way too small for a toddler, though. It made me realize she hadn't seen her son in so long, she probably had no idea what he wore or how big he'd gotten. "Said he wouldn't make them citizens unless I married her."

I heard the keys clicking on his keyboard and Wire muttered to himself for a few minutes. While he was busy, I caught Zoe's attention. "*Princesa*, get a few things for Luis. Whatever he'll need when we bring him home. Just remember he's grown some and is not the *bebé* you left behind."

She gave me a nod and moved over to some bigger clothes, things that looked like they would fit her son. I hated to remind her it had been so long since she'd seen him, not that I thought a moment went by she didn't worry about him. It was clear she'd done what she had out of love for the boy.

"You like her," Wire said softly.

So? It wasn't like she was ugly or mean. Zoe was a sweet woman, but she deserved to be loved, and I wasn't sure I knew a damn thing about that emotion. It had been a long time since someone had loved me. I'd seen the way my mother and father were together, and my grandparents. I'd always wanted what they had, but I didn't know how to get it.

"Is she nearby?" Wire asked.

"Yeah, she's right here."

"Let me talk to her," he said.

I handed the phone to Zoe, who looked at it like it might bite her. I explained who was on the phone and she took it from me, but I could tell she was nervous about speaking to a strange man, even if I did vouch for him. She spoke softly and I took a few steps away. I didn't know what Wire needed to ask her, but I thought she might want some privacy. As much as she could get in the middle of a large store.

When she handed the phone back to me, her cheeks were flushed and she wouldn't hold my gaze. Curious, I put the phone back to my ear. "What the hell was that about?"

"Congratulations, Daddy. You're now a husband and father, or you will be in a few hours. By morning at the latest. International shit takes a little longer, even with Lavender helping me. She chose you, Dagger. Don't know if that's what you wanted, but I'm betting she'll bend over backward to make you happy."

Shit. Shit. Shit. I glanced at Zoe, but she still wouldn't look at me. I'd left it up to her, and it seemed she'd made her choice. Now I had to man up and deal with it. I wasn't sure if she only wanted me, or if she was open to having another man in the relationship. Now wasn't the time to ask, but we'd be talking about it soon. Really fucking soon.

"I told her I'd get what you needed to bring him home," Wire said. "Without her having to be your wife. If that tells you anything. So don't be pissed at her. For whatever reason, she wants you by her side."

I gave a grunt of acknowledgment and hung up the call. It seemed I had a wife and kid. Zoe was holding a pair of small shorts, but she hadn't put them in the cart. Just kept staring at them. I moved closer to her. Reaching out, I took the shorts, and grabbed her hand to pull her against me.

"Zoe, look at me."

She shook her head. "*Lo siento.* I'm so, so sorry."

"*Princesa*, eyes up here." Her gaze lifted to mine and I saw she was close to tears. "I'm not mad. I told you the choice was yours and you made it."

"But I ruined your life. I'm not who you wanted," she said. "He said I didn't have to marry you, but I..."

"*Corazoncito*, I walked away because I didn't want to scare you. I was hard as fuck, and it wasn't because of Jared. Did I hope for something different? *Sí*. But that doesn't mean I won't treat you with the respect you deserve. Now, let's get what our boy needs, then I'm going to do whatever it takes to bring him home."

A tear trickled down her cheek and I wiped it away. I brought her against me, holding her tight. I didn't know what to do with a crying woman, or a kid for that matter, but it looked like I'd be figuring that shit out real soon. Oh, fuck. Grizzly. He was going to have my ass. The second Outlaw had given me that damn ultimatum, I should have called the Pres. I didn't know why I hadn't, except I wasn't too keen on him finding out Zoe was in my house.

Griz was going to be pissed.

"Come on. Let's finish shopping and go get some food. You have to be hungry."

She took a step back, but the dejected look on her face nearly ripped my heart out. I made a decision I hoped I wouldn't regret. Reaching out, I cupped the back of her neck with my hand and held her still as I lowered my mouth to hers. The kiss was soft, brief, but I hoped it was enough to make a point. She touched her lips as I backed away, an awestruck look on her face, and I had to wonder if that was her first kiss. If it was, then I'd just fucked up even more because it was hardly a kiss.

I took her hand and we picked out a few more things for Luis. I also made sure she had two pairs of shoes. I was hoping Adalia or one of the other ladies might want to go shopping with her, so she could pick out something else. Maybe even go to a real shoe store or hit the mall. If Zoe was going to be a part of my life from this point forward, then I wanted her to feel like part of the family. I might not have blood relatives still alive, but I did have my brothers at the club and their women. I hoped it would be enough for her.

Chapter Four

Zoe

I'd expected Dagger to be angry, even though he'd said the decision was mine. Then he'd kissed me. I knew it wasn't the same kind of kiss he'd shared with other women, or even other men. The ones I'd seen him give Jared were hotter, but it was my first kiss. To me, it would always be special. After Dagger paid for my purchases, he pulled out one of the new outfits and handed it to me.

"Go change, then we'll get a bite to eat," he said.

"I made this," I murmured, feeling like he thought my dress wasn't good enough.

He tipped my chin up. "And you did an amazing job, but I told you I can see through your dress, *corazoncito*. I don't like the idea of other men checking out what's under it. You're mine, Zoe. That means only I get to see those beautiful curves. Now, go change."

My heart gave a thump. I knew he didn't care about me, didn't even really know me, but I liked that he didn't want other men looking at me. I'd never mattered to someone before. My son had been too small when I left to even miss me, but I was no less determined to bring him home. I carried the items into the bathroom and stepped into a stall. I closed and locked the door, then changed into the new clothes. I'd have preferred to wash them first, but it seemed Dagger wasn't ready to go home yet.

Home. Was I supposed to move into his house? What would the club think? They'd been nice to me, except for the one who'd grabbed me. My chest got tight and hurt. I rubbed at the spot. What if that man said something? Or got angry? I picked up the dress and fingered the fabric. Dagger had been right. It was threadbare, and even though I'd made it with my own hands, I didn't really want to keep it. Besides, I had others. I could always put one aside just to remember how I'd gotten to this point. Forgetting your past was never the answer.

I let myself out of the stall and tossed the dress into the trash. Keeping Dagger's shirt in my hand, I stared at my reflection, marveling at how different I appeared in the new clothes. My hair was long and tangled, but Dagger hadn't seemed to mind. Taking a breath, I straightened my spine and went back out to my... fiancé? It seemed a little surreal. He wasn't where I'd left him and for a moment I panicked, thinking he'd left me. I scanned the area, my heart pounding. Starting for the door, I paused when I heard my name. I looked around again and saw Dagger heading toward me, pushing the cart, but I didn't understand why he'd gone back into the main part of the store.

"I thought you'd left," I said.

"Sorry. There was something I forgot."

He didn't say anything else, just headed for the exit. I tried to keep up, but his legs were so much longer than mine. I tripped over my own feet, and he slowed a little, making sure I didn't fall. When we reached the SUV, he put my new things into the cargo area. I climbed into the front seat and waited, putting his shirt in the back seat. I'd expected him to get in and leave, but he sat there a moment, almost as if he were gathering his thoughts. He reached into his pocket and pulled something out, but I didn't get a good look.

"I wanted you to know I was serious when I made that offer, and I'm going to stand by you, *princesa*." He reached for my hand, then slid a ring onto my finger. I couldn't help but gasp as I stared down at it. Not only was it gorgeous, but he'd somehow gotten the fit just right. "My beautiful wife deserves a beautiful ring. I didn't know if it would fit, but they said we could have it sized if necessary. All the rings in the display case seem to be the same size."

He thought I was beautiful? I stared at the sparkling diamonds on my finger. It was a silver band, or maybe white gold, with four diamonds embedded across the top. They were small, but I didn't care. It was too much! I'd never had anything so gorgeous or expensive before. It felt wrong accepting it when this marriage wasn't real. Although, he'd said that it was. I knew he didn't really want me as his wife. He might have gotten turned on when he saw me in his yard, but men wanted to sleep with women all the time. It didn't mean they wanted to keep them forever.

"Dagger, I…" He reached over and placed his fingers over my lips.

"Call me Santiago when it's just us. Once the hacker gets done marrying us, you'll be Zoe Afoa, and Luis will be mine as well." He reached into his pocket and pulled out something else, then slid a sliver band onto his own finger. "Want to make sure everyone knows I'm not available. I don't cheat, *corazoncito*."

He didn't cheat, and I'd backed him into a corner. By telling that man I wanted to be Dagger's wife, it meant he couldn't be with Jared anymore. Unless I was open to being with both of them. I didn't know how I felt about that. The only experience I had was with the man who raped me, and as Dagger had said, that wasn't sex. Going from nothing to two men at once was a bit much for me to handle at the moment. I didn't want to just outright say no because it wasn't fair to Dagger, and Jared really did seem like a sweet man. So maybe not no, but not right now?

"Do you have a preference for dinner?" he asked.

"Anything is fine. As long as it doesn't have mushrooms. I'm allergic."

He gave a nod. "All right. I'll make sure I never order you anything, or bring anything home, that has mushrooms. Any other allergies for you or Luis?"

"No. Just the mushrooms." My brow furrowed. The last time I'd seen my son, he was still on a bottle. "I don't know about Luis. How can I not know if my son has food allergies?"

It made me feel like a horrible mother. Yes, everything I'd done was for him, but it had been so long since I'd last seen him. Would I even recognize my own kid? There was no way he'd know who I was. What if he didn't want to come with me? It hadn't occurred to me until now that he might prefer to stay with the people who had him. The woman had kids. Had he made friends with them? Did he think *she* was his mother?

Dagger pulled up in front of a place called *Betty's Diner* and parked near the door. He got out, and I remembered this time to wait for him. When he opened my door, I held his hand as I slipped out of the truck. It felt a little like the ground was rushing up at me, but oddly, I trusted him to not let me fall. We may not have exchanged vows, but he'd offered his protection just the same.

He kept his hand at my waist as he led me inside. There were a few women in uniforms, but only one looked our way. The moment she saw Dagger, she sneered and walked the other direction. I didn't understand. He looked a little scary, but no one had ever treated me better, even if he had handcuffed me to his bed earlier. I still didn't quite understand why he'd done that. So what if I'd seen him kissing Jared?

Anyone walking past could have.

"I think you're scaring them," I murmured as another waitress looked our way, then dismissed us. "Maybe it's the leather vest with all the patches?"

He shook a little and I realized he was silently laughing. At me? What had I said?

"It's called a cut, *princesa*, and as my woman, you need to know that. Technically, you'll be not only my wife but my ol' lady, and you'll get a property cut. It will look similar to mine but say *Property of Dagger*."

I remembered seeing a few women wearing those. The club didn't seem to have a lot of women who were there all the time. Mostly the ones who were there to party. What if the other ol' ladies didn't like me? I'd never really had friends, not since coming to this country. The people I worked with always looked out for themselves. You learned to do that or risk losing your spot, or even your life. With Dagger by my side, I no longer had to worry about such things. As long as he planned to keep me, I knew I'd be safe. I just wasn't sure about my place within his club. What if they didn't accept me?

"I don't think they're going to seat us, Dagger." My stomach rumbled and I felt my cheeks warm. His gaze met mine, and I saw a flash of irritation before he glowered at the room in general.

"There are at least a dozen empty tables and booths. Is there a reason my wife is standing here hungry and we can't get a table?" His voice boomed throughout the space and I noticed a few people jumped.

An older woman came from the back, easily in her late sixties or early seventies, except she wasn't like the older women I'd met before. Her hair was a vibrant pink, ink covered her arms, and she wore a black T-shirt tucked into a pair of ripped jeans. The boots on her feet looked similar to what Dagger wore.

"What the hell is going on out here? Who's being so Goddamn loud?" the woman demanded.

"You Betty?" Dagger asked.

Her gaze zeroed in on him. "I am. What's the problem?"

He pointed at the women nearby wearing the diner uniform. "They won't seat us, and my wife is so hungry her stomach is growling. If bikers aren't allowed, you should probably just put that on the door. Although, I can't promise the safety of this place if you discriminate against such a large group of people. Your business could suffer."

Had he just threatened her? I looked up at him, but he was still staring at Betty. Other than looking pissed, he seemed like the usual Dagger. I couldn't tell if he truly meant to do something to her diner or not. I was worried how the woman would react to his statement, but she tossed her head back and cackled, before slapping the counter.

"I like you," she said. "You'll have to ignore the bitches who work for me. Good help is so hard to find these days. Looks like it's time for me to clean house again."

I heard several of them gasp, but I kept watching Betty. I'd never met someone like her before and found her fascinating. She came toward us, grabbed two menus, and motioned for us to follow her. Dagger pointed to a booth by the window, and she set the menus down.

"What do you want to drink while you decide what to eat?" Betty asked. "And don't worry. I'll personally handle your order."

Dagger skimmed her from head to toe and she

smirked. Turning her arm over, she showed him a mark on her inner forearm. I couldn't see it clearly, but the words *property of* stood out clearly. Did she belong to a biker? Whatever the rest of the tattoo had said, it seemed to set Dagger at ease.

"What do you want, *corazoncito*?" he asked me.

Since being left with the Devil's Fury, I'd found myself partial to sweet tea. I ordered one and Dagger asked for coffee, then we were left to read the menu. Everything sounded good, but I worried about ordering too much. I'd been careful with my meals, knowing I needed to lose some weight. Except, no matter how little I had, I never seemed to lose a single inch. I might be short, but I was also a bit plump. I couldn't remember ever having a defined waistline, unless round was considered definition.

When Betty returned, I ordered a salad. Or tried to. Dagger glared at me, growling softly. My eyes went wide as I stared at him.

"*¿Por qué ordenaste una ensalada?*"

Why did he think I'd ordered one? "*Porque estoy gorda.*"

He brought his fist down on the table, making the silverware rattle, and I admittedly jumped at his display of anger. I didn't understand it. I needed to lose some weight, and a salad was a perfectly reasonable thing to order. It was healthy.

Dagger leaned over the table. "Let's get one thing straight right now, *princesa*. You are not fat. I don't ever want to hear you say that shit again, understood? You're beautiful and don't need to change a fucking thing."

Betty patted my shoulder. "Listen to him. He's right. You're gorgeous, and he clearly likes you as you are. Don't go changing because fashion these days says you need to be a size two."

"What do you really want?" Dagger asked. "Don't look at prices, count calories, or any of that shit. Tell me without thinking too hard, what sounds good right now?"

"A cheeseburger and onion rings," I said.

Betty patted me again. "I'll bring it out. What about you, big guy?"

"Same. But extra onion rings."

"Be out in a jiffy." Betty walked off and I suddenly found the table fascinating. I didn't know why he'd gotten so upset by what I'd said. I'd seen the women who went to the clubhouse. They were all thin, or at least a lot slimmer than I was. He had to have been with some of them at some point, or at least women like them.

"Zoe, look at me," he said, his voice soft yet holding an edge that made me comply. "Do I look like the kind of guy who would have an ugly wife? Or would get hard if a woman wasn't sexy and appealing? Is there anything about me that says I want a stick-thin woman with no tits or ass?"

I slowly shook my head. No, he'd made it clear he liked my curves, as he'd called them. I hadn't realized that extended to the part around the middle where I carried my extra weight.

"Then stop putting yourself down. You're mine, *princesa*, and I think you're *muy hermosa. ¿Entiendes??*"

"Yes, Dagger. I understand. I'm sorry. I just..." I took a breath and tried to gather my thoughts. "I've never had anyone want me. The man who... He told me I was fat, unattractive, and he was doing me a favor because no one would ever find me pretty. I don't regret my son for a moment, but that man's words, and his actions, have haunted me since it happened."

My throat grew tight when I remembered that day. Dagger had told me of his past, and it only seemed fair that I share that part of myself with him too. It was something I'd been ashamed of, even though I'd had no choice in what happened. I knew Dagger hadn't truly had a choice either. If anyone could understand, it would be him. "He covered my face and even left most of my body covered. Said he couldn't look at me and stay hard."

"Motherfucker," Dagger muttered. "If I ever find him, I will make him pay, and then I'll ensure he never harms another woman ever again."

Find him? I didn't even know who the man was. The tattoo on his neck had been enough to tell me he was part of the cartel, but that's all I knew. It wasn't possible for Dagger to find the man who had hurt me, but the thought was still sweet. Sort of. I wasn't sure it could be considered such since I was almost certain he'd meant he would kill the man. Maybe it made me a bad person, but I'd feel relieved if such a thing were to happen. I didn't like the idea of Dagger taking a life and ending up in jail, but that he would do something like that to get justice for me and keep others safe made me feel warm inside.

Our food arrived faster than I'd anticipated, and I had to admit it looked and smelled delicious. While we ate, I took the time to study my fiancé. It still felt odd thinking of someone like that. Even without the ceremony, it seemed I would still legally -- or illegally? -- be his wife. I only hoped he didn't come to regret his decision.

"There's something you need to know," he said. He tapped on his phone screen, then slid the device across the table. A little boy was on the screen, and even though I hadn't seen my son in years, I instantly knew it was Luis. "The woman you've been paying doesn't have him anymore, but I know where he is."

"She doesn't have him?" I asked.

Dagger shook his head. "She sold him. Wire said he seems to be okay, for now, but I'll need to go get him. Just waiting on Wire to get me the docs I need for Luis to come here legally. Or at least appear to be legal."

"How can he do that?" I asked. When the man had said he could marry me and Dagger, I hadn't really understood. Didn't that require a ceremony of some sort at the very least? I didn't know how everything in this country worked, but I didn't think I could get married without having to do anything at all.

"The government goes to Wire when they need a favor. He's the best at what he does, and they damn well know it. If anyone could change someone's name, drain their bank account, or hack into another government's systems, it would be Wire and his wife. They're the dynamic duo when it comes to hacking."

I stared at the image on the screen. My son. He'd gotten so big! Tears misted my eyes and my heart hurt. Everything I'd missed, and that woman hadn't even been caring for him? His first steps. First words. I didn't know what he liked to eat, if he was allergic to anything, or anything about him at all. At the store, I'd guessed on sizes for the clothes we'd bought. It was my hope if we left the tags on, we could return anything that didn't fit.

But that all hinged on Dagger being able to bring him home. If the people who had Luis now had bought him, they wouldn't be likely to give him up. Would they? I'd think they'd want to hold onto him. I knew the authorities down there would be useless, unless Dagger was able to bribe them into helping. At least, that had been my experience with them. The town where I'd lived was very corrupt.

"Can I go with you?" I asked.

"No, *princesa*. I need you to stay here, just in case things don't go smoothly. I may need to grab Luis and make a run for it. I'll take a few guys with me, and I'll have someone stay with you. If you don't want anyone at the house, I'll at least make sure a Prospect checks in every few hours."

Which reminded me of Jared and the mess I'd created for Dagger by accepting his marriage proposal, if you could call it that. I didn't know when he was leaving, but maybe I could use that time to figure out what to do. I didn't want to keep him from Jared, but I needed to do a little soul searching first, and determine if I could handle being with two men. For all intents and purposes, I was still a virgin. One act of violence may have stolen my hymen and given me a child, but I still wasn't very knowledgeable when it came to men and sex. I had no experience at all, and I didn't even know if I could please Dagger, much less another man as well.

We finished our meal and Dagger took me home. It looked like I'd have to figure out how to be a wife rather quickly. I only hoped I didn't disappoint him.

Chapter Five

Dagger

I hadn't even thought about furniture for Luis' room. I put the two bags of clothes inside his doorway, and knew I'd either need to arrange for a Prospect to go buy something and put it together, or I'd have to order online and have it delivered. I didn't want Zoe worrying about it while I was gone. If Wire were true to his word, I could have what I needed as soon as tomorrow. I hadn't told Zoe where Luis was being kept, and for good reason. If she knew her son was with the cartel, she'd have panicked.

I'd made room in the closet and dresser for her, then left her to get settled. She'd still need her things that she'd brought with her, and whatever she'd bought before today, which was apparently next to nothing. We could get it later. Everything she'd need for tonight and the morning had been purchased earlier. When she appeared in the kitchen doorway with her new clothes clutched in her arms, I wasn't sure what to make of it.

"Something wrong with the things we bought?" I asked.

"I wanted to wash them before I wear them. Is there a washer and dryer here?"

I showed her where the laundry closet was in the hallway. There was a set of folding doors that hid the washer and dryer, with a rack over the top of them where I stored the laundry detergent and dryer sheets. They were basic machines, so I didn't think she'd have any trouble with them. Hell, if they were more complicated, I couldn't have done my own damn laundry all this time.

Shit. I still hadn't told Griz about Zoe. I went

back to the kitchen to grab a beer, because the conversation would require alcohol for certain. Then I dialed the Pres. I took a gulp of the ice-cold drink to brace myself. He answered almost immediately.

"Dagger, what the fuck is Zoe doing with you? A Prospect said he saw her get into a club vehicle with you."

Right to the point as usual. I was surprised he hadn't called the moment he'd heard about it, which made me wonder what he'd been dealing with. "I took her shopping for some things. Found out she'd sent all the money you gave her back to Mexico."

He sighed. "Oh, well that's all right, then."

Don't relax too much, Pres, because there's more and you won't fucking like it. I took another swallow of my beer, wondering if I should drain the bottle and get a second one. Griz was about to go through the damn roof over what I said next, I just knew it.

"And she's my wife." The silence after that statement was nearly deafening. I waited. And waited. Checked the screen and the call was still connected, but I didn't even hear him breathing. "Um, Pres? You still there?"

"She's what?" he asked, his voice deceptively calm. Yeah, he was ticked. I had a feeling we'd be getting a visit shortly, and it wouldn't be the fun kind. "How the fuck did you marry her? *Why* did you marry her?"

I rubbed the back of my neck. I'd need his permission to go after Luis, but I didn't like that it put Zoe in a bad light, only marrying me because of her son. For that matter, it made me look like a jackass who had required that of her. Fuck Outlaw and Wire. They caused more trouble than anyone else around here.

"Wire is working on it right now. There's more.

She has a son. Luis. He's been sold down in Mexico. I'll need to go get him and bring him home, and I'll need a few guys to go with me. I'm just waiting on Wire to finish whatever the hell he's doing."

I heard him shifting around and then a door slam. Sounded like he was on the move, and most likely heading my way. Good times. I probably should have bought more alcohol while we were shopping.

"You know I need to speak to Zoe and make sure this is what she wants," Griz said. "I don't think you'd force any woman into being with you, but we agreed to help those women."

"I know, Pres. I figured you'd be stopping by." I took a swallow of my beer, then another. "Also need a property cut for her. Do I need to take that shit to the table for a vote? Or are you just going to give me this one?"

"If you're already married, not much point in voting," Griz said. "I'd say to do things the right way next time, but there better damn well not be a next time. No divorce. You made her your ol' lady. She's it for the rest of your life or hers. Got me? There might be clubs out there who drop their women and get a younger one, or even keep one or two on the side, but that's not the way Devil's Fury works."

"I know, Pres." I also knew that was a big reason he didn't have a woman in his life. His wife had died from cancer, and Griz hadn't even thought of finding another woman. May was his one and only. If he'd been with any of the club whores, I didn't know about it, and I doubted anyone else did either. I couldn't imagine being celibate the rest of my life if Zoe died, but if Griz was getting action somewhere, he was keeping that shit private.

"She up for company?" he asked.

"She's doing laundry. If you want to come by, come on over." Like he needed an invitation. I had no doubt he was in his driveway just waiting to get on his bike.

"Be there in a bit. I won't stay long. I'm sure the two of you have a lot to... discuss."

I nearly snorted my beer. Discuss. Right. That was a good one. I'd told her if she decided to be mine it wouldn't be in name only, but I wasn't a heartless enough bastard to expect her to spread her legs right off. Especially not with her background. If she wanted some time, I was fine with that, as long as she didn't leave me hanging forever. Blue balls would make me cranky as shit, and I knew from experience my hand didn't do a good enough job relieving the tension.

I hung up and glanced at the doorway to find Zoe shifting from foot to foot. I nodded to the table by the window and she pulled out a chair. Even though the Pres had been keeping tabs on the women, I wasn't sure how she'd feel about him dropping in. I sat in the chair next to her and set my beer on the table. What was left of it. I'd damn near drained the bottle.

"Grizzly is coming by for a minute. Wants to talk to you," I said.

Her shoulders tensed. "Did I do something wrong?"

"No, *princesa*. He wants to make sure I didn't coerce you into marrying me. I explained about Wire handling the marriage, and the adoption of Luis, but he needs to speak with you and make sure I didn't force you to be with me."

Her lips parted and I saw her pulse flutter. Her cheeks flushed. "Force me? He honestly thinks you'd be capable of such a thing? Santiago, you're the last person who would ever do that. You've been so nice to me."

I reached for her hand, covering it with mine. "Easy, *corazoncito*. He's just watching out for you."

"*Nunca me lastimarías.*"

No, I wouldn't hurt her. Or any woman. Well, except for truly evil bitches who deserved it. If I got my hands on the woman who was supposed to care for Luis, I'd gut the fucking whore. I didn't think Zoe needed to know that, though. Last thing I needed was her sleeping with one eye open, scared I'd kill her in her sleep. I hadn't gotten my name by being an angel.

"It seems the two of you are getting along well," the Pres said, alerting me to his presence. For someone his size, the fucker moved silent as a damn cat, at least when he wanted to.

"Pres. Didn't see you there."

He smirked. "I'm aware. Give me a moment with Zoe."

I stood, but Zoe clutched at my hand. Her chest rose and fell rapidly, and it looked like she might pass out. I hunkered down next to her chair, smoothed her hair back from her face, and tried to get her to focus on me.

"Easy, *princesa*. The Pres won't hurt you. I'll be in the other room. He needs to hear from you that you want to be here, with me. Whatever he asks, just tell him the truth. *¿Entiendes?*"

She gave a quick nod and released me. I pressed a kiss to the top of her head and left the room, giving the Pres some time with her. And if I lurked just outside the doorway, out-of-sight but not out of hearing, that was for me to know. If it sounded like he was upsetting her, I'd step in.

"I wasn't even aware you knew Dagger," the Pres said.

"I noticed him last night."

"And where were you when you saw him?" Griz asked.

It was quiet and I knew she didn't want to admit to being near the clubhouse. I also knew she'd never tell him one of my brothers tried to force himself on her. One way or another, I'd figure out who it was and put my fist through his damn face.

"Zoe, I need you to be honest with me. Where were you when you noticed Dagger?" Griz asked again.

"Behind the clubhouse," she said softly. "I followed the music and ended up there. He was outside."

"Did you approach Dagger then?" Griz asked.

"No. I followed him, though, and knew he lived here. I walked to his house today, wanting to speak with him. Before I could get the courage to knock on the door, he found me in his yard."

Griz made a noise that was part rumble and possibly a rusty laugh. "And how did he handle that?"

I closed my eyes. Shit. I'd cuffed her to my bed. That's how I fucking handled it. I braced myself, not sure if Griz would find it funny, or if he'd be pissed. Whatever she said, I couldn't hear her. Grizzly was quiet. I cautiously moved closer to the doorway and tried to listen. Was he going to remove her from the house? Even if he said she couldn't stay here, I'd still go get her son. He wouldn't deny her that. I didn't think he would at any rate.

"He's been wonderful," she said. "I feel like I'm taking advantage, and I'm worried he'll wake up one day and realize he made a mistake. I wouldn't blame Dagger if he threw me out and told me to get my son on my own."

Griz pitched his voice low enough I could only hear the rumble of his words, but couldn't understand a damn thing he said. What the hell was he telling her? I shifted, but without walking into the room with them, I couldn't make out anything. Would he talk her out of being married to me? She'd be better off with someone else. If Zoe wanted to remain mine, I'd keep her, and treat her like a queen. Her son would be mine in every way that counted. I just couldn't help but feel she deserved more. Like love. I didn't know that I would ever come to love her. Wasn't that something women always wanted? Hearts, flowers, and all that shit?

"Dagger, get in here," Grizzly bellowed.

I took a breath, trying to prepare for whatever happened next, then walked into the kitchen. The Pres didn't give anything away, didn't even look at me. Instead of sitting, I stood behind Zoe's chair and placed my hand on her shoulder. She reached up, putting her fingers over mine, and I felt the way she trembled. Whatever they'd discussed, she was still shaken. I felt my muscles tighten, but I wasn't about to lash out at the Pres. Not if I wanted to keep my head attached.

To some, Griz might seem like a big teddy bear. With his girls, he was a softie. The rest of us knew better than to piss him off. He'd earned the name Grizzly and anyone who forgot would pay the price. Didn't mean that I liked him scaring Zoe.

"I'm giving you permission to get Luis from Mexico and bring him home," Griz said. "And I'm going to send Colorado, Steel, and possibly Matt with you. I know Matt is only a Prospect, but he has a military background and might be of some use if shit hits the fan. If not him, I'll find someone equally competent."

I gave Zoe's shoulder a slight squeeze. Three wasn't quite as many as I'd hoped for, considering what I'd be up against, but it was better than going in alone. I'd ask for Dragon to come with me, but I knew he didn't want to leave Lilian and his kids. There was no damn way Badger or Dingo were leaving their women either. Although... I could think of one scary fucker I wouldn't mind having on this trip.

"What about Blades?" I asked.

"You want me to ask Blades to leave China behind for what? Close to a week? Maybe more, depending how things go when you get to Mexico. You even know where you're going?" Grizzly asked. The way he said it made me think he'd gotten more information on the way to my house. Maybe Wire had spoken to him.

I did, but if I said the name of the town, Zoe could flip out. It was a known hotbed for criminal activity. I tried to convey that with a look, but I could tell the Pres was going to be stubborn on this one. If it were up to me, Zoe would never know exactly where her son was being kept, or by whom. It seemed Griz was of a different opinion.

"Would you have told your wife?" I asked.

His gaze narrowed, but I saw the flash of fury that went through him. Yeah, he hated it when we brought her up, unless it was a happy memory. I knew it had to suck balls to have lost her to cancer. She'd been a sweetheart, and had been good for Griz and the club. I might not understand the love they shared, but I knew he still felt her loss deeply.

"Dagger, what's going on?" Zoe asked.

"Tell her," Grizzly said.

Goddamnit! I didn't want to tell her. She'd worry herself to death until I brought Luis home. And that's if

Wire's intel was still good by the time I got there. They could move him and I'd never know it. Even if I opened up my bike, it would take me three days to get there. Then I had to figure out how to bring him back home. I could use one of the club trucks, but they weren't as fast.

"I'm not going to have her worried for that length of time. It will take me days to get there, and days to return after I've secured Luis. You want to put her through hell?" I asked. "Why? What's the fucking point?"

"The men who have your boy are into human trafficking among other things," Griz said. At least he hadn't outright told her who had Luis, but I still wasn't happy he'd even said that much about them.

I heard Zoe sob, then felt her body go lax. If I hadn't reacted fast enough, she'd have ended up on the floor. Lifting her into my arms, I cradled her close to my chest and tried really fucking hard not to knock Grizzly's teeth down his throat. Whatever he'd hoped to accomplish by telling her that, I hoped he was pleased with himself.

"That was a dick thing to do," I said.

"Remember who you're talking to."

"I know exactly who, Pres. Doesn't change the fact she didn't need to know that until her boy was home safe. I'd have told her, when the time was right."

"Luis," Zoe said softly.

"I'll bring him home, Zoe," I promised.

She shook her head. "He could have been sold already. What if you get there and he's gone?"

"No offense, Pres, but get the fuck out. I need to calm Zoe down, and I'd rather do it without an audience."

He snorted and stood. It seemed like he wanted

to say something, then thought better of it. Grizzly let himself out of the house, the door closing softly behind him. I didn't know what to do with Zoe, but I remembered Dingo once saying that a hot bath would calm Meiling whenever she'd get upset or have nightmares. I hoped something like that would work now for Zoe.

Carrying her to my bedroom, I paused next to the bed, reluctant to let her go. I eased her down onto the mattress, but she clung to me when I tried to pull away.

"*Princesa*, I'm going to run a bath for you. Nice big tub in there. Might make you feel better, but you need to let go for me to do that."

She gripped me harder and shook her head.

I toed off my boots, then managed to remove my cut and set it on the bedside table. Nudging her over a little, I settled on the bed next to her and just held her close. If this was what she needed, or wanted, I'd give it to her. I stroked my hand down her back, hoping it would soothe her. I heard her sniffle and felt her tears soaking my shirt. I fucking hated that Griz had said that shit to her, and that it had terrified her. She'd done everything she could to try and give her son a better life, and it had blown up in her face. I knew there were no guarantees in life, but I wanted to bring Luis to his mom, reunite them, and make sure he had everything he could ever need or want for the rest of his life. Both of them. Somehow, Zoe had wormed her way past my defenses.

"I meant what I said, Zoe. Where he's being kept doesn't make a difference. I won't come home without him."

"You don't understand," she said, lifting her head and wiping at her tears. "It's not just him I'm scared for. If you go down there and try to bring him home, they could kill you. Men like that don't play around, Santiago. If they're willing to sell children, I can only imagine what else they're capable of. What if they're angry and kill you for interfering? It would be a long and painful death. I don't want anything to happen to you. Either of you."

"I'm coming home to you, Zoe, and so is Luis. I'll bring our son home. No matter what it takes."

"That's the part that worries me." Her hand fisted my shirt and her mouth tightened into a hard line. "I don't want you to die getting him back. If you can't get him home, and keep yourself safe, leave him for now. It pains me to say that, but I can't lose you both."

I ran my fingers over her cheek. "Trust me, *corazoncito*. I'm going to walk through the door with our boy in my arms, and we'll both be perfectly fine."

My phone chimed in my pocket, and while I was hesitant to stop and see what the message said, I knew it could be from Wire. If he had any information that might set Zoe at ease, I wanted to know. I reached into my pocket and pulled the phone out, then quickly accessed the text.

Congratulations. You're officially married.

I showed her what Wire had said and she gave me a faint smile. It was a start. I knew nothing short of having Luis here would bring the light back to her eyes. Then the phone dinged again.

Give us three hours and Luis should officially be your son.

She read that one too, and her body marginally relaxed. "Us? I thought it was just Wire working on it. You said something about his wife. Is she helping somehow?"

"I'm sure they're tackling it together."

"That's kind of sweet."

Maybe in a diabolical sense. I knew Wire and Lavender could wreak havoc if they ever decided to. Thankfully, they used their skills to help their club and others, like mine. Anyone who pissed them off or came after the Dixie Reapers? They were fair game, and Wire and Lavender made sure they paid.

"If everything is in order by morning, I'll make the arrangements to get Luis," I said. "Will you be okay here?"

"Do I have a choice?"

"Nope. I'll make sure someone stops in to see if you need anything." Although I didn't have a fucking clue who to ask. Before Jared had stormed out of here, I'd have asked him. With the way things stood, I wasn't about to put that on him. I might be an asshole, but not enough of one to rub my lover's face in the fact I had a wife now.

She snuggled closer. The scent of her, and the feel of her soft curves, was making me hard as fuck. I wasn't about to act on it. I might have told her this would be a real marriage, but I wasn't going to demand that of her the first damn night. It wasn't like we had a real wedding, or got married because we loved each other. We were still strangers, even though I knew a secret from her past and she knew mine. It wasn't enough for me to even attempt anything with her. I'd give her time. However much she needed.

Fuck my life. I was going to have blue balls. I could always go tug one out, but that's as good as it would get until she was ready to take things further. Couldn't remember the last time I hadn't been able to get off with one of the girls up at the clubhouse, or lately with Jared.

Welcome to monogamy, asshole. You chose this.

Chapter Six

Zoe

My mind was racing with everything that could go wrong. What if Dagger did find Luis, but died trying to bring my baby home? I never should have told that man I'd like to marry Dagger. I'd put him in danger, and what was he getting out of it? Nothing, that's what. I'd stolen his chance to find happiness with someone, put him at risk, and saddled him with a woman with no sexual experience.

It hadn't escaped my notice he'd gotten hard while we'd been lying in bed. I knew he was only trying to comfort me, and I had no doubt Dagger wouldn't make the first move. He might want me, but he was trying to be a decent guy. I'd have never thought someone like him would care, and while he'd made it clear we would have a regular marriage, he wasn't pushing for that to happen right now.

He'd given me something I hadn't had in a while. Hope. Even more than that, he'd opened his home to me, made sure I had everything I needed, and claimed Luis as his own. The more I thought about it, the more I realized he'd shown me more kindness than anyone had since I'd discovered I was pregnant with Luis. My parents had disowned me for shaming them, even though I'd had no choice in the matter. For them, I was pregnant and unwed. It made me a sinner in their eyes.

Being with Dagger wasn't the same. We were married, sort of. The handcuffs hanging on the bed gave me a few reservations about being intimate with him, but I didn't think he'd ever hurt me. Not on purpose. The moment he'd shackled me to his bed, he could have done whatever he wanted. He hadn't.

Instead, he'd released me. Then he'd shared a part of himself that he claimed no one else knew. A bad man didn't do things like that. It didn't matter what he'd done in the past, or what he planned to do to get my son back. No one could ever convince me Dagger was anything other than honorable.

Which meant if I wanted things to progress between us, I'd have to let him know that's what I wanted. Somehow. I'd never tried to seduce a man before, or flirted with one. I didn't know the first thing about any of that. For years, I'd done my best to be as unnoticeable as possible. He'd made it clear he found me attractive. I knew that wasn't enough to make a marriage last, not a happy one. Neither was sex. I could only hope somewhere along the way, we'd find a middle ground and a way to genuinely enjoy being with one another.

"Santiago." He shifted and met my gaze. "Would you kiss me? Like earlier? It was my first, and... I liked it."

He closed his eyes a moment, his body tightening, then he nodded. It was almost as if my request had caused him physical pain, but I didn't understand how, unless he truly didn't like kissing me. Dagger shifted so that he was leaning over me, his weight braced on his forearms. His gaze was intense as he studied me. If he was waiting for me to back out, it wasn't going to happen. I wanted him to kiss me, and I thought it might be a way to break the tension I felt building between us.

Slowly, he lowered his head until his lips brushed against mine. It was whisper soft, and not quite what I'd had in mind. I didn't know how to ask for what I wanted. I reached up, placed my hand on the back of his neck, in case he decided to pull away.

Parting my lips, I hoped to encourage him to kiss me the way he wanted. He'd said before what he'd given me wasn't a real kiss.

"Kiss me, Santiago. A real one."

"You don't know what you're asking for," he said. "My control isn't the best right now, *princesa*."

I held his gaze. "Then lose control. I'm your wife, aren't I? I won't break. If you do anything that scares me, or is too much for me to handle, I'll tell you. I trust you, Santiago. I know you won't hurt me. You've had ample opportunity, but all you've done is treat me with kindness."

It was as if my words released whatever had been holding him back. Heat entered his gaze, along with a darkness that should have terrified me. My heart thrummed in my chest and I braced myself as he claimed my mouth. Or maybe devoured was a better word. My nipples hardened and I felt my panties dampen. No one had ever made me feel the way Dagger did. Not once had I ever desired someone, not really. I might have held some infatuations when I was younger, but this was so much more.

When he pulled away, I tried to follow, not wanting the kiss to end. Was he finished already? No, the way he looked at me said he was far from done. His gaze skimmed over me only to return to my face a moment later.

"I need to know exactly what you're asking for, *corazoncito*. It's just us in this room. You don't have to be shy. Tell me plainly what it is you want from me right now."

I licked my lips and tried to find the courage to put my desire into words. "I want you to be my first for other things too. I want you to… I want…"

Why was it so hard to ask him to have sex with

me? Plenty of women threw themselves at men around here. I'd seen them do it when I'd crept up to the clubhouse. I didn't know why it was so difficult for me to do that with Dagger.

"You want me to fuck you, *princesa*? Want my cock inside you?"

I nodded. "Yes. I want that. Want *you*, Santiago."

He still hesitated. "All of me? Because what I want, *corazoncito*, is to strip you bare, cuff you to my bed, and do whatever I want. I'll make you scream in pleasure, push you, make you take more than you think you can. I don't know if you're ready yet."

"You won't hurt me," I said.

"No, I would never hurt you, not in the sense you mean. Sometimes a little pain can enhance your pleasure."

"I don't know that I'd like pain, not even if it's supposed to feel good, but I want to try. I want to be a real wife to you, Santiago. I'm worried I'll disappoint you."

He kissed me again, slower, deeper. "You could never disappoint me, *corazoncito*."

I let him undress me, even though it felt like my heart was racing so hard it might explode. My cheeks burned as he stripped me, and I tried to cover myself. He gripped my hands and tugged them away, leaving me exposed. Dagger pulled my arms up over my head and I felt the cool metal of the handcuffs as he clicked them into place. He shifted and got off the bed. He removed his shirt, then took off the rest of his clothing. The moment I saw how large he was I started to have second thoughts.

He smirked. "It will fit."

I wasn't convinced, but I didn't have the experience he did. I'd keep trusting him, unless he gave me a reason not to. It was hard not to curl up and try to hide. I'd never let anyone look at me like this. Dagger reached down and started stroking his cock as he eyed me. A little thrill went through me and I shifted on the bed. Before, if a man looked at me like that, I'd felt ashamed. With Dagger it was different.

Every inch of him was hard. His broad shoulders looked strong and capable. The muscles in his chest flexed as he tugged on his cock. If a man could ever be described as beautiful, it would be Dagger. The ink on his body gave him a sexy, dangerous vibe. Except I knew he really was dangerous. I'd seen enough guns and knives since coming to the Devil's Fury to know these men didn't abide by the laws.

Dagger moved closer and reached out with his free hand to tweak my nipple. I gasped, a little zing shooting through me. My clit started to throb and I wanted his hands on me. No, I wanted more than that. I needed him. The sensations swirling through me were nothing I'd ever experienced before, and I didn't want the feelings to stop.

"Spread those legs, *hermosa*."

Only Dagger had called me beautiful. More than once now. No one had ever said that to me before. Not even my parents. My mother had often told me how I should improve my looks if I ever wanted a husband. Now I had one, and he seemed to like me just as I was. I felt a tremor rake me from head to toe as I parted my thighs. Dagger groaned and yanked on his cock harder.

He trailed his fingers from my breast down my belly until he brushed the hair between my legs. My cheeks warmed again. I'd heard the women talking about waxing and shaving down there. I hadn't been brave enough for any of that, but I'd found a pair of trimmers in the bathroom cabinet and had cut the hair really short. I only hoped whoever had left them wouldn't want them back. I'd hidden them in my room after I realized I liked the shorter hair.

"So wet." He parted the lips of my pussy and stroked his fingers over my clit. I cried out, my body going tight. Everything inside me clenched, and pleasure rolled over me. "Christ! Never had a woman as responsive as you, *princesa*."

I whimpered, feeling nearly breathless from anticipation. I knew he was far from finished with me. If that had been a small taste of what I could expect, I eagerly awaited the rest. I spread my legs farther, inviting him to do as he pleased with me.

He swirled his fingers over my clit again before easing one inside me. Dagger curled it a little as he withdrew, and it was the most incredible sensation I'd ever felt. He did it again. And again. When he added a second finger, I nearly saw stars.

"I'm close to coming just watching you. Feeling you." He worked his fingers in and out of me faster and harder. Before I knew what was happening, I'd come again, this one even stronger than the last. "Need you to take the edge off, *solo te necesito a ti*."

"Santiago, please..."

He pulled his fingers free and knelt on the bed next to me. "You deserve more, *dulzura*."

"You can take more time later. Right now, I just want... you. I want all of you." I took a breath to steady myself. "Make me yours, Santiago. In every way."

He covered my body with his, and I felt his cock brush against me. Dagger shifted his hips and slowly pushed into me. It burned as he stretched me, yet there was a hunger inside me that demanded to be filled. I lifted my hips, trying to pull him in deeper. He chuckled and kissed me, his lips and tongue dominating me. With one hard thrust, he entered me. I cried out and my body tightened, but the sharp burst of pain quickly warmed into so much more.

With my hands bound, I couldn't reach for him, couldn't hold on. He started thrusting, his strokes long and deep. Every time he bottomed out, he ground his pelvis against me, creating friction against my clit, making me beg for more.

"*¡No pares!*" I cried out, not wanting him to stop. I needed everything he had to give.

He growled and powered into me. It felt like I was electrified as I came again, my muscles clenching on his cock. He gripped my hip with one large hand, taking what he wanted. I felt the warmth of his release as he came inside me. My body trembled and I felt as if I were gasping for breath. As he withdrew from me, I realized he was still hard. I hadn't known it was possible for a man to remain in that state after having an orgasm.

Fire lit his gaze as he flipped me over, then lifted my ass in the air. He drove into me again, taking me as if he were possessed.

"Mine!" Our bodies slapped together as he did as I'd demanded. Claimed me. He spread my ass cheeks and my heart stuttered a moment, worried he'd try to take me there, but he didn't. "Need you to come again."

I didn't think I could. I felt wrung out. Dagger proved me wrong. He slid a hand down between my legs and worked my clit as he fucked me. He not only made me come again, but he pulled another two orgasms from me. My legs were barely holding me up when he started thrusting faster. He grunted as he came again, slamming into me again and again.

When he stilled, I heard his breath saw in and out of his lungs. I felt a little dazed, thoroughly used, and a million other things. I'd have to analyze my emotions later. I only wished I could see his face. Had this been enough for him? He'd said his ideal relationship would be with him, a woman, and another man. I felt as if I'd robbed him of that, of his future happiness. I closed my eyes and tried to picture Jared here with us.

I'd thought I would feel disgusted, or unsure. Honestly, the thought of the other man here, watching what Dagger had done to me, only made me ache. I didn't think I could handle any more, my pussy was already sore, but my clit throbbed again. Maybe when Dagger returned with Luis, we could discuss our relationship again. Or more importantly, discuss the possibility of asking Jared to join us.

Dagger ran his hand down my spine, then leaned over, our bodies still joined, and pressed kisses along my shoulders. "*Eso fue increible!*"

It made me feel warm inside that he felt that way. It had been amazing for me, but I had nothing to compare it to. Dagger was the first man I'd ever wanted. Sex hadn't been a concern for me, especially since having Luis. I'd have been content to never pair off with anyone, but Dagger had proven how wrong I'd have been. Anything that felt that amazing should be enjoyed as often as possible.

He withdrew from my body and got the keys, unlocking the cuffs. He gently rubbed my wrists and crawled back into the bed with me, pulling me against his chest. I went willingly, still trying to unjumble my thoughts. I felt the stickiness between my legs and realized we hadn't used protection. He'd said he got tested regularly and was clean, and he wanted more children. There was a moment of panic before I realized that if we'd just created a child, I would love him or her with all my heart.

"What happens now?" I asked.

"What do you mean, *corazoncito*?"

I nibbled at my lip, trying to figure out exactly what I wanted to ask. "If I said I would be willing to try a relationship with you and Jared both, how would that work?"

He went completely still, only the thump of his heart making a sound. I worried I'd said something wrong, but then he started stroking my arm. Dagger took a breath, and another. It felt like forever before he spoke, and I knew he had to have been weighing his words. "I'd have to talk to Jared. He was pissed when he left here. It's possible he wouldn't want to be a part of this."

That was true. He'd been angry when he slammed the door. "But what if he does?"

Dagger shifted us so that we lay on our sides facing one another. He cupped my cheek before running his fingers through my hair. "I'd make sure he understood it could be a one-time thing. If it was too much for you to handle, I wouldn't ask you to keep him in our bed. You might be married to me, but if we included Jared in this relationship, you'd be married to him too. Maybe not on paper, but he'd be your husband just as much as I am."

Luis would have two dads. It wasn't conventional, but Jared had been sweet, and Dagger had proven to be willing to do anything for my son. I couldn't imagine two more perfect men for the task of raising Luis. I didn't know if I could handle both of them at the same time. And what would people say when we went out places? For that matter, what if their club didn't like it?

I heard a door slam and scrambled under the covers. I didn't know if people always dropped in unexpectedly, or if Dagger had merely forgotten to lock the door. Whatever the case, he reached for his underwear and pulled the boxer briefs on. He'd barely managed to cover himself before Jared entered the room. He froze inside the doorway, his gaze on me, then Dagger. I didn't know what he was looking for as he studied Dagger, but his gaze swung back to me and he moved farther into the room, not stopping until he was next to the bed.

"Did he hurt you?" Jared asked.

I bolted upright, clutching the sheet to me. What the hell? Did he seriously think Dagger would hurt me? On purpose? "What? Why would you ask that?"

Jared's jaw tightened and something flashed in his eyes I couldn't quite discern. I wasn't sure if he was worried about me so much as he was pissed that Dagger had slept with me. "He can be rough. I heard the two of you went out tonight. You didn't have to sleep with him as payment for dinner, or whatever else the two of you did while you were gone."

I blinked. I was not only offended for myself, but for Dagger as well. I saw my husband's shoulders tense, and knew he'd felt those words as if they were actual blows against his body. I reached for him, placing my hand on his shoulder. My left hand. Jared glanced down, saw my ring, and it seemed as if every part of him tensed.

"You're fucking married?" he demanded as he focused on Dagger again. "So that's it? I get pissed and walk out, so you marry the next convenient person?"

Dagger stood so fast the mattress sprang up and toppled me over. "I should beat the shit out of you for that. Take it back right fucking now! Zoe isn't anyone's second option. If you'd stuck around, all three of us might have ended up in this bed tonight, but no. You got bent over what I said and ran off like a little bitch."

Jared sucked in a breath, then it was like he just physically and emotionally deflated as his head dropped, his shoulders hunched, and any fight he might have had left him. "I didn't mean to disrespect your wife, Dagger. I came to apologize to you for running out earlier. It was a shock to find the two of you together in bed."

I could only imagine how he felt. Even if the two of them hadn't been exclusive, they'd still been together. Maybe Jared had hoped it would become more. It was clear he was hurting right now.

"I think the two of you need to talk," I said. "Um, Jared, could you turn your back? I need to get dressed."

Dagger turned toward me, braced his hands on the bed, and kissed me softly. "We'll go in the other room. Why don't you shower, then you can come join us? I think this might be a discussion for all of us."

I nodded, and kissed him again. I pulled him closer and whispered in his ear, "I'll accept the both of you, or at least try. He's hurting and I feel partly responsible."

He gave a nod and pulled away. I watched him put on his jeans before walking out with Jared. He pulled the door shut behind him, and I scurried out of the bed and into the bathroom. After taking the world's fastest shower, and putting on some clothes, I braided my hair and tried to prepare myself for whatever would happen next.

I only hoped I was ready if Jared wanted to be part of our relationship. I'd opened that can of worms by telling Dagger I might be willing to take that step. Now it was time accept their decision, whatever it might be. He'd said we could try being together once and see if I could handle it. I had a feeling it would crush Jared to be kicked out after that one time, but I was grateful Dagger had given me an out.

I took a breath to steady myself, then went to find my men.

My men? Shit. I was already thinking of Jared as mine, as well as Dagger. Guess I was jumping in with both feet, and I'd just hope it didn't blow up in our faces.

* * *

Jared

My mind was reeling as I tried to process everything. Dagger and Zoe were *married*. I knew they couldn't have been legally married at the courthouse in front of a preacher because there hadn't been time to get through all the red tape. But still... the fact he'd agreed to marry her still hurt like a bitch. Had he even thought about how it would affect me? Had he cared?

Sure he said if I'd stuck around all three of us could have ended up in bed together, but was that really the case? We'd talked about sharing a woman before, but not once in any of those discussions had we talked about getting married. How would something like that even work?

It felt like the room was closing in on me as I waited to hear more from Dagger, and possibly Zoe. I wasn't running this time. I'd stay and listen, see what they had to say. But it didn't change the fact they were together, had slept together, and I hadn't even known about it until I'd walked in and found them in bed.

Dagger hadn't so much as taken the time to send me a text or try to call me. That didn't exactly make me feel as if they wanted me to be part of their lives. The opposite, in fact. I felt like I'd intruded on them. Now Dagger felt like he owed me an explanation, or maybe it was more that Zoe was encouraging it.

I couldn't remember ever feeling this fucked up or confused before. I clenched my hands so I wouldn't rub my chest, where my heart lay aching. We'd never really said how we felt about each other, but I'd known for the last few weeks I was falling for Dagger. I just wasn't so sure he felt the same about me. Especially now.

Chapter Seven

Dagger

Jared sat on the couch, his head in his hands as he stared at the floor. I'd never thought he'd find out about my relationship with Zoe by finding us in bed together. Even if we hadn't been exclusive, I knew that had to have hurt. It was a dick thing to do. Next time, I'd make sure I locked my fucking door. At least then I could have prepared him better.

I honestly didn't know what to do right now. Zoe had said she might give it a try, having a relationship with both of us, but I was concerned after Jared's reaction both now and earlier. I didn't know if him being a Prospect would cause issues with a long-term relationship. As long as he didn't fuck up, I knew he'd eventually patch in, but for now I outranked him. He'd still know more club business than Zoe would, but I didn't want it to cause problems between us. It hadn't in the past, but we hadn't been committed to each other either. Bringing him into my marriage as an equal could cause issues.

"You said you came to apologize," I said. "Let's start there."

Jared sighed and looked up at me, regret clearly written across his face. "I shouldn't have left the way I did. I know there are times you aren't the Dagger I've been intimate with, that you have to be the Dagger who's a patched member of Devil's Fury. It hasn't come up before when we weren't around the club. It was wrong of me to walk out."

I sat on the coffee table, facing him, and tried to think of what I wanted to say. Yeah, he'd pulled a bitch-ass move, but he wasn't some pussy-whipped guy who'd want to sit on the sidelines either. He might not be as dominant as I was, but he wasn't a pushover. In fact, I knew Jared could hold his own in a fight. But like it or not, if we were going to have a relationship with Zoe, he wouldn't be the one in charge. If he couldn't handle that, then I needed to know now.

"I get it. I really do," I said. "But if you wanted something long-term with me, pulling shit like that wouldn't fly. There will be times I give you an order as a member of this club, and other times I might give you an order that has nothing to do with Devil's Fury and everything to do with me trying to keep you and Zoe safe."

He held my gaze. "Me and Zoe?"

"She's not sure if she can handle being with two men, and I don't want to force that on her. If she wants to give it a try, then you'd have to go into it knowing it might be a one-shot deal. Without getting pissed or acting like a bitch if she says she can't do it, that she just wants me."

Jared shifted and I could see the spark of hope in his eyes. "But she's willing to try?"

I nodded. "Yeah. Which brings me to another matter. I need to leave in the morning to get Luis. I'll be gone at least a week, possibly longer. I don't like the idea of leaving Zoe here alone. Would you be willing to either come check on her, or stay in the guest room so she has someone here when the club doesn't have you doing shit?"

He rubbed his hands up and down his thighs and glanced away. I knew it was asking a lot of him. I'd had no intention of requesting Jared keep an eye on Zoe, but since he was here... Maybe I should have kept my mouth shut and asked someone else. I'd thought since he was familiar to Zoe, and he'd been nice to her before, maybe he would be the right choice. It seemed I may have been wrong. I could have flat out told him to do it, but that's not what I wanted.

I caught sight of Zoe in my peripheral vision and held my hand out to her. She came into the room, took my hand, and I pulled her down onto my lap. Jared looked at her, and I could see he was undecided on what he should do. Right now, Zoe was the most important person in my life. I may not have chosen her as my wife, but that's what she was just the same. With some luck, I'd already planted a baby in her. It had been shitty of me to take her bare without getting tested again, even though I'd gotten the all clear in the last few weeks. I should have protected her better, but I couldn't deny I'd loved being inside her without a barrier between us. I'd never done that with anyone.

Zoe had promised to keep my secret, but if Jared ended up being a part of our lives, he'd need to know about my past. I wasn't sure how he'd react, or if he'd end up blabbing to my brothers. I didn't think he would, but I couldn't be certain, which was part of why I hadn't said shit to him about it yet. Wasn't his business. That would change if he became a permanent part of my life with Zoe.

"We've talked before about having a woman as part of our relationship," I told him. "And while we weren't exclusive, if you decide to pursue something with me and Zoe, I'd have to ask you not to fuck around with anyone else. I won't put her in danger if you can't fully commit."

"Can I have time to think about it?" he asked.

Zoe leaned into me and I tightened my hold on her. "Of course. What about the other thing? You willing to check on Zoe or stay here with her while I'm gone?"

I didn't know which of my brothers had tried to

hurt her, which meant I didn't know who to trust. She'd said she hadn't seen a name. Did that mean it was a Prospect who hadn't had a name stitched on their cut? Or was it an actual brother and she was too scared to tell me? Sooner or later, I'd find out who it was and beat the fucker. The Devil's Fury might not be law-abiding citizens, but there was some shit we didn't tolerate.

"Don't make him stay if he's uncomfortable," Zoe said softly.

I gave her a slight squeeze, hoping she'd catch the hint and keep quiet. Now that we weren't discussing a possible relationship and were focused on her safety, she didn't get a fucking say in the matter. I'd do whatever it took to keep her safe. There was no negotiating when it came to that, and if she decided to argue, I'd just spank her ass and do whatever was necessary to get the point across that she wasn't in charge -- I was.

I shifted, my dick getting hard at the thought of needing to punish her. *Shit.* I seriously needed to think of something else. Having her on my lap was already enough to turn me on. I hadn't lied when I'd said she'd made me hard the moment I'd stepped outside and seen her in my fucking yard. I may like both men and women, but Zoe had a body that would have starred in my fantasies for a while. As it was, I now got to sleep next to her at night, and make her scream my name as she came. Only thing better would be having Jared there with us, or someone else if he decided he couldn't handle it.

Jared held Zoe's gaze. "Would it bother you if I stayed in the guest room?"

She shook her head and I felt her relax against me. Maybe I wasn't the only one concerned about her safety while I was gone. I hadn't realized until that moment she'd been a little tense. There was something I needed to take care of before I left her here. Maybe she and Jared could have a little test run right now to see how they got along without me around. I tapped Zoe's thigh and she stood, giving me the chance to get up without dumping her on the floor.

"Need to run to the clubhouse for a few. Stay with Zoe?" I asked Jared.

"Yeah. I can hang here until you get back."

I pulled Zoe against me. "Need to take care of something. I'll be back."

The way she chewed her lip told me she was nervous. I smoothed it with my thumb, tugging it free from her teeth. She leaned in closer, pressing tight against me. It was tempting to say fuck it and take her back to bed. But I knew damn well I'd worry about her while I was gone, and I needed to know if anyone would fess up about trying to get in her pants.

"Maybe Zoe would want to take a walk?" Jared suggested. "I'd stay with her, make sure she's safe."

I tugged on her hair. "Would you like that, *corazoncito*?"

She nodded.

I brushed my lips over hers, then took a step back before I was tempted to do far more. With a chin lift to Jared, I went to the bedroom and pulled on the rest of my clothes and my boots. I grabbed my keys and headed for my bike in the driveway. I was just far enough from the clubhouse that I didn't want to walk. I could hear the music pulsing before the clubhouse even came into view, which meant it was likely a wild night. Normally, I'd partake of the pussy inside, get shitfaced, and have some fun. Tonight was different. I wasn't here to get trashed or wet my dick. I wanted to know who the fuck put his hands on my woman.

Demon was out front smoking, and by the smell, it wasn't tobacco. He eyed me as I went up to the door, then held out his hand. I stopped, waiting to see what he had to say. If he'd been anyone other than the Sergeant-at-Arms, I'd have flipped him off and kept going. Demon had earned his fucking name, and I knew he was one of the last brothers I wanted to piss off.

"Heard you have a woman now," he said.

"Yep."

He glanced at the clubhouse doors, then back to me. "And you're already here? Doesn't sound like you're too happy with your choice."

"Not here to party," I said. "Just need some information."

He grinned and took another drag off his joint, then rolled his neck until it cracked. Even though his gaze wasn't on me, I knew he was still watching. I didn't know what the fuck he wanted. After a moment, he waved me off so I went inside to see what I could find out. I didn't even know where the hell to start. Making my way up to the bar, I waited for Beau to head over. He already knew what I liked to drink and slid a cold beer to me, but I wanted more than a drink.

"You notice anyone paying special attention to our newest batch of ladies?" I asked. He looked around, but I shook my head. "Not the club pussy. The women who are hands-off."

He rubbed at the back of his neck. "This have anything to do with Grizzly yelling something about you having a woman now?"

"Maybe. What have you seen or heard?" I asked.

"Nothing really. I know some of the guys have been talking about them. A few seemed to be eyeing them in a way they shouldn't. At least, according to the Pres. He wanted everyone to give those ladies a wide berth, but I know some want under their skirts."

And that's what I needed to know. "Anyone specifically mention Zoe?"

He shook his head. "No names. Just shit talk in general about their tits and wanting to give those girls a good fucking. They don't do it around the Pres or even around Demon and Wolf. Anyone can tell those three have a soft spot for them. Who'd have ever thought Demon could be nice?"

I snorted, knowing he wasn't wrong. The SAA wasn't exactly known for his tact. Nor did he have a gentle side that I'd ever seen. Demon liked to get bloody, whether it was putting his fist through someone's face or ripping out their insides. And the fucker would laugh while doing it.

"Something happen to your woman?" Beau asked, his brow furrowed.

"Yeah, and I want to know who the fuck is responsible. She was scared shitless when she showed up at my house, wanting my protection so she'd be safe at the compound. We don't fucking hurt women. Not unless they're deceitful, cold-hearted bitches who earned it like that whore who could have gotten Lilian killed. I'm surprised Demon didn't do worse."

Beau smiled a little. "He wanted to. I heard Grizzly talking him out of it. When he found out a woman had died not too far from where he'd picked up Lilian, he wanted to kill the bitch."

I couldn't blame him for that. The club pussy was expendable, but Lilian most certainly wasn't. Not only was she Grizzly's adopted daughter, but she was Dragon's ol' lady. And a mother. Yeah, the bitch had fucked up when she'd tried to put a wedge between

Lilian and Dragon.

"Someone put his hands on Zoe, and I want to know who the fuck did it," I said.

"Wish I could help, Dagger, but I haven't heard shit. I might only be a Prospect, but I wouldn't stand around and not stop something like that."

I knew he was right. Beau was a good kid. I ran a hand down my beard and scanned the room. Unfortunately, it seemed one of the whores thought it was an invitation. She hustled over and pressed her naked tits to my arm, batting her fake eyelashes at me.

"Want to party?" she asked. Her lips parted and she slid her tongue over her bottom lip. "I'll let you put it anywhere."

I shoved her away. "Didn't call you over."

She pouted, but wandered off. At least she wasn't pushy like some of them. With some luck, the latest batch were only here to have some fun. The ones who'd thought they would get claimed had left after Demon made an example of Cheri. Guess they hadn't wanted one of us quite that bad. Good riddance as far as I was concerned. Even though I wouldn't be dipping my dick in any of them anymore, the last thing the club needed was a bunch of troublesome women.

I gulped down my beer, tapped the bar, and walked out. I could have tried talking to someone else, but they were either too fucking drunk, or had their dicks out. Whether they were drinking or fucking, I wouldn't be getting much from them right now. I knew it had been a gamble, but I wanted this shit settled before I left.

I didn't want to go home, not yet. It wasn't that I was trying to put distance between myself and Zoe, but I didn't like the thought of looking her in the eye when I left tomorrow and not being able to guarantee her safety. Yeah, I had Jared watching over her, and she'd get a property cut. Already wore my ring. Didn't feel like it was enough. Not even close.

My bike was only a few feet away when I heard the panicked scream. I jolted, scanned the area, then heard it again. Down the road that led to my house. I got on my bike and tore out of the lot in front of the clubhouse, hoping like hell one of the women wasn't hurt. When I heard her scream Jared's name, my heart nearly stalled. *Zoe.*

I pushed my bike, going faster, until I whipped around a curve in the road and came to a skidding halt. Jared was down, knocked the fuck out, and someone wearing a Devil's Fury cut was advancing on Zoe. Except it wasn't someone I recognized. I put down the kickstand and got off. The man barely glanced my way, not seeming to be concerned someone else had come along. What the fuck?

"Get away from her," I demanded.

The guy flipped me off. "Bitch wants it. She's just playing hard to get."

"No, she fucking isn't. That's my wife, asshole. Back the hell off," I said.

He paused and turned to face me. Even in the darkness, I could see clearly enough to know this man *wasn't* one of my brothers. I didn't know where he'd gotten the cut, or how he'd made it into the compound, but I was sure the fuck going to find out. He stood straighter, but I noticed he swayed a bit. Drunk. Or high. Maybe both.

I approached, keeping Zoe in my peripheral, but not willing to take my gaze off this ass. No way would he get away with this. Whoever he was, he'd just signed his own death warrant, and I was going to be the Grim-Fucking-Reaper who delivered him to hell.

He'd touched what was mine. Frightened Zoe. Knocked out Jared. I wasn't about to let that shit stand.

My gaze scanned him and I noticed the name on his cut. *King -- Treasurer*. Son of a bitch. Where the fuck had he gotten that? I might not have known King personally, but I'd heard of him. And this asswipe was nowhere near old enough to be King, even if the man wasn't dead already.

"You're not King," I said. "So who the fuck are you?"

He sneered, then spat at me. "I'm fucking royalty. All of you are in for a world of pain before I'm done. Starting with your bitches. I owe this one. Stupid cunt kneed me in the nuts."

"Too bad she didn't kill you. Would have been kinder than what I have in mind." I slipped my phone from my pocket and unlocked the screen with my thumbprint, then tossed it to Zoe. She clumsily caught it, nearly dropping it twice. "*Corazoncito*, call Demon and tell him where we are and to bring backup."

She hastened to obey while putting more distance between herself and whoever this shithead was. I'd be finding out before the night was over. He'd be spilling all his secrets and crying like a baby. Begging for his life. Wouldn't do any good. He was dead as far as I was concerned.

It didn't take long for Demon and four other brothers to arrive. While they took down King, I checked on Jared. He was still breathing, but his face was already bruising. Fucker must hit like a sledgehammer. I looked over at King in time to see Demon hit him with a crowbar. I didn't know why he'd brought it, but I wasn't going to complain. Better than shooting him. That was the easy way out, and this little shit wasn't getting off without some major pain.

"He's mine," I said. "Put his hands on Zoe. Twice."

"Sorry, brother. I get him first. Need to find out where he got this cut and how he got in here. You can have whatever is left, assuming he's still breathing when I'm done," Demon said. "Right now, take care of your woman. I'll get someone to drag Jared's ass back to the clubhouse."

Zoe whimpered, her tear-filled eyes on Jared. I was about to say something that could damn me, but I didn't like seeing that look on my woman's face. "Take him to mine. I think Zoe wants to be there when he wakes. He tried to protect her."

Demon gave a nod. I got my phone from Zoe and called Nox. I needed him to bring a truck, and have Henry ride along. I'd already heard one of my brothers called for a truck to transport the imposter. While I wanted Demon to leave him alive, give me a chance to get vengeance for Zoe and Jared, I knew my priorities should be with my family, even if the club didn't know that last part.

I waited until Nox arrived with the truck, and once Jared was loaded, I helped Zoe onto the back of my bike and headed home. She clung to me, her face buried against my back. As much as I loved having her ride behind me, I hated the reason for it. Once the shitstorm was over, and Luis was home safe, I'd have to take her for a ride. At the house, she got off the bike but looked like she was seconds from collapsing. I lifted her into my arms and carried her inside, knowing the Prospects would bring Jared in.

"Put him in the guest room," I called over my shoulder. I took Zoe straight to the bedroom and pushed the door mostly shut. I set her down on her feet, but kept my arms around her.

- 91 -

"He wasn't part of your club?" she asked.

"No, he wasn't. You lied to me, didn't you? You saw his name, knew who he was. Or at least who he was pretending to be."

She shook her head. "I didn't see a name, but I did see his title. I worried he'd try to hurt me, or do something to you if you confronted him. I'm sorry, Dagger. I only wanted to protect you. And... I was scared."

I tipped her chin up and pressed my lips to hers. "You're going to pay for lying to me, *corazoncito*. I'm going to spank that ass, but not right now. Jared needs us. Can you hold it together a little while longer?"

"*Sí.*"

I leaned in closer and dropped my voice. "I won't be forgetting that spanking. Might not happen right now, but sooner or later, your ass is going to be red. By keeping shit from me, you put yourself and the club in danger. Can't have that, Zoe."

A flash of fear entered her eyes and I felt like an ass, but I couldn't let this slide. If she'd spoken up, I could have confronted our current Treasurer, Savage, and we would have quickly discovered something was incredibly wrong. Maybe if we'd known there was an imposter, we could have found him sooner. What if he'd hurt someone else while he was here? Shit. I needed to have someone check on the other women.

I traced her nose with mine. "And, *corazoncito*, when I'm done spanking that ass, I'm going to fuck you until you can't stand up. I'm fucking furious. You could have been hurt or even killed. When I realized that was you I heard screaming, I about had a Goddamn heart attack. I could have lost you."

She reached up, her fingers trembling as she touched my jaw. "I'm sorry, Dagger. I promise, I won't lie to you again."

I kissed her once more, then walked out to check on Jared. If he was down for the count, I couldn't very well leave him to watch over Zoe. But the longer it took me to reach Mexico, the worse my chances became of actually bringing our son home. And yes, Luis was *our* son. Not only Zoe's, or even Zoe's and mine. He belonged to Jared too because whether he wanted to admit it or not, Jared was just as much mine as Zoe was.

Just had to convince the stubborn fucker of that.

Chapter Eight

Zoe

When I'd seen the man coming out of the shadows, I'd recognized him, and been terrified. Then he'd hit Jared. Not once. Not twice. Three times. Rapid punches that had knocked Jared out cold. If Dagger hadn't heard me, hadn't come to save me… I shivered, not wanting to think of what could have happened. Would Jared have died? Would I? It never occurred to me the man wasn't really part of the Devil's Fury. Dagger was right. If I'd said something sooner, then maybe they could have found the man before he hurt Jared.

Dagger sat on the edge of the guest room bed, holding an ice pack to Jared's battered face. I lurked in the doorway, not wanting to interrupt. Even though Dagger had said more than once he and Jared weren't exclusive, I could tell the other man meant something to him. No one had ever been as tender with me as he was right now with Jared. Except maybe Dagger, as I thought back to the gentle touches and nice things he'd done for me. But this was different. I could clearly see the connection between them. Dagger might have been married to me on paper, but I knew I didn't have his heart. The man who lay unconscious had more of a claim to him than I did.

The big biker came off as gruff and a bit scary, but deep down, I had a feeling he was capable of love. Despite his past, and the way he kept people at a distance, one day Dagger would fall for someone and fall hard. I swallowed the knot in my throat, when I realized that person might very well not be me, and I'd trapped him. It was clear he cared for Jared, maybe even loved him on some level. While Dagger was good to me, it wasn't the same. Might never be.

It felt wrong, watching them, like I was intruding on their time together. Even though Jared hadn't woken, I didn't think Dagger would want me in there with them. I backed up and decided to make some coffee. Now that Jared had been injured, I didn't think my husband would be leaving in the morning for Mexico. In fact, it was possible he'd changed his mind entirely. My heart ached at the thought of my son. If I hadn't seen a picture of Luis, then I wouldn't have even known what my own child looked like. I might have come to this country with the best of intentions, but the fact remained that I'd abandoned him.

What kind of mother did that?

"A rotten one," I muttered to myself.

My hands shook as I prepared the coffeemaker, and I spilled grounds across the counter. Once the pot was brewing, I cleaned up the mess I'd made and sat at the table, uncertain what I should do. Maybe it wasn't too late to fix things. I didn't know who had my son, or if Luis was in trouble, but it wasn't fair to ask Dagger to go after him. Yes, their President had said the men who had Luis were into human trafficking, but part of me hoped that wasn't why they had Luis. It was too much for me to handle, the possibility my son could be sold or hurt. But Dagger needed to be here right now, especially now that Jared was injured. And it had been my fault. He had every right to be angry with me.

A tear slipped down my cheek, then another. I hastily wiped them away. Crying had never solved anything. It wouldn't make Jared wake up. Wouldn't bring Luis to me. And it wouldn't make Dagger ever fall in love with me. I'd been selfish, only thinking of myself, and I'd possibly ruined two other lives. They both would have been better off if I'd never come to this house.

The coffee finished brewing and I poured a cup, then carried it to Dagger. I set it on the bedside table. He didn't even acknowledge my presence. It was all I needed to know that I had to fix the mess I'd made of things. I walked out and kept going. Leaving his home hurt, but it was for the best. I didn't know where I was going, so I wandered through the compound. The path meandered past the clubhouse and I kept going. I didn't know how far I'd gone, or how much time had passed. The sky started to lighten and I knew it was morning.

Outlaw had given Dagger the ultimatum to marry me. If I could find him, then I could make it all right again. I just didn't know which house was his. One of the guys wearing a vest that said *Prospect* was heading toward me. I didn't know his name, but maybe he could help me.

"You lost?" he asked as he stopped a few feet away.

"I need to find Outlaw."

He tipped his head to the side, and at first I thought he wouldn't say anything. He lifted his chin and pointed back the way I'd come. "You passed his house. Go back three homes, but it's really damn early to be waking him up unless it's an emergency."

It was. At least, I thought it was. I thanked him and went back to the home he'd pointed out. My hands trembled as I knocked on the door and waited, hoping he wouldn't be angry I was here so early in the morning. The man who answered wore a scowl, and had a scar on his cheek that made him look fierce. I took a step back and nearly toppled off the steps, but he reached out and grabbed my arm.

"Easy," he said as he steadied me.

"I need your help," I said. "I need to take it back."

"Take what back? Who are you?" he asked.

"Zoe. You made Dagger choose between marrying me or leaving my son in Mexico. Wire did something, married us. I need to fix it."

Outlaw sighed and rubbed at his eyes. "It's too damn early for this shit. Why don't you want to be married to Dagger?"

I thought of Jared and the tender way Dagger had cared for him. Remembered how angry he'd been when he realized I'd known the man who attacked us. If I could undo everything, I would, but I couldn't go back in time. But maybe I could fix just one thing and give Dagger his freedom.

"I made a mistake," I said. "Several. He's been kind to me, but… he deserves to be happy."

"Trust me. Having a woman in his bed every night will be enough to make him happy. Unless you have a problem with that aspect of being married to him?" Outlaw asked.

"He already cares about someone else," I said softly. "I've ruined things and I need to fix it. He left the choice up to me. Agreed to marry me, even though I know he didn't want to. I want a happy marriage, Outlaw, not a husband who's stuck with me. I don't want someone who will wake up one day and hate me for ruining his life, for taking away his chance to find his perfect match."

Outlaw reached out and cupped my cheek. "What did he say to you? Did he do something to make you feel like this?"

I couldn't tell him without revealing Dagger's love interest was another man. I wouldn't do that to the man who had been so nice to me, had given me a chance, and done everything he could to help me. But I had to tell Outlaw something.

"He didn't say anything. I know he's angry I didn't speak up about the man who tried to hurt me, but he didn't ask me to leave if that's what you mean. He was taking care of the man who was injured trying to protect me. I snuck out when he wasn't paying attention."

Outlaw gave a soft chuckle. "I see. Then I'd imagine he'll be looking for you. Zoe, you may not know Dagger that well, but I do. I know more than he realizes."

I stiffened and tried to pull away from his touch. What did that mean? Did he know about Dagger and Jared? Or did he mean Dagger's past? I'd promised I wouldn't say anything, and I'd keep my word, but I wanted to know exactly what this man thought he knew about Dagger.

"Do you know what Dagger wants more than anything?" he asked.

I did, or thought I did. I wasn't about to tell Outlaw. What I thought Dagger wanted most was to be with Jared, openly, without worrying the other men here would kick them out or make them feel bad for loving each other.

"A family," Outlaw said. "The Pres had a daughter who recently left. Shella had Dagger's eye for a while now. I knew it. Everyone did. For whatever reason, he never made a move, and I have my suspicions as to why. I think it has a lot to do with the man in his house right now. Jared. Because Dagger doesn't just want a wife and kids. He wants to share that woman and those kids with the Prospect in his home."

Maybe he did see far more than Dagger realized.

Did anyone else know? He'd believed no one knew their secret, but it seemed that wasn't the case. But if Outlaw knew that already, why had he forced Dagger to marry me in order to save my son? I didn't understand any of it.

"You're confused," Outlaw said. "And you should be. It's really damn early and I'm guessing you never went to sleep. My wife isn't up yet, my daughter has only been asleep an hour, and I'm still exhausted. You can crash on the couch for now, but I can promise Dagger will be coming for you. He cares more than you think he does."

"He feels responsible since you backed him into a corner," I said.

Outlaw smiled. "We'll see. Come inside and get some rest. I'll get a blanket for you."

I followed him into his home and eased down onto the couch. I suddenly felt like I'd run for miles and exhaustion set in. He handed me a blanket and a pillow before leaving me alone, most likely heading back to his own bed and his wife. I hoped I hadn't woken her when I'd knocked on the door. After I kicked off my shoes, I got comfortable and covered up. The moment my head hit the pillow I closed my eyes.

Despite the fact I was tired to the point I wanted to cry, I couldn't sleep. Outlaw hadn't said he would help me. He seemed to think Dagger wanted to keep me, but I didn't think that was true. It wasn't like the man had feelings for me. We were still strangers. Yes, we'd slept together, but I knew that didn't mean anything for a guy like Dagger. He'd slept with a lot of people. For him, it was just a release. With me, it was different. He'd given me a special moment I would always cherish.

My eyes felt like they had sand in them, and my

body felt heavy. I must have drifted off at some point because the next time I opened my eyes, the sun was streaming through the windows and I smelled breakfast cooking. I stretched and got up, careful to fold the blanket I'd borrowed. I put my shoes back on. As much as I wanted to go thank Outlaw for letting me stay, I thought it would be best if I left. It was obvious he didn't plan to help me.

I crept out the front door, attempting to be stealthy, and shut it as soundlessly as possible. Rushing down the steps, I made my way back to the apartment I'd been using until I'd gone to Dagger's house. I knew the door would be unlocked and I let myself in. The fact my things were still here should have been a comfort to me, but it wasn't. I sat on the edge of the bed and wondered what I should do next. I couldn't stay, but I didn't have anywhere to go either. Or money for that matter. I'd sent every penny to the woman in Mexico, who didn't even have my child anymore. I was furious with her! My hands curled into fists at my sides and I wished I could hit her. But more than that, I was angry with myself. I'd entrusted my child to her, without truly knowing her. Even if my family hadn't wanted me, I didn't think they'd have turned Luis away if I'd left him with his grandparents. They could have lied and said they were helping someone or had adopted him.

One of the women stopped in the doorway, her arms folded and her hip leaning against the frame. "Heard you got yourself a biker. Why are you back here?"

"It was a mistake," I said. "He didn't really want me."

She snorted. "Really? Just wanted in your pants and now that you've given it up he's done? Figures.

It's why I'm keeping my distance."

No, Dagger wasn't like that, but I couldn't make her understand. He hadn't asked me to leave, or thrown me out. I'd left because it was the right thing to do. Maybe if I could find a way to Mexico, I could check on Luis. There was a chance the people who had bought him had wanted a child to raise. Or at least I told myself that. It made it easier on my heart and my conscience. I didn't know how I'd get there. I had no money, no transportation. Even I knew hitchhiking was a bad idea, and besides, who would take me all the way to another country?

"If you didn't have money, how would you get back home?" I asked.

"Home?" The woman's eyebrows rose. "I'm not going back to that hellhole. One way or another, I'm staying in this country. I was trying to bring my husband here, but he's dead. No reason to go back."

I blinked, not quite sure what to say. "Dead? Who told you that?"

She waved a hand. "One of the guys here. Outlaw? Something like that. He checked into all our families back home. I'm not the only one who lost someone. Except for me, it's no great loss. I hadn't wanted to make that deal, to work in a shop and earn my husband's way here. No, that was all *his* idea. Probably thought I'd be earning it on my back."

I opened and shut my mouth. What exactly was the correct response? It sounded like her husband had been a horrible man. She'd probably be better off without him. And with only herself to worry about, she'd land on her feet. It seemed the bikers were going to help us. Although, they probably wouldn't want to help me right now.

My stomach rumbled and I realized I hadn't

eaten since dinner last night. I went into our small kitchen and dug through the cabinets. There wasn't a lot in there, but I pulled down a box of macaroni and decided to make a pot. Something was better than nothing. When we'd gotten here, I'd remembered seeing chicken breasts and pork chops in the fridge, but it seemed everyone had eaten them already. Even though there were two of us in this particular apartment, I'd seen all of them eating together and knew they took turns making meals. I'd just never been invited. After not getting much in the way of food for so long, it was hard not to want to consume everything in sight.

While the noodles boiled, I prepped the amount of butter and milk I'd need, and stirred the pasta frequently. I drained the macaroni, then mixed in the milk, butter, and powder mix. It wasn't the most appetizing of meals, but it would be filling. Whoever had bought the groceries for these places must have loved this stuff because the cabinet had a dozen boxes in there. And cans of something called Spam. I hadn't been brave enough to try the canned meat.

I sat at the small table and ate my food. Since it was breakfast, I'd have preferred bacon, eggs, and hash browns. Or better yet, chilaquiles, but I didn't have the ingredients to make those. There were some things I missed about Mexico. Mostly the food, but I'd also enjoyed the festivals I'd been able to attend. When I was younger, I'd been permitted to go if my chores were finished, or if we could manage to enjoy the parades and festivities without it costing too much. Later, I'd struggled, and things had been hard, but at least I'd been independent. Here, I had to rely on other people to give me what I needed.

I'd barely eaten half my food when someone

pounded on the door so hard it rattled on the hinges. Everything in me froze as I stared at it. Whoever was out there seemed pissed. Were they here for me? Was I going to be punished for not telling someone about the man who'd tried to touch me? My heart started racing and my hands shook. Someone, likely my roommate, let one of the bikers inside.

I remembered him. Demon. I dropped my fork and tried not to pee on myself. He was so imposing, and so very angry. The way he watched me made me want to bolt from the room, or from the compound entirely. He stomped over, reached down and gripped my arm, then hauled me out of the chair. As he dragged me from the apartment, I wondered how bad it would hurt. I didn't know what he'd do to me.

"Do you have any idea how much trouble you're in right now?" he demanded.

"I-I'm sorry."

"You're going to be."

I tried not to whimper. I wouldn't cower or beg. I'd take whatever punishment was coming, and then I'd figure out my next move. I couldn't stay here. They probably wouldn't let me anyway. I'd need a job. A place to stay.

He dragged me to the front of the clubhouse, then tossed me down on the ground. I sprawled at their President's feet. The gravel from the parking lot dug into my hands and broke the skin on my palms, but I stayed where I was, not sure what he would do if I tried to get up.

"What the fuck, Demon?" Grizzly asked.

"Little bitch was hiding at the apartments. We've been looking all over this place for her. Do you have any idea how much time we've wasted trying to find her?" Demon asked.

"I'm sorry," I muttered, over and over. I rocked back and forth, fighting not to let the tears fall that were burning my eyes.

"Jesus, Demon. I think you broke her," someone else said.

A hand gripped me and hefted me to my feet. I was led over to a truck and placed in the passenger seat. I didn't know where they were taking me, but I hoped it wasn't somewhere to kill me. Oh, God. Had Jared died? Was I responsible for killing him and now they wanted to return to the favor? My hands were shaking and my stomach felt like it was in knots.

The biker got in and drove, not saying a word. I didn't know where we were going or why. I stared down at my lap, thinking it was best if I didn't see our destination. When the truck came to a halt, the biker got out, then tapped on my window. I opened the door, but I didn't think I wanted to go any farther.

"Get your ass in the fucking house before Dagger starts ripping everyone's heads off," the guy said, yanking me from the truck. I stumbled and looked up to see that we were indeed in front of Dagger's home.

I went inside, worried about what I'd find. When his gaze fastened on me, there was a wildness in his eyes. His hair stood on end, and it looked like he hadn't slept all night. His throat worked as if he had trouble swallowing, and then he was striding toward me. I tensed, not sure what to expect, but he folded his arms around me and held me close.

"You scared the shit out of me," he murmured.

Wait, what? He'd been... worried about me? I tried to pull back so I could look at him, but his hold was too tight.

"Dagger, I..."

"She was at the apartments," the guy said who'd

tossed me into the truck.

"You can go," Dagger said.

I heard the front door shut. Someone yelled from the back of the house. "Is she back?"

"She's back," Dagger answered, then looked down at me. "Come on, *princesa*. You had us both worried. Let's show Jared that you're in one piece."

He took me by the hand, and I winced. Dagger stopped and let loose a slight growl as he examined my skinned palms. He led me to the bathroom and gently washed the debris and blood away. Once they were cleaned, they didn't look so bad. After pressing a kiss to my forehead, he led me to the guest room. Jared, shirtless, reclined in the bed against a bunch of pillows. The bruising on his face had to be painful, but he smiled when he saw me. Dagger gave me a nudge and I moved closer to the bed. Jared reached over and took my hand, tugging me down onto the mattress. I sat, not quite sure what was going on.

"Why did you go to the apartments?" Dagger asked. "Did you leave something you needed? I'd thought you didn't have much of anything."

I looked from Jared to Dagger, then back again. Then I took a breath. I owed him an apology. "I'm sorry, Jared. It's my fault that man attacked you."

I felt the heat of Dagger's body as he came up behind me, then his hand fisted in my hair, forcing my head back. "Excuse the fuck out of me?"

"You were right," I said softly. "It was my fault. All of it. If I had told you sooner that I'd seen his title, then you could have found him. Jared wouldn't have been injured."

"Is this because I said I was going to punish you?" Dagger asked. "I wasn't pissed because Jared got his ass handed to him. It infuriated me that you'd put yourself in danger, *corazoncito*. You could have been raped. Killed."

Tears filled my eyes, and then I was back in Dagger's arms. He sat on the side of the bed, pulled me onto his lap, and stroked my hair.

"Why did you leave?" Jared asked. "Because you felt guilty?"

"I left because it was the right thing to do. I went to Outlaw and asked him to undo everything."

Dagger stiffened. "Undo what exactly?"

"Our marriage. I know you didn't really want to marry me. It was sweet of you to agree to it, but I can't be the cause of your unhappiness. I watched as you took care of Jared, and I realized that while you'd love someone someday, it wouldn't be me. I wanted to make it right."

"Fuck," Jared muttered. He shared a look with Dagger and gave him a nod. I didn't know what that meant, but then Dagger was standing and setting me down on my feet. He turned to shut and lock the door, then faced me again.

"Undress, Zoe. Right the fuck now."

My heart hammered against my ribs. He wanted me naked? Why?

"Don't disobey me, *corazoncito*."

I removed my clothes. My cheeks warmed, knowing it wasn't only Dagger watching me but Jared as well. I didn't understand what was going on, or why I had to do this. Was he trying to humiliate me? Would he punish me in front of Jared?

Dagger began to remove his clothes and Jared tossed off the blankets. I gasped when I saw he was naked under the covers. Were they… were they going to share me? Or was I supposed to watch while they… A warmth started to spread through me. It had been sexy before, watching Jared suck Dagger's cock when I'd been spying through the kitchen window.

"On the bed, wife," Dagger said.

I scrambled onto the bed, then felt his hands at my waist as he positioned me between Jared's splayed legs. The Prospect's cock was hard and upright. My cheeks burned and I knew I was blushing furiously. Dagger fisted my hair and tipped my head so I had no choice but to hold his gaze.

"You're going to be a good girl and *show* Jared how sorry you are. Not because he was knocked unconscious, but because he was worried when we couldn't find you. You're going to take every inch of his cock into your mouth, and suck him dry."

My nipples hardened and I felt myself grow slick between my legs. Dagger leaned closer to me, his voice dropping to that sexy rumble making me want to beg him to let me come.

"And while you're doing that, you're going to put this pretty little ass in the air. I'm going to spank it until you can't sit down without remembering you fucked up, then I'm going to fill that pussy. You like that idea, *princesa*? A cock in your mouth and one in your pussy?"

I nodded, my breath catching in my throat.

"Then show me," Dagger said.

"Yes, Santiago."

Chapter Nine

Dagger

I could see how turned on my little wife was over the thought of having both Jared and me at the same time. She might have thought she couldn't handle it, but I knew she could. No, not just that she could, but that she needed it as much as we needed her. When I'd discovered she was missing, my heart had nearly stopped. Then Jared had freaked the hell out when I'd told him she wasn't in the house. I'd known then I'd found my woman and my man. The three of us together were going to be a family, whether the club liked it or not. If they had an issue with it, then we'd leave and go somewhere else. I'd put the brotherhood ahead of my needs long enough.

I gripped Zoe's hair and lowered her head to Jared's cock. There was a bead of pre-cum on the tip and her tongue flicked out to lick it off. Jared groaned and my own cock twitched. She parted her lips and Jared thrust upward. When he reached for her, I released her hair and let him take over. He guided her motions, forcing all of his cock down her throat. She gagged more than once, but he didn't let up.

I stood behind Zoe at the foot of the bed, admiring the view. Her ass moved with every bob of her head, but it was how fucking soaked she was that held my attention. It seemed she enjoyed being with Jared, and having me watch. But I was done being a bystander. I got onto the bed behind her, and ran my hands down her back. Her ass was about to be really damn red, and I knew she'd be hurting for a few days, but I hoped she'd think twice before running off again.

My hand cracked against one ass cheek, then the other. She squeaked and jolted, but Jared wouldn't release her, just thrust harder into her mouth. I spanked her ass until I could feel the heat coming off her skin, and still kept going.

Crack. "Every time you make me worry." *Crack.* "I'm going to spank this ass." *Crack. Crack.* "And next time, I may damn well fuck it afterward."

I spanked her three more times on each cheek, then lined my cock up with her pussy. I surged forward, going balls-deep on the first stroke, and gripped her hips tight. While she sucked Jared off, I pounded into her, taking what I needed. She'd scared the shit out of me when I couldn't find her, and needed a reminder she was mine. Not just mine. She belonged to both of us.

"You're mine, *corazoncito*. If you run, I will find you. And when I get you home, I will punish you how I see fit. This pussy is mine, and I'm going to fill it with my cum so you remember that." I slammed into her harder. Deeper. "Your mouth and ass are mine to claim, and I will. But you're also Jared's, and you will bend over and beg for his cock whenever he asks you to. Understood?"

She hummed around the cock in her mouth.

"You close?" I asked Jared. He nodded, his eyes fever bright. "Pull her off. You're not coming yet."

Jared made Zoe release his cock, and I came inside her, grunting as my hips jerked and my release filled her. When I pulled out, I lifted Zoe until she straddled Jared. His eyebrows rose, but I simply stared him down. He wanted to be part of this, then he would be. After he'd woken, we'd talked. I knew he planned to stay faithful to Zoe and me, he was clean, and that was all I needed to know right now.

I leaned in closer to Zoe, putting my lips by her ear. "Take his cock into your pussy, *princesa*. Show him he's part of this relationship, part of our family. He needs to know you belong to both of us."

She sank onto his cock and started riding. I reached between her legs, feeling where they were connected. Using my cum, I lubed the tight little hole between her ass cheeks. Zoe gasped and her body tensed, but I ran a hand down her arm, trying to relax her. I worked my finger into her, wishing it was my cock, but I wasn't exactly small and we'd need to build up to that.

"She feels good, doesn't she?" I asked Jared.

"Like fucking heaven." He groaned, his eyes sliding shut. Bliss crossed his features and his hips jerked as he came. I reached around Zoe and rubbed her clit in small tight circles until she found her release.

I helped Zoe off Jared, and she sank to her knees next to him on the bed. I gripped her chin and made her look at me. Her cheeks were flushed and her eyes were bright, and she looked really damn happy. I brushed my thumb across her lips, then kissed her. My cock was already getting hard again, but I didn't think she'd be ready to go another round immediately.

"Dagger." My gaze jerked to Jared, who was eyeing my cock. "Even though I just came, I'm feeling a little left out where you're concerned. Why don't you put that to use?"

We'd fucked many times, but never with someone else in the room. I released Zoe and left to get the lube from my bedroom. When I came back, her thighs were spread and Jared was playing with her pussy. Her nipples were so fucking hard I wanted to bite and suck on them. I shut and locked the door again, in case anyone decided to wander into the house uninvited.

"You sure?" I asked Jared.

"Yeah. Our *princesa* is going to let me make her come while you fuck me. And I think she'll enjoy watching."

A flush spread across her breasts and up her neck. It seemed Jared was correct. She liked the idea of seeing me fuck him. I took my time prepping Jared, and kept an eye on what he was doing to Zoe. It wasn't long before she was trying to ride his fingers, and I could tell she was close to coming again.

Jared tossed the pillows from behind him and lay flat on the bed, then bent his legs giving me more room to work. When he was easily taking three fingers, I slicked my cock with more lube, then pressed the head against his tight hole. I pushed in, getting even harder when he groaned and lifted his hips. Yeah, he wanted it. Probably needed this as much as I did. We'd always used condoms in the past, but now that I knew the three of us were exclusive, we didn't need those anymore.

I thrust into him, using long deep strokes. Jared's cock twitched and I knew he'd be hard again soon. I braced my weight on my knees and reached down to stroke his shaft.

"Christ, Dagger! So fucking good," he murmured. His eyes opened and he looked over at Zoe. "Come on my fingers, pretty girl."

Zoe's hips bucked faster, her movements jerky, and then she was crying out her release. She collapsed on the bed, her chest heaving, her legs splayed. Seeing her wet pussy, filled with my release and Jared's, made my control snap. I fucked Jared harder, not stopping until I'd come, filling his tight ass. His cock jerked and twitched. I gripped him tighter and stroked faster until his cum covered my hand and his body.

"I think the three of us need a shower," I said.

"Only if our *hermosa esposa* lets me eat her pussy while we're in there."

Zoe shivered, but she didn't say no.

"I'll go get the water ready. The two of you rest in here until I call for you." I leaned down and kissed Jared, pressing my hips tighter against him. When I straightened, I withdrew my cock from his body and got off the bed. "You two get better acquainted while I'm gone."

I saw Jared lean down to Zoe for a kiss as I walked out, a smile on my face. I finally had what I wanted. Mostly. I still needed to find Luis and bring him home. The thought of leaving Zoe and Jared wasn't pleasant, but the boy was mine, which meant he was my responsibility. I couldn't ask someone else to retrieve him.

The water in the shower warmed quickly and I yelled out for Jared and Zoe to come join me. I washed off while I waited for them. But when a few minutes turned into several more, I got curious what they were up to. I left the water running, but padded down the hall to the guest room. I peeked around the open doorway and grinned when I saw Jared was enjoying our woman again. I'd already gotten her to myself once, so it was only fair he got the same treatment.

I finished my shower, standing under the stream of water, letting it beat down on my head and shoulders while I waited for them. When they joined me, they both looked content and completely sated. We put Zoe between us, washing her together. One day we'd fuck her together too. I couldn't wait to have her between us. I rinsed the soap from her body, then Jared knelt at her feet. I wrapped my arm around her waist, lifting her as he positioned her legs over his shoulders, then I held her as he ate her pussy and made her come again. Her cries of pleasure were the sweetest I'd ever heard.

Zoe was nearly boneless when we got out of the shower. I tucked her into bed, kissed her brow, then pulled on my clothes. I'd had every intention of getting us some food, until my damn phone went off.

Grizzly.

"Everything okay, Pres?" I asked.

"Church in five. Bring Jared with you, but leave Zoe at home."

My gut clenched. Not knowing if anyone else was lurking inside the compound, I wasn't about to leave my wife alone. She seemed to be a magnet for trouble. "Are you sending someone here to watch her?"

After that asshole made it into the compound, I wasn't taking any chances with her safety. I didn't want to risk that he had an accomplice, especially since it seemed he'd been tight-lipped and refused to talk. Demon had handled the impersonator last night, but whatever secrets the asshole had, he'd taken them to his grave. And I knew Demon could be a persuasive bastard.

"I'll send Beau over to keep an eye on her," Grizzly said. "Just get your asses here, assuming you're done fucking your woman into submission."

The Pres hung up the phone and I stared at it. What exactly had that meant? Did he know Jared and I had been with Zoe together? There was no fucking way. We'd made sure to keep things quiet, to not flaunt our relationship. No one knew I was fucking him, did they? No, maybe he'd meant I'd been with Zoe alone. That had to be it.

"Get dressed," I told Jared. "Church in five, and the Pres said you have to go too."

Jared froze in the middle of pulling his jeans up his legs. "What? Prospects aren't allowed in Church."

Yeah, no fucking shit, which made my stomach clench. Just what the hell were we walking into? I couldn't think of a single damn reason for us both to be called in. My only hope was that it had to do with Zoe, or Luis. Maybe Grizzly wanted Jared there to talk logistics since he was going to remain here with her.

I glanced at the bed and smiled when I saw Zoe was already asleep. We'd worn her out, but then, she didn't look like she'd slept much if at all. I was pissed that she'd worried herself so much, and us as well. If she'd just come to talk to me, then we could have avoided the entire issue. It was something we'd have to work on. That was twice she'd kept something from me. I couldn't protect her if she wasn't completely honest with me. And in this case, I'd needed to save her from herself. I still couldn't believe she'd thought I didn't want her.

There was one thing she'd gotten correct, though. I did care about Jared, more than I'd been willing to admit. I knew if I confessed my feelings this very moment, he'd freak the hell out. I'd bide my time, and when an appropriate time presented itself, I'd talk to him. He was in this for the long haul, exactly like me, but throwing around words like "love" was another matter entirely.

Once Jared and I had finished dressing, and I made sure someone was outside to watch over Zoe, we got on our bikes and headed for the clubhouse. I couldn't help but feel that something was off. My instincts had kept me alive thus far, and I generally didn't ignore my gut. And right now it said we could be walking into trouble. I hoped like fuck I was wrong. Griz had been cryptic, which didn't usually bode well.

At the clubhouse, we parked our bikes at the end, in case we needed a quick escape. It looked like everyone was already present, and it made me wonder if I'd been called last.

"You ready for this?" I asked.

"For what?" Jared asked.

"My point exactly. I have no fucking clue what's about to happen."

Jared squared his shoulders and walked up the clubhouse steps, then entered the building. I followed at a slower pace, trying to judge the overall vibe as I assessed my brothers. No one seemed to be in a rush to get into Church, so maybe I'd been worried for no reason. I was the last through the doors and shut them behind me, then claimed my seat at the table. Jared stood off to the side. Since he wasn't a patched member, he didn't have a seat.

Grizzly banged the gavel and called everyone to order. I tried not to shift in my seat as unease ate at me. I also did my damnedest not to look over at Jared. We'd tried to keep our relationship a secret, and I'd thought we'd done a damn good job. Now I had to wonder if I was wrong and the club knew. Was I about to be tossed out, and Jared along with me? If that happened, I didn't know what I'd do about Zoe and Luis. I'd promised to bring him home to her, and I needed this club to make that happen.

"I have a few orders of business for today, but I'll try to keep it short," Grizzly said. "As everyone knows, a man made it into the compound wearing a Devil's Fury cut. Worse, that cut belonged to King who's been dead for over two decades. I've checked with every brother who was around back then, and none of them remember what happened to his cut when he went inside. Could merely be an issue of his woman dumping his shit at the thrift store and this asshole bought it. Or it could mean something else."

"Won't be finding out now unless you conduct a séance," Demon said. "I put that fucker in the ground. Wasn't for a lack of trying to get him to talk. No matter what I did, he simply grinned like a damn psycho."

"Did we ever figure out how he got inside?" I asked.

"Hot Shot found a piece of fence someone had cut toward the back of the property," Grizzly said. "Anyone coming from that direction had to cut through the woods for miles, which meant he came here for a reason. This wasn't just a matter of an opportunity presenting itself."

"Do we know if he was alone? Anyone else going to pop out of the dark?" I asked. "I need to know if Zoe is even safe inside these fucking gates. How can I leave her to bring our kid home if I can't be assured of her safety while I'm gone?"

Talon leaned his elbows on the table. "I've had both brothers and Prospects scouring every inch of this place. Far as I can tell, this guy was acting alone. We've already repaired the fence, but to be honest, there just aren't enough of us to watch every fucking section of fence line all day every day."

Outlaw tapped the table. "Which is why I prepared some numbers for Grizzly. I know cameras aren't foolproof, and someone could still find a way to either cover the lens or cut the feed entirely, but it would be better than nothing. Found some low-profile ones that shouldn't be all that easy to spot."

"Aren't you supposed to notify someone the property is monitored by cameras?" Jared asked, then paled a little when he realized he'd spoken on matters that didn't concern him. "Sorry. Merely thinking out loud."

Grizzly and Slash both eyed him, but Jared didn't squirm. If anything, he lifted his chin a notch and stared them down. Made me want to smile, but I refrained. Sort of. A slight smirk might have slipped free for a brief moment before I was able to control myself.

"And that brings me to the next order of business," Grizzly said. "I know Jared hasn't been prospecting for long, but he was willing to protect Dagger's woman at any cost. The fucker might have gotten the drop on him, but I think it's safe to say Jared is the kind of guy we want by our side when shit happens. I'm calling a vote. All in favor of Jared patching in."

Every damn hand around the table went up, and my heart swelled with pride. I glanced his way and saw the shock on his face, but it quickly changed into a broad smile. Neither of us had expected this when we'd come here today. Sometimes guys had to prospect for years before they patched in, if they ever did. But Jared hadn't been with us all that long. The two of us had clicked almost immediately, even though we'd hidden it from the others, and even from each other at first. One drunken kiss had changed everything. Thank fuck we hadn't been out in the open when it happened.

"Congratulations, Jared." Grizzly stood. The doors opened and Magda peeked inside, then hurried over to give the Pres a cut. No, she gave him two. He held one up for everyone to see as Magda rushed back out. "From this moment forward, Jared will be known as Guardian."

Griz handed the cut to Jared. He removed the Prospect cut and put on his new one. He couldn't contain his smile, even though he tried. Every time he'd drop the grin from his face, a moment later it would be right back. I could tell he was proud, excited, and probably felt a million other things. But it was the other cut that held my attention. Griz held it up and my breath caught when I read it. It felt like the words were burning into me.

Property of Dagger and Guardian.

My gaze met the Pres' and he winked. Fuck! He'd known? I glanced around the table and saw several smirks, including Dingo, Outlaw, and Slash. Demon looked resigned, but not exactly pleased by the turn of events. I hoped like hell we weren't going to have a problem later.

"How long?" I asked.

"Do you mean when did the club know the two of you were --" Slash smacked Demon in the back of the head. "Together," the Sergeant-at-Arms said.

"Yeah, when did you know Jared and I were together?" I asked.

Dingo gave me a half-smile. "Noticed it a few times, but didn't think much of it. It was the day Demon branded that whore it really hit me the two of you had something going on. You were watching Shella, but Jared was watching you."

"I've known for a while," Outlaw said. "Caught the two of you a few times when you didn't know you weren't alone."

I swallowed hard. "And none of you said anything?"

Grizzly reclaimed his seat. "Son, there are a few here who aren't too happy about the fact you're bisexual. As far as I'm concerned, as long as you refrain from any PDA that doesn't involve your woman, then it's none of our business. What you do in your own home is entirely between the three of you. But out here? The only kissing or groping had better be either with you and Zoe, or Guardian and Zoe. Am I clear?"

I nodded. "Crystal."

I didn't like the fact I couldn't show how I felt about Jared, but the fact the club had given their blessing for us to be together would have to be enough. I knew the only reason they'd accepted the relationship was because it included Zoe. If we'd tried to make this work without her, we both might have been asked to leave. Then again, it seemed they'd known for at least several months, and yet we were still here.

"One more order of business," Grizzly said. "Your boy. Luis."

"I still need to ride down to Mexico and get him."

"Or you could fly," Slash said. "Getting your boy back isn't going to be easy, so we called in reinforcements. You'll have both Casper VanHorne and Specter at your side. I know Casper is mostly retired these days, but his name still strikes fear into most men. And it's his jet."

I tried to wrap my brain around that one. Two of the deadliest men I'd ever heard of, and they were going to help bring my son home? Why? I didn't understand what they would get out of it. The question must have been written on my face because Slash decided to elaborate.

"Specter has a little sister, one who needs protection. While he's more than capable, he still gets called away for long stretches on jobs. The club offered to keep her here."

Grizzly snorted. "That's one way of putting it."

"You, Guardian, Outlaw, Dragon, and Dingo

don't have anything to worry about. You're already taken," Slash said.

"Taken. So, he wants one of us to what? Claim her? Marry her?" I asked.

"She'll be staying here a few months," Slash said. "During that time, Specter is hopeful one of us will decide to keep her. Permanently, in every way possible. He said the only way he'll stop worrying about her is if he knows she's protected. I guess a bodyguard wasn't good enough."

Blades rapped his knuckles on the table. "Count me out. I know China and I aren't official, but it's not because I don't want to be. She's still badly broken, even though she's improved a lot. One of these days, I'm claiming her. Just don't want to move too fast and scare her."

"Count me out too," Steel said. "Not getting leg-shackled anytime soon. If I want pussy, there's plenty around here."

Slash waved a hand. "Not an issue right now. Let's wait until she arrives and we'll play it by ear. I'm hoping some of our current guests will be gone before she gets here. Then she can use one of the apartments."

"If not," Griz said, "my girls can double up in a room for a short while and she can stay with me. We'll figure it out. Dagger, the jet leaves in the morning at six o'clock. Don't be late getting to the airstrip. Guardian is to remain here with Zoe. I'll send a handful of men with you, but Casper said he had some contacts that would meet all of you in Mexico. One way or another, Luis is coming home."

Griz banged the gavel. "Now get the fuck out of here!"

I wanted to hug Jared, to kiss him and tell him how proud I was that he'd patched in. Sadly, I didn't even want to attempt holding his hand after we'd been told to keep any displays of affection behind closed doors. It fucking sucked, but at least we could be together without having to hide. I'd take what I could get right now.

"Let's go home and share the news with Zoe," I said.

Guardian grinned and gave me a nod. I had a feeling our woman was about to be even more tired. At least she'd have someone here with her when I left tomorrow. With some luck, I wouldn't be gone too long, and I'd be bringing our son back with me.

"So, what do you know about putting together a room for a little boy?" I asked.

"You're bringing our kid home and he doesn't even have a room? When I'd heard you went shopping, I figured that had been part of it. Did you not order anything at all?"

I shrugged. I'd had other things on my mind. I'd honestly planned to have it handled, then I'd been distracted first by Zoe, then by Jared, and finally by both Zoe and Jared. No, not Jared. Guardian. It was going to be damn hard to remember to call him that in front of our brothers. When the others had patched in, it wasn't an issue. But then, I hadn't been sleeping with any of them.

"Let's go home and figure everything out while breakfast cooks. I have a feeling our woman is going to need some nourishment."

Guardian grinned. "Our woman. I like the sound of that."

Yeah, I did too.

Chapter Ten

Jared

I'd felt the bed dip when Dagger got up, and I'd opened my eyes only to have him motion for me to stay in bed. Zoe was wrapped in my arms, and I had to admit I liked having her there. I could tell Dagger didn't want her awake for his departure. Personally, if I were about to leave and go to another country for who knew how long, I'd want to tell my woman bye.

"She's going to be upset when she realizes you're gone," I said in a whisper so as not to wake her.

"It's for the best. If she cries, I don't know that I can walk away. Always hated a woman's tears, but when it's Zoe I feel like my heart is being ripped out."

I nodded, understanding completely. She might not have been ours for very long, but already I felt like she was part of us. Dagger might be married to her on paper, but she belonged to us equally, at least in the eyes of the club. I still couldn't believe they'd accepted our relationship. I'd been scared shitless I was about to get kicked out.

"You'll let us know you got there okay?" I asked.

"I'll keep in touch as much as I can. I doubt I'll have time to call you, the Pres, and keep up with everything happening. I'm hoping we get in and out pretty quick, but you know how that goes. If nothing else, I'll keep Griz up-to-date, and you can keep in contact with him," Dagger said.

I hated that I wasn't going on the trip with him, but I knew one of us needed to stay with Zoe. She was strong, far stronger than she realized, but if we were both gone she'd likely worry herself to death. Just having Dagger gone would be bad enough. While we'd both fucked her last night, she seemed to have a better connection with him than with me. I knew it was because they'd spent more time together, and being left alone with her would help put me on equal footing a bit quicker, but I'd have preferred that he stay here.

Going up against the cartel was going to take some serious firepower. I knew he had backup, some seriously badass men, but it didn't mean I wouldn't worry about him. How the fuck was I supposed to keep Zoe calm if I was freaking out inside too? I couldn't let her see that. I'd have to fake it the best I could, and keep her distracted. Hell, I'd need to distract both of us.

Right now, I didn't feel like some tough biker. I was simply a guy worried about the man he was falling for, who was about to run off into a dangerous situation. I didn't care what papers he had. The cartel wouldn't give a shit if Dagger claimed Luis belonged to him. Wouldn't stop them from gunning him down, or worse.

"Be careful," I said.

Dagger leaned over Zoe and pressed his lips to mine. "I always am. Keep her safe."

"You know I will."

He gave me a slight smile, then cast a tender look at Zoe. Yeah, I knew exactly how he felt. Having her between us was beyond amazing. I'd always thought it would be pretty fantastic to share a woman on a permanent basis with Dagger, but until Zoe had come into our lives, I hadn't realized how great it would actually be.

The only thing more perfect would be having Luis with us. I'd never thought I'd have kids. It wasn't that I didn't like them, even though I had no experience with smaller ones, but I'd never figured I'd find the right person to raise a family with, much less find two of them.

"Soon as she wakes, I'll take her out to find some things for Luis," I said. "And yes, I'll make sure we have some brothers or prospects with us. I won't take any chances with her safety while you're gone."

"She's not just mine," he said. "She's yours too."

I nodded. I knew it, even though it still seemed a bit surreal. And it wasn't only Zoe who was mine, but Luis would be as well. And any other kids the three of us had together. Wouldn't matter if the kid had my DNA or Dagger's. They'd have two dads, and I knew we'd love them equally.

After the shitty way we both grew up, I knew our kids would be spoiled. While there was still a lot I didn't know about Dagger, a few times he'd talked about losing his family and not having anyone until finding the club. I'd seen the darkness in his eyes and wondered what was in his past that haunted him, and one day I hoped he'd share it with me. Until then, we had a new family, and a little boy we could dote on. Nothing wrong with that. Just had to make sure Dagger and Luis made it back in one piece. I'd never been one to pray, but I was tempted to start right about now.

"I'm heading out before she wakes," Dagger said. His gaze lingered on Zoe, then he quickly kissed me again, before backing away. I watched as he gathered his stuff, cast one more look our way, then walked out.

With some luck, he'd be coming right back through that door within the next seventy-two hours, but I had a feeling that was just wishful thinking.

* * *

Zoe

I'd gone shopping with Guardian and two other men to pick out stuff for Luis' room yesterday, which had been fun. Something told me Guardian had been trying to distract me from the fact Dagger was gone, or maybe we'd both needed the distraction. It felt wrong picking out items for our son's room when Dagger couldn't help. Although, if he were anything like Guardian and the others who had gone with me, he wouldn't have been much help. It had been amusing to see the big tough bikers looking decidedly uncomfortable around all the toddler items.

Guardian sat in the middle of Luis' room, his legs spread, as he screwed together the toddler bed we'd purchased. I had to admit, it was a rather sexy sight, and I suddenly yearned for another child. If my men were willing to go to such great lengths to not only bring Luis home, but make sure it actually *felt* like his home when he arrived, I could only imagine what they would be like with a baby we'd created together. But small steps. Although, if they didn't start using condoms, we might very well end up with a baby sooner rather than later. I knew Dagger wanted a family, so I didn't have any doubt he was doing it on purpose.

Having Luis here might change his mind. I hadn't seen my son in so very long, but I knew young children could be full of energy and cause a bit of mischief. Our son could easily run us ragged, and make Dagger second-guess having a baby right now. Or maybe it would make him want one even more.

"Dinner is done," I said.

"Just give me about fifteen minutes. If I stop in the middle of this, I may never remember what goes where. Last thing we need is the bed to fall apart the first time he lies down on it. That wouldn't exactly make a good first impression on our son."

Our son.

I stepped into the room and ran my fingers through his hair. It amazed me when Dagger and Guardian referred to Luis as their son. They'd claimed him, even knowing he wasn't theirs and the circumstances behind his conception. It warmed my heart, and made me realize choosing to marry Dagger, and accepting Guardian as well, had been the right decision. I didn't know if they would ever love me, but maybe what we had would be enough. We already shared a closeness, and they were affectionate with me. Maybe that's all we really needed.

"You're already so good to him and you haven't even met him," I said.

He glanced up at me. "Zo, he's our son. Of course I'm going to be good to him. Doesn't matter he's not mine biologically. He's part of you. You're mine, so that means he is too. I know on paper it looks like you only belong to Dagger, and that he's Luis' adopted dad, but you both belong to me too. Doesn't matter if it's official outside these gates or not."

I dropped to my knees next to him. He was right. I did belong to both of them, and so did Luis. My property cut they'd given me even said as much, but the ring I wore, and the papers with the US government, said I only belonged to Dagger. I wondered if that bothered Guardian.

"I wear my ring from Dagger all the time, but I'll only wear the cut when I leave the house. It doesn't feel right. As you said, I belong to both of you."

He stopped what he was doing, frozen in place, and slowly his head turned toward me. "Are you saying you'd be willing to wear something to show you're mine too?"

I ran my hand down his arm. "Why wouldn't I?"

"Don't move. No, better yet, come with me." We got up and he walked into the guest room. Since Dagger had left so soon after making things official with us, he hadn't had a chance to clean out any space for Guardian's things, which meant they were currently scattered around the guest bedroom. He went over to a duffel on the floor and dug through it a moment, then withdrew a small velvet box.

I waited in the doorway, feeling almost as if I were intruding. He caressed the small box, looking lost in thought. Whatever was inside had to mean a great deal to him. It made me wonder where it had come from, or for that matter, where *he* had come from. I knew nothing about his past. Dagger had shared his with me, even though I didn't think he'd told Guardian yet.

That wasn't a conversation I wanted to be part of. I didn't think Guardian would look at him differently, or refuse to be part of this family anymore, but the fact it had been kept from him wouldn't go over well. He'd hated not feeling like an equal, and now that the club saw him as such, he would probably feel Dagger had betrayed him by not being completely honest.

Guardian came closer, the jewelry box clutched in his hand. His eyes were haunted and he hadn't met my gaze yet. Was he about to share a part of his past with me? Would I finally learn something about him?

Even though we'd done things I never imagined doing with someone, and were officially a couple, I still felt like I didn't know him. There were times I felt like Dagger was still keeping secrets as well. I knew it was possible I'd never know much about either of them, but I hoped over time they would trust me. They had to know I would never look down on them for the things they'd done, or any past sufferings. To me, they were strong, brave, and mine. That's all that mattered.

"I grew up in foster homes," he said. "When I was fifteen, an older woman took me into her house. I'd thought she'd be like all the others and I'd be on the move to a new location within a few weeks, or maybe a few months. She proved me wrong. She was strict, but fair. As a retired schoolteacher, she didn't put up with anyone's shit, but she also taught me that I could become anything I wanted as long as I put in the effort to get there."

He opened the box and stared inside, but the lid blocked my view. It was small, so I thought it was probably a ring, but it could have been earrings or a necklace. I hadn't exactly seen a lot of boxes shiny things came in since I'd been too poor to buy anything like that, and I certainly had never had a man give me jewelry until Dagger had put a ring on my finger. When Guardian turned the box toward me, I saw a plain band inside. I didn't know if it was silver, white gold, or something else. Didn't matter. The way he held it told me it meant the world to him.

"This was her wedding ring. When she got sick, she removed it and placed it in this box, then gave it to me. She said since she'd never officially adopted me, there was a chance I'd never be given the ring when she passed. I was supposed to keep it and give it to the woman I married. Her husband had given it to her, and she said they had over fifty years together. She hoped I found that same happiness."

"Her husband was already gone when you went to live with her?" I asked. He hadn't mentioned him before so I assumed that was the case.

Guardian nodded. "She'd been a widow for two

years when she decided to take me in. I was seventeen when she died. Bounced around to three more homes before I aged out of the system. Turned eighteen a few months before my graduation. My social worker made sure I had the tools I needed to graduate, and I worked some minimum wage jobs just to stay off the streets." He smiled faintly. "I've made it to the age of twenty-seven without ending up dead in a ditch, so I guess that's all that matters. And now I'm a patched member of the Devil's Fury. As far as I'm concerned, I'm a success."

I reached and placed my hand on his forearm. "I think she'd be proud of you."

He nodded. "Maybe. Anyway, I'd be honored if you'd wear her ring, Zoe. As far as I'm concerned, you're my wife too. There won't ever be another woman in my life."

Since Dagger had only given me a wedding band and not one of those sets with multiple rings, I held out my left hand. Both rings should fit on the same finger, as long as this ring was the right size. Guardian slipped it onto my finger, sliding it up against the band already there. A perfect fit.

"I promise I'll be careful with it," I said.

"I think she'd have liked you." He leaned down and kissed me softly. It was the first kiss he'd given me since Dagger left. I fisted his shirt and tugged him closer, pressing my lips to his again. I took a step back when I released him.

"Finish the bed later. Come eat before dinner gets cold."

He nodded, but I noticed the corners of his lips twitched as if he fought back a smile. When I turned to go back to the kitchen, he reached down and took my hand. To some it might not have seemed a big deal, but for us it was. I had a feeling the three of us might blunder through this relationship until we found our footing, but it seemed to be off to a good start.

I fixed Guardian a plate and set it on the table before making my own. Pulling two sodas from the fridge, I set them down and got forks and knives from the drawer. He pulled out my chair and winked at me as I sat down, then he claimed his own seat. The moan that came from him with the first bite was enough to make my cheeks warm, and it filled me with happiness. I hadn't had a lot of opportunities to cook since coming to this country, but it seemed I hadn't lost my touch. Growing up in a large family, I'd learned to cook early so I could help with my younger siblings. It seemed those skills would come in handy with two large men to feed. "Any word from Dagger?" I asked.

"No, but he's probably focused on getting Luis. I doubt he has much downtime right now, and when he does, he's probably resting. Considering the men who are with him, he'll be fine and he'll bring our boy home. I don't doubt it for a second."

"How long do you think he'll be gone?" I asked.

"I don't know, Zoe. Could be a few days, or could be longer. It depends if Luis is where we think he is. If he's been moved, it could take some extra time to locate him. Then Dagger either has to negotiate, or find a way to extract him." Guardian ran a hand through his hair.

Extract? That didn't sound right. Just who had that woman given my son to? My brow furrowed and I pushed my food around my plate. Something didn't feel right. I was missing an important part of all this, and I didn't know what it was. Mostly because the men in my life wanted to keep me in the dark. I understood they were trying to protect me, but I didn't like it.

"Who has Luis?" I asked. "And please don't lie to me, Jared. I need to know."

He set his fork down and studied me a moment. I started to think he wouldn't tell me, when he finally spoke. "The cartel has him."

It felt like all the air went out of the room. Everything spun and I couldn't breathe. Dots swam across my vision and I felt my body sway. Before I could topple from my chair, Guardian had me in his arms.

"And this is why no one told you," he muttered.

"Cartel," I whispered. "Luis... the man who..."

Guardian sat back in his seat, cradling me against his chest. He smoothed my hair back from my face, and I saw the moment he understood. Digging into his pocket, he pulled out his phone and dialed a number, putting the call on speaker.

"No word," said the man who answered.

"Pres, there's something they need to know. Can you get a message to Dagger? I didn't want to chance calling him in case he's in a spot that requires silence."

"Does it pertain to his mission? Or your woman?" Grizzly asked.

"Luis is the product of rape. I know we didn't tell you because it didn't matter. He's ours like Zoe is, and that was that. Except when I mentioned the cartel to Zoe, she said the man who raped her was in the cartel. It's possible Luis is with his sperm donor, in which case..."

"He won't give him up willingly," Grizzly finished.

"Right. The team down there needs to know what they're walking into. If the guy knows about Luis, then he's going to be pissed if Dagger goes down there waving around papers saying the kid belongs to him."

"I'm on it." There was a moment of silence. "Am I on speaker?"

"Uh, yeah. Sorry. I thought Zoe might feel better if she heard you were going to handle it. I know I shouldn't have done that without saying something first."

"We'll talk about it later. Zoe, I'm going to make sure they know the man who hurt you is part of the cartel. It could be a coincidence they have Luis, or he could have been picked because of his connection to one of their men. Do you know the man's name? Or his rank?" Grizzly asked.

"No. I only know he was part of the cartel because there was a tattoo I could see before he covered my face." I felt sick thinking about my poor boy down there with those monsters. If they hurt him, I'd never forgive myself for leaving him behind. Just the thought of what he could have seen, or been forced to do...

I bolted off Guardian's lap and ran for the bathroom, barely making it before I threw up. I heard booted steps rushing toward me, then Guardian was on his knees, the heat of his body pressing against my back. He pulled my hair back and wrapped an arm around me while I emptied my stomach until there was nothing left.

"I'm sorry," I murmured.

"You have nothing to apologize for, baby. You have every right to be worried or scared, but I promise you that Dagger won't come home unless Luis is with him. There's no way he's leaving that boy down there. You hear me?"

I nodded. "I'm worried he'll get hurt, or that the cartel may have harmed Luis already. They're so evil.

They rape, murder, and profit off other peoples' pain and suffering. I don't want our son exposed to that."

"Let's focus on bringing him home right now. When he gets here, we can get him whatever help he needs, baby."

I knew Guardian was right. I only hoped Dagger came home in one piece, and brought Luis with him. If anything happened to either of them, I'd never forgive myself. Once again, I'd kept something to myself and it had put someone in danger. If Dagger had known when he left that the man who'd raped me in Mexico had been part of the cartel, then he would have been better prepared.

"He's going to be angry," I said.

"Who? Dagger? Why would he be angry?" Guardian asked.

"Because I didn't tell him everything. Again."

He hugged me tight. "Baby, he'll probably spank your ass, and he might be upset, but there's no damn way Dagger would ever hurt you. And I know he couldn't stay mad at you for long. You're just too damn sweet."

I didn't know if Guardian was right or not, but I'd have to wait and see. With some luck, Dagger wouldn't be gone too long, and he'd bring Luis with him. My son hadn't seen me since he was a baby, and I doubted he'd know who I was. Infants didn't retain enough for him to remember me, did they? It was going to hurt, being a stranger to my own child, but I'd brought it on myself. I should have fought harder to bring Luis with me, or remained in Mexico and made the best of it. But if I'd done that, I may have never met Dagger and Guardian.

Please bring them home safely. I closed my eyes and prayed, and hoped someone was listening.

Chapter Eleven

Dagger

My wife was going to have a red ass when I got home. I'd have still come down here to get Luis, even if I'd known his biological father might have him, but not walking into that blind would have been a big help. Thankfully, Grizzly had gotten word to us before I'd marched in there and started demanding shit. Like my boy. Not knowing which of these fucks had sired Luis didn't help matters any.

"New plan?" I asked Specter and Casper.

"More like option two," Casper said. "We knew you didn't have a snowball's chance in hell of walking out with the boy. Even if he's there by coincidence, they won't release him. You could possibly buy him back, but that's not much fun."

I stared at the man, and the creepy ass Specter who was grinning. Not in a happy way, but in an *I can't wait to fuck shit up* kind of way. I should be thankful these two hadn't already started a bloodbath. They weren't exactly known for leaving men standing. Someone got in their way, don't bother looking for them. You'd be lucky to find a few pieces. Unless they wanted you to.

"Anyone ever plan on telling me about option two?" I asked.

"We'll create a diversion, then you and your men go in and grab the boy," Specter said.

A diversion. Christ. I wasn't about to fucking ask what that meant. With these two, I had a feeling it would end in a high death toll. Granted, they were taking out the cartel's men, so I was okay with that. Long as my brothers made it back home, and I was able to get Luis out of there, that's all that mattered.

Going home empty-handed, or in a body bag, wasn't an option.

"When are we doing this?" I asked.

Casper looked at his watch. "In about fifteen minutes. Everything should be in place by then."

Fifteen... I narrowed my eyes at them. "You two had this planned all along. You knew your option two would be the *only* option, didn't you?"

Casper shrugged and looked away, but a smile spread across his face. The fucker. Everything would have been simpler if they'd just laid out this plan from the beginning. I went to tell my brothers we needed to move fast, except I wasn't sure what to expect. I had four Devil's Fury members with me, and Casper had arranged for some of his acquaintances to help as well. Although, they were missing at the moment, which meant they were probably a big part of his plan.

I should have known something was up when they all walked off.

"Watch for the signal," Specter said. "I'll cover you from above."

I glanced around and didn't have a damn clue where he planned to hide. As long as he kept me from getting shot, I didn't much care. Although, I was a little concerned about the payment Casper would expect. I already knew what Specter wanted, but Casper VanHorne? The man didn't do anything out of the goodness of his heart. Fuck, I wasn't even sure he *had* a heart.

"I don't like this," Wolf said. "It feels wrong."

I knew exactly what he meant. The hair on my nape pricked, and I hoped shit wasn't about to go sideways. The ground rumbled, and then an explosion had us covering our ears and ducking our heads as debris rained down. The gate and surrounding walls were nothing but rubble, but before the men inside could rush in our direction, another bomb went off. At least, I assumed that's what was causing the damage and noise. As I rushed toward the gate, my brothers were at my back.

A man charged me, his arm raised and a gun in his hand, but before he got a shot off, crimson stained the front of his shirt and he fell face first onto the ground. Each man that came for us met the same fate, and I knew Specter had kept up his end of the deal. I entered the cartel's compound and didn't have a fucking clue where they would hide Luis. Wolf came with me, while Steel and Colorado went the other direction.

I entered the building on the left, my gun in my hand, as I cleared each room. A man yelled as he saw me, taking aim and getting off two shots before I took him down. He'd missed me, for which I was thankful. But the distraction cost me. Another seemed to pop up out of nowhere. He got off five shots, one of which clipped me in the shoulder. I heard Wolf grunt, then the man dropped with a hole in the center of his forehead. I glanced back long enough to make sure my brother was fine. He gave me a slight nod and we kept moving.

Wolf watched my six as we made our way through each building. Steel and Colorado were standing in front of the last building when we approached it. If they hadn't found Luis, and we hadn't either, he was in the building in front of us. Unless he'd been moved before we even made it to Mexico. The only thing working in our favor right now was that these assholes didn't know why we'd hit their compound. They had no clue what we wanted. If they knew I wanted Luis, I had no doubt they'd either move him again, or kill him.

"If he's not in there..." I let the thought just hang there. Honestly, if he wasn't in this last building, I had no fucking clue what to do next. The cartel could have moved him anywhere. For that matter, they could have sold him and he could be long gone from Mexico. I couldn't go home without him. It would destroy Zoe.

"He's there," Steel said. "And if he's not, we'll find someone who can tell us where they moved him. We'll get your boy."

Chaos surrounded us as Casper and Specter waged war on the cartel, keeping them busy while we searched for Luis. Anyone got close, and Specter took them down. Or maybe one of Casper's men did it. Hard to say since they were all like fucking ghosts and I didn't see a damn one of them.

Steel kicked in the door ahead of us and we went into the building, guns drawn. Steel took point with his AR-15 and I followed, a Glock in one hand and my knife in the other. Wolf backed me up and Colorado took the rear. We systematically cleared the building, saving one place for last. The tower. As we made our way up the stairs, I hoped like hell we weren't walking into an ambush.

Steel pushed the door open and stepped inside. I was right on his heels and drew up short when I saw the man holding a gun on a room full of young boys. It seemed Luis wasn't the only one they'd bought or taken.

The man started speaking in rapid-fire Spanish. "You're not taking our children."

"Not your kids, asshole. I just want my son," I said.

He hesitated and scanned each of us. "¿*Hijo*?"

"Yes, my son. Luis." I scanned the boys behind

him and noticed a pair of blue eyes were watching me. I held out my hand to him. "Luis, your mom misses you. I'm taking you home."

I saw his eyes flare and knew I had his attention. He might not remember his mother, but it was clear he wanted to see her. I only hoped he didn't think the bitch who'd sold him was his mom. It would gut Zoe. She had to expect a bit of resistance from Luis, or at least some distance. The kid didn't know her, or me for that matter. With some luck, he wouldn't put up a fight.

"Not your son," the man said. "Juan's boy."

Juan. I wondered if that was the man who had raped Zoe, or if he'd merely claimed Luis as his own after purchasing him. I slowly reached into my pants pocket and retrieved a copy of the official documents showing Luis belonged with me. No way I'd give this fucker the real thing. He could rip it up, and then I'd be screwed.

"I have paperwork saying otherwise." I held it out as far as my arm would reach. "Take it. See for yourself."

He snatched the papers and looked them over, before throwing them on the floor and spitting on them. It seemed we weren't doing this the easy way. The only good news was the gun no longer pointed at the boys. He'd been distracted enough to drop his guard. I saw Steel's finger gently squeeze the trigger and the man staggered as the bullet ripped through his shoulder.

Wolf and Colorado moved fast, making sure the guy went down and stayed down. As much I wanted to slice into the asshole with my knife, I sheathed it and hurried over to Luis. He trembled and his shoulders hunched as I got closer. I dropped to my knees, hoping if I seemed smaller he might not feel threatened.

I doubted he knew English, or much of it, so I made sure to use Spanish when I spoke to him. "Your mother is at home waiting for you. I'm her husband. Your father. Will you come with me, Luis? I'll take you somewhere safe. Your mother has been worried about you."

He slowly reached his hand for mine. With his fingers wrapped in mine, I stood and walked to the door, but I hesitated. Glancing at the other boys, I had to know.

"Anyone else not belong here?" I asked in Spanish.

Five more boys came forward, all ranging in size and age. They left with me. I saw Wolf shadow us as we went down the steps and made our way out of the compound. Dead bodies littered the ground, and I hoped the sight wouldn't give these kids nightmares. I didn't know what they'd been exposed to already. Luis tightened his hold on my hand as we left the compound. Casper was standing just outside, hands in his pockets, as if he hadn't a care in the world.

"That your boy?" he asked.

I nodded. "These others said they don't belong here. Any way you or your men could find their homes? Or see that they get somewhere safe?"

He looked at them and smiled. A genuine one. "Yeah, we'll see they're taken care of. I'll remain behind to handle it. The jet is fueled and waiting."

"Steel and Colorado are tying up a loose end. There's more kids in the building too," Wolf said.

"Get your boy out of here, Dagger. Don't wait for the others. When the jet gets back to Georgia, they'll refuel and come back for us. I promise your brothers will come home, just not right this minute. They can help me get the kids settled where they belong." Casper straightened. "It's not negotiable."

I didn't like the idea of leaving anyone behind. I looked over my shoulder and saw Steel and Colorado coming out of the building, the kids following behind them. I waited, needing to hear from them that they were all right with the plan. I wasn't heading back without them any other way.

Casper told them the same thing he'd said to me, and Colorado shrugged. Steel eyed the kids behind him, then my boy. When his gaze met mine, I knew he was fine with the plan.

"All right. I don't like it, but I agree I need to get Luis home sooner rather than later," I said.

"There's one thing you need to know. Something you won't like," Steel said.

I braced myself, wondering what the hell he could have found out in the short time since I'd left with Luis. Had the man he'd shot decided to talk?

"Juan isn't in Mexico anymore," Steel said. "The woman who sold Luis to him reached out when Zoe sent money from a new return address. He's going for your woman. I couldn't make heads or tails of the rambling, but it seems he plans to use her as a breeder for more kids. Guess he liked the looks of Luis or something. She didn't know when he left. Could have been today, or he could have been in our territory for a while now."

I growled and my body tensed. No fucking way would he get his hands on my wife. I'd show him exactly why they called me Dagger if he even thought of harming her. Lifting Luis into my arms, fire spread through my shoulder from the bullet wound, but I ignored it and I headed for the vehicles. Casper had arranged for us to use a few Humvees, and I was grateful right now. I climbed in with Luis while Wolf got behind the wheel. It seemed he was coming with me, and I was glad. If we ran into trouble, I didn't want to face it alone.

One of Casper's men got in on the other side and gave me a nod. "Just going along for the ride. I'll bring the Humvee back after you've boarded the jet. Might need an extra set of hands."

It went unsaid we could run into trouble between here and there. It was likely someone had noticed the cartel compound getting hit. I was a little confused about something, though. I hadn't seen any drugs, guns, or anything else the cartel could profit from. Except the kids. Were they dealing in children? Or had that place been something more?

Luis started to relax a little, and I hated to scare him, but I needed a few questions answered. I kept to Spanish when I spoke in case that's all he knew.

"Luis, why did they have you at that place?" I asked.

He blinked up at me, but wouldn't speak. The kid was two. Three? I couldn't remember what the birth certificate had said, what Zoe told me before, or what was written on the papers Wire had provided to bring him stateside. Probably should check on that so I didn't get tripped up if we were stopped at the airstrip. I didn't think anyone would bother us, just because Casper seemed to have shit in hand.

"Kid's scared," Wolf said. "Give him some time, Dagger. That place is possibly all he's ever known. Let's get him to his mom and go from there."

I knew he was right. We had no idea what they'd made Luis do, or what he'd witnessed while he was at that place. I pulled my phone from my pocket and shot off a message to Guardian. *Coming home. Watch Zoe.*

It didn't take long to get a response.

What's going on?

I didn't want to say too much over the phone, not in a text, but I didn't want to try calling right now either. *There's a man coming for her. Knows her current location.*

When Guardian answered, it made me smile. *Fucker isn't taking our wife.*

Damn straight he wasn't. It sounded like maybe he and Zoe had gotten closer while I'd been gone, which was a good thing. I'd worried how they'd handle being alone together. With everything still so new, I'd wanted to stay longer. But Luis needed to come home. If I hadn't come here when I did, we might have lost him. They could have moved him, sold him, and he could have possibly vanished without a trace. Time was of the essence.

At the airstrip, I waited in the vehicle with Luis while Wolf and Casper's guy checked out the area. I didn't want any surprises while I had precious cargo. The boy leaned into me, and I held him closer. I hoped he understood what was happening, and that he'd be safe where we were going. Even though Juan was apparently heading into Devil's Fury territory, I knew my brothers would handle him. I didn't have any idea how long ago he'd left Mexico, but if the man didn't strike until I arrived, even better. My knives and I would love to have a little chat with the guy who'd raped my wife.

Wolf gave the all clear and I exited the vehicle with Luis in my arms. We boarded the jet, and I took my seat, buckling Luis next to me. I rubbed his back and tried to casually check the neck of his shirt for a size, in case we'd bought the wrong things for him. Once I had his size, I sent a quick text to Guardian so he could ensure Luis would have clothing ready. I gave my best guess on the size of his foot in inches and hoped they could figure it out from there.

I didn't hear a sound other than the jet's engine, but I didn't breathe easy until we were in the air. Once the kid was calm, and the flight was smooth, I'd do something about my shoulder. It could wait for now. The flight would only be around three hours, but that was entirely too long when I'd already been gone for days. I couldn't wait to see Zoe and Guardian again. To be home. I hoped they had everything ready for Luis. And I really hoped he didn't tense up or hide when he saw Zoe for the first time. I knew it would break her heart. To Luis, she'd be a stranger, but she'd been waiting a long time to see her son again.

Chapter Twelve

Zoe

I peered out the front window for the hundredth time in the last twenty minutes. When Guardian had received the text from Dagger about the size clothes and shoes Luis needed, he'd insisted we go get what our son needed. The clothes I'd picked out before were the wrong sizes, so we'd returned them and bought some new things. Then I'd tossed the new things into the washer so they'd be clean and ready to wear when Luis arrived.

"Baby, they'll get here when they get here," Guardian said, wrapping his arm around my waist and tugging me from the window. "Staring down the road isn't going to make them move faster."

"What if he doesn't like me?" I asked. "What if he hates me for leaving him?"

"He's three, Zoe. He's probably scared, confused, and he's going to need time to adjust. I don't think he understands you left him, and he may not remember you. We just need to give him some time, all right?"

I knew he was right. I was overthinking everything, and panicking a little. It didn't help that Guardian had said a man was heading this way, someone called Juan. I wondered if it was the man who had raped me, or if he was merely part of the cartel. Whoever he was, I'd been assured he wouldn't get anywhere near me. When we'd gone shopping, four other men had been with us. They'd kept their distance, but I'd felt safer knowing that it wasn't just me and Guardian out there.

Guardian led me to the kitchen, then gently shoved me down onto a chair. "Sit and I'll get you something to drink. Decaf, I think, since you're already jittery."

"So, water?" I asked.

He grinned. "Yeah, water. And maybe a snack so your hands are occupied. You look like you're about to crawl out of your skin. It's going to be fine. Promise."

Guardian popped a bag of kettle corn, gave me a glass of ice water, then claimed the seat next to me. He seemed so calm. Why wasn't he freaking out? He'd seemed excited at the store, and had even bought a few toys for Luis in addition to the clothes and shoes, but now he was all laid back and... I watched him. No, he wasn't. He was pretending. I saw the way he slightly vibrated and realized he was bouncing his leg under the table.

"You're just as nervous," I said.

"Never had a kid before. I don't want to fuck up. Besides, you're scared your own son won't like you. If he doesn't like you, why the hell would he want to be around me?"

I hadn't thought of it like that. A door slammed outside and I jolted, but Guardian reached over and clamped his hand around my wrist to hold me in place. My heart was racing, and I wanted to run out and greet them, but I held still. The front door opened and I heard Dagger murmuring, the timbre of his voice soothing. I turned to face the kitchen doorway and I wanted to cry when my husband walked in with our son in his arms.

Luis seemed at ease, and looked at both me and Guardian in curiosity. It had to be a good sign he appeared so relaxed. He'd only spent a few hours with Dagger and had already accepted him. Maybe that meant I'd been worried for no reason. Guardian released me and I stood, walking slowly toward my son.

"Luis, do you remember me?" I asked. He didn't so much as blink. I looked at Dagger, feeling helpless.

"Luis, *esta es tu madre*," Dagger said.

My son peered at me, but didn't seem overly eager to release Dagger. I couldn't really blame him. I rather liked being in those arms too. When Dagger held me, I felt safe and secure, and I realized my son felt the same way. I ran my fingers through Luis' hair, but tried not to scare him. I felt a presence behind me, and noticed Luis lock his gaze onto something. Guardian. I glanced over my shoulder and realized he'd come to meet his new son.

"Does he understand any English?" I asked. As far as I knew, Guardian didn't know Spanish. I didn't want him to feel excluded from anything we said to Luis.

"I'm not entirely sure," Dagger said. "I found him at a compound owned by the cartel, hidden in a tower room with other boys. They'd left a guard up there, and the asshole pointed his gun at them when we entered. I don't know what he's been exposed to in the last few years. So far, he hasn't said a word."

My heart ached for my little boy, and I wondered what horrors he'd faced. I didn't know why they'd wanted him, or the other kids, but it couldn't be for anything good. Those men were rotten to their very cores.

As much as I hated leaving Guardian out of the conversation, I decided to only use Spanish when I spoke to Luis until he opened up a little more. I hoped that was the right decision.

"Are you hungry?" I asked my son.

He curled tighter into Dagger, but gave a slight nod. Progress! I'd made tamales for lunch yesterday, and we had some left over. While I warmed them,

Dagger sat at the table with Luis still in his arms, and Guardian reclaimed his chair. I listened as Dagger introduced Guardian as Luis' second dad, and explained he had two and one mother. I didn't dare turn to watch them, for fear I'd be tempted to snatch my son. It had been so long since I'd held him.

I plated the tamales, putting only one on a plate for Luis, and four on Dagger's plate. If Guardian was still as nervous as I was, then I doubted he was hungry right now, but I'd warmed enough he could have some if he wanted to. Taking the seat next to Dagger, I pushed his plate toward him. I cut a small bite from Luis' tamale and offered it to my boy. He slowly leaned forward and accepted the food, his eyes lighting up as he chewed.

"There wasn't much in the way of child-appropriate beverages and food on Casper's jet. Luis nibbled on some pretzels and had a bottle of water, but that's it. I don't know how often they were fed," Dagger said. "He's probably starving."

"I'm sure you are too," I said.

He shrugged. "Been a while since I had a chance to eat, but Luis was more important. Now that he's home, I know that I have two others helping me with him. Wolf came home with me, but he's about as clueless as I am when it comes to kids."

"What about Juan?" I asked.

Luis tensed when I said that name and his gaze darted around the room. Everything inside me screamed that asshole had somehow hurt my child, and I wanted him dead, but I didn't have proof. Yes, he'd bought Luis, or at least money had exchanged hands for some reason, but I still didn't know for what purpose, or know the woman's connection to Juan.

Dagger tightened his hold on our son. "I'll check

with the club and see if they've heard anything, but I think tonight the four of us need to get acquainted and have a relaxing evening. We can show Luis his room. Maybe you can talk him into a bath and put one of his new outfits on him, show him whatever toys we have for him."

I nodded, knowing he was right. As much as I worried about the threat that could be lurking in the shadows, I knew we needed to focus on Luis at least until tomorrow. Even then, my main concern needed to be Luis. I made sure he ate most of the tamale, and when he turned his face away for the next bite, I decided not to push. If he got hungry again, we had plenty of food for him.

"I'll get a bath ready. Why don't the two of you show Luis his room?" I suggested. As much as I wanted to see his face when he realized all that stuff was for him, I knew Guardian and Dagger needed some time with him too.

Dagger got up with Guardian following. I cleared the table, then went to run a bath for Luis. I added a little of the bubble bath we'd grabbed and the rubber duck. I hadn't known what my son would like, so I was hoping someday soon I could take him shopping to select his own bath toys. And anything else we'd missed. It was quiet. Too much so. I peered into the hall and saw Guardian leaning against the doorway of Luis' room, but his face was set into hard lines. Whatever was going on in there, it didn't seem like a joyous moment.

"Bath is ready," I said.

He pushed off and went into the room, and I heard him say something to Dagger. A moment later, they were both heading my way with Luis. Dagger set him down. If Guardian hadn't been blocking the doorway, Luis may very well have bolted when I pulled his shirt off. The boy shrieked, his eyes wide in fear, and tears rolled down his cheeks. I looked at my men, not having any idea what to do.

Dagger murmured to him in Spanish. "You're okay. No one here will hurt you. It's just a bath, Luis. Then you can wear your new clothes."

Luis sniffled, but gave a slight nod. I finished removing his clothes, and everything in me went still. It felt as if the temperature in the room dropped fifty degrees as I shared a look with Dagger and Guardian. It was clear Luis had been through hell. A number had been carved into his skin on his hip, and bruises covered his back.

"Find him," I said. "And end him."

Dagger held my gaze. "Won't be pretty. Got my name for a reason."

"He brutalized our son. I don't care what you do to him, as long as he hurts and isn't breathing when you're done. A monster like that doesn't deserve to live."

"I'll handle it," Dagger promised. "I'm going to go speak with Grizzly and Slash. Guardian will remain here with you. Don't leave the house. I'll make sure all the doors and windows are locked before I take off. I don't plan to be gone that long."

I helped Luis into the tub and gently washed him. No matter how hard I tried to get him to play with the duck, he wouldn't. My poor boy just sat in the tub, frozen like a statue. The thought of what he could have suffered tore me apart. I'd thought I left him with someone trustworthy, that he'd be safe. I'd been so horribly wrong, and my small son had paid the price.

Tears slipped down my cheeks, no matter how hard I fought to hold them in. Soon I was openly sobbing. I felt arms close around me and pull me back against a hard chest. Guardian's scent washed over me.

"Easy, baby. You're going to scare him even more. He doesn't know why you're crying," he said.

"I-I know, but... this is all my fault. If I'd never left him..."

"You don't know that," Guardian said. "What if you'd stayed and Juan decided he wanted your son? He could have seen you anywhere. If you'd refused to sell your child, he'd have taken him, and possibly you as well. You could have ended up in a brothel or worse. You can't tear yourself apart second-guessing your decision to come to this country."

He was right. And I couldn't undo the past. Whatever it took, I'd see Luis had a happy life from this moment forward. I knew Dagger and Guardian would protect him with their lives, and I could already tell they would love him. I hoped it was enough to undo whatever damage the *culero*, and the other cartel men, had done to my boy.

I pulled Luis from the tub and dried him off, then helped him into his new clothes. Guardian lifted him, and Luis went to him without issue. It made my heart hurt that my own son didn't want me to hold him. After the way he'd reacted to Juan's name, it was surprising to me he'd go to a man. For whatever reason, he trusted Dagger and now Guardian. While it was disappointing he wasn't at ease with me, I was grateful he'd been willing to let his daddies hold him.

I followed them into the living room where Dagger was sprawled at the end of the couch. Either he'd never left, or he really hadn't taken that long to speak to the others. Guardian sat next to him and Luis seemed content with both men nearby. I took the remaining spot. Luis watched me and I gave him a smile.

"I missed you," I told him. "So very much. I never thought we'd be apart this long."

Dagger cleared his throat and I turned my gaze toward him. "Spoke to Griz. The club will handle our little problem, or at least round him up. I'll take it from there, but I told him tonight was family time. There is one thing. Dr. Larkin is going to stop by and make sure Luis is in good health. From what Wire could find, he's not had any vaccinations and he'll need quite a few. I don't imagine he'll enjoy the visit very much."

Guardian leaned forward and grabbed the remote off the coffee table, then clicked on the TV. "Then I guess we'd better give him some happy memories first. Otherwise, he may hate us."

He flipped through channels until he found an animated movie, then settled back with Luis still clinging to him. It didn't take long before the TV caught our son's attention. He eventually relaxed even more and cuddled between Guardian and Dagger. We watched two movies, then there was a knock at the door. I got up to answer, but Dagger beat me there, giving me a fierce glare.

"You were just going to open the door?" he asked.

"You were expecting someone."

"*Sí*, but it could have just as easily been someone else. One man made it into the compound before. Who's to say Juan won't as well?"

He had a point. I nodded my understanding and let him answer the door. He welcomed the man on the doorstep, which meant it was probably the doctor. When the man stepped into the house, I saw he wore a white lab coat and carried a bag with him.

"You must be Zoe," the man said, holding out

his hand. "I'm Doctor Larkin."

"It's nice to meet you," I said, giving his hand a quick shake.

"Luis hasn't spoken more than a word or two, and he's very reserved," said Dagger. "Worse, he has a number carved into his body and bruising. I don't know what all those bastards did to him."

"He may associate my visit with unpleasantness. I'd hate for him to have those memories in a common area or even his new room. Is there somewhere else I could examine him?" Dr. Larkin asked.

"The guest room," I suggested.

Dagger nodded. "Perfect."

He got Guardian, and they carried Luis into the guest room with me and the doctor following. Dagger introduced our boy to the man in the white coat, explaining he was a doctor and what would happen. Luis fidgeted and tears rolled down his cheeks. Our son never screamed, and didn't fight, but I could feel his fear. Guardian and Dagger wore tense expressions, not liking this any more than I did.

When the doctor said he needed to remove Luis' clothes for the last part of the exam, I knew I needed to leave the room. I couldn't take it another moment, and I was too scared of what he might discover. By the time the visit was over, and Luis was cradled in Dagger's arms, my heart felt like it was going to beat right out of my chest. My neck hurt from the tension in my body.

"He took some blood to run some tests," Guardian said as Dagger carried Luis into another room. "The exam wasn't pleasant for any of us, but the doc saw no signs of sexual assault. I've never been more grateful for something in my life. If those assholes had done that to our sweet boy…"

He swallowed hard and I saw the fury in his

eyes. I knew exactly how he felt. It was bad enough Luis had been harmed in any way, but at least he'd been spared in some way. I had a feeling what he'd seen or had done to him was bad enough to give Luis nightmares. Only time would tell.

"I'm going to contact Outlaw and give him the sequence of numbers on Luis' hip and see if he or Wire can figure out what it means," Guardian said. "Dagger suggested you start dinner, and we'll all sit at the table for the meal. None of us thought to get a booster seat for Luis, so I'm going to have a Prospect run and pick one up."

"I don't even know what to make," I said.

"Anything you want, baby. Hell, order pizza. Every kid loves that shit, right?"

I didn't know about that, but I could easily order pizza. It would provide us with dinner, and I wouldn't have to lose any time with Luis. While I would have preferred to provide my son a home-cooked meal his first night in the house, there would be plenty of other opportunities.

Provided Juan was captured and taken care of. Otherwise, our happy family could quickly unravel.

* * *

Jared

Watching Luis withdraw into himself during the exam had about gutted me, but it had been the look on Dagger's face that hurt the most. I could tell something was going on, but I didn't know what. It was possible he'd simply formed enough of a connection with the kid during the flight here that he felt our boy's pain more than I did, but I had a feeling it wasn't just that. I could only hope he'd open up at some point and let me in.

Even worse, I could see the fear and pain in Zoe's eyes and I didn't know how to help. I could hold her, tell her everything would be okay, but that wouldn't be near enough. She felt like she'd done this to her son by leaving him behind, and nothing I said would ever change that. She'd have to come to terms with it on her own. As far as I was concerned, she'd done what she felt was right, and if she'd put her faith in someone trustworthy, then everything would have ended differently. Instead, she'd gotten suckered by a con man who only wanted nearly free labor, and didn't care if her son ever made it out of Mexico or not. The small pittance he'd given her had gone back to Mexico for Luis.

If Ramirez hadn't already handled that asshole, I'd be tempted to go after him. What he'd done to Zoe was unforgiveable. Because of his refusal to let Zoe bring her son with her, Luis had suffered, and now Zoe felt responsible for it all. I wanted to break the man in half, literally snap his bones, but I had a feeling he was already dead. Ramirez wouldn't have removed the women, and wouldn't be acting as if he were in charge, if his boss were still breathing. I'd have to hope the bastard suffered a great deal.

I listened to Zoe order dinner, but I kept an eye on her. She flitted around, her hands trembling a little. The slight quiver in her voice confirmed how anxious she was, either over Luis having been harmed, or the fact he didn't seem too quick to go to her. I had to imagine it hurt like hell to have your own flesh and blood prefer someone else. As far as I was concerned, he was my son, as well as Zoe's and Dagger's. I didn't have much experience with kids of any age, and none with someone as small as Luis, but I'd do what I could to show him he could trust me.

Without knowing exactly what he'd been through, it was hard to say how long it would take for him to recover. I didn't know the first thing about helping a kid heal from emotional or physical trauma, especially one who wouldn't talk. Whatever he needed, I'd see he got it. Even if it he only needed lots of cuddles.

Zoe finished placing the pizza order and set the phone down. Her shoulders slumped and I watched as she hung her head. I hated that she was beating herself up. Not knowing what else to do, I walked over and pulled her against my chest, wrapping my arms around her waist.

"He's a strong kid, baby. He'll be okay." I kissed the top of her head. "He has you, me, and Dagger. Not to mention the rest of the club. We'll make sure he has whatever he needs."

"Doesn't stop me from feeling like I failed him," she said softly.

"You didn't. No one can see the future, Zo. You did what you felt was right at the time, and if the man you'd trusted had been honorable, or the woman you'd thought was taking care of Luis, then all this might have turned out different. But playing the *what-if* game isn't going to do anything but make you hurt more. We can't change the past, baby, but we can make sure he has a safe and happy future."

She sighed and leaned more of her weight against me. "I know you're right, but I'm struggling. I promise I'll get there. It hurts to know I couldn't protect my son."

"I know." I hugged her tighter. "We're here for you, and for Luis. Remember that. You aren't in this alone, baby."

She nodded, then turned in my arms and hugged me. I'd do whatever I could to keep our family happy. If that meant playing peacemaker sometimes, then I would. Right now, I'd lend my strength to Zoe so she could get through whatever we were about to face with Luis. No matter how strong she was, I knew she'd need help in the days to come. We all would, but none of us were alone anymore, and together I knew we could face anything.

Chapter Thirteen

Dagger

I knew it was time to speak with Guardian about my past. I should have done it before now. At first, I'd been worried how he would react, then there hadn't been time. It wasn't something I needed to hide any longer. Not from him. I still didn't plan to share what happened with the entire club.

Luis had been asleep for the last hour. Even though Zoe knew what I'd been through, I didn't think she wanted to hear it again. I went to our bathroom and started the tub, filling it with hot water so she could soak and relax. She'd had a trying day, and there were shadows under her eyes. We were all on edge after finding out Luis had been hurt, but until we knew everything, I knew none of us would sleep well.

After I shut off the water, I went to get Zoe. She'd curled against Guardian on the couch, but the stress and tension were evident in her body. I didn't say a word, just walked over and lifted her into my arms. I carried her to the bathroom, helped her strip down, then gave a nod to the tub.

"Don't even think of arguing. Just get in the tub and try to relax, *princesa*. I know everything going on makes it seem impossible. I'm worried about you." I smoothed her hair back and leaned down to brush my lips against hers. "I'll come check on you shortly."

I walked out, pulling the door mostly shut, then went back to the living room. Guardian sprawled on the couch, one of his booted feet on the coffee table. I shook my head. There were times I wondered if he'd been raised in a barn. "Our wife will skin you if she sees your feet on the table," I said as I took the seat next to him.

"She going to be okay?" he asked.

"She blames herself. It's not her fault. Yes, she left him, but she was trying to give him a better life. It's not much different than someone giving their kid up for adoption. There are no guarantees in life. She sent every penny she had to that woman, but the bitch sold our boy. Zoe couldn't have predicted that would happen, and I don't believe she realized her debt would never be paid and Luis would still be in Mexico years later."

"You think he's going to be okay?" Guardian asked. "We have no idea what he's been through. Since he won't talk, and I have no idea if he understands English, I'm not sure if there's anything I can do. Does he have any idea what I'm saying to him?"

"I don't know. We need to give him some time, and get him some help. I'm sure they have therapists for small kids. Maybe we should check into one, find someone Luis is comfortable with and maybe they can help him process whatever he's seen or experienced."

Guardian nodded. "Not a bad idea. I may actually know someone who could point us in the right direction. If she'll take my call."

"She?" I asked.

"My sister." He turned to face me. "I know you and I never talked before about where we came from. My family threw me out when I was thirteen, after they caught me with another boy. None of them would talk to me. I crashed where I could until I found out my parents were dead. The state rounded me up and dumped me in foster care. It took me a little while to find my sister, and I've reached out to her a few times. She's a therapist now and seems more open to speaking to me, but I've kept my distance because of the club life. I don't want any ugliness touching her."

"She work with kids?" I asked.

"I don't know. If she doesn't, she may know someone who does. Want me to call now?" He looked at the screen of his phone. "Or maybe send a text. I didn't realize it was so late."

"You can text, but there's something we need to talk about first. Or rather something I need to say. First, know I didn't keep it from you for any reason other than I was worried you'd see me differently. And the club doesn't know. They don't need to."

His gaze narrowed slightly. "You've kept something from me? Didn't you tell Zoe you owe her a spanking for not telling you about Luis' sperm donor? Now you're hiding shit too? Does she know what this big secret is?"

"Actually, she does." I rubbed the back of my neck. "I told her before she agreed to marry me. I wanted her to know who I was before she took that leap."

"I didn't warrant the same consideration?" Guardian asked.

"Things were casual with us, and then they suddenly weren't. When she disappeared that night, I wasn't thinking straight. And I don't think you were either. What happened, it wasn't planned. I'd had every intention of telling you about my past before you committed to this family, and I'm sorry I took that from you."

He sighed and waved a hand for me to continue.

"When I was a teenager, I lost my family. Bounced around foster homes until I couldn't handle it anymore. The system wasn't kind to a kid like me. Ended up on the streets. A man took me under his wing, for a price. It wasn't horrible, and he didn't abuse me. Until the day someone offered him money for some time with me. After that, he became my pimp. I was scrawny and fighting back wouldn't have done me any good. At least Rick made sure I wasn't hurt."

Guardian's hands fisted on his thighs. "Not hurt? Did you want to be with him or the others?"

I shrugged, but the answer was no. I'd done it out of necessity.

"They raped you," he said. "You didn't have a choice. It was take it and survive, or what? End up in a worse position?"

"Something like that. Anyway, I managed to get away when I was eighteen and Grizzly found me. I bulked up a few years later, and by then I had a home here. I never told anyone what I'd been running from. Guess I was too ashamed. Not to mention, I didn't think the club would look kindly on me fucking other men."

Guardian reached over and took my hand. "Is that why... you're always the top? I assumed it was because you were kind of dominant in the bedroom."

"I was never given the choice before. Being in control keeps me from reliving those moments. If I were bottom, I'm not sure if I'd have a flashback or some sort of attack. I probably have PTSD."

He nodded. "Wouldn't surprise me. Thank you for sharing that with me. I understand a little more why you need the things you do. That sense of control isn't just to get you off. It's what you need to feel safe when you're with another man. Was it always men?"

"Yeah. If women were hiring prostitutes, they weren't hanging in my part of town. Only women hitting the corners there were either looking for a fix or spreading their legs."

Guardian gripped the back of my neck and tugged me closer, kissing me. His lips barely brushed mine before he deepened the kiss. When he pulled away, I saw the acceptance in his eyes, as well as affection. "Whatever you need to feel safe, I'm okay with it. If that means you always need to be the one in control, then fine. I won't say I've never wondered what it would be like to fuck you, but it's not something I'll push for. If you decide you want to try, let me know, but I won't bring it up."

"Thank you, Jared. I guess I was worried you'd see me as dirty or something. And the club... I never expected them to accept the two of us together, so the thought of confessing that to them wasn't something I could even contemplate. It terrified me."

He kissed me again, then pulled back. Our thighs brushed together even though we weren't touching in any other way. It was enough. I checked my phone to see if Outlaw had messaged me, but I didn't have any missed texts or calls. Guardian tapped on his phone and I assumed he was texting his sister. I hoped she would know someone who could help Luis. Poor kid. "I'm going to call Outlaw. I know he hasn't had much time to dig up anything, but I'd like to at least get some sort of update."

Guardian gave me a nod, but kept texting. I didn't know if his sister had responded, or if he was just sending a really long damn message. I dialed Outlaw's number and waited for him to answer.

"You don't give anyone a lot of time, do you?" Outlaw asked as he picked up.

"Just concerned about my boy. Find out anything at all?" I asked.

"Wire and Lavender are working on it. My hands won't cooperate today. Dropped my fucking coffee cup this morning and can't grip anything for shit. Wire said he'll message you once he has something."

"Thanks, and sorry it's a shitty day." Ever since Outlaw had sacrificed himself for Wire's woman, he'd had a lot of issues with his hands. Some days were better than others. The club had worried about him, until he'd found Elena. Now he had a reason to get up every day. More than one. His daughter, Valeria, was only a month old and absolutely adorable.

I started to message Grizzly, but something made me pause. I listened, feeling as if something was out of place. Had Luis woken? I got up and moved closer to the hall, but everything was quiet. I felt Guardian at my back and lifted a hand to keep him silent, then went to check on our son.

I pushed Luis' door open and peered inside. The sheets were mussed, but the bed was empty. Even worse, the window was open. *Motherfucker!*

I ran to the bedroom, opened the safe in my closet, and pulled out several guns, arming both myself and Guardian. I strapped four blades on my person, along with a set of throwing knives. "Stay here with Zoe."

A quick glance toward the bathroom was enough to assure me she was still in the tub. I saw her knees bent and barely showing over the top of the tub. Except... Zoe was a tiny thing, barely five feet if even that. A feeling of unease pricked at me and I moved toward the bathroom. When I opened the door fully, my heart stopped.

"No! Goddamnit!" I dropped the gun I'd still clutched and reached for Zoe, jerking her out of the tub. "Please, *corazoncito*. Don't do this to me."

My hands shook as I swiped her hair off her face and tipped her head back. I put my face near her nose and mouth, but didn't feel the stir of her breath. I placed my ear against her chest and realized her heart had stopped beating. I was seconds from losing it, and I knew I needed to get Luis back as well, but I couldn't just leave her...

"Move, Dagger. I know CPR. Go get that fucker," Guardian said.

"Bring her back. Whatever it takes." I stood and forced myself from the room, but it was the hardest thing I'd ever done. How the fuck had that asshole gotten in undetected, not only the compound but my fucking house? He'd killed Zoe without us being any the wiser, and snatched Luis. I'd failed my family.

I pulled my phone from my pocket as I exited the house. I sent one text, but included all the club officers. *Luis is missing, and Zoe isn't breathing.*

I put the phone on silent, then made my way around to Luis' bedroom window. I saw the boot marks of someone with a smaller foot but a heavy tread. They were deep, but he had to wear a size seven, maybe an eight. Cigarettes littered the ground, which meant he'd been out here a while. At least long enough to smoke five of them. Had he been here when we'd put our son to bed? Just waiting for the moment to strike?

I'd put off searching for him, wanting to have a nice evening with my family, and look what it had cost me. My heart ached, and my throat burned with unshed tears. He'd taken everything, and I'd make him fucking pay. I heard the roar of bikes and knew help was on the way, but was it too late? Were both Zoe and Luis lost to us already?

I followed the steps to the road, then noticed they continued on the other side. I waited, as much as it pained me to do so, until my brothers arrived. I could tell by the sound of the pipes they were drawing closer and would be here any second. I heard them pull up to the house.

Around the side. I sent the message, then started following the prints. Demon, Slash, and Hot Shot joined me. "Left Stitches at your house," Slash said. "Called an ambulance too. So if we're catching this asshole, we need to do it fast. I have no doubt the police will come too, or follow up at the very least."

"Tracks lead toward the back of the compound," I said.

We tracked Juan, stopping at the back fence. The prints abruptly halted, or so it seemed. I scanned the area and realized he'd somehow managed to hold onto Luis and climbed the fence. Except he hadn't gone over. The footsteps started back up about eight feet away.

"Look," I said, jerking my chin that direction.

"What's that direction?" Hot Shot asked.

"Nothing. Just an old cabin that used to be part of the original property. Damn thing is falling down. Just four decaying walls, a roof with holes, and a dirt floor. Probably was used as a line shack or something back when all this was farm and ranch land," Demon said.

"Think he'd take Luis there hoping we'd leave the compound to search for him?" I asked. Most people would have seen the tracks end at the fence and assumed he'd gone over.

"It's possible. Let's go find out. Only wish those damn cameras were installed everywhere already. Outlaw ordered some, but he didn't get nearly enough. This entire section is still a blind spot," Slash said.

After this, there had better be fucking cameras everywhere. We'd had too many things go wrong, and now that we had women and kids here, things needed to change. I wasn't about to risk our families for any reason. My chest ached and I rubbed at it before checking my phone.

She's alive! Those two words from Guardian meant everything to me. It felt like a weight had been lifted. As long as Zoe was still breathing, then I could handle the rest. Luis would be back home safe and sound in no time, and I'd be having a little one-on-one time with Juan. I had no doubt he was the one who'd tried to drown our wife and who'd snatched our son.

We followed the footprints for another mile. The building that stood in front of us, if it could be called that, looked like a stiff breeze would knock it over. I took another step and the dirt at my feet kicked up.

"Did that fucker just shoot at me?" I asked.

"Yep. And he's using a silencer," Hot Shot said. "Well, there's four sides to that building and coincidentally there's four of us. He can't shoot everyone at once."

"That's your great plan?" Demon asked. "Only one of us can get taken out at a time? Fucking awesome."

Hot Shot flipped him off, but Demon only grinned. Since it was my boy in there, I'd take the front. Maybe he'd be so focused on me, one of my brothers could get in there and subdue him.

"I want him alive," I said. "Get Luis out of there, and knock the asshole out if you need to, but he's mine. I get to end his miserable life."

"Let's do this," Slash said. They fanned out, each taking a side of the building, and I kept heading for the front door. Either the man inside couldn't aim for shit, or he was toying with me. Several shots landed within inches of my toes, but he never hit me. I was within feet of the building when pain pierced my shoulder, and it felt like fire engulfed my arm. *Motherfucker!*

Same damn arm, and the previous wound hadn't had time to heal. I didn't even spare it a glance. Didn't need to. Fucker had actually shot me.

Blood ran down my arm, but I didn't let that slow me. I breached the building just as Hot Shot came through a back door. The windows on either side exploded on impact as Demon and Slash busted them out and trained their weapons on the man who'd snatch Luis and tried to kill Zoe. I wasn't sure if he was brave or stupid for coming alone. If he'd had an accomplice they were either long gone or didn't care what happened to him.

"Juan, I presume?" I asked.

The man spat at my feet and started cussing at me in Spanish. I just smiled and waited until he was finished, then planted my fist in his face. The crunch of bone as his cheekbone gave way was satisfying to say the least. His screams were even better. "You tried to kill my wife. Stole my son. You should have never come here," I said.

"She's a fat *puta*. I watched the women who come here. I did you a favor," Juan said.

"Tried?" Demon asked. "Zoe made it?"

I nodded. "I don't know what kind of shape she's in, but Guardian said she's alive."

"Your son is fine," Hot Shot yelled from outside.

"Not your son." Juan spat on the floor again. "Fucked that bitch good. Knocked her up. Luis is mine."

A red haze settled over my vision. It was as I'd suspected. This asshole had raped Zoe, and was proud of the fact. He was going to die, but not just yet. I wanted him to suffer. I also needed information from him. If he wouldn't talk, I'd have to convince him.

"What do you want to do with him?" Demon

asked. "I have a few ideas, but he's yours. If there's anything left, I'll play with him."

I could only imagine what Demon wanted to do to him. He was a sick fucker and got off on causing others pain. Or at least, our enemies. I was grateful to have him by my side, and certainly didn't want to go up against him. As the Sergeant-at-Arms, he could have claimed Juan's life. I knew I only got my chance to make this *culero* pay because Demon permitted it.

"Let's take him to the clubhouse. I think he needs to see our special room," I said.

"Right." Demon started dragging Juan from the building.

I stepped outside and saw Hot Shot with Luis. My boy looked so damn scared. I knelt and opened my arms, and he rushed toward me. I hugged him, holding him close, and murmured what I hoped were words of comfort. I'd never been around kids much until my brothers started reproducing like rabbits, but those were all tiny babies.

"Luis, I'm going to take you home, but Hot Shot is going to stay with you while I take care of something. I need to make sure that man will never hurt you again. Then we'll go see your mom." I lifted him with my good arm and started for the house. Then translated to Hot Shot, who gave me a nod. I didn't know how many, if any, of my brothers knew Spanish.

At the house, I carried Luis inside and left him with Hot Shot, then grabbed my kit from the closet and took my bike to the clubhouse. It was time to make sure Juan never hurt another person ever again. I doubted Zoe was the first woman he'd ever raped, or that Luis was the first child he'd kidnapped. No, this guy had a soul as black as pitch. Devil's Fury might not walk the straight and narrow, but there was some shit we just wouldn't do.

Grizzly waited for me outside when I arrived. I gave the Pres a nod, and carried my kit inside. I headed down to the secret room and smiled when I saw Demon had stripped Juan before shackling him to the chair. The man wasn't very big. Maybe five inches taller than Zoe, and while he was a bit thick around the middle, his dick was the size of a toddler's. Blood smeared across his lips and ran from his nose. His eyes were turning black, and I knew Demon had gotten in a few hits.

"Regardless of what you think, Luis doesn't belong to you. He's my son, and I want to know what the fuck the numbers on his hip mean." I unrolled my kit and studied the contents, trying to decide what I wanted to use first.

Juan grinned, showing two missing teeth and a mouthful of blood. "Think of it as a transaction number."

Transaction? I had a feeling what I discovered tonight was seriously going to piss me off. But I needed to know. Not only for Luis, but I needed to make sure all those children back in Mexico were no longer in danger. If that meant bringing them here, then so be it. As far as I knew, Steel was still there, along with Casper and Specter. I knew they'd make sure the kids were safe. "What kind of transaction?" I asked.

"You think that bitch was the first I fucked?" Juan asked. "She wasn't even the first that day. I had three *putas* after her."

"How many of those kids were yours?" I asked, thinking of all the boys at the compound.

"Six," he said. "The girls are sold to brothels and trained early. But the boys... they're special."

"Tell me about the boys."

He smiled. "I think I'm done."

Oh, no. He wasn't anywhere near done. I selected my smallest blade and approached Juan. He sneered at the small knife in my hand. Oh, it wouldn't kill him unless I stuck it in the right spot, but that wasn't my intention. I wanted to make him hurt. I gripped the handle and slammed the blade into the top of his thigh. He squealed like a pig and thrashed in the chair. I yanked the blade free, then brought it down again. By the fourth time, he was blubbering like a fucking pussy. "I'll talk!"

Damn right he would.

"The boys have two roles. Some are trained as future soldiers. Those who are too weak, too pathetic, are sold to men with particular tastes."

I wanted to rip this shithead apart with my bare hands, but I waited. I needed to know everything. Then I needed to get that information to Steel so he could make sure none of those kids were within reach of the cartel.

Juan licked his lips. "Little Luis is too pretty for fighting. Sold him six months ago. His new owner was waiting for him to ripen a little more, but I made sure he got a good show every week, let him see the merchandise."

I was shaking as fury snaked its way through me. I set my knife down and pulled a different one. This one was special. It wasn't for stabbing, or killing. Not directly. No, this one was perfect for peeling the flesh off his body.

I worked on Juan for an hour. When I got a text from Guardian, I decided I'd done enough. Zoe had asked me to end this man's life, and I wanted to keep my word, but I needed Demon's approval. He'd already said he wanted a piece of this guy. Killing him wouldn't bother me. Wouldn't be the first time I'd taken a man's life, and it wouldn't be the last. I did whatever was necessary to protect my family.

"On the off chance the cartel knew he was coming here, send them a message. Make sure they know this same fate awaits anyone who dares fuck with us," I said.

Demon snorted. "You telling me how to do my job now?"

"No, but I need to tell my wife she's safe, that no one else is coming for her or our son. I need to give her peace of mind, Demon."

He nodded. "Want me to finish up?"

"She asked me to do it." I pulled my largest, sharpest knife, and waited for Demon's okay. He gave a nod and I drove the blade straight into Juan's chest, piercing his heart -- if he even had one -- and ended his miserable life. "Can you have someone clean my stuff and return it to the house? I need to shower and go see Zoe."

"You going home like that?" Demon asked, eying the blood covering me.

"Yeah, I am. If Luis gets scared, I'll tell him why I look like this. I want him to know I will always protect him. Although, not all of it belongs to Juan. He shot me in the shoulder."

"Go get your family. I hope Zoe makes a full recovery." Demon slapped my back. I winced, but gave him a nod.

I went upstairs and out to my bike, then rode straight home. I paused as I entered the house, and noticed Luis looked me over, but he didn't seem frightened. I needed a shower, then we'd go to the hospital to see Zoe. It didn't take me long to scrub myself clean. I wrapped a towel around my waist and wiped the condensation off the mirror.

My shoulder hurt like a bitch, but I checked the wound and was grateful the bullet went straight through. It was still bleeding, but it wouldn't be the first time I'd taken care of myself. Hell, if I called the doc every time I got hurt, I'd just need to build a room onto the house for him.

I pulled the sewing kit from under the sink. It might not be medical grade, but it would close up the wound. I managed to stitch the front side, then realized I'd need help to close up the back. I shouted down the hall for Hot Shot.

"You got shot?" he asked.

"No, just thought I'd decorate my body with holes. What the fuck do you think? Stitch that up. I can't reach it."

Hot Shot flipped me off, but took the needle and thread from me. Once I'd been patched up, Hot Shot went to check on Luis while I put on fresh clothes. My cut had blood on it, and I wiped it down best I could. I'd have to do a better job later, but right now, I had other priorities.

"I called for a truck," Hot Shot said. "You'll need one if you're taking Luis with you. Griz had someone get a car seat and it's already installed."

"Thanks, brother." My gaze locked on Luis. "You ready to go see your mom?"

I held out my hand and he hurried over to me, his little fingers closing around mine. I only hoped I didn't end up regretting taking him with me. Zoe might be alive, but Guardian hadn't shared anything else with me, other than a message to get my ass to the hospital. I hoped like hell that didn't mean she'd taken a turn for the worse.

Epilogue

Zoe

I'd come to the conclusion I loved my husbands. If I didn't, I'd have murdered them by now. Guardian and Dagger hadn't left my side. I must not have been in the water for very long before Dagger had found me. Even though I'd been resuscitated and coughed up water before the paramedics arrived, I'd had to stay in the ER for six hours while they made sure my lungs were clear and I would remain breathing on my own. It had been terrifying, not just for me, but for them as well.

Dealing with the police hadn't been fun either. I hadn't known what I should or shouldn't say when they'd shown up in the ER, but thankfully the hospital staff had told them I needed time to heal before they asked more questions. Dagger had spoken to the officers at some point, or so he said, and that had been the last I'd seen of them. Whatever he'd told them must have been enough to satisfy them.

I hadn't had any lasting issues from drowning, except annoyance at the men currently flanking me on the couch. The doctors had released me three weeks ago, and still they treated me like I was made of glass and would shatter at any moment. Neither of them had touched me, or given me more than a quick peck on the lips, since I'd been home. While I understood they were worried, I was fine. More than fine.

Since Dagger and Guardian had glued themselves to me like ticks while I'd been in the hospital, Hot Shot had helped take care of Luis. Our boy now had a favorite uncle. Even though he'd been slowly opening up around the others, Hot Shot was his go-to person if his daddies weren't nearby. He even preferred Dagger and Guardian over me, but I couldn't hold it against him. They were pretty amazing.

In fact, Luis was with his Uncle Hot Shot right now. Guardian's sister had arranged for a child psychiatrist to meet with Luis. Our son still wouldn't talk, but I thought the visits were helping. The doctor was using play therapy because of how young Luis was, but as long as she helped our son I didn't care what means she had to use. As long as it didn't hurt him more.

"I love you," I said, taking both of their hands. I felt Dagger stiffen and Guardian shifted toward me.

"What?" Guardian asked.

"I said I love you. Both of you."

Now that I had Dagger's attention too, I started to squirm. His gaze was focused on me, and it made me feel warm all over.

"You love us?" he asked.

I nodded. "*Sí.* If I didn't, the both of you would be dead already."

"Uh, baby, how exactly did you come to that conclusion? Because I revived you and Dagger got our boy back, so…"

"Because the two of you are driving me insane! You won't touch me, kiss me. You act like I'm going to break at any moment. If I didn't love you, I'd have hit you both over the head with a shovel and asked someone to bury your corpses."

Dagger snorted, then started laughing.

"I'm so glad you're amused."

"*Corazoncito*, we were waiting for a sign you were ready for more." Dagger tightened his hold on my hand. "You *died*. Even though you seem fine now, we didn't want to rush you. What if you'd had complications? The doctors could have missed something. We don't know for sure how long you were dead. Being cautious didn't mean that we didn't want you, but our relationship isn't just about sex, *princesa*. We love you, too."

"No, it's not based on sex, but that doesn't mean I don't *want* sex," I said. I ached for them. In fact, I'd woken in the middle of the night more than once with my clit throbbing and the need to orgasm. A few times I'd managed to make myself come without either of them waking, but usually I ended up feeling frustrated because my fingers weren't what I wanted.

I'd never experienced that before. I wasn't sure if they'd woken something inside me, or if it was something else. I had this niggling feeling I might be pregnant, but we'd only been together such a short time. Even though I'd only started having sex with them a few weeks ago, I'd missed my period. At first, I'd thought I was just late when it didn't show last week, but my breasts were more tender than usual, and this crazy need for sex made me think there could be a baby growing inside me. I remembered the massive mood swings and hormone surges when I'd carried Luis, even though sex had scared me back then.

So I'd gotten an early detection pregnancy test. Or more accurately, I'd asked China to get one for me. Meiling's mother was quiet, but once she'd learned my parents had tossed me out on my rear, she'd taken me under her wing. In the last few weeks, I'd met all of the Devil's Fury ladies, but China remained my favorite. I knew that wasn't her real name, but it's what her man called her, and everyone else seemed to refer to her that way as well.

"In fact, I think I'm going to want a lot of sex. At least until I'm too big for us to be intimate." Dagger's brow furrowed and even Guardian looked perplexed. I sighed and stood up, then turned to face them. I pointed to my belly. "Congratulations, Santiago and Jared. One of you knocked me up. We're having a baby."

"Are you sure?" Dagger asked, coming to his feet and gently placing a hand on my belly.

"Took a test. It came back positive, and there are a few signs I can't ignore. Missed period. My breasts are sensitive. And I want sex. Lots and lots of sex."

Guardian stood, then lifted me into his arms and walked off. He called back over his shoulder, "You heard our wife. She wants sex."

I giggled as he carried me to the bedroom, then stripped off my clothes and his. Dagger wasn't far behind, and soon all of us were naked and piled on the bed. Guardian lightly dragged his fingers over my nipples, making me gasp and arch into his touch. Dagger wedged his hand between my thighs and tugged them apart, then stroked my pussy. I knew I was already wet because my panties had been soaked when Guardian had removed them.

"What do you want, *corazoncito*?" Dagger asked.

"I want you. Both of you. Need to feel you inside me. Please, Santiago. Please, Jared. Don't tease me right now."

"You heard her," Dagger said. "Let's make her feel good."

Dagger flipped me onto my hands and knees, making me squeal in surprise. With a nod of his head, Guardian knelt by my face. His cock was hard and twitched twice, almost as if it anticipated what was to come as much as I did. I felt the head of Dagger's cock enter me, stretching my pussy wide. He felt so incredible!

"More, Santiago! Don't hold back!"

His hand came down hard on my ass, first one cheek, then the other. "I still owe you some spankings for withholding information again."

My heart raced at his words.

Smack. Smack.

"You're not going to lie anymore, are you, wife?" he asked. "Even by omission."

Smack. Smack.

Guardian chuckled. "She already did. She could have told us she thought she was pregnant, but she somehow got a test and took it without us."

"He's right. You've been very, very bad. This ass is going to hurt when I'm done."

He spanked me at least a dozen times before he started fucking me with hard, deep strokes. I screamed in pleasure, begging and pleading for more.

"I think she needs something to occupy her mouth. Gag her with your cock, Jared," Dagger said.

Guardian fisted my hair and tilted my head. "Open."

I parted my lips and he thrust between them. The salty taste of his pre-cum coated my tongue. With Dagger pounding into my pussy, and Guardian making me take all of his cock, it felt like my body exploded when I came. I cried out around my mouthful, and Guardian thrust faster. He came down my throat as Dagger filled my pussy.

I tried to pull away, but Guardian held me still. "No, baby. Not yet. Keep sucking. Get me hard so I can feel that pussy wrapped around me."

I did as he commanded. Dagger stayed buried inside me as he strummed my clit, making me come again. When he pulled free, he trailed kisses down my spine. I felt Guardian get hard again, his shaft swelling in my mouth. Before I could process what was happening, I'd been flipped around and Guardian was balls-deep inside me, taking me as if he were possessed.

Dagger got up and stood next to the bed. I glanced over my shoulder and saw his heated gaze focused on Guardian's cock as he took me. I shuddered in pleasure and came twice before Guardian found his release.

Even though I'd wanted sex with them, it had completely drained me. I collapsed onto the bed, and felt as if my legs were made of jelly. "Shower."

"No," Dagger said. "You're going to wear our cum for a while. In fact, after you've rested, we're going to fuck you again. You said you wanted lots of sex, so prepare to get your wish."

I groaned and buried my face against the bedding. They were going to kill me, but it would be an amazing way to go. I rolled to my side, and stared at the men I adored. I wasn't sure when exactly I'd fallen for them, but they were perfect for me, and were amazing dads. Not only was Luis blessed to have them, but so was I, and the unborn child growing inside me.

I'd come to this country in the hopes of giving my son a better life, but I never could have predicted how well it all would end. It hadn't been a smooth, easy path, but I was so grateful I'd found them.

"I love you. Both of you."

"And I love both of you," Guardian said, sliding his gaze from me to Dagger.

Dagger shook his head. "I never believed in love, just hoped we'd all find some happiness together. But the two of you have proven to me that love exists, because I sure the fuck love both of you. And our kids."

They both touched my belly, looks of awe on their faces. I didn't know how Luis would handle the news, but I hoped it would draw him out a little more. I'd make sure to tell him that as a big brother, he'd have a very important role. And we'd have to make sure he knew that we would all love him, that he wasn't being replaced.

"When my family threw me out, I never thought I'd have a family of my own," Guardian said. "I figured if my parents couldn't accept me, then no one else would. To have both of you, Luis, and now a baby on the way is more than I'd ever hoped for."

"You both know I don't have the best past, and I was scared shitless that I'd be a bad dad, but being around Luis has proven that isn't true. I would do anything for him, and for any other children we may have. The club might be family, but the two of you and our kids are the most important people in my life."

I smiled. "Just three misfits who discovered we weren't really misfits after all, because the three of us fit together perfectly."

I snuggled between them, and soaked up all the love they wanted to give. I didn't know what tomorrow would bring, or if the cartel would come after us again. Or if some other darkness would encroach on our lives. All I could do was hope we'd have a happily-ever-after. I wasn't a princess, and my husbands weren't princes. Ugliness and pain had brought us together, but it was our love that would keep us together.

Whatever the future brought we'd deal with it. Together.

Steel (Devil's Fury MC 5)
Harley Wylde

Rachel -- Getting pregnant in high school hasn't exactly made my life easy, especially since my daughter's father wants nothing to do with us and his parents hate us. Starting over in a new town sounded easy enough, but finding work and a place to stay isn't so simple in Blackwood Falls. I never counted on a knight in shining armor coming to my rescue, or that he'd be riding a Harley. There's something about the sexy silver fox that makes me feel safe. Steel might be some big, tough biker, but anyone who rescues a pug and names her Victoria can't be all bad, right? I only hope I'm not falling for the wrong guy yet again. My heart can't handle it, and neither can my daughter's.

Steel -- I may have seen a lot of sh*t in my time, and done things that would give most people nightmares, but I'm admittedly a softie when it comes to kids and animals. Little Coral might have enchanted me at first, but her mom is the one I can't get off my mind. I can tell she's running from something, and I'll find out what one way or another. She thinks she's all alone, but she's wrong. She has me -- because I always go after what I want and I'm going to make her mine. Doesn't matter I'm more than two decades older than her. I pity anyone who stands in my way or dares to harm any of my girls -- I won't hesitate to put the bastards six feet under.

Prologue

Steel

It was a Friday night and I should have been at the clubhouse. Except it was getting a bit old. Or maybe I was. The club pussy had been fun, but the past year or two, I'd not seen the appeal. Besides, those bitches could be downright evil at times. I didn't need drama in my life, especially of the catty female variety. At my age, it was doubtful I'd ever claim a woman, but the more of my brothers I watched fall, the more hope I had maybe someone was out there for me. Hell, if a woman could take on both Dagger and Guardian together, then surely someone could put up with my cranky ass.

I could admit it. At fifty-five, I was set in my ways. I'd spent over a decade in the military, first Air Force, then the Army, and I liked everything done a certain way. I might not have any say over how the club ran, but when it came to my house, I liked everything in its place. There was also the issue of me needing to be in control more than most women liked. I'd dated, but it never went anywhere. After getting called a controlling asshole one too many times, I'd given up on finding a forever kind of woman, and settled for getting off with the club whores when the need arose.

So now my brothers, those who weren't at home with their families, were having a grand time at the clubhouse and I was out walking the streets of Blackwood Falls. The town was quiet most of the time, but we had our share of trouble. There were bad elements no matter where you lived, and this sleepy little town was no different. Hell, Badger had done time for killing a man he'd caught raping a young girl.

In fact, it had happened in an alley not too far from my current location. Then we'd found out about the human trafficking ring -- one run by men at town hall -- when Meiling had shown up at the clubhouse.

I was starting to think there was nowhere safe anymore. Murderers, rapists, pedophiles... they lurked in the shadows of even the most respectable places. Fuck, how many times did the news report teachers preying on their students? Or police officers who were rotten to the core? I'd once believed everyone had the ability to be good and some chose to be evil. After all I'd seen and done over the past four decades, I'd learned it wasn't the case. No, some people were just born without a soul, with a darkness so deep there wasn't even a hint of light anywhere inside them.

A sound caught my attention, and I stopped in the middle of the sidewalk, straining my ears. There. A soft whimper, but it sounded more like an animal than a human. I hunted for the location and entered a dark narrow alley between two buildings. I heard a *thud* and the hair on my nape prickled. I pulled the knife I kept at my waist. The blade wasn't exactly legal, but it wasn't like I gave a shit.

As my eyes adjusted, I saw a young punk draw his foot back and the *thud* echoing off the brick walls had me growling. The little fucker was literally kicking a puppy, or at least a small dog. I approached, knowing it was time someone taught this kid a lesson. He'd obviously never learned right from wrong, and I was happy to have the honor of correcting his behavior.

"What the hell did the dog ever do to you?" I asked.

The dick jerked his head my way, clearly not having heard me before now. "It's none of your business. Move on, old man."

Old man? I narrowed my eyes and moved in closer. I'd show this little shit just how this *old man* could kick his ass. "Move away from the dog."

The jackass kicked it again, and something in me snapped. It was like a red haze settled over my vision as I launched myself at him. The blade in my hand sank into his side, and I gave it a little twist before yanking it out. He stumbled away from me, and I went after him again, landing a blow across his jaw and another to his temple, knocking him out cold. It would serve the little shit right if he bled out. I'd made sure the wound wouldn't heal easily, if at all.

The whimpers from the dog drew my attention. I cleaned my knife off on the punk's clothes, then sheathed it before easing closer to the little dog. I could now see it was a pug, or at least a pug mix. Inky black fur made it damn near impossible to see in the darkness, but its large eyes were hard to miss.

"I won't hurt you," I murmured, hunkering down and holding out my hand. It struggled to stand and fell back to the ground, telling me it might be too far gone to save, but I was going to fucking try anyway. I moved in closer and slowly reached out my hand again. The dog gave me a tentative lick, and I gently lifted it, holding it against my chest. "Let's get you to the vet."

I'd ridden my bike, and there was no damn way I was going to carry this dog on there, so I walked the six blocks to the vet's office. Even though they were closed, I knew they kept someone on staff at night for emergencies. This wasn't the first animal I'd tried to save, and it wouldn't be the last. I rang the bell and waited, hoping the little bundle of fur in my arms was a fighter.

The young vet opened the door and frowned when he saw the dog. "What happened?"

"Caught some idiot kicking this dog. It doesn't seem to be able to stand so I thought I'd bring it in to get checked out." I stepped inside and walked past him, then down the hall to the only room with a light on. I eased the dog onto the metal table and stroked its fur. "Don't care what it costs. Just help the little thing."

"Are you keeping this one, Steel?" Dr. Morgan asked.

"Maybe. Let's see if she pulls through first. I don't know what kind of damage the kid did before I found the punk."

"Should I be worried about the condition he's in now?" Dr. Morgan asked.

I arched an eyebrow and stared at him. "You really give a shit?"

"Nope. I figured it was my civic duty to attempt to care, but anyone who hurts an innocent creature like this one deserves whatever you did to them."

It was one of the things I liked about the vet. Being the youngest at this particular clinic, he was always here at night when I needed emergency care for some wounded beast or other, and we seemed to agree on how animal abusers should be handled. The other vets were bleeding hearts who would be horrified I'd stabbed the kid and left him for dead. But Dr. Morgan wasn't just anyone.

As a kid, he'd been on the receiving end of abuse often enough he could sympathize with this animal more than most. I'd tried to keep an eye out for him when he'd been younger, and even helped him prospect for the club. He'd been patched in before he'd graduated high school, then he'd left for college on a full scholarship, only to return with a veterinary degree. Even though he was still technically a member of the Devil's Fury, Grizzly didn't ever call on him. I knew the Pres was hoping young Zachary would walk the straight and narrow since he had more options now.

I couldn't have been prouder had he been my own son.

"How's life treating you these days, Doolittle?" I asked, using his club name. Even as a teen, he'd had an affinity for animals.

"Okay, I guess. The woman I was seeing left town to be with a plastic surgeon up in New York. Met him online or something. I'm sure it means she wasn't the right one for me."

The kid could try to convince himself all he wanted, but I could tell by the look in his eyes it had hurt when she'd left. I knew despite all he'd accomplished, down deep, he was still the scared boy getting beat up by his father on a regular basis. We all carried some emotional or mental baggage from our pasts, but Zach hadn't been able to let his go, especially since he'd come back to Blackwood Falls. He would have been better off staying long gone from this place, but I knew he liked having the club nearby. Griz might not ask him to handle shit for the club, but we were family, and Zach needed that as much as the rest of us.

"The dog seems to be either full pug or at least mostly pug. Looking at her teeth and gums, as well as her eyes, I'd say she's probably around five give or take a year or two. I'm not seeing any graying fur yet, so I don't think she's quite a senior. I need to do an X-ray to check her ribs, but it doesn't feel like she has internal bleeding. I'll know more after some tests," Zach said.

"You keeping her overnight?" I asked, running

my hand over the dog's head.

"Probably for the best. I'll see how badly she's injured, get her treated, then put her in a kennel to get some sleep. Want me to call in the morning after I find out more?"

"Yes. I'll take responsibility for her. Since I have a house over at the compound, no reason she can't come live with me as long as she pulls through. Got plenty of space for her."

Zach smiled. "I knew you were an old softie, at least when it comes to animals and kids."

I flipped him off, but he grinned bigger. I let myself out and walked back to my bike. With some luck, the little dog would pull through, and I'd need to have some supplies when she came home with me. Even if the pug didn't make it, I wouldn't mind adopting a dog over at the shelter. It would be nice to have some company at home.

After I'd stayed behind in Mexico to help the kids Dagger had found, I'd realized despite the club my life was rather lonely and solitary. I didn't have a woman or kids waiting for me, not so much as a goldfish. For the longest time, it hadn't bothered me. Then my brothers had started to pair off.

Badger claimed Adalia after he'd gotten out of prison. Dingo had taken one look at Meiling and decided she was his. Then there was Blades and China, even though he hadn't officially made her his. Everyone in the club knew they were destined to be together. Outlaw had fallen for a little shy bookworm. Then Dragon had gotten the Pres' daughter pregnant and claimed her. Hell, even Dagger and Guardian had a woman. One by one, my brothers were finding their other halves.

I didn't know if I'd ever find a woman who

could put up with me, much less love me. I could hope she was out there. Maybe she was, but I could also spend the rest of my life alone and never find her. If the best I could do for companionship right now, other than my brothers, was a dog, then I'd make sure the little pug had everything she could ever want or need.

I rode over to the twenty-four store and picked up a few doggie essentials, only the stuff I could fit in my saddlebags, and figured I could get the rest when I picked up the pug. She'd need a name. Something strong. If she came through this, then she was a fighter. Maybe I'd call her Victoria after the Roman goddess of victory.

Now I just had to hope she made it.

Chapter One

Rachel

I'd only been in Blackwood Falls a few days, but already I could see the charm of living here. At least for those who had an actual home, and a job. Both of those things were currently lacking in my life, but I was determined to make the best of things. There wasn't a homeless shelter, not one I could find at any rate, and my money was disappearing fast. I'd found the cheapest motel in the area and rented a room, but it was eating up my funds, what little had been left after the bus fare to get this far. The only upside, other than a place to sleep at night, was the room at the motel gave me running water and I could keep a loaf of bread, peanut butter, and some jelly so there was something to eat.

"Come on, Coral," I said, holding my hand out to my six-year-old daughter. She was the one bright spot in my life these days. "Mommy needs to apply at a few more places today."

"I'll be quiet," she said, her voice nearly a whisper as she grasped my fingers.

She'd never been any trouble, not even as a baby. It broke my heart her father not only didn't want anything to do with her, but her grandparents had made it their life's mission to cause problems for us. They hated me, and I wondered if they didn't hate their grandchild too. In exchange for Patrick signing over his rights, I'd agreed to not receive child support from him and never to ask his family for help. Apparently, it wasn't good enough.

We left the motel room, and I made sure the door locked behind me, then we headed down the main strip toward the restaurants and businesses. I wasn't entirely certain what I'd do with Coral while I worked. School was out for summer break for at least another few weeks. I'd hoped the money would last until the middle of August, give me time with Coral and set up a job to start after she started first grade, but I hadn't been lucky enough.

I'd checked the local diner when we'd first arrived in town, and there hadn't been any openings. The manager had been busy at the time and wouldn't accept an application, but I hoped my luck might change today. I'd managed to graduate before Coral was born, barely, but there were still very few jobs available for someone who only had a high school diploma and no extra skills or training. I'd waited tables in our hometown, not only through high school, but I'd switched to full-time once I'd graduated. Until the restaurant had closed and I'd been left without a job.

A bell over the door jangled as we stepped inside, the icy air conditioning was welcome against my heated skin. Coral held on tighter as she looked around. Instead of waiting to get someone's attention, I approached the register, hoping the manager might be available this time. A young girl stood behind the counter, her hair up in a bun, and a stained uniform clinging to her like a second skin. With her curves, I was willing to bet she raked in the tips.

"I'd like to get an application," I said when she finally noticed me.

"I'll go get Rick." She stepped away and went into the back, only to return a few minutes later with a man following behind her.

He eyed Coral, then held out his hand to me. "Rick Gilbert. I'm afraid I'm still getting up to speed since I accepted the manager's position a week ago.

Laura said you'd like to apply for a job."

I nodded. "I've been waiting tables since high school. I'd hoped you might have an opening, or maybe would at least take my information in case something opens up."

His lips tipped up on one corner. "Since high school? Was that last month?"

I straightened a little, trying to make myself bigger, knowing at slightly under five feet I wasn't the least bit imposing. My lack of breasts never helped my cause, but everyone always assumed I was younger than my twenty-three years. "I can assure you I graduated a while ago. I'm more than qualified."

Rick lifted his hands. "I didn't mean any offense. Who's this little beauty with you?"

"Coral. My daughter." I waited to see how he would react. I'd been sneered at plenty of times when people realized I'd gotten pregnant in high school.

"It's nice to meet you, Coral. Why don't you sit at the bar right here," he said tapping a place to his left, "and I'll get Laura to make you a milkshake while I talk to your mom."

Coral looked up at me and I gave her a nod. I didn't know what the milkshake would cost, but if it meant I was employed when I left here, it would be worth every penny. I knew we were on borrowed time before we were living on the streets. And without a car, I couldn't even keep my daughter out of the heat or rain if we lost the motel room.

Rick motioned for me to follow him, and I stepped into the back of the diner. His office was cluttered, with stacks of paper falling every which way. I eased down onto the chair across from his desk while he dug out an application. He handed it to me on a clipboard, along with a pen.

"Go ahead and fill that out so I'll have something official, but if you honestly have experience, then you're exactly what I need right now. The last manager was something of a sleaze from what I understand, and a hard ass. Pardon my language. He ran off all but three waitresses, and that's honestly not enough for a place that's open twenty-four hours."

I paused in the middle of filling out my information. "Wait. You mean I'm hired?"

He nodded. "Although, I have to ask you something. Since you brought Coral with you today, does that mean you don't have childcare available when you're working?"

I chewed on my lower lip, hoping I wasn't about to lose my chance at this job. As bad as the motel seemed, I couldn't leave Coral there. Not only was she too young, but I worried she wouldn't be safe there. "No, I don't. Should I stop filling this out?"

"Not necessarily. Coral seems old enough to attend school."

"She's six," I said. "She'll be starting first grade this year, but school won't start for several more weeks."

"In Blackwood Falls, it will be a bit longer than that. Try another three to four weeks."

I winced, not knowing they started so much later than where we'd come from. He might have let me work and place Coral in an out of the way spot for a week or two, but an entire month? I knew it was asking too much. I signed and dated the application, then handed it over to him. Rick scanned the document, his eyebrows lifting at one point, and I wasn't sure if it was a good or bad thing.

"You're living at the motel on the edge of town?" he asked.

"It's all I've been able to afford, and honestly, if I don't get this job, then we won't be living there much longer." I rubbed my hands up and down my thighs. "I promise I'm not a bad mother, but my last job disappeared overnight. What little I had in savings I used to get us here, and I've been searching for a job the last three days. I came by my first day job hunting, but I was told the manager was busy."

He ran a hand over the back of his neck. "Yeah, I was probably trying to dig my way through all this crap. I'm sorry they didn't at least give you an application to complete. I could have hired you sooner than today."

"But I still don't have anywhere to leave Coral," I said.

"Let me go over some details first, make sure this is the job you want, then we'll figure something out." He leaned back in his chair. "The job pays three dollars an hour plus tips. That being said, in the state of Georgia, if your tips and wages don't come out to minimum wage, the diner has to make up the difference. So regardless of how slow a shift is, you're guaranteed minimum wage per hour you're on the clock."

That sounded more than reasonable to me. I knew it wouldn't be a fortune, unless I made some really amazing tips, but at least it would help keep Coral fed and a roof over our heads. That's all I wanted right now.

"You're allowed one meal on the house during your shift, and you'll get a thirty-minute break for a meal during an eight-hour shift. If you work overtime and you're here for either both breakfast and lunch, or lunch and dinner, then you'll get two meals for the day. Typically, you'll get whatever is on special for the day, unless you're allergic to what's on the menu. It doesn't include pie, milkshakes, or anything extra. You can order those things, but you'll have to pay for them."

Getting a meal sounded like heaven. That alone would make it worth working at the diner. And if I worked enough to get two meals, maybe I could box one to take home to Coral. My previous employer had made us pay for anything we ate during our shift. I was already liking this place.

"Now, about your daughter. Until school starts, or you're able to afford daycare, you can bring her with you. I'll make sure she gets something to eat during your shift, but you'll be responsible for giving her ways to stay occupied. If you have to tend to her more than your customers, then I'll have no choice but to let you go."

Again, entirely fair. He did have a business to run, and the fact he would let Coral come with me at all was a miracle. I'd been worried where I'd put her while I worked, and he'd already resolved the issue for me. Things were looking up for a change.

"How much are you paying per night at the motel?" he asked.

I hesitated, unsure why he needed to know. Although, he'd been incredibly nice so far. Maybe he was worried I wouldn't make enough to keep living there?

"It's forty dollars per night, which I know is incredibly cheap, even for a small town."

"There's a reason for that," he muttered. Rick pulled a calculator closer to him, then started punching buttons. "If you stay at the motel, you'll end up paying around twelve-hundred dollars a month if you stay on the nightly rate. What they didn't tell you is they offer a weekly rate for long-term guests. It's still not cheap, but it would save you a lot in the long run."

He was right. I hadn't known about the discount. Of course, I hadn't known how long we'd have to stay there when we'd arrived in town. Maybe if the motel clerk had known we'd be there for a while, he would have offered the cheaper rate. Then again, he hadn't looked like the sort to care.

"There's an apartment over the diner that used to be rented to wait staff who needed a place to stay, but it's currently occupied. It was part of the paperwork I reviewed this morning, and I'm afraid their lease isn't up for another three months. If you'd like the apartment when it becomes available, I'll reserve it for you, but the cost is four hundred per month, and there's only one bedroom and one bathroom."

"We don't need anything big," I assured him.

"Then I'll make a note to let you have first option of renting whenever it's available again. Until then, I'd suggest you tell the staff at the motel you need to book your room by the week. It's about the cost of your room for three nights at the daily rate."

I did the calculation in my head and knew I'd need around one-hundred-twenty dollars to accomplish that. While I did have enough left, it would only leave me about thirty dollars for other essentials. But if Rick gave me this job, which it sounded like he would, then at least one meal would be covered for both me and Coral until she started school, unless I pulled a double and got two meals, or I made other arrangements for her. Once I started getting tips, then I could stock a few more things in the motel room for us to eat.

"If everything sounds agreeable, I'll get the employment forms and you can fill them out now.

Could you start as early as tonight? Dinner is usually our biggest rush, and I'll go ahead and let you know I only have one other person handling that shift today. You'll be extremely busy, but we'll make sure there's a spot for Coral at the end of the bar. You'll need to be here by five and you'll get off at eleven. I know that's only six hours, but I want to see how you handle things the first few shifts."

"Yes! Thank you, Rick. I really appreciate the opportunity to work here."

He pulled out a bunch of papers, attached them to the clipboard, then handed them over. "I'll need a copy of your driver's license and social security card."

I removed both from my wallet and handed them over. He turned to a printer in the corner of the office and lifted the lid, using it as a copier. Once he'd finished, he handed back my two forms of ID, then waited for me to complete the paperwork. When I'd given him everything, and shaken his hand once more, he found a uniform in my size.

"You'll have to be responsible for keeping it clean," he said. "We only give out one per employee, but they can acquire a second one for a flat fee of fifty dollars. If you quit working here and return both uniforms, then that charge will be reimbursed and included in your last check."

"I don't have enough to keep the motel, feed Coral, and get the second uniform right now, but I'll try to put some money aside for one." I thanked him again, then went to check on Coral. She'd finished her shake and was speaking to an imposing-looking man next to her. His hair was pulled back and a short beard covered his jaw. The leather vest over his shoulders said his name was Steel.

Neither noticed my presence, or at least Coral

didn't. I had a feeling this Steel person didn't miss anything. He had the look of someone who'd seen the darkness in life. I'd seen the same look on cops, military guys, and even the mafia men who ran my hometown. Coral wasn't one to trust just anyone. The way she smiled at him and chattered told me she felt safe with Steel. I only hoped she wasn't talking to someone who would kidnap her or worse. Not knowing anyone in this town meant we were surrounded by strangers, and didn't know who to trust.

"Coral, stop bothering the nice man. It's time to go," I said, reaching for her hand.

She hopped off the stool and grabbed my fingers. "It's okay, Mommy. Mr. Steel is really nice. He said maybe one day I can pet his puppy."

My gaze jerked to his. I hoped he really did have a dog and it wasn't a euphemism for anything else. Of course, I'd never heard a man call any part of his person a puppy before. Steel stood up, his height towering over me. He held out his hand, but with Coral holding onto me and the uniform clutched in my other palm, I couldn't exactly shake. He smiled when he saw my dilemma.

"You have a very sweet little girl," he said. "My name's Steel, and I promise I'm not going to hurt either of you."

I backed up a step. Wouldn't someone who *would* hurt us say the exact same thing? I cast a quick glance toward Laura, but she was ignoring us as she refilled a customer's drink. She didn't seem worried about the man speaking to me, so maybe he wouldn't hurt us. Or she was so oblivious she didn't even know he was here.

Steel nodded and backed up. "You're right to be

cautious. I see you'll be working here. I come in here rather often, so I'm sure we'll see one another again. You run into any trouble, you stop by the Devil's Fury compound on the other end of town. Ask for me."

He tossed some money onto the counter next to his half-eaten burger, then turned to walk out. I saw the back of his vest and realized he was a biker. *Devil's Fury MC* was stitched on the back with a rather ominous-looking logo, or whatever they called it. He walked out, not pausing to turn back toward us, and went over to a motorcycle parked nearby. As he started it up and the engine made a loud rumble, I held onto Coral and watched him ride off.

"Those men aren't exactly harmless," Laura said as she came to stand next to me, "but none of them would hurt your daughter. They're all rough around the edges, and into some stuff that isn't exactly legal, but they protect kids."

So, she had been paying attention. It was good to know the man could be trusted, and apparently anyone else from the Devil's Fury. At least Coral hadn't been talking to a pedophile while I'd been trying to land this job. It made my stomach stop knotting, and I led my daughter outside. As we walked back to the motel, I told her about my job and let her know she'd get to eat dinner there later. I only hoped the one coloring book and few crayons she had would be enough to keep her occupied during my shift. I'd picked them up at the dollar store before we'd boarded the bus to come to Blackwood Falls, and I knew she'd colored most of the pages already.

Whatever it took, I'd keep this job, and I'd make sure my daughter was fed and cared for. She was my entire world and I'd do anything for her.

Chapter Two

Steel

The redhead at the diner had intrigued me. Her daughter had been the sweetest thing, and I'd enjoyed talking to her. Children were so innocent, and seldom came with a filter so whatever they thought came out of their mouths. I'd learned more from her than I probably would pull out of her mother even if I'd lured her into a lengthy conversation. Like they were new in town, and didn't know anyone here. It's why I'd offered my help if they ever needed anything. That and I couldn't deny being attracted to the mom.

Once Coral had learned about Victoria, she'd asked a million questions about the pug. It hadn't escaped my notice Coral had a massive amount of energy, and for every bit of it, her mother seemed equally worn down. The dark smudges under her eyes told me she hadn't slept well lately. I'd thought my time for having a family was long past, and maybe it still was, but I hoped I'd get to see more of Coral and her mother. Maybe even convince them to go to dinner with me one night, or have breakfast somewhere. I'd simply have to get the woman to trust me first.

I'd spent the rest of the day checking the security cameras we'd added to the compound, then I'd checked on our guests. The ladies, who'd been dropped at our gates a few months ago, seemed reluctant to leave. I couldn't blame them. We'd made sure they had some cash for clothing, shoes, and any other necessities, and none of them paid rent or for their groceries. I wondered how long the Pres would let them stay, but he didn't seem in a hurry to toss them out. I figured it had more to do with the two teens he'd adopted than the ladies staying in the apartments.

Steam billowed from my shower and I stripped out of my clothes. I'd left my cut on my bed, and tossed the rest into the hamper. I stepped under the spray and pulled the glass door shut. My home might not be as big as some of the ones inside the compound, but I'd made sure my bathroom had every luxury. My shower could easily hold four people and had a bench across the back wall. There was a tub big enough for soaking, and I had two sinks with a lot of counter space on the off chance I ever found a woman who could handle being mine.

The water beat down on my neck and shoulders, and I felt the tension ease from my body. When Dagger and Guardian had claimed Zoe, we'd run into a bit of trouble with the Mexican cartel, but thankfully they'd given us a wide berth since Juan had broken into the compound and snatched Zoe's son, Luis. Might have had something to do with us delivering his head back to the cartel. Demon had wanted to ensure they knew not to fuck with us, and they'd apparently received the message loud and clear. The fact we'd hit their compound and freed the kids hadn't hurt. I was certain it had pissed them off, but they knew we meant business and wouldn't take their shit lying down. Either that, or they were regrouping and would strike again later.

Since I'd had a rather large role in making sure all the young children they'd stolen or bred had been placed in safe homes, I had no doubt they'd love to get their hands on me. Wouldn't happen, but the fuckers could try. I'd bury every last one. Anyone who trained kids to kill, or sold them to pedophiles, needed to die a slow and painful death. I was only too happy to help.

Thinking of those kids reminded me of sweet

Coral. She'd taken after her mom with all that pretty red hair and her green eyes. The smattering of freckles across her nose and cheeks had been pretty damn adorable. I wondered where Coral would stay while her mom worked. The little girl had mentioned living at the motel, and while there was more than one in town, I hoped like hell they weren't in the one at the far edge of Blackwood Falls. It was mostly filled with drug dealers and whores, and definitely not a safe location for such a sweet child or her mom.

I washed quickly and got out, deciding I wanted to do something nice for them. With my luck, the mom would freak the hell out, but I didn't like the idea of them being alone. Did they have everything they needed? Their clothes had looked a little worn out, but I'd noticed they were clean. Even if they were struggling, it was obvious they were doing the best they could. But everyone needed help every now and then. Even tough single moms. Or maybe it was *especially* tough single moms.

After I'd dried off, used a little beard balm, and run a brush through my hair, I stopped and stared at my reflection.

"What the hell are you doing? You're too damn old for someone like her." I leaned on the counter and tried to convince myself to abort my plan, but something told me not to.

I pulled my hair back and got dressed before heading out to my Harley. My saddlebags weren't huge, but I hoped they'd be sufficient for what I planned to purchase. Coral had mentioned she liked to draw and loved puzzles. I had no doubt if I'd bought something for her mom, the lady would have refused, but I knew she'd have a hard time saying no to a present for her daughter.

As I neared the front gates, I came to a stop and studied the chaos in front of me. What the fuck was going on now? It looked like the clubhouse was packed, but it was the sight of Lilian throwing shit at Dragon making me pause. It was no secret when she lost her temper, he got the brunt of it, but Dragon usually deserved it. I walked the bike closer, then put down the kickstand and shut it off.

"Are you trying to kill him or maim him?" I asked as I got closer.

Tears slipped down her cheeks, and I glared at Dragon. What the hell had he done this time? While I'd have him at my back in a second, he had a habit of saying or doing the wrong thing when it came to his woman.

"I want to knock him unconscious," Lilian said as she sniffled. "He's an asshole."

"Well, darlin', you knew that before you agreed to be his. Little late to change your mind," I said. "What did he do this time?"

"He bought me a new dress." I waited because there was no damn way she was pissed he'd purchased new clothes for her. Had to be more to it. "Two sizes too big! He thinks I'm fat!"

Oh fucking hell. I shook my head and pinched the bridge of my nose. I loved Lilian, we all did, but her hormones were all over the fucking place. I'd thought she'd calm down after her twins were born, but it didn't seem to be the case. Speaking of... I scanned the area and saw little Mila in Wolf's arms and Blades had Ronan. The babies seemed oblivious to their mother's meltdown, for which I was thankful.

"Lilian, you know damn well this boy doesn't think you're fat. Hell, he about lost his damn mind when you disappeared up to Tennessee, then got yourself kidnapped. Did he not come after you? Claim you? Stay by your side this entire time?" I asked.

"Well, yeah," she said softly.

"I told her it was an honest mistake," Dragon said. "I don't know shit about woman's clothes. I saw something pretty and grabbed one."

"He's not too smart, Lilian, but he's yours. Now stop throwing shit at your man, get your kids, and take your ass home," I said. "What would your daddy say if he saw you throwing a fit in front of the clubhouse?"

She winced and glanced around, almost as if she feared Grizzly would appear at any moment. I reached out and grabbed her arm, giving her a tug. I put her right in front of Dragon, and he wrapped his arms around her, held her close, and whispered in her ear. Her shoulders drooped and she relaxed against him. Good. One issue resolved for the day.

Before I got back on my bike, I went to get a look at little Mila and Ronan. They were too damn cute. I knew Mila had an operation for her cataracts not too long ago, but she seemed to be doing well. Her little fist waved in the air as she babbled at Wolf. As much as I wanted to hold those babies, I knew if I stuck around, someone would decide they needed something. I went back to my bike, started it back up, and pulled out of the gates before anyone could stop me.

I didn't want to take the time to drive all the way over to the twenty-four-hour store, so I pulled into the pharmacy parking lot. I knew they had a toy aisle and carried things like gift bags. Parking my bike near the door, I surveyed the area before I shut off the engine and locked the Harley. I didn't think anyone in Blackwood Falls would dare mess with any of our bikes, but I didn't want to take a chance. I went inside and grabbed a gift bag with a princess on it, then located the toy section.

Not having ever had kids, I felt a little lost as I looked over the selection. I didn't see a drawing tablet, but there was a box of crayons and a handful of coloring books. The crayons went into the sack, as well as two coloring books. Coral had said she liked puzzles, but they didn't have many of those either. I picked out one I thought she could put together with kittens in a basket, and added it to the bag. As I was heading to the register, something pink caught my attention. A display of small stuffed animals was nearly overflowing. The splash of pink had been a swan on the top rack. I grabbed it and added it to the bag before going to check out. If I lingered much more, I'd surely find something else.

The woman smiled as I handed her the sack. "Your little girl is going to love all this."

I knew I should correct her, but I liked the thought of Coral being mine, and especially of her mom belonging to me. "I hope so. I know she likes drawing and puzzles, but the stuffed animal was an afterthought."

The woman laughed. "It's hard to come in here and only get what you planned to buy. People check out all the time with several items they had no intention of getting."

I paid for the purchases while she put them all back into the gift sack. When I got outside to my bike, I carefully put it in my saddlebags and drove to the diner. Even though I didn't know when I'd see Coral or her mother again, I hoped the manager might at least hang onto the sack until the redhead was scheduled to work. Imagine my surprise when I walked through the door and saw Coral at a table in the back corner. Alone. And looking entirely too bored, since she was currently spinning the saltshaker on the table.

"You're back." I jerked my gaze to the woman addressing me and realized it was Coral's mother. The nametag on her uniform said *Rachel*. At least I had a name now, instead of referring to her as "Coral's mom" or "the redhead."

"Thought I'd grab a bite to eat, and I was going to leave this for your daughter," I said, lifting the bag. "I hope it's okay. She mentioned liking puzzles so I picked up a few things for her."

Rachel's face softened as she looked at the bag and a slight smile curved her lips. "That was so sweet of you. She must have really talked your ear off earlier."

"I enjoyed it. Kids are precious. They always tell you exactly what they think, whether you want to hear it or not."

Rachel threw her head back and laughed. "You're so right."

"Look, I know I'm a stranger and all, but if you're okay with Coral having this stuff, I'd really like to give the bag to her." And if she said no, then I'd find some other way to make sure the sweet girl got her present. At first, I thought she'd balk, but then she gave a nod.

I made my way to Coral's table and set the bag down. Her eyes lit up and she started to reach for it, then stopped. Her gaze held mine. "Is that for me?"

"Yep. Thought you might like a little welcome present since you're new to Blackwood Falls."

Coral picked up the bag and pulled out the items inside, her smile growing with each one. The way she reverently handled everything, it made me wonder how often she'd received gifts, if ever. I saw a coloring book and crayons on the table, but the crayons were down to nubs and the book was so thin I doubted there were many pages she hadn't yet colored. Maybe my little treat would at least give her something to do while her mother worked.

"Thank you, Mr. Steel," Coral said, hugging the little swan to her chest.

"You're welcome, Coral."

I walked off and Rachel seated me at a table nearby. It allowed me to keep an eye on the little girl, and on her mom as well. The crime rate in Blackwood Falls wasn't as great as in larger cities, but we still had our issues. If any troublemakers came in, I wanted a clear view of the door, and the girls I felt the need to protect.

Rachel handed me a menu, then pulled a pen and pad from her apron. "Do you know what you'd like to drink?"

"Glass of water and some coffee," I said.

She scribbled it down and walked off, giving me time to decide what I wanted to eat. I don't know why I bothered looking. Every damn time I came in here for dinner, I ordered the same thing. Hell, I got it for lunch most days too. Couldn't go wrong with a burger and onion rings. Most days, I tried to eat somewhat healthy, but sometimes I simply needed something greasy.

When Rachel came back, I placed my order and sipped my coffee. I noticed Coral was using her new crayons and coloring book, and I realized if she had to sit here every time her mom worked, she would quickly go through all those pages. If she liked puzzles, maybe she'd like some of those word search books. I knew they had some easy ones even a little kid could do. Coral had informed me, rather proudly, she was six and would be starting first grade in the fall. I didn't know shit about six-year-old little girls, but she seemed rather bright and inquisitive. Maybe it was only unique to Coral, or it was possible all six-year-olds were like her.

Rachel stopped by my table to refill my coffee and swayed on her feet. I reached out to grip her waist and hold her steady. A quick glance at her face was enough to tell me she was beyond exhausted. I didn't know how long her shift would be tonight, but I worried about her safely getting home. Hell, I wasn't sure she wouldn't pass out in the middle of the diner.

"How long you been up today?" I asked.

"Since before five," she murmured.

"You're not going to last much longer, Rachel. I can tell you're worn out and need some rest."

She shook her head. "Don't have a choice. I need this job. I'll be fine once I get some sleep. Now that I'm employed, I won't be quite so stressed."

I looked at the clock on the wall and wondered if she'd already had her break. As much as I wanted to force her down into a chair, I didn't want her to lose her new job either. It wasn't my place to tell her what she could or couldn't do, but if I'd ever seen someone who needed a person looking after them, it was Rachel. I had a feeling she used up all her energy making sure Coral was taken care of and didn't worry about her own health and well-being.

"If you get a break before I leave, come sit with me. And don't worry about Coral. I'll keep an eye on her while I'm here."

She gave me a tired smile. "Thanks, Steel."

Rachel started to walk off, then turned around to face me again. I could tell she wanted to say something, but couldn't seem to find the words. Whatever it was, she must have thought better of it because she heaved a sigh and walked off. I stayed true to my word and kept close watch over Coral, but I also made sure Rachel was doing okay. The moment I saw her grip the counter to stay upright, I knew I had to do something.

Tonight might have been her first shift, but if she passed out, it could very well be her last for a while. I stood and hurried over to her, reaching out just in time to keep her from falling to the floor. She sagged against me, and I could tell she didn't have a drop of energy left. Whatever had kept her going this long had completely dried up. The new manager, Rick, came from the back at the perfect time to see me lift Rachel into my arms. I had no fucking clue where I'd put her. It wasn't like I could carry her and Coral on the back of my bike, especially while she was so far gone.

"What the hell happened?" Rick demanded as he rushed over.

"Think she's too worn down. Probably needs a day or two of rest."

"I got the impression that wasn't a luxury she could afford," he said.

Maybe not, and she'd probably be pissed at me when she was able to think clearly again, but I wasn't about to drop her by the motel. And I sure the hell wasn't leaving her here. I carried her over to Coral's table and set her down on the seat. The little girl eyed her mom with concern, and I couldn't blame her. I pulled out my phone and shot off a quick text to one of the Prospects at the club, asking for a truck to be brought over to the diner. I knew there would be questions, but I was going to take these two over to my house for the time being.

Rick had followed and stood off to the side, his arms crossed as he studied Rachel. He didn't look pissed that she wouldn't be able to finish her shift, but I could tell he was worried about her. So was I. I didn't know how long she'd been pushing herself, but it needed to stop now. It wasn't long before one of the club trucks pulled into a parking space out front and Matt climbed out. When he came in and saw me at a table with a woman and little girl, he nearly couldn't hide his smirk. I knew I'd be hearing about this from my brothers later, unless the Prospect kept his mouth shut.

"Rescue mission?" Matt asked as he came closer.

"Not quite. Rachel is overtired and needs to rest. I'll carry her to the truck, then I need you to take her and Coral over to my place. I'll be right behind you." I turned to look at Coral. "Sweet girl, I need you to ride with Matt here. He'll take care of you, and when we get to our destination, you'll get to play with Victoria."

Her eyes lit up. "The puppy?"

I smiled. "Well, she's not quite a puppy, but yes. She even has a ball she'll occasionally chase if she's motivated enough. But her favorite thing is scratches behind her ears."

Coral started to shove all her things back into the gift bag, as well as the items she'd already had on the table when I'd arrived. I dropped some cash on my table to cover my meal, but withheld the tip until Rachel was more awake. I'd either hand it to her personally, or slip it into her purse.

"She have personal items in the back she might need?" I asked.

"I'll go grab her purse from her cubby," Rick said. "If you want to carry her out, I'll bring it to you."

I lifted Rachel again and Coral scampered out of

the booth, reaching for Matt's hand. He seemed surprised when her little fingers closed around his, but he took it in stride. When we reached the truck, I eased Rachel down onto the front seat and buckled her in. Smoothing her hair back from her face, I saw she'd completely passed out. I only hoped she didn't wake up before we reached my house or she might freak out over being in a vehicle with a strange man. Couldn't really blame her.

Once both girls were buckled up, I went over to my bike and followed them back to the compound. Matt pulled through the gates and turned in the direction of my house as I'd requested. He stopped in the driveway and I parked my bike in the one-car garage. Most of the homes either just had a driveway and parking pad, or had a carport, but I'd enclosed mine and added a door. Best way to keep my bike out of the elements because even a cover wasn't one-hundred percent foolproof. If a hurricane came up the coast, it would still send bad weather our way, rough enough that I knew a few of my brothers had dealt with fallen trees and other things during those storms. One had nearly wiped out Cobra's bike once.

Coral clung to Matt as I carried Rachel inside. I started to put her on the couch, but I didn't know how long she'd be asleep, so instead I eased her down onto the bed in the guest room. I didn't really get company, but it was nice to have the room on the off chance I ever needed it. Like now. I removed Rachel's shoes and covered her with a blanket before stepping out of the room.

"Is Mommy okay?" Coral asked, with her eyes wide and her lower lip trembling.

"Your mom will be fine, Coral. She needs to sleep for a bit. Has she been extra worried lately?" I asked.

Coral nodded. "My grandparents are mean to Mommy, and to me. We had to leave and come here."

Well, there was one piece of the puzzle. Now I needed a few more so I put everything together. If Coral and Rachel were in trouble, I damn well wanted to know, and then I'd handle it. No one was going to scare them, or try to hurt them. I wouldn't fucking let them.

"Coral, I'm going to get the motel room key from your mom's purse, but you can watch if you want so you can tell her I didn't take anything else," I said. Rachel would be freaked enough when she woke in a strange place. Didn't need to add any more stress.

"I trust you," she said. "You're not like my daddy and his family."

What the fuck? Not like her daddy? Who the hell had gotten Rachel pregnant? It wouldn't be the first time I'd dealt with unsavory types, and it sure the hell wouldn't be the last, but the woman lying in my guest room didn't seem like the type to belong in a world of darkness. Had she slept with the wrong guy and then tried to run? Or was something else going on?

I shared a look with Matt, and I knew his curiosity was piqued. It was wrong to pull information from sweet little Coral, but I needed to know if the Boogieman was coming for her. Little kids might be scared of what went bump in the night, but I sure the fuck wasn't.

"Coral, what can you tell me about your daddy and his family?" I asked.

"Daddy didn't want me. He's mean and always angry. Mommy doesn't know I've seen him a few times. The lady who watched me while Mommy worked would let Daddy in. They'd go into another room and shut the door, then I'd hear her screaming."

I hoped like hell my face remained expressionless. It sounded like dear ol' dad was fucking the babysitter. How cliché could you get? But it seemed that Coral's parents weren't together, and hadn't been even then. So what was going on?

"Coral, what did your daddy say when you saw him?" Matt asked.

"He said I was a mistake. He told me he hates me." Her lower lip trembled and her eyes filled with tears. "Then he said that someone important wanted me, and he'd see they got me. If I told Mommy, he would kill her."

My gut clenched, and I saw the fury in Matt's eyes as well. I didn't know what piece of shit had donated sperm for Coral, but he was no father. It took a real man to be a true dad, and the fucker Rachel had slept with didn't seem to qualify. Only pussies preyed on little kids.

"I won't let anything happen to your mommy," I promised.

Matt hunkered down next to her. "Coral, you're safe inside the gates here. We won't let anyone take you. Steel is right. Your mom is protected here."

She sniffled, then nodded. "Where's the puppy?"

I laughed softly and went to the kitchen. I'd discovered Victoria was good about going out, unless I was gone for any length of time. When that happened, I'd come home to a puddle or two on the floors, so I'd started putting a baby gate across the kitchen doorway so the mess would be contained. I let her out back, watched as she did her business, then whistled for her to come back inside. The moment she saw Coral, she became a wiggling mass of wrinkles. With every gyration of her body, her skin would gather up near her neck.

It must have amused Coral because she giggled as she sat on the floor, motioning to Victoria. "Here, puppy. I want to pet you!"

Victoria danced over to Coral, and sprawled across the little girl's lap in complete bliss. It seemed the two had made fast friends already. If only Rachel were as easy to win over. I had a feeling I'd have my hands full when she woke up. Matt brought her purse inside, and I dug around for the motel key. He glanced down at Coral before holding out his hand to me. I placed the key in his palm and knew he'd go clear out their stuff.

I didn't know how I'd convince Rachel to stay here, but there was no fucking way she would return to the motel. It was too dangerous, and it was a damn miracle she hadn't been hurt in the days she'd remained there. Since they'd arrived on a bus, I knew they didn't have transportation. She'd likely be worried about getting to and from work, but we'd figure it out later. Right now, she needed to focus on resting her body. I had no doubt she'd been missing meals too, all so Coral could eat.

"You want to watch cartoons?" I asked. Even though I hadn't watched an animated show in forever, I'd seen the channels in my cable package.

Coral stood up so fast Victoria rolled across the floor, only to scamper back over to the little girl. I led Coral over to the living room and she plopped back down on the floor, with Victoria eagerly crawling into her lap once more. After I turned on the TV, I scouted for the kids' channels, then let Coral pick something to watch. I didn't know if she had a bedtime, or where I'd put her. The bed in the guest room was only a full, and while Rachel and Coral were small enough to both fit, I thought the little girl might like her own space.

I walked down the hall and opened the third bedroom. A few boxes were stacked against the back wall, a few holdover memories from my days in the military. They would easily fit in the garage with my bike. Lifting them two at a time, I carried them out so I could clear the room. Once it was empty, I placed a call to Matt, hoping I'd catch him before he returned to the compound.

"Did I forget something?" he asked by way of answering.

"No, but I did. You know that mattress store, the new one with all the discounts going on?" I asked.

"What about it?"

"Can you stop and get a twin mattress set and a bed frame? Then stop by a store and grab some bedding appropriate for a little girl," I said.

Matt was quiet a moment. "You're going to keep them, aren't you?"

Was I? Wouldn't be the worst idea I'd ever had. At least they'd be safe. Couldn't deny there was something about Rachel that called to me. One look was enough to tell me she was too damn young for someone like me, but time had taught me something important. Age was only a number. Yes, people might give us weird looks, but so what? I'd dealt with worse.

"Maybe," I finally said.

"I'll get a few toys too." I heard the truck door slam. "By the way, when I cleaned out their motel room, there wasn't a lot there. Safe was empty. Only a handful of clothes between the two of them, and there wasn't a damn toy anywhere to be seen. Found a few slices of bread and some peanut butter."

Fuck me. I'd had a feeling things were bad. Anyone staying there was down on their luck, but I hadn't realized how much trouble the girls were in. Rachel was obviously a fighter and had been doing her best to take care of herself and her kid, but everyone needed help now and then. She'd likely never admit it, and I'd have to play devil's advocate to keep her here, but I'd handle the situation when it arose.

"Use the sizes on the clothes you picked up and grab a few more things for them. Just simple stuff like T-shirts and jeans are fine. Get at least three more outfits for each of them."

"Um, no offense, Steel, but if you're going to claim those two, there is no fucking way in hell I'm buying bras and panties for your woman. So if you want her to have more of that stuff, you'll have to get it yourself or take her shopping. The shirts and pants I can handle."

"Fine. I'll order some shit online after you get back. And don't take no for an answer at the mattress shop. Make sure let you leave with that bed tonight."

"Steel, it's nearly eight o'clock. I don't even know if they're still open."

Dammit. He made a good point. I hadn't realized how late it was. "Fine. If they're closed, I'll figure something out for tonight. But I want that damn bed no later than noon tomorrow. Hear me?"

"Yep, got it."

I disconnected the call and checked on Coral. She'd fallen asleep watching the animated movie, but I wasn't going to move her until I knew if she'd have a room of her own for tonight. At some point, she'd moved to the couch. I'd slept on it often enough to know it was comfortable as hell, so she'd be fine there for a little while.

What the hell was I going to do with the two of them? As I watched the little girl sleep, I couldn't deny the thought of making her my daughter was more than just a little appealing. Hell, even the dog liked her. At some point, Coral had pulled Victoria onto the couch and the little girl had her arm around the pug. I typically didn't let the dog on the furniture, but I didn't see the harm in it just this once.

While I waited on Matt to return, I went about checking the kitchen to see what I'd need to restock, then did the same for the hall bathroom. I wanted to make sure they had everything they'd possibly need. And part of me hoped what they needed most was me.

Chapter Three

Rachel

I groaned and slowly opened my eyes. My body ached and my head was pounding. The lights were off, and the bed felt far more comfortable than it had in the previous days. As my eyes adjusted and I took in my surroundings, my heart started to race. Where the hell was I? This wasn't the motel. I quickly patted my body and felt my uniform, but that didn't mean someone hadn't done anything vile to me.

Sitting up, I waited for the room to stop spinning, then swung my legs over the side of the bed. Someone had removed my shoes and covered me with a blanket. I padded barefoot across the room and out into the hallway. The racket coming from the room next door must have woken me, and I heard a man cursing. I tiptoed to the next doorway and peered inside, unable to stifle my gasp as I saw Steel kneeling in the floor as he put a bed frame together.

He glanced my way and a smile spread across his lips. "I see you're awake."

"Where am I? Where's Coral? How did I get here?"

He held up a hand. "Slow down. First, you passed out at the diner. I brought you to my house so you could rest. The thought of leaving you at the motel didn't sit right with me, especially with the criminal element that hangs out down there. Coral is asleep on the couch with my dog, but once I get the bed put together, I was going to move her into here."

I opened and shut my mouth a few times, trying to process what he'd said. "You bought her a bed?"

He nodded, then went back to putting the frame together. As he tightened the last screw, he put his tools aside, then stood. I saw a mattress and box spring leaning against the wall, and he placed them onto the frame before grabbing a plastic sack near the closet. Steel withdrew a package of sheets, tore them open, and started making the bed. I knew I should say something, or at least help, but I'd never felt so confused in my life. Or so touched. He'd done all this for Coral?

I looked around the room and noticed more sacks. One looked to contain a blanket, another a pillow. But it was the bags of clothes and toys that made my eyes mist with tears. I couldn't remember anyone ever buying my daughter something, other than myself, and now Steel had not only brought a treat to her at the diner, but he'd given her so much more. Everything in me begged for caution, to not believe he was so nice. I'd learned the hard way that people seldom did anything without wanting something in return. For the life of me, I had no idea what it was Steel wanted from us.

He finished making the bed, then pulled a stuffed bear from a sack and leaned it against the pillow. I didn't know what other toys he'd purchased, but there looked to be a few dolls and puzzles, as well as more things I couldn't quite see without opening the bags fully. Steel gently took my hand and led me to the living room, where Coral lay sleeping on the couch with Steel's little dog. They looked so peaceful, as if the two of them belonged together. My heart ached, knowing I hadn't been able to give her the one thing she wanted most. Well, two. A dad and a pet.

"I'm sure you have questions, and you're probably hungry. Kitchen is that way," he said with a nod over my shoulder. "Go sit down and I'll be right there. I'm just going to tuck Coral into bed and let

Victoria out once more for the night. I have a feeling the two will be sleeping together and I want to make sure she doesn't leave puddles anywhere."

Almost in a daze, I went to the kitchen and sat at the large table. I'd assumed he lived alone, but there were six chairs. Who needed something this size if they didn't have a wife and kids? I hadn't noticed a ring on his finger, but that didn't really mean much these days. When Steel walked into the room, he immediately went to the fridge and pulled out a pitcher of tea. He poured two glasses, then set one in front of me. I sipped at it, pleasantly surprised that it was just the right amount of sweet. I'd found sweet tea generally went one of two ways. You either had to add sugar, or there was so much already in it you had to practically chew your drink.

"I'm sure you're hungry," he said. "I don't have a lot here right now. Need to make a run to the store, but I do keep stuff on hand for sandwiches. How's a ham and turkey on wheat sound?"

It sounded amazing, and my mouth started to water. "Really good."

He pulled out the two containers of meat, along with some lettuce, a tomato, mustard, mayo, and some cheese. Steel shut the fridge and grabbed some bread from a cabinet, then started making sandwiches. I hoped he didn't think I could eat everything, since he was apparently making four.

"Anything you don't want on it? Or any allergies?" he asked.

"Everything is fine. I'm not allergic to any food or drinks."

He plated two of the biggest sandwiches I'd ever seen and placed them in front of me, then went back to finishing up the other two. I was a bit relieved when he put everything away, then sat across from me with the other plate. At least he hadn't expected me to eat all four! I might have been hungry, but even if I'd been starving I couldn't have handled that much food at once.

"Go ahead and ask," he said.

"Ask?"

"I'm sure there's a lot going through your mind right now. Ask whatever questions will put you at ease. If I'm unable to answer, I'll at least give you a reason why."

That seemed fair, if a bit suspicious. Why offer to answer questions, then tell me he might not be able to? It made me wonder about who Steel really was, and just who were the Devil's Fury? It was obvious they were bikers, and the girl at the diner had said they protected kids. Did that make him one of the good guys?

"I'm assuming this is your house?" I asked.

"It is."

I looked around a moment. "Lots of space for just you. Do you have a wife or kids?"

"Nope. Just me." He set back a little. "Always wanted a family, but at my age I figured it wasn't in the cards."

At his age? His hair might have been mostly silver, but I'd known men who were thirty and had just as much. The lines bracketing his eyes didn't give much of a clue either. The way he'd scanned his surroundings at the diner still made me think he was possibly military. Not to mention the camo pants he had on right now. I knew not only military men wore those, but it was the vibe I got off him.

"Why did you think I would be safer here than at the motel?" I asked.

"Because I won't let anything happen to you or your daughter, and neither will my brothers. You're safe behind the gates at the Devil's Fury compound. Quite a few of us have military training. I can assure you, only dumbasses attack us, and none of them walk away."

I digested that a moment. He hadn't outright said he killed people, but it was implied. Granted, I'd imagine anyone trying to break into this place probably didn't walk the straight and narrow. It had to be suicide to go up against a guy like Steel, and he'd said there were others like him. I couldn't imagine there being more than one guy like him. No one had ever been so sweet to Coral before, and so far, he didn't seem to want anything in return. I hadn't realized there were still good people in the world.

"You bought my daughter a bed," I said softly.

"That I did. And you may as well know, I ordered some stuff to be delivered in the morning for both of you. I asked Matt to get a few basics to get you by. Looked like neither of you had much."

I bristled at the implication. "I do perfectly well taking care of my daughter. We don't need handouts!"

I'd fought hard for everything we had, and while it might not be much, it was ours. My job might not be glamorous, but I'd worked for every cent I had, every toy Coral had ever owned, and the clothes on our backs. I didn't like anyone thinking I couldn't take care of my kid. We might not be rich, but we did okay.

Steel leaned in closer, folding his hands on top of the table. "First of all, no one said you weren't taking care of your kid. Secondly, letting people help you isn't a sign of weakness. Everyone needs help sometimes, Rachel. Even me."

And now I felt like a bitch for snapping at him. I

closed my eyes and hung my head, trying to sort out all the emotions tumbling through me. I couldn't remember anyone ever trying to help us just because they were nice. The one and only time a man had offered to buy dinner for us, he'd expected compensation in the form of a blowjob after. I hadn't given in, and had ended up with a black eye for my trouble. It was the last time I'd trusted a man. As if Coral's father and grandparents weren't enough reason to never believe anything someone ever said to me.

"I'm sorry. I know I have a hard time accepting help, but I honestly haven't had too many people offer. The ones who did seemed to want something in return."

He narrowed his eyes and his jaw tightened. "I'm not helping you and expecting payment of any sort. I only want to keep you and that little girl safe. You're exhausted, Rachel. Anyone can see it. You nearly dropped at the diner tonight. I can tell you take excellent care of Coral, but the problem is no one seems to take care of *you*."

I couldn't exactly argue with him. He was right. As much as I loved my daughter and tried to give her everything she needed, there was no one to help me along the way, and more often than not, I was beyond exhausted. I'd known it was only a matter of time before I collapsed, but I'd hoped getting the job at the diner would lower my stress enough I'd be okay. Obviously, I'd been wrong.

"How long do you plan for us to be here?" I asked.

He stared me down and wouldn't answer, which told me enough. Indefinitely, it seemed. There was a part of me that wanted to balk and run the other way, but deep down I wondered if being here with Steel would be the best thing for both me and Coral. For one, he seemed to want to protect us for whatever reason. Neither of us had had that in so long. For that matter, there hadn't been someone in my life who cared since Coral was born. The moment my family had heard I was pregnant, they'd merely tolerated my presence. Now it was just me and Coral. Or had been.

"Why would you help us?" I asked. "We're strangers."

"My father was in the military. He was killed in action during the Vietnam War, leaving my mother alone and pregnant. She raised me on her own, and I know exactly how damn hard it was for her. I don't want that for you, or any woman. If I can help, then I will."

I digested that a moment. He'd said his father was killed during the Vietnam War. I wasn't the greatest at remembering historical facts, but I thought it had occurred in the nineteen-sixties. Which meant Steel was likely in his fifties, and that put him at roughly thirty years older than me. The only men I'd been attracted to were close to my age, but those hadn't exactly turned out so great. I wasn't sure what to think of Steel yet, but I couldn't deny there was something about him that made me want to know more.

"If you're really worried about single moms, why not start a shelter for them? Or some other assistance program?" I asked. "This town doesn't have a homeless shelter, which means those who can't afford a motel room, apartment, or house are just left on the streets to fend for themselves. I'd imagine a lot of those people are women and children."

He nodded. "You'd be right. Starting up

something like that isn't easy as snapping my fingers. Even if I had the funding for it, there's a shit ton of paperwork and red tape with the government. It would need to be a non-profit so we could accept donations, which means lots of legal work."

I leaned back in my chair. It seemed he'd thought about it, more than just a little. Was he really as nice as he seemed? I glanced at the leather vest over his shoulders and the various patches. I didn't know what any of them meant. What if he was luring me in, making me feel safe, and then he planned to hurt me or Coral? If my family didn't want us, and Coral's father had walked away, why would this stranger do so much for us?

I couldn't remember ever feeling so conflicted in my life. I wanted to believe he really was as amazing as he seemed, but my past experiences taught me not to take things at face value. If we stayed, would he change over time? Was all this an act? I wanted to trust Steel was the real deal, a true knight in shining armor, but I'd been wrong before.

"I don't know what your life has been like up to this point," he said, "but I can guess it hasn't been easy. It's clear Coral's father isn't in the picture. She told me he didn't want her. I also think you're running from something. I don't expect you to trust me overnight, Rachel. It's good you're cautious, especially with your little girl counting on you. I only ask that you let me help at least a little. Stay here for a bit. Get your strength back, rest as much as you can, and save up some money so you don't have to return to the motel."

"And you don't want anything in return?" I asked.

"Not a thing."

It seemed too good to be true, and over the last six years, I'd discovered it meant I needed to run as far and as fast as I could in the opposite direction. What kind of person bought all this stuff for strangers, let them into his home, and then expected nothing in return? Maybe fifty years ago someone would have been as helpful, but today? Not a chance.

"When I left the diner earlier, did you ask about me? Or my club at the least?" he asked.

"The waitress said your club protected children."

He nodded. "And we do. I don't expect you to take my word for it. If you want to share a room with Coral tonight, and lock yourselves in, it won't hurt my feelings. I'd imagine you've run across a lot of assholes wanting to take advantage of your situation. I'm not one of them, but you'll learn that for yourself in time."

I knew Coral would be excited to have her own bed, and to see all the things Steel had bought for her, but I also wanted her with me for tonight. I got up and put my plate in the sink, then went into the living room and lifted Coral into my arms. With one last glance at the man who left me so confused I was nearly dizzy, I went into the bedroom and eased Coral onto the bed before locking the door. We'd sleep in here tonight, and tomorrow I'd assess things better. He'd been right when he said I needed to rest.

I smoothed Coral's hair from her face and smiled at my sleeping angel. She was the best thing to ever happen to me. "Sleep, my sweet girl. Maybe Steel is as amazing as he seems. For your sake, I hope so. I could really use the help he's offering, but I'm too damn scared to take it."

I'd trusted her father, and look where it got me. He'd signed his rights away, and still his parents made my life a living hell. I didn't think it would ever end.

Even being in another town, there was still a chance they would come for me. If they did, I didn't know what I'd do. There wasn't enough money for me to run this time. I'd be stuck here, with no way to fight back.

It would have been nice to know Coral's dad had ties with criminal elements before I'd slept with him. I never would have gone on a date much less let him get any closer to me. Because of my poor judgment, we'd been on the defensive for six years. Would it ever end? Or would his family keep coming after me until they managed to bury me?

"Whatever it takes, I'll keep you safe," I murmured to my daughter. She was my life, my everything, and I'd do anything to keep those monsters away from her.

Even trust a man I didn't really know.

Chapter Four

Steel

It hadn't surprised me when Rachel had locked the bedroom door. I should have gotten some sleep while everyone else rested, but there was too much to do. Wouldn't be the first time I'd stayed up for more than twenty-four hours, and I doubted it would be the last. I did know one thing. It was time to learn more about my houseguests so I could better protect them. I'd thought I was only saving Rachel from herself, but I had a feeling there was more going on. Since Rachel's purse was still in the living room, I pulled out her license and snapped a picture before texting it to Outlaw along with a short message. *See what you can find on her. I need to know everything.*

The girl on the license looked younger but no less haunted. *Rachel Williams.* According her date of birth, she was twenty-three. I'd known she was young, but having a six-year-old, I'd thought she was closer to twenty-five or twenty-six. Didn't matter. Either way, she was entirely too young for an old bastard like me. It looked like she'd traveled here from Alabama, not too far from the Dixie Reapers. If Outlaw couldn't find anything, maybe Wire would be able to.

While it wouldn't be the first time one of us brought a woman home to keep her safe, Rachel was a complete unknown. It had worked out well for Outlaw, when he'd claimed Elena, but I knew sooner or later we'd try to save the wrong woman. Rachel might seem sweet and down on her luck, but it could just as easily be a ruse. Although, if she was attempting to gather intel on a club, I'd have thought she'd go to the Reapers since they'd been closer to her hometown. Our club might have enemies, but none were in

Alabama that I knew of.

"Who exactly are you, Rachel Williams, and what are you running from?" I muttered. I put her license back and went to make breakfast. It had been a while since I'd had company and even longer since I'd been around kids, but I had a feeling little Coral would wake up hungry. Even if I didn't know quite what to make of her mom yet, I knew without a doubt that little girl was innocent.

I made pancakes and sausage links while I thought about their situation. It was clear Coral's dad wasn't in the picture, and from what little I'd heard, I wondered if he might be dangerous. Would he track them here? Assuming Rachel hadn't been sent here on purpose. As much as I wanted to wrap those two in cotton and keep them safe, I kept reminding myself Rachel might not be as innocent as she appeared.

Once the food was ready, I set everything in the center of the table and pulled down plates from the cabinet. I placed a fork and butter knife next to each setting, then grabbed some glasses. The fridge might be getting bare, but I did have juice and milk in there. I set out the butter and syrup, then went to check on the girls. Before I'd even reached the spare room, the door opened and a sleepy Coral stumbled out, rubbing her eyes and yawning widely.

"Morning, sunshine," I said.

She blinked at me and went into the bathroom, closing the door behind her. When she emerged again, she seemed a little more awake. I noticed she hadn't shut the bedroom door and I peered inside, seeing that Rachel was still sleeping soundly. I wasn't sure if I should wake her, or leave her be. It was clear she'd been exhausted when she passed out last night.

"Should we let your mom sleep?" I asked.

"There's breakfast on the table."

Coral's eyes lit up. "I'll get her."

She practically ran back to the bedroom and I decided to head to the kitchen. I didn't know what sort of mood Rachel would be in today, and having me hover in the hallway might bother her. Yes, it was my damn house, but until I knew what was going on with those two, I didn't want to run them out of here.

My phone chimed with an incoming text and I saw it was from Outlaw. *Rachel Williams, age 23. Single mom to Coral Williams. It's Coral's dad we need to worry about.*

What the hell did that mean? I responded to his message: *Who's the dad?*

Patrick Mulligan. His parents are Cait and Sean Mulligan. They have ties with the Irish mob. Court docs show he signed away his rights.

Shit. That put a new light on things. I didn't see Rachel working with someone like the Mulligans, not with Coral caught in the middle. If there was one thing I'd discerned right away, it was how much she loved her daughter. Anyone mixed up with the Irish mob was on borrowed time. I knew they wouldn't hesitate to use Coral in any way necessary, which might explain why Rachel was in the middle of nowhere, so far from home, and didn't know a damn soul in this town. She'd been on the run.

My phone went off again. *What are you going to do?*

Fuck if I knew, but I wasn't about to leave them defenseless. What if the Mulligans knew exactly where Rachel was hiding? If they came for either of them, she wouldn't stand a chance. Those people would snatch Coral and run, and Rachel would be lucky if they didn't do worse, like sell the pair of them. Although with Coral being of Mulligan blood, my money was on them using her to sweeten a deal by offering her hand in marriage when she came of age. Wasn't unheard of in crime families. Hell, corporate types did the same damn thing, even if they wanted to put a fancier spin on it.

I finally sent a message back: *No damn clue. But they need protection.*

Coral and Rachel came into the kitchen, each taking a seat. Rachel twisted her hands in her lap and had a haunted look in her eyes. The pink pajamas she wore were cute, even though they were a bit threadbare. I wondered if she was ready to come clean about why she was in Blackwood Falls, or where she'd come from. Had she decided to trust me yet? She'd likely change her mind if she knew I'd taken a picture of her license and had her investigated. Couldn't be too careful, though. Just because she was pretty and looked sweet didn't mean shit. People with no morals, and no heart, didn't care if a woman or kid got caught in the crossfire. But I sure the fuck did.

"Hope the two of you are hungry," I said, adding pancakes and sausage to each of their plates. I let them add the butter and syrup on their own, but it had been obvious Rachel wasn't going to help herself.

"All this is for us?" Coral asked softly.

I forked a few pancakes onto my plate and added some sausage links. "Well, it's for me too, but yes, Coral. You can have as much as you want. I'll need to get some groceries before we make lunch, but there won't be a food shortage around here."

I held Rachel's gaze, and I saw the exact moment she decided to let me help. She smiled down at her daughter, tucking Coral's hair behind her ear. "Sweetheart, Mr. Steel bought you some things last night. You'll have your own bed to sleep in tonight, and there are some toys and clothes in there too. The room next to where we slept last night."

Coral practically bounced in her chair, and I could tell she wanted to bolt from the kitchen and go look for herself, but I knew she needed to eat first. I gave her as stern a look as I could muster in the face of such cuteness, and she settled back down.

"Eat your breakfast, then you can see your room," I said.

It wasn't until I'd uttered the words I realized I wasn't her parent. Yes, they were in my house, but I wasn't sure her mother wanted me to give orders to her kid. A quick glance at Rachel told me she hadn't minded in the least. If anything, she still looked a bit dazed. I wanted to kick the ass of every person who had let her down over the years, starting with Coral's sperm donor. I couldn't even think of the man as her father because it was clear he'd never acted as such. How could he not want his own child?

"It's really a room just for me?" Coral asked.

I nodded. I had no clue how long they'd be here, but I wanted the little girl to feel welcome. More than that, I wanted her to feel safe, and like she belonged somewhere. The few conversations I'd had with her, I could tell the life they'd led had been a bit stressful on her, especially of late. I might not have a magic wand to fix everything right away, but I'd do what I could.

Coral ate so fast I worried she'd make herself sick, but I could tell she was excited. When she finished her food, Rachel excused her from the table. I remained behind, hoping Rachel would open up and talk to me a bit. Even though I'd learned about her circumstances from Outlaw, I wanted to hear it from her.

"Thank you," she said. "For everything. No one's

cared what happened to us in a while. I'm sorry if I seemed suspicious before. I've learned no one does stuff without wanting something in return, but you've proven there really are good people in the world still."

I held up a hand. "I'm not a saint, Rachel. No, I don't want anything in return for helping you, but don't make me out to be something I'm not. I drink, I cuss more than I should, and I have blood on my hands -- both from serving my country and from protecting my family. I will do whatever it takes to keep you and that little girl safe, but don't put me on a pedestal."

She gave a nod. Standing, she gathered her dishes and mine, then moved to the kitchen sink and started rinsing them. I couldn't remember a time someone had loaded the dishwasher for me, or cleared the table. Having lived alone since I'd left home, it was a little strange having someone else in the house. Not in a bad way, though.

She sat across from me when she'd finished, her hands clasped on the table. The way her gaze darted around the room and her fingers trembled, I could tell something was bothering her. I didn't push. If she wanted to say something, she would when she was good and ready. While I waited, I got up and made a pot of coffee. I took down a mug and wondered if Rachel wanted a cup.

"Want coffee?" I asked.

She gave a slight nod, so I pulled down a second mug. After the coffeemaker finished brewing, I poured two cups, then placed them on the table. If she wanted milk or sugar, she didn't say. I sat down and sipped mine, waiting patiently for her to gather her courage. When she finally spoke, I was glad I hadn't pushed. I could tell it was difficult for her.

"When I was in high school, I thought I was head over heels in love with one of the football players. His name was Patrick Mulligan, and he seemed charming. Didn't hurt he was popular," she said, a faint smile on her lips. "Until I found out I was pregnant with Coral. That's the day I realized I'd been dating a monster. I should have known before that, since he wanted to keep our relationship a secret. He tried to make it sound romantic, like he wanted me all to himself."

My hands tightened on my cup. I wanted to reach for her, or ask if he'd hurt her, but I held back. If I did anything at this moment, it could stop her from telling me her story, and I needed to hear it firsthand.

"He became hateful, calling me names, telling me to get rid of the baby. Even threatened me and my family," she said. "When I told him I was keeping Coral, he signed a document giving up his rights to her. It meant I wouldn't get child support, and neither Coral nor I would have contact with him again, except for what was required at school until we graduated. My family let me live with them until I received my diploma, and then I was on my own."

"Your family threw you out?" I asked before I could stop myself.

"Yes. They were ashamed of me. It didn't help that I couldn't tell them who the father was. It had been part of Patrick's agreement, which I'd also had to sign. Something his family lawyer had drawn up. I upheld my end, never contacting him or his parents, never asking for anything, and I never breathed a word of who Coral's father was, but it wasn't enough." She took a breath, her hands trembling as she sipped her coffee. "Little things happened over the years. I always chalked them up to bad luck, but lately I started to worry my daughter might be in danger. Something fell off a building and nearly hit me. A car nearly ran me over. It seemed to escalate with each incident."

"Why did you think she was in danger?" I asked.

"I started to see not only Patrick but his family when I'd go somewhere with Coral, and his mother tried to pick her up from daycare shortly before we left. I don't know why they suddenly are showing an interest in her, but they haven't approached me, which makes me think…"

"They're up to no good?"

She nodded. "The Mulligans are a powerful family where I come from. While I was dating Patrick, I didn't realize just how rotten they all were. I know this sounds completely crazy, and like something off TV, but I think they have ties with the mob."

"That's because they do," I said. Her gaze lifted to mine and I saw the stark terror. "The Mulligan family is part of the Irish mob, Rachel. And before you ask, no, neither my club nor I have any dealings with them."

"How do you know about them?" she asked.

And here's where it got sticky. If I admitted I'd snooped in her purse, then she could possibly run from me. But keeping it from her made me no different from anyone else she'd known and trusted.

"While you were asleep, I looked at your identification. And before you get all irate and shit, just know while you were unsure about me, I was just as uncertain about you. Wouldn't be the first time a pretty woman was used to lure in a man for nefarious purposes. I had to make sure you really did need my help and you weren't bait."

It took a moment, but her body finally relaxed. "Fine. I can understand why you'd be concerned. But how did you tie my name to the Mulligan family?"

"One of my brothers in the club is a hacker. He traced your name and Coral's, then found the document on file showing Patrick Mulligan had given away his rights to his daughter. From there, it was easy enough to figure out exactly who Patrick was, or more accurately, who his family is. And, girl, you are in a world of trouble."

She gulped the rest of her coffee and held out the mug. I got up to refill it, then waited for her to process what I'd told her. It was clear she knew her ex was bad news, but I wasn't sure she had a grasp on what exactly the man, and his family, was capable of. I didn't think they necessarily cared about Rachel, but they definitely wanted Coral. While I had my suspicions as to why, it wasn't anything I knew for certain. The last thing I wanted to do was scare Rachel more, but she needed to know what she was up against.

"Crime families tend to use children to barter deals. They most likely want Coral to offer her hand in marriage, when she's of age, to another family in the Irish mob. As for you, I doubt they give a rat's ass about you, unless you get in their way."

"And then?" she asked.

"They'll make you disappear, either by killing you and hiding the body, or they'll sell you. I'm not trying to scare the shit out of you, but I want you to understand the amount of caution you need to use if you're out and about. It won't be a matter of *if* they find you but *when* they find you."

Rachel paled and swayed a bit, but I saw the moment she braced herself for whatever might come her way. Her spine straightened and a look of determination entered her eyes. I'd known she was strong, but I hoped she was strong enough. If the

Mulligans truly wanted Coral, I knew they'd stop at nothing to get her. Changing their location wasn't enough. Hell, even changing their names wouldn't stop those people.

"I know I'm a stranger, Rachel, but I want you and Coral to stay here for a while. At least until you're on your feet and can afford a place in a safe area. You can keep the room you slept in last night, and we'll get the other one fixed up for Coral. The only thing I ask is that you tell my club as much as you can about your time with Patrick Mulligan, and anything that's happened since, and not the glossed-over version you already gave me."

"Why?" she asked.

"Because we can't keep you safe if we don't know everything. You can't run from the Mulligans, Rachel. The only way to get away from this situation is to stop it for good. We need to find out if they'll consider something in trade for Coral. Even though they don't have a legal leg to stand on, these people don't play by the rules. They'll take her and never look back, so we need to give them something they want more than her."

"I don't have anything," she said softly.

"You let my club worry about it when the time comes. If you want to keep working at the diner, someone here will drop you off and pick you up. I don't think Rick will mind you taking another day or two off. I know he's shorthanded, but he doesn't want you passing out at work either."

She smiled. "I slept more last night than I have in years. I'm sure I'll be fine to go back tomorrow."

I wasn't going to tell the woman she couldn't work. If she wanted to be at the diner for a shift, then I'd make sure she got there. It wasn't like she was mine. Hell, even if she were, I'd feel like an ass if I put her on lockdown unless it was absolutely necessary. My brothers might prefer to keep their women home, but I'd lived longer than most of the ones who had paired off, and I liked an independent woman who wanted to take care of herself. Well, older than all except Blades. Even though he and China weren't officially together, and her circumstances were different. There was a chance he'd never claim her, despite the fact they lived together.

"Find out when your shift starts and ends," I said. "I don't want you trying to get there, or back here, on your own. It would only take a second for someone to snatch you off the street."

"I thought coming here would mean a fresh start," she said.

"It will, but not until the Mulligans are handled. They're not the kind of people you can hide from, Rachel. I'm sure Patrick was charming in high school, but you really stepped in a nest of rattlers when you paired off with him."

Rachel finished her coffee. She stared at the table as if it were the most fascinating thing ever, and I wondered what thoughts were swirling through her mind. I knew hearing about the Mulligans had to be a bit overwhelming. She had to have figured out they were bad news. She'd run from them after all.

My phone rang and I answered when I saw it was the Pres calling. "You need something, Pres?"

"Is there a reason I'm hearing secondhand that you have a woman and kid in your house?"

I winced. Shit. I should have called or texted him last night. "Rachel passed out at the diner and little Coral was with her. They've been staying at the motel on the edge of town. You know as well as I do it's not a safe place for the two of them. Brought them here for the time being."

Grizzly growled and I heard him stomping, then a door slam. Great. I'd be willing to bet he was on his way to my place. "Don't fucking move. Any of you. And, Steel, you know you can't do shit like this."

Yeah, I knew it, but I'd done it anyway. And I'd do it again in a second. I hung up and waited for the Pres to show, and hoped like hell he didn't scare the shit out of the girls.

Chapter Five

Rachel

I didn't know who, or what, a Pres was, but the look on Steel's face said whoever was heading this way wasn't happy. Since I'd been sitting within feet of him, I knew the call had been about me and Coral. Was Steel in trouble for bringing us here? It hadn't even occurred to me he'd need permission. He'd said this was his house. If it was his, why did someone else have the authority to say whether or not we could be here?

Before I could gather the courage to ask, I heard the front door open and heavy steps entered the house. There was a pause and I heard my daughter speaking. My heart nearly stopped and I started to jump up, but Steel reached over to grab my wrist, holding me in place. He gave a quick shake of his head and I sat down. It seemed Steel trusted Coral with whomever had entered his house.

A large mountain of a man with a long beard came into the kitchen and took the seat between me and Steel. My heart slammed against my ribs as I wanted to bolt from the room. Steel kept his hand on my wrist, holding me in place. The man studied me, no hint of a smile on his face. Was it Steel in trouble? Or me? I didn't want to be on this man's bad side. He looked like he could break me in half without the slightest bit of effort.

"You're scaring her," Steel said. "Her pulse is racing."

The man leaned back in the chair and folded his arms over his large chest. "My name's Grizzly and the Devil's Fury is my club. I'm the President, and you, little girl, are on my turf."

Oh shit. Had I just traded one set of criminals for

another? Steel had said his hands weren't clean, but I'd figured he'd been protecting someone. What if these people were no better than the Mulligans?

"Pres." There was a warning tone in Steel's voice, but I didn't understand it. "Would you back the hell off? She's not here for nefarious purposes. She's in trouble, much like every other woman living at the compound."

"We'll talk later," Grizzly said, narrowing his gaze at Steel before turning back to me. "Saw your daughter in the living room. If the two of you need help, you'll find it here. We might be rough around the edges, but we'd never turn away a woman or kid in need."

"So, all the growling, stomping, and glaring was what? A scare tactic?" I asked.

"Something like that," he said, a smile crossing his lips. "Needed to make sure you have what it takes."

I glanced from Grizzly to Steel, then back again. "What does that mean?"

He reached into his pocket and pulled out a folded piece of paper, then slid it across the table to Steel. I didn't know which of them to watch, but when Steel started cussing and jumped up from the table, I wondered if I needed to worry. What the hell was on that paper?

"Are you shitting me right now?" Steel asked. "What the fuck was Outlaw thinking?"

"You'd have to ask him," Grizzly said. "I'll give you some time to explain things to your girl here, but let me know when you're ready for a property cut."

I could hear the words coming out of his mouth, but it was like he was speaking a foreign language. I had no idea what he was talking about, or why Steel looked pissed. The man had been calm and cool since I'd first met him, but he looked ready to put his fist through a wall. Or a person. I didn't know who Outlaw was, but I hoped he was fast because if Steel went after him, I had a feeling he'd beat the poor man.

Grizzly stood and walked out, and I heard the front door shut. Steel kept pacing and looking at the paper in his hand, then muttering under his breath. I was so damn confused. Who was Outlaw and what did he have to do with me being here? What was a property cut? And why had he called me Steel's girl? We were complete strangers. It was nice of him to help me, but that's all it was.

"You're going to wear a hole in the floor," I said.

He stopped and sat again, the paper crumpled in his hand. "Seems you're about to get a crash course on what it means for me to be part of this club, and for you to be here."

That sounded... ominous.

"This club is my family, one I chose. We don't follow the letter of the law, not the ones outside these gates anyway. We make our own rules. Grizzly is in charge, and there are other officers of higher rank than me, but they're under the Pres. I should have asked before bringing you here. This is my house, but it's on Devil's Fury property."

"And he's mad you didn't ask before bringing me here?" I asked.

"Not exactly. Oh, he's pissed I didn't follow protocol, and I'm sure I'll be fined or assigned some shit job I don't like as penance. Thing is, the women in this compound typically fall into two categories. The club whores and the old ladies."

My brow wrinkled. The word whore made that one self-explanatory, but old ladies? Were there senior citizens running around this place? It seemed a little odd.

Steel smirked. "Old ladies as in women claimed by club members. Most marry their women, but some don't. At least that's how it's working for this club. And before you ask, the club whores are here of their own free will. They aren't forced to come here. For whatever reason, they're here because they want to be."

I couldn't imagine willingly sleeping with a bunch of men, but other than my time with Patrick, I hadn't been with anyone else. We'd only slept together a few times, and I hadn't much cared for the experience. I still didn't understand why he was telling me all this unless... My eyes widened. "Am I expected to be a club whore?"

Steel closed his eyes and a look of pain crossed his features. "No. Not just no, but hell no. You are not now nor will you ever be a club whore."

"Then why did you tell me all that?" I asked.

He smoothed out the paper in his hand and slid it over to me. I read it. Four times, but I still didn't understand what I was seeing. It was a marriage certificate for me and someone named Isaac Crowley. Who the hell was that? I'd have remembered if I married someone. The only guy I'd seriously dated in my entire life was Patrick Mulligan, and look how it had turned out!

"I don't know Isaac Crowley," I said.

"Actually you do. Just not by that name." He sighed. "Isaac Crowley is my given name. I go by Steel around here. To call me anything else in the presence of my club or even out around town would be considered disrespectful. I earned my road name."

Wait. Had he just said..."We're married?"

"Thanks to the club hacker, yes. I have no fucking clue what the asshole was thinking when he pulled this stunt, but I know damn well he'll refuse to reverse it. Ever since he found his woman, he thinks the rest of us need to settle down too. Doesn't matter that *you* might not have wanted this. I'll talk to Outlaw, but I already know it won't do me a damn bit of good."

Married. I was married to the man sitting across from me. Someone I'd just met. We hadn't even gone on a date or kissed! How could we possibly be husband and wife? What the hell kind of place had I come to? Normal people didn't do things like this. They just didn't.

Steel placed his phone on the table, then tapped the screen until the name Outlaw lit up and I heard it ringing as he placed the call on speaker.

"Steel, I take it Grizzly gave you the good news," the man I assumed was Outlaw said by way of greeting.

"Good news? You asshole! Did it ever occur to you Rachel might not want to be saddled with an old goat like me? She's not said much of anything since I showed her the marriage certificate. I think you traumatized her. You undo this shit right the fuck now," Steel said with a hint of growl in his voice.

"Can't. And I won't," Outlaw said.

"Why not?" I asked.

The line went quiet a moment. "Now who's the asshole? You didn't tell me she was listening to this conversation."

So he'd wanted to keep me in the dark about all this? My lips pressed together and I felt the blood pumping through my veins. If that man had been here in this kitchen, I might have throttled him. I wasn't some pawn in a game. I was a person! And I had Coral to think about too. What right did he have to mess with our lives this way? Or Steel's life for that matter.

"She's looking a little homicidal," Steel said. "I'd tread carefully."

"Fine. You want to know why I married the two of you? I'll tell you, Rachel. It's because you and that little girl need as much protection as possible. Since Patrick Mulligan signed away his rights, it means Coral can easily be adopted... by your husband."

Everything in me went still. Coral adopted by Steel? My gaze lifted to his and I saw he was just as surprised as me. But the idea didn't seem to repulse him. For that matter, he'd only seemed angry over the marriage because he'd worried how I would react, thought it wasn't fair to me. What had he called himself? An old goat? He had to know that silver foxes were sexy, didn't he?

"Steel can adopt Coral?" I asked. "So he'd be her father? And Patrick couldn't touch her?"

"Technically, he's not supposed to have contact with her already. Steel being her adopted father wouldn't change much, except the law would be on our side if we needed them to step in. More than that, if you and Coral belong to Steel, then this club will go to hell and back for the two of you. Because you're family," Outlaw said. "How long has it been since you had one of those?"

Too long. I held Steel's gaze, trying to judge how he felt about all this. The thought of being married to a stranger was a bit frightening, but he'd been so good to us. I might have had reservations about his motives before, but things had changed rather quickly. Actions spoke louder and all that.

"Looks like we need to talk," Steel said. "I'll call you back in a bit."

"I have a feeling I know where this is going. I'll start on the adoption paperwork. You'll be Coral's dad, officially, by tonight."

I heard a squeal, then my darling little girl raced into the room and threw herself at Steel. He caught her easily, a smile on his face. It seemed he wasn't the least bit worried about suddenly becoming a father to Coral. And judging the look of pure bliss on my daughter's face, she was thrilled to have Steel as a dad. Since she'd never truly had one before, I had to wonder if she'd secretly yearned for a father all this time and just never said anything to me.

I reached over to press the button to end the call, and Steel gave me a wink. Coral clung to him. My heart ached over the fact she'd been without a father all these years. It hadn't seemed to bother her, but now I knew differently. No matter what I'd done for my child, it wasn't enough. I hadn't been able to give her the one thing she apparently wanted most. Until now, and making Steel her dad wasn't even my doing. It was all thanks to a man I'd never met.

"Are you really my daddy?" Coral asked.

"Is that all right with you?" Steel drew back enough to look down at her in his arms. Coral nodded eagerly. "Then yes, I'm really your daddy."

Coral shot a smile my way, a smile that lit up her entire face. "I have a daddy!"

Tears misted my eyes and I felt my throat grow tight. "Yes, you do, sweetheart."

Steel caught my gaze, squeezed Coral a little tighter, then set her back down on her feet. "Why don't you give me and your momma a few minutes? Pick out something to wear. You can watch a little TV, but you'll need to take a bath soon. We'll all get cleaned up and go somewhere to celebrate."

Coral shot out of the room, more excited than I'd seen her in a while. If ever. I knew Steel making her his daughter had to be the highlight of her life. I twirled the coffee cup on the table in front of me, wishing it was full so I'd have something to do, even if I wasn't necessarily thirsty.

I didn't know what to say to him. According to that paper, we were married, even if we hadn't said vows. We didn't know much about one another, and I had no idea if he meant for this to be a real marriage or one of convenience. He'd mentioned club whores. Maybe that was a good place to start. Did he intend to keep sleeping with those women? Because if he did, there was no way I'd welcome him into my bed, not now and not ever.

"Probably not the way you saw yourself getting married," he said.

"Not exactly. Although, to be fair, I hadn't really thought about getting married. Coral has been my main focus, and with the Mulligans causing problems, dating wasn't high on my list of things to accomplish."

"I've told you how the club works, or the basics. I'm sure you still have questions."

I nodded. I did, but I wasn't sure how to voice them. "What do you expect from me?"

"At my age, I figured I'd never find a woman and settle down. I'm not some randy twenty-year-old hanging out at the clubhouse every night, and I don't date that often. I'm set in my ways and like everything just so. Then there's the not-so-legal side of my life. There are women out there who wouldn't mind. My brothers are proof of that since five of them have women. But finding one to accept me and my club? Didn't think it was in the cards."

"But you wanted someone to share your life?" I

asked. "Kids?"

"Yeah. I wanted a woman and kids. Spent some time in Mexico not too long ago. Found some children the cartel was either going to train as soldiers or sell to the highest bidder. I stayed until I'd made sure each one was safely relocated and would have a shot at a decent life." He drummed his fingers on the table a moment. "I'm not a saint. Just a man who believes women and children should be protected. And before you ask, yes, I would kill to keep you and Coral safe, or my brothers and their families."

"Would or have?" I asked.

"Both." His lips twitched as if he fought back a smile. "I killed in the name of defending my country. I've killed to defend this club. I have my own sense of right and wrong that doesn't always mesh well with law enforcement, but I've never spent time in jail and I don't plan to start now."

"You still didn't answer my other question," I reminded him.

"What I expect is for you to be faithful. If I find out you're running around behind my back, there will be consequences. And before you get all riled up, I'm not saying you're the type to do such a thing, but it's been known to happen, especially when someone as young and pretty as you ends up with an old bastard like me."

"You're not old," I said. "Haven't you heard that silver foxes are hot?"

He snorted and ran a hand over his beard. "Got the silver part right at any rate. Look, I know you don't know me, but that's the beauty of a marriage. We have plenty of time to learn more about one another. I don't expect you to share my bed right now. Eventually? Yes. But from this moment on, I won't kiss or sleep with another woman. That paper from Outlaw might not mean much to you, but it does to me. And for the record, I'm clean. Haven't been with a woman in a while, and I've been tested since then. So that's one thing you don't have to worry about."

I looked at the paper in the center of the table. It wasn't that it didn't mean something to me, but it scared me. The only relationship I'd had was still haunting me. I wasn't sure I could trust my judgment when it came to men. Putting those fears aside, I really didn't have a clue how to be a wife to someone. There were days I didn't think I even had the mom thing figured out.

"One day at a time. Right now, we should get cleaned up and head out. I promised Coral we'd celebrate, and I intend to keep my vow to her."

I reached across the table and placed my hand over his. "Thank you. Not just for bringing us here last night, but for… everything."

I stood and started to leave, but something held me back. The only man I'd been intimate with had been Patrick Mulligan. I hadn't even kissed many men other than him. Steel and I were married. What would it be like to kiss him? Before I could talk myself out of it, I walked around the table and leaned down to press my lips to his. He held still at first. I started to draw away, but he reached up and threaded his fingers in my hair. Our lips were mere inches apart.

"That's not a kiss, wife."

"It's not?" I asked, my voice a near whisper.

"No. This is a kiss." He pulled me closer and I tumbled into his lap. Steel held me as his mouth ravaged mine. Everything inside me started to warm and I pressed my thighs together. My nipples tightened and I couldn't contain the whimper that left my lips. And still he didn't let up. I'd never felt so thoroughly claimed before, and he'd barely touched me, other than his mouth on mine.

I pulled back and touched my fingers to my lips. They tingled and I fought not lean into him and beg for more. What had just happened? No one had ever kissed me like that, or made me feel so... needy. He placed a hand on my hip and slid it up to my waist. My breath caught and I held his gaze as he slid his palm higher, brushing the outside of my breast.

"When you're ready, I'll give you kisses like that and so much more." He pulled his hand away. "But for now, I think that's enough. It's clear there's something between us. I don't think that was all one-sided."

I shook my head. No, it definitely hadn't been. My panties were damp and my clit pulsed with need. I leaned in again and pressed my lips to his, needing one more taste. He held me close, but this was a bit softer. I still felt it all the way to my toes and wished it would never end.

"Steel, I..." He placed a finger over my lips, silencing me.

"When we're in the house and it's just us, call me Isaac. Around the club or out in public it's Steel."

"Isaac," I said softly. "I just wanted you to know I don't go around kissing every man who looks my way. I haven't been with anyone since Patrick. He was my first and only. I have kissed one or two men since then, but it felt wrong and I ended it. But with you... everything feels so incredibly right. So much it scares me."

"Does Coral know how to bathe herself? Start a shower or anything?" he asked.

I nodded. "I taught her how to start the shower."

He raised his voice to yell out for our daughter.

Our daughter. It felt strange thinking of Coral as anything other than mine, but it was clear Steel adored her. When she scampered into the room, he told her to take a shower and get ready. I didn't know what he was up to, but the moment we heard the bathroom door shut, I found out.

"Not pushing for more than you're ready to give, but I'm going to make you feel good. When's the last time you came?" he asked.

My cheeks burned. "Never."

"Then I'll have to rectify that. Immediately."

Before I could ask what he meant, his lips claimed mine again. He tugged at the waistband of my pajamas and I lifted my hips. Steel slid the material down to my knees, then shoved the pants to the floor. My heart raced and I trembled as I sat on his lap in nothing but my pajama top and panties. His fingers caressed my legs from knee to hip, leaving goose bumps in their wake.

He didn't let up from his kiss, and I felt like I was drowning in sensations. I felt his fingers dip between my thighs and I spread them a little. He groaned as he cupped my pussy through the damp material. Steel pushed the panties aside and ran his fingers along my lips before spreading them open and flicking my clit. I gasped and my body tightened.

The kiss ended abruptly and I stared up at him, dazed and slightly confused as to what was happening. He rubbed the bundle of nerves again and I nearly came just from that alone. My breasts felt heavy and ached, wanting his touch too. His gaze dropped to my chest and he growled softly.

"Unbutton your top."

My fingers shook as I obeyed his command. The cool air made my nipples tighten even more. I reached up, cupping my breasts and tugging at the hard peaks. I could feel the hard length of Steel's cock pressing against me and I spread my legs a little more. I'd never felt so out of control, especially when it came to a man. He made me nearly mindless with pleasure.

He plunged a finger inside me and I cried out. Steel was quick to silence me by pressing his lips to mine again. He stroked in and out as his thumb worked my clit. It was too much, and yet not enough. Within seconds, I was coming, so hard that I felt my release soak his hand and his pants. He drew back and cocked his head a moment, and I realized he was listening for Coral. I could faintly hear the shower still running.

"You good now, or you want more?" he asked.

"M-more. Please."

He added a second finger to my pussy, pumping them in and out. "More of my hand, or do you want something else? I said I'd wait, and I will, but I will give you anything you want, Rachel. Want to come on my hand again? Or on my cock?"

I gasped and arched my back when he hit just the right spot. Oh, God! I wanted him. More than what he was giving me now. I wanted to experience everything with Steel. Maybe it made me a woman of questionable morals to let him do this to me so soon after meeting him, but the paper on the table said I was his and he was mine. He twisted his fingers on the next stroke and I came again. When he tried to pull his hand back, I trapped it between my legs.

"No, I want more."

He smiled. "I think I created a little monster. You want to come again?"

I nodded. "B-but not on your fingers."

His eyes dilated. "Not on my fingers. You want

my cock?"

"Yes, Isaac. Please. I-I think I need it. Need you. I've never… no one's ever…" My cheeks warmed again.

"As much as I want to savor our first time together, it will have to be quick. Coral can't stay in the shower forever," he warned. "And I'm sure the fuck not taking you in the kitchen."

He stood with me in his arms and carried me down the hall to what I assumed was his bedroom. He nudged the door open with his foot, then kicked it shut, stopping long enough to twist the lock. The moment my feet touched the floor, he slid the pajama top down my arms and shoved my panties to my ankles. I reached for him, pulling at his clothes, but he pressed his hand over mine, trapping it against his chest.

"No time for all that, darlin'. Not right now." He jerked his chin toward the bed. "Lie on your back with your ass near the edge of the mattress."

I hurried to do as he said, having to jump slightly to reach the damn bed. Why the hell was it so big? I heard him chuckle behind me, but finally, I was on my back and waiting eagerly for what came next. I heard the clink of his belt and the rasp of his zipper, then he was leaning over me.

"Just so we're clear, no woman has ever been in this bed, and if you'll let me later, I'll make this up to you."

Before I could ask what he meant, he spread my thighs wide and I felt his cock press against me. My breath caught as he pushed inside. It burned and yet I didn't want him to stop. It had been so long since I'd been with Patrick, it was almost like I was a virgin all over again. His body tensed and his lips firmed.

"So damn tight," he murmured. Then he was stroking in and out of me, rubbing my clit with his thumb. Steel leaned down and took my nipple into his mouth, gently biting down. I nearly saw stars and held him to me. He did the same to the other nipple, then pulled back and worked my clit faster.

I came, crying out his name as another orgasm took me over the edge. I gasped for breath as he pounded into me. It wasn't until I felt the heat of his release that I realized we hadn't used protection. Granted, we were married, sort of, and he'd said he wanted a family. Steel leaned down and kissed me, his cock still buried deep.

"You still want me later, I promise I'll do better." He withdrew from my body, but held my legs open as he stared at my pussy. I wanted to squirm away and slam my thighs together, but I liked the flare of heat in his eyes. No one had ever made me feel so desirable.

"If it gets any better, I won't be able to walk," I said.

Steel leaned down to kiss me again. "Challenge accepted. Use my shower. I'll grab some things from the other room and lay them out on the counter for you. Coral and I will watch cartoons while we wait, then I'll rinse off and change before we head out."

He backed away, giving me one last lingering look, before unlocking the bedroom door and pulling it shut behind him. I hurried into the bathroom and started the shower, then stepped under the hot spray. What had I just done?

You had sex. Incredible, mind-blowing sex.

I reached between my legs and felt his release and mine. My clit still throbbed, and I knew if it weren't for Coral, I'd have begged him to make me come again and again. He was right. He'd created a monster by showing me what I'd been missing all these years, and now I wanted every bit of pleasure he could give me.

I'd lived the last six years of my life for my daughter. Maybe it was time to live a little for me too.

Chapter Six

Steel

What the hell had I done? It was one thing to treat the club whores like a toy to be used, but my wife? She hadn't uttered a word of complaint. In fact, every time she'd glanced my way, her cheeks had flushed and she'd given me a shy smile. We'd taken Coral to the park before having lunch, and now we were shopping even though Rachel had balked at me spending more money. Whether she liked it or not, she needed clothes. I'd ordered some things to be delivered, but they'd need more.

"Can we have ice cream?" Coral asked as we waited for Rachel to try on a few outfits.

"How are you still hungry?" I asked, smiling down at her. I poked her belly. "There can't be any room left after everything you had for lunch."

She giggled and climbed onto my lap. "There's always room for ice cream, Daddy."

Every time she called me that, my throat got tight and I was a little overwhelmed with emotion. Wouldn't admit it even if someone called me on it, but it's how I felt. I'd never thought I'd have kids, and Coral was a gift I'd treasure always. Same for her mom. I could blame Outlaw for this all I wanted, but the truth was Fate had stepped in and put Rachel and Coral in my path.

"Let's make sure your mommy has enough clothes for at least a week, and then we'll get ice cream. Any special requests for dinner later?" I asked.

"Pizza?" Her eyes got comically wide. "The kind you order."

"All right. We'll get pizza, but it's not going to be an everyday thing. It's not healthy for you."

She got a mutinous expression on her little face. "It has cheese. Mommy said they use milk to make cheese, and she always makes me drink my milk because it's good for me."

I chuckled softly. Couldn't argue with that logic. "Pizza once a week. Any more often and you might turn into a pepperoni."

Coral giggled and cuddled closer to me. Rachel stepped out of the fitting room, her hands twisting in the skirt of the sundress she'd tried on. It hugged her curves and stopped just below her knees. To some, it was modest, but damn if it didn't make me eager to get her out of it. While it covered everything important, it hinted enough at what lay beneath to make a man want to find out on his own. I'd never cared for the women who barely clothed themselves. Maybe it was my age, but if you could see everything on offer, what was the point? Didn't mean I hadn't looked, and I didn't disparage them for wanting to flaunt their bodies. It just didn't turn me on. Not like my wife wearing this dress.

"You need it, and one of every other color or pattern they offer," I said.

"You don't think it's too much?" she asked, turning slowly. The back had straps that crisscrossed over her shoulder blades, but it still covered her from mid-back and down. From the way I was currently feeling, something told me I was about to become a jealous, possessive asshole when it came to this woman. I didn't like the idea of other men looking at her. All that beauty and sweetness was mine.

"It's perfect, just like you." I winked. "Now get whatever fit and let's check out. A certain little girl wants ice cream."

Rachel placed her hands on her hips and patted

one of them. "You seemed to like these just the way they are. If you keep feeding me this way, they'll expand."

I stood up, setting Coral down, and approached Rachel. I pulled her against my body, and placed my lips near her ear. "I will want you even if your hips expand. In fact, I hope to one day see these beautiful tits swell to twice their size and your belly round with my baby. And even then, I won't want to keep my hands off you. You're a sexy, sweet, smart woman, Rachel. Any man would be lucky to call you his."

She licked her lips and I couldn't stop myself from giving her a quick kiss. Then before I started getting hard enough I wouldn't be able to hide my arousal, I backed away and took Coral's hand, leading her over to the register to wait for Rachel. When she came to the counter, her arms were nearly overflowing and I felt like an ass for not thinking past my dick. She'd needed help. I took the clothes from her and placed them on the counter, then sent her and Coral outside while I paid for everything. I knew this store wasn't cheap, because I'd been with Outlaw when he'd bought a present for Elena from here, and something told me Rachel would have a fit if she saw the total.

I swiped my card and waited for the woman to hand me the receipt and bags, then met my girls outside on the sidewalk. I stowed the bags in the truck we'd borrowed, since I couldn't very well have Coral and Rachel riding on my bike with me, then I took Rachel to one more place. The lingerie store. She worried at her lip as I nudged her inside.

"Pick out whatever you need, or anything you *want*. I'll wait outside with Coral, and I'll come in to pay when you're finished." I kissed her cheek, then took our daughter back out of the store. I had a daughter. My heart swelled at the thought. Coral might not be mine by blood, but that didn't matter to me. I'd raise her as my own, and hopefully I wouldn't fuck up.

"Why couldn't Victoria come with us?" Coral asked.

"Because she's too lazy. Besides, dogs aren't allowed inside stores unless they're service animals, and Victoria doesn't have the right temperament for that."

Coral scrunched her nose. "What's a service animal?"

I tried to think of a way to explain it so a six-year-old would understand. "Some people have illnesses we can't see on the outside or something that doesn't present itself all the time. Some of those people, and even those with visible illnesses, require a service animal. Anxiety, PTSD, maybe they suffer from seizures. Dogs, and occasionally other animals, are trained to sense when their human is about to have one of those episodes, and they alert them to the problem, or keep them calm."

She seemed to think it over, and while I knew there was so much more to service animals, I wasn't sure how to put it into terms Coral would understand. Eventually, she shrugged and skipped off a few paces only to come bouncing back. It was clear she had abundant energy, and maybe it made me an ass, but I hoped I could run it out of her by bedtime later. Even though Rachel might very well change her mind about coming to my room later, or our room if I could get her to move in there permanently already, I was hopeful she still wanted me as much as I wanted her.

"Can Victoria sleep with me tonight?" Coral asked.

"As long as she goes potty before bedtime." I winced when I realized I'd forgotten to pen her in the kitchen when we'd left. With my luck, she'd leave a puddle on the floor. Or in her case, a lake. I'd never seen so much pee come out of something so small.

"Can we stop at a pet store and get her something?" Coral asked.

I could tell that for every bit I planned to spoil Coral and Rachel, our daughter wanted to make the pug completely rotten. Then something occurred to me. "Coral, have you ever been inside a pet store?"

She shook her head. Well, damn. Now I couldn't say no. Every kid should experience a pet store, even if they didn't have a pet yet. Granted, Victoria seemed content to belong to Coral. Maybe when I'd rescued the pug, it had been the Universe trying to tell me something great was heading my way. Rachel and Coral were the best gift I could have ever received.

Rachel came out of the store, her cheeks flushed, and a smile on her face. I headed inside to pay for whatever she'd purchased, then went back outside to my girls, carrying the pinkest shopping bag I'd ever seen. I quickly handed it to Rachel before lifting Coral into my arms. Once everyone was back in the truck and buckled, I decided we'd get ice cream first and stop at the pet store second. And God help me if Coral asked for a pet because I didn't think I could say no.

At the ice cream shop, Coral bounced on her toes as she peered into the glass case. Being a privately owned place and not one of those chain stores, they didn't have a large variety, but it didn't seem to bother the little girl in the slightest. We placed our order and found a table near the window. As Coral licked her cone, she got more on her face than in her mouth, but I found it rather adorable.

"Bet you didn't know what you were getting yourself into," Rachel said.

"I'm loving every second." I smiled at Rachel, more content than I'd been for as long as I could remember. They would still need to meet the rest of the club, but I knew the other old ladies would welcome them with open arms. Even reserved China wouldn't be able to resist little Coral.

"Don't forget the pet store," Coral said.

Rachel narrowed her gaze in my direction, but I pretended not to notice. She could get mad if she wanted. This was my first official day with a family and I was going to enjoy it to the fullest. If my newly adopted daughter wanted to go to a pet store, that's what we'd do. As we tossed our trash and headed to the truck, Rachel leaned in closer to whisper to me.

"You're not giving her another pet. The dog is enough."

I shrugged. I wasn't about to make any promises I couldn't keep, and if little Coral begged for another pet, she'd get one. Might not be the best way to start out my role as her daddy, but I'd make it clear after today she'd only get things in moderation unless it was a special day like her birthday or Christmas.

"I'm allowed to spoil the two of you today." I kissed her cheek, then helped them both into the truck.

Had I realized the moment Coral entered the pet store she'd take off like a squirrel on crack, I may have rethought the extra trip. She flitted from one animal to another, even cooed at the cats in cages along one wall. I didn't think Victoria would take too kindly to a cat and steered Coral in another direction. She tapped on the fish tanks, no matter how many times I pointed out the signs that said not to touch, and pressed her face to the hamster habitats. The only thing she didn't want to see were the snakes and lizards.

"Victoria needs lots of toys," Coral said.

"She already has toys. You can pick out one new one, something that's just from you to her," I said. "And maybe a bag of treats that can be special between the two of you."

Coral ran off to the dog aisles and came back a moment later with a stuffed purple giraffe and a bag of pug-sized treats. Before she could beg or plead for anything else, Rachel guided her to the checkout line. It didn't escape my notice Coral kept looking longingly at the fish, and I had no doubt I'd find myself back here soon specifically for a fish tank. She needed a dresser first, and more clothes. But fish were definitely in her future.

"Time for a nap," Rachel said.

Coral whined but her mom gave her that look only mothers seem to manage, and Coral quieted down. When we reached the house, Rachel took our daughter straight to her bedroom and tucked her in. I cleaned up the mess Victoria had made while we were gone, let her out, then placed her on the bed with Coral. The two snuggled together and I knew they'd both be sleeping soon enough.

I leaned against the wall in the hallway wondering where someone so tiny got so much energy. I'd been around kids before, but not for as long a time as Coral had been here. Still, I wouldn't have traded a second of today for anything in the world.

"You're good with her," Rachel said as she pulled the bedroom door mostly shut.

"Kids are easy. It's adults that tend to be a problem."

Rachel pressed herself against me, wrapping her arms around my waist. "I don't know. I think you're pretty good with adults too."

"Does Mommy need a nap too?" I asked.

"No, but what I need is generally easier if done on a bed." She smiled at me, then stepped back, taking my hand and leading me to the bedroom. I was assuming it was now our room. It seemed whatever time she'd thought she needed was now a thing of the past.

I shut the bedroom door and turned the lock. Folding my arms over my chest, I leaned back and watched as Rachel stripped off her clothes. The little tease was removing each item as slowly as humanly possible, but I liked seeing this side of her. She'd gone from overly tired and scared to more confident.

"What's that smile for?" she asked as the last article of clothing hit the floor.

"Just admiring my sexy wife."

I pushed away from the door and shrugged out of my cut, setting it down on the dresser, then started to remove the rest of my clothes. She licked her lips and I watched as her eyes darkened. Her nipples hardened to little points, and from the way she squeezed her thighs together I had no doubt she was already wet and ready. I wasn't about to rush this, though. No, this time I wanted to make it last a bit longer.

"Coral should be asleep any minute. She'll nap for at least an hour," Rachel said.

"I only get an hour? Then I better make it count."

I placed my hands on her hips and pulled her closer, then claimed her mouth. She tasted sweet, and I knew I'd never get enough of her. I loved the feel of her soft skin under my calloused fingertips as I caressed her hips. Walking her backward, my lips still stroking hers, I toppled her to the bed. Her eyes were wide as she stared up at me, but she'd made it clear earlier she had little experience when it came to sex. I planned to remedy that.

I trailed my lips along her neck, pausing a moment to tease the tender skin with my beard. She sighed and gripped my arms tightly, almost as if she were afraid I'd walk away. Not fucking likely. Only an idiot would leave when there was a sexy woman lying in his bed, and while I'd been known to do stupid shit from time to time, there wasn't a chance in hell I was leaving Rachel. I lavished attention on her breasts and nipples, smiling to myself when I saw the beard burn on her skin. Even if she wasn't inked and didn't have a cut just yet, I'd still marked her as mine.

I sank to my knees next to the bed and spread her thighs wider. Parting the lips of her pussy, I held her open as I leaned closer and flicked her clit with my tongue. Rachel cried out and her body went tight before she relaxed again.

"Isaac, what are you… I…"

Good. She'd been rendered speechless, or near enough. Meant I was doing something right. I thrust my tongue into her tight channel, then went back to teasing the hard little bud. I circled, flicked, and sucked until she was crying out my name and thrashing on the bed. She was so damn wet, and it was making me hard as a damn rock. Within moments, she was coming. As she lay trembling, I stood and wiped her release off my beard before gripping her hips.

One hard thrust and I was buried inside her. She reached for me, her hands gripping my wrists, as I drove into her again and again. I'd meant to draw this out more, make her come multiple times, but no one had ever gotten me this hot this fast. Her gaze fastened on mine. I hoped everything I felt in that moment was reflected on my face for her to see. Even though we'd only known one another a short time, she'd already turned my life upside down and burrowed her way under my skin.

"Need you to come for me again," I said, reaching for her clit once more. It only took two strokes before her pussy clenched down on my cock and she screamed out my name. I felt the gush of her release and fought not to follow her over the edge.

She panted for breath, a light sheen of sweat coating her skin. I withdrew from her body only long enough to flip her over. Rachel fisted the covers and held on as I thrust hard and deep. Each drive of my hips pushed her up on her toes, but she didn't utter a word of complaint. The opposite.

"Please, Isaac. I need more."

I pounded her pussy like a man possessed, barely holding on. When she came again, I let go, filling her with my cum. My heart hammered against my chest and I struggled to draw a breath. Hell, I'd run ten miles and not felt this level of exertion. My cock twitched inside her, and I was loath to pull out, but I knew she couldn't be comfortable. Slowly, I withdrew from her body and Rachel rolled to her side. I lifted her into my arms, settling her onto the pillows, then stretched out beside her.

"Is it always like that?" she asked.

I didn't pretend to not know what she meant. I curled a tendril of her hair around my finger. "No. Only with you."

It wasn't a line I was feeding her. The pint-sized woman with curves for days packed a serious punch. I'd been with my fair share of women over the years, and not a damn one came anywhere close to what I experienced with Rachel. The moment I'd seen her at the diner I'd known she was special. The fact the sex between us was phenomenal only proved my point. If ever there was a woman meant for me, it was this one.

I kissed her brow, the tip of her nose, then her lips. "Rest a moment, then we'll get cleaned up."

She cuddled closer and sighed, her eyes sliding shut. I knew exactly how she felt. Content. Utterly and completely content. There wasn't much that could make my life more perfect right then. Except the Mulligans falling off the face of the earth. I'd have to handle that situation soon enough, but for now, I'd enjoy the sweet woman in my arms and try to come up with a plan. Because there was no fucking way I'd ever let anyone get their hands on my wife or daughter. If they even tried, I'd bury them in a shallow grave. Several, in fact, because I'd cut them into pieces first.

Chapter Seven

Rachel

Steel wasn't anything like I'd expected. When I'd first met him, I couldn't deny I'd found him attractive, but I hadn't trusted him. Not because he was a stranger, but more because he was a man. Every man in my life had let me down, including my father. Didn't help the last guy I'd trusted had given me an amazing daughter and a ton of trouble. The last few days had proven Steel was different.

Maybe he'd scrambled my brains with his kisses and everything that happened after. Regardless, we'd been at his house for over a week now and I couldn't remember ever being happier than I was right now. It was possible Steel could be acting, but I didn't think so. I'd woken this morning to a small jewelry box on the bed next to me. The most beautiful wedding set had been nestled inside. I didn't think the man would do something so wonderful only to become a monster the next day. Then there was Coral. She worshipped the ground he walked on.

He'd been gone all day so I'd made breakfast and watched TV with Coral for a little while. She'd asked to go outside with Victoria and I hadn't seen the harm in it. Steel had a fence out back so the dog didn't wander far so I felt secure letting Coral out there on her own. At six, she was attempting to be more independent. Part of me wanted to keep her little forever, but the other half of me was proud that she was growing up into a sweet, responsible little girl.

I peeked out back a few times. Victoria chased after the ball Coral would throw, then ran circles around my little girl before collapsing at her feet. After a great amount of petting, they'd do it all over again. I didn't think it would be long before both of them were ready for a nap. Steel's house was immaculate, or had been before a six-year-old moved in. I spent a good bit of time putting Coral's toys back into her room, then wiped down the kitchen and swept the floors.

When I'd put my new things away, I'd noticed Steel seemed a little OCD, or maybe it was his military background. His shirts were not only folded with a precision I found a bit intimidating, but they were in the drawers by color, what few colors he owned. It was mostly a sea of black, gray, and navy. His jeans hung in the closet, perfectly positioned on the hangers and lined up from lightest to darkest. Then his camo pants, of which there were more than a few. Even his underwear was organized by color. His socks most likely would have been too, if they hadn't all been exactly the same.

It worried me a little. Coral wasn't the messiest of children, but she wasn't overly neat either. What if she left her things out and he got mad? Would he yell at her, or worse, if he tripped over her toys? He hadn't seemed like the type so far, but could I really know a man after so little time? I'd known Patrick for a year before I'd slept with him, even if we hadn't been dating that entire time, and it hadn't turned out as planned.

"You're thinking awfully hard," said a deep voice from behind me.

I yelled out and spun to face the intruder. He wore the same leather thing Steel did. He'd told me it was a cut, and this one said the guy's name was Guardian. I hadn't met anyone other than Matt and Grizzly. I backed against the kitchen counter, my hands trembling as I glanced around for a weapon. The fact this guy was part of Steel's club should mean I was safe, but what if I wasn't?

"Relax," the guy said. "Just came to see if you were up for some company."

"Company?" What the hell did that mean? Company like friends coming over, or company like... Oh God. He didn't want me to sleep with him, did he?

"My wife and son wanted to meet you and your daughter. Steel has kept the two of you to himself, but I thought you might like to meet another woman at the compound."

Wife? The tension drained from my body. So he wasn't here for nefarious purposes. He only wanted his family to meet us. I didn't see the harm in it, although, I did have to wonder why Steel hadn't invited them over already. Was there a reason he didn't want me to meet the other members of his club or their families? He'd said our marriage, no matter how strange, was a forever kind of thing. Had it been a lie? If we were a permanent part of his life, he'd want us to know the other people who were important to him, right?

"Would they like to join us for lunch? I usually put Coral down for a nap just after, but I can have her rest before then."

He nodded. "Lunch would be good. Um, there's something you should know beforehand."

"Something bad or good?" I asked.

"I guess it depends on how open-minded you are. My family consists of more than just my wife and son. I also have a husband."

A husband. I let that sink in a moment, then the lightbulb went off in my head. "Oh, you mean she's not just your wife but someone else's too?"

He shrugged. I had a feeling it was more complicated than that, but I couldn't quite wrap my mind around how something like that would work.

Didn't matter to me how many men she had in her marriage. As long as Steel didn't plan for us to do that too, then I was fine with it.

"You're all welcome," I said. "But thank you for telling me ahead of time so I didn't say something stupid in front of your wife."

He grinned. "I'll bring Zoe and Luis by in a little bit. Dagger and I have a job to tackle this afternoon but our home isn't far from here. They can walk back or bring the car over here."

"Are there others? Other women and children?" I asked.

Guardian hesitated a moment. "Steel hasn't told you much about this place?"

"He's mentioned his brothers and families, but I haven't met anyone other than a Prospect and Grizzly."

"Can't really blame Steel. He's been alone a long time. Even though there are women up at the clubhouse most nights who are more than willing to give a guy some relief, I haven't seen him with any in a while."

I wasn't sure what to say to that. He'd just told me there were women who would gladly sleep with my husband. Was Steel at this clubhouse place now? He hadn't left a note as to where he was going or how long he'd be gone. I didn't have a cell phone and I hadn't found a landline in the house, which meant even if I did have his number, which I didn't, I still wouldn't have been able to call.

"There are five other ladies here who are paired with patched members of this club, even though Blades hasn't technically claimed China, but it's a long story and it's theirs to tell. You'll also see a few Mexican ladies who are trying to find their footing. Grizzly is just helping them out a bit. And he has two teens at his house."

It was a lot to take in, and I had so many questions. I simply nodded and hoped I'd remember all that when I met his wife later, or anyone else around here for that matter.

"You'll meet Adalia and Lilian at some point too. They're both Grizzly's daughters and paired off with club members. Adalia is with Badger and Lilian is with Dragon."

I bit my lip, but couldn't contain my question. Steel had told me his real name and explained he went by a road name around here. I just didn't quite understand what a road name was or why they had them. Nor did I understand how they'd gotten their names.

"Steel told me about road names, but I don't understand them," I said.

"My name is Guardian because I protect those weaker than me. My husband, Dagger, got his name because of his preferred way of dealing with our enemies. Same with Dragon. Badger's name suits his personality."

"And Steel?"

"That's for your husband to explain. Now, I'm going to head out and let Zoe know it's okay for her to stop by with Luis at lunchtime. If you need anything and can't reach Steel, your neighbor to the left is Colorado."

"Thank you, Guardian. I look forward to meeting your family."

He gave me a nod, then let himself out. I checked on Coral again before I looked in the refrigerator to decide on lunch. I didn't know what Zoe and her son liked to eat, but most kids seemed to enjoy pasta. I'd put cheese and spinach tortellini on my grocery list the other day and knew I had enough to feed four or more people. Since I wasn't sure when Steel would return, I wanted to make sure I had enough for him too just in case.

I hated sauce that came from a jar. There was at least two hours until lunch, which gave me plenty of time to put Coral down for a nap and make some sauce. Alfredo would have tasted better with it, but my little angel always turned up her nose if I put white sauce of any sort on pasta. I had cans of crushed tomatoes, tomato sauce, and paste. I set them all out on the counter, then called Coral into the house.

"I'm still playing," she said, giving me the most indignant look a six-year-old could manage.

"We're going to have company soon. You need to lie down and rest so you'll be able to play when Zoe and Luis come over. I don't know how old Luis is, but I bet he'd like to go out and play with you and Victoria."

She nodded eagerly, opened the door for Victoria to come inside, then raced down the hall to her bedroom. The little pug stopped long enough for some water, then trotted after Coral. Not only had Steel given Coral a daddy, but he'd given her a pet as well. I wondered how Steel felt about his little dog preferring Coral over him. He hadn't seemed to mind so far.

While Coral and Victoria took a nap, I started the sauce. If I'd been making spaghetti, I'd have added some ground chicken or turkey to the sauce, or maybe meatballs. Since we were having tortellini, I just made a basic red sauce. As much as I preferred using fresh garlic, the jar of minced garlic Steel had picked up would be sufficient, as were the little jars of spices and seasonings he'd gotten for me. When I'd been employed before, I hadn't had a lot of extra money, but

I'd made sure to feed Coral decent meals. It had meant learning to cook, and I'd found that I sometimes enjoyed the experience. Maybe not on days I'd been on my feet working for eight or more hours, but the rest of the time it was almost fun.

I stirred everything together and let it simmer on the stove. I checked the time and realized there would be plenty of time for me to shower and change clothes. If I was going to meet my first potential friend, I wanted to wear something slightly better than a T-shirt and leggings. Since I'd been cleaning and putting things away, I'd dressed for comfort. I turned the sauce down so it wouldn't bubble over and checked on Coral. Satisfied that the house wouldn't burn down and no one would need me for the next twenty minutes, I laid out a pair of jeans and one of my nicer shirts, then started the shower.

Steam billowed out of the glassed-in stall. I removed my clothes and put them into the hamper before climbing under the spray. The hot water eased my tense muscles and I wished I could stay in the watery paradise for a while. I shampooed my hair, digging my fingers into my scalp, then rinsed it. The bubbles slid down my body and spiraled the drain. I squeezed a generous amount of conditioner onto my palm and worked it into my hair. While it set, I washed the rest of me and shaved. It wasn't the leisurely shower I'd have loved to take, but I was already feeling more human.

By the time I'd finished and dried off, I heard Coral and Victoria moving around in her bedroom. I knew my hair would take a while to dry and didn't want to look like a drowned rat when Zoe arrived, so I quickly braided it and put on my clothes. I'd always hated wearing shoes if I didn't have to and after a quick glance at the pairs Steel had insisted I needed, I didn't see the harm in remaining barefoot. I checked on Coral and decided to leave her be. She spoke animatedly with Victoria while she flipped through a book.

I checked on the sauce and started the tortellini. Once the pasta was boiling, I rummaged through the pantry and pulled out the loaf of Italian bread. After I sliced off four thick pieces, I put the remainder back and got the butter out of the refrigerator. Garlic toast was simple enough. Coral loved it so I hoped Luis would be a fan as well. I'd just put the finishing touches on everything when the doorbell rang.

Coral raced past me to the front door and yanked it open before I could stop her. I didn't think we were in any danger since there was a fence around the compound, but I'd prefer to use caution. A woman and little boy stood on the porch, both grinning broadly. Coral immediately grabbed the boy's hand and pulled him into the house, chattering away.

"Well, that was easy." The blonde woman held out her hand. "I'm Zoe, and your little girl just took off with my son, Luis."

"I think she plans to show him the dog and go out back. Are you all right with that?" I asked. "Sorry. Manners. I'm Rachel, and it's nice to meet you."

"If pets are involved, Luis will be in heaven. Something smells delicious. I hope you didn't go to any trouble."

I waved off her concern. "I like to cook. Besides, we needed to eat anyway. I just made a little extra. I have no idea when Steel will be home. He was gone when I woke up and I haven't heard from him all morning."

Zoe followed me to the kitchen and sat at the

table. The kids ran through with the dog, going straight to the backyard. Since Zoe didn't seem worried about her son eating right away, I decided to let them play for a bit. Coral hadn't had a playmate in a while, not since school ended. I dished up some food for both of us, grabbed two glasses from the cabinet, and poured sweet tea into them. Sitting across from Zoe, I wondered if her men vanished like mine had. Was this a normal thing? Or was Steel doing something bad, something he might not come back from? I still didn't know much about this place or the people here.

"So you and Steel are a new thing," Zoe said, "but I heard the two of you are married."

"I guess we're married." My brow furrowed. "Steel has a piece of paper that says we're husband and wife, but neither of us actually spoke vows or anything."

"Outlaw," Zoe muttered. "Did he force you into this? That man is such a menace. It worked out fine for me, but one day he's going to marry off some woman who is going to be pissed as hell about it."

"Wait. He's done this before?"

"It's kind of their thing from what I understand. The guys try to protect someone, or fall for a woman, and Outlaw swoops in, works a little magic on the computer, and marries them."

I wasn't sure what to make of it. How could someone do that? Was it even legal, or binding in any way? If I went to a lawyer and asked for a divorce, would he even find an official record of our marriage? It didn't really matter. As far as Steel was concerned, we were married. He claimed Coral as his daughter, and was even going to sign papers to adopt her. Or however it worked since Outlaw seemed to work magic. Nothing else mattered. He was good to us, and I'd be stupid to walk away. Maybe he didn't do things the legal way, but he hadn't hurt us. It was more than I could say for Patrick and his family.

"What's that look?" Zoe asked.

"If Outlaw married us over the computer, which I still don't understand, is the marriage even legal?" I asked.

"From what I understand, he hacks into the government websites. If anyone goes to look, it will show you are legally married to Steel. The question is whether or not that's good enough for you, or do you want a real wedding?"

I'd not thought about a wedding since Patrick turned his back on me. I hadn't expected him to marry me back in high school, but I'd thought he'd at least be part of my life and Coral's, and maybe one day things would head that direction. Then he'd shown his true colors. I hadn't let anyone get close enough since then, until Steel. Although, I hadn't *let* Steel do anything. He'd sort of bulldozed me, even though he did have good intentions. To some women, it might have been a deal breaker, or even pissed them off. To me, it was just nice to have someone care that much.

"If it makes a difference, I've heard he hasn't been with any of the women at the clubhouse," Zoe said. "I asked Dagger when I heard Steel had brought someone home. The fact he wants you here speaks volumes. What little gossip I've heard is that Steel has always wanted a family and thought he'd never have one. So while he may be your knight in shining armor, or whatever, you're the answer to his prayers."

"I'm wanted," I said softly. "We both are."

Zoe nodded. "Yes, you are. Now let's eat and have some girl talk. Better get used to it because the other ladies will be on your doorstep soon enough."

I spent the next hour talking to Zoe, and we fed the kids. Luis was several years younger than Coral, but it didn't seem to matter. They played with Victoria and ran around the backyard. Their squeals and laughter made me smile, and I felt like I was truly home for the first time since those two pink lines had changed my life forever.

Nearly two weeks ago, I'd been scared and alone. I hadn't known where we'd sleep, if I could feed my child, or whether or not I'd find a job. Now I had a home, a husband, and a new friend. Things weren't perfect, but they were certainly looking up. Coral and I were no longer alone. I wouldn't go so far as to say Steel loved us, or at least me. Coral was pretty easy to love. I hoped that one day I'd fall head over heels for him and he would the feel the same about me. For now, I was content. Happier than I'd been in years.

Whatever, or whoever, put Steel in my path, they'd given me the greatest gift ever.

Chapter Eight

Steel

I eyed the men around the table, thankful they hadn't had an issue with me claiming Rachel. Outlaw may have married us, and Grizzly had known about it, but if the club hadn't accepted her, we'd have had to move outside the compound. It wouldn't have bothered me, much, but I liked the safety the gate provided for my family. It wasn't perfect, as we'd learned numerous times already, but each incident brought us closer to making the compound stronger and safer.

"There's something else," I said. "She came here because she's on the run. I'm officially adopting Coral, courtesy of Outlaw, but that little girl's biological dad is Patrick Mulligan. It seems his family has been causing some problems for Rachel. The little punk signed away his rights to his daughter, but his parents seem to have found a use for her. I don't know what or why they suddenly want her now."

"I'll get with Wire and Shade to see what we can find," Outlaw said. "No one will hurt your new family, Steel."

"We installed more cameras along the perimeter," Grizzly said. "If the Mulligans show their faces around town, or send anyone after your girls, we'll do whatever is necessary."

"And by that you mean..." I arched an eyebrow, hoping he wasn't implying what I thought.

"Guns for hire," Grizzly said. "But not just anyone. I'll call Torch and see if he can get Casper's help selecting some men. We'll have to figure out where the fuck to put them, but I'm hoping it won't come to that. Maybe we can resolve this the easy way."

Yep, that's what I'd feared. It would be too easy for the Mulligans to slip someone into the compound, a man we actually hired. I knew Griz trusted Torch and Casper, but unless we received a photo of every man they were sending our way, there was no guarantee. I wasn't convinced even then. I had something precious and I'd be damned if I'd lose my family.

Dingo snorted. "Yeah, Pres, because anything having to do with our women is oh so easy. We had to take down nearly everyone at town hall to keep Meiling safe. What's a few Irish mobsters?"

"No one said anything about the mob." At least, I didn't think Outlaw had disclosed that part yet.

Dingo gave me an *are you stupid* look. He had a point. I wouldn't have brought up a particular family if they didn't have ties to some bad criminal types. With the name Mulligan, the Irish mob wasn't too far of a leap. Well, for ordinary people it might be, but not for us. I knew the Bratva had paid a visit to the Dixie Reapers when Sarge claimed one of their women. Why not the Irish mob?

"I tried to dig up something on my own," Outlaw said. "But my damn hands wouldn't cooperate. I didn't want to get caught, so I backed out. I know Wire will be up for the challenge, so I'm sure he'll help."

I tapped the table. "He might be, but make sure he knows these people aren't too far from the Reapers territory. They could cause problems for the Dixie Reapers a lot easier than coming all the way here to Blackwood Falls. It's not without risk."

Outlaw nodded.

"Any word on the little Mexican ladies?" Colorado asked. "Not that I mind them being around, but are they just staying indefinitely or what? I thought this was just a layover."

He wasn't wrong about them being here longer than anticipated, but I'd noticed the way Wolf looked at one of those ladies. There was no fucking way Grizzly was going to send them out on their own unless it was deemed necessary. Demon had seemed sweet on one of them, but lately he'd kept his distance. I didn't know if they'd argued or he'd just lost interest. Not my problem.

"You want me to toss them into the gutter?" Grizzly asked.

"No," Colorado said. "But they can't just live here forever. Are they even working on a way to improve their lives, or just living off us? Because we pay for where they live, their utilities, and even the food they eat. I'm all about helping those who need it, but this is just dragging on, Pres. What Ramirez gave us only went so far. It's been months."

"Franny is doing her part," Wolf pointed out. "She has a job, even if it's only part-time. She's saving her money and making plans. Yeah, the shit we offer is helping her get there faster, but she's not trying to drain our finances. So just shut up with that shit."

"Rosa has a job," Demon said, but the way his jaw tightened told me he wasn't happy about it. Was that why he'd stopped spending time with her? Just where the fuck was she working?

"Fine. So two of them have jobs. What about the others?" Colorado asked. "Isn't it possible some may be taking advantage?"

"We'll discuss it at another time," Grizzly said. "I'll give the women a nudge who don't seem to be moving forward. The girls at my house are fine where they are. I'm hoping to enroll them in school this fall. It's time they had a chance at a childhood and not shoulder so much responsibility."

Couldn't argue. He was right. Those girls did deserve a chance at a somewhat normal life. And if Grizzly could give it to them, then he had my support one hundred percent. If he decided they were his kids, then heaven help anyone who got in his way. The big guy loved taking in strays. I often wondered if it was a way to remember his wife. They'd adopted Adalia, and after May passed from cancer and Adalia moved in with Badger, he didn't hesitate to take in Lilian and Shella. Speaking of...

"Hey, Pres, you have my support whatever you decide, but what about the girl you took in? I know you sent Shella to the Devil's Boneyard to visit with her baby half-sister, but I haven't seen her since. She not coming back?" I asked.

Grizzly rubbed the back of his neck. "Shella is being... difficult. In fact, she's not at the Devil's Boneyard anymore. She stopped there for a few weeks, then packed up her car and took off. Outlaw has a tracker on her vehicle and assures me she's safe. I tried to raise her right, but I guess I gave in too much when she wanted shit. It's time for her to figure out how to stand on her own two feet."

"She hasn't talked to Lilian," Dragon said. "We tried to call her about the babies, but she wouldn't answer the phone and hasn't called back. Lil feels pretty fucking bad about it."

"Shella's a damn brat," Dagger said. "No offense, Pres, but you should have spoiled her less and spanked her more."

Grizzly grunted, but I could tell he was in agreement. He'd overcompensated for her shitty life before she'd come here, and it had backfired in a horrible way. I didn't understand it. He'd done the same with Adalia and Lilian and both had turned out fine.

"Steel, the cut for Rachel will be ready in a few days. You want anything special for Coral? Maybe a T-shirt or something so she doesn't feel left out?" Demon asked.

"Little Coral would love that. I'd appreciate it." I smiled, remembering how much her face lit up every time she called me Daddy, and she found plenty of reasons to use her new name for me. I rather liked it too.

He nodded, then focused on Griz again. The Pres looked like he'd aged ten years just in the last few months. I knew Shella leaving had weighed on him, and he'd had so much on his plate since then. It seemed we couldn't catch a break. If one of us ever claimed a woman who wasn't in trouble, it would be a fucking miracle. Adalia might not have had issues when Badger claimed her, but he'd rescued her as a teen from a rapist. So yeah, we all had a type.

"When Outlaw finds out more about the Mulligans and why they want Coral, we'll reconvene. Until then, everyone keep an eye out. Anyone suspicious starts hanging around, you tell me or Demon," Grizzly said. "Steel, you need to introduce your woman to more people. She needs to know she has an entire community here, a family, who will support her. We'll keep the clubhouse cleared out tomorrow for a family gathering. No club whores permitted inside the gates. Anyone living inside the compound will be welcome."

"I sent Zoe and Luis over for lunch," Guardian said. "It's why I was late. Thought the kids might be close enough in age to be able to have a playdate."

"Appreciate it," I said. Even if that did mean I

might have extra people in my house when I got home. I'd enjoyed my time alone with Rachel and Coral, but it couldn't last forever. Grizzly was right. They needed to know they weren't alone.

"Everyone get the fuck out. Except you, Steel," Grizzly said.

I hung back, waiting for the room to clear. I had a feeling I knew what he wanted to discuss. When Dagger and Guardian had claimed Zoe, a lunatic wearing a Devil's Fury cut had slipped into the compound. Except it belonged to a man long dead, and none of us had a fucking clue we'd had a psycho in our midst. He'd only shown himself to Zoe, and she hadn't known the man claiming to be King wasn't really a member of this club.

"What did you find out?" he asked once the doors closed behind everyone.

"Traced King's widow to Missouri. Only problem is her current residence is a cemetery. I found her last known address and spoke to a few neighbors, but none of them knew much about her. Said someone showed up a few days after her death and cleared out her place. It was on the market a day later."

He sighed and pinched the bridge of his nose. "Fucking great. So we aren't any closer to figuring this shit out. I doubt Demon thought to take a picture of the nut job wearing King's cut before he let Dagger redecorate the man's face."

"If he did, I didn't have a copy. I just had a general description, but none of the neighbors remembered what the man looked like. It was a male, though, so it's possible it was the same guy Dagger and Demon tortured and killed."

"I don't like it. King isn't the only member who's passed on. What if more cuts are out there? We need to make sure every single person inside the gates knows everyone else. If another imposter sets foot in this place, I don't want there to be any doubts," Grizzly said. "We have enough issues to deal with as it is."

So fucking true. I wouldn't be opposed to a few quiet months without drama or any bullshit going on. I doubted anyone else in the club would either. I knew Grizzly had hoped for a different outcome from my little trip, and so had I. Sadly, it seemed King's widow had died alone with no friends and no family. I didn't know why she'd moved away from Blackwood Falls, but I wished she'd stayed. The club may have been different back then, but we'd have still watched over her. By being King's wife and old lady, she was family.

"I know you're anxious to get back to your woman and kid," Grizzly said. "But there's one thing I need you to do first."

"What's that, Pres?" I asked.

"Doolittle. I know you saw him the night you found Victoria, but I'm worried about the kid. I've tried my best to keep him away from the club and all the shit going down around here, but like it or not, he's one of us. Saw him around town not too long ago and he didn't look quite right. I know the two of you are close. Go check on the kid and make sure everything is okay. If he's in trouble, you bring him here. We'll find a spot for him."

I gave him a nod and got up to leave. If he thought Doolittle was in trouble, then he likely was. I just didn't know if it was club related, woman related, or something else, but I'd damn well find out. Like Grizzly said. Once you were part of this club, you were family. Only way you left was by death, or by fucking up so royally you ended up dead anyway, by the hands of your brothers. The Devil's Fury wasn't the type of club you joined, then walked away from, not without a price. Doolittle was still a patched member, but he'd been so damn young I knew Grizzly wanted more for him than this life, and he'd done it. Or so I'd thought.

I got on my bike out front and started her up, then pulled through the gates. First place I checked was the vet clinic, but I didn't see his truck in the lot. I couldn't remember a time Zach took a day off. Not voluntarily. He rented a duplex not too far off the main strip so I went there next. The driveway was empty and the stack of newspapers on the porch made the hair on my nape prickle. It looked like he hadn't been home for days, but Griz had seen him in town. So where the fuck was he?

"You looking for the vet?" a neighbor called out.

"You seen Zach lately?" I asked.

She shook her head. "Got in his truck a few days ago with a duffle bag and I haven't seen him since. Even loaded up his pets."

The Zach I knew wouldn't do something impulsive, but if he'd taken everyone with him, he didn't plan to return anytime soon. The question was where the fuck had he gone? And why? I thanked the woman, then pulled out my phone and tried to call him. When he didn't answer, I waited a moment, then called again. The third time, he finally picked up.

"Steel, I'm a little busy," Zach said.

"Griz was worried about you and sent me over to your clinic. Except you weren't there and you aren't at home. In fact, the neighbor said you packed up and left. What's going on, Zach? And don't tell me it's nothing."

He sighed. "I was going to call Grizzly if I couldn't handle it on my own."

"What's the issue?"

"A girl I went to college with called me. She sounded frantic and once she calmed a little, I found out her piece of shit boyfriend beat the hell out of her. The cops released him after twenty-four hours because one of his buddies gave him a false alibi. She's scared and alone, Steel."

"How far out?" I asked.

"We're in Reckless Kings territory. I already called so they would know I'm here. Got a motel room for a few nights. She was in rough shape, and I didn't think she could handle the drive."

"You bringing her to your place?" I asked, hoping like hell he didn't want the club to put this girl up. We were fast running out of room, and we weren't a damn hotel or halfway house for abused women.

He was quiet a moment and I knew he wasn't taking her home. No, he was about to ask me if she could stay at the compound. Fucking hell. Grizzly would no doubt tell him yes, then we'd have to scramble to figure out where the hell to put her. With the other ladies already in the apartments, there really wasn't another spot open. Unless...

"If you want her to stay at the compound, you'll have to be there too. There's still a few of the smaller homes available. Just say the word and we'll make sure it has the basics. Enough for you to get by until you figure shit out," I said. "But don't wait until the last minute. The club is dealing with a fucked-up mess or two right now."

"Do you need help?" he asked. "I'm still a patched member, even if the lot of you try to keep me out of everything."

"For good reason, boy. You have a good life. Don't fuck it up."

"Steel, you didn't answer my question."

"My woman has some bad people after her. And yes, I said my woman. Got a wife and daughter. We've also had some other issues crop up, namely that some asshole got into the compound wearing the cut of a dead member. Someone who's been buried for decades. We still don't know where he got it, or if there are others out there. So you come to the compound. Just know there's trouble brewing and coming at us from multiple sides."

Zach cleared his throat. "Steel, I know you think I'm just some kid, but I earned my patch same as everyone else. Just because there's a DVM after my name now doesn't make me any less Devil's Fury than you. If there's trouble, I want to help."

Grizzly was going to have my ass for this, but I didn't want Zach to think we didn't want him. Hell, we were all proud as fuck of what he'd accomplished. As the youngest patched member, he'd been a bit like a surrogate son to some of us. We'd all attended his high school graduation, and a few of us had even traveled to his college one as well. I didn't want him to screw everything up by associating with us, but it sounded like he'd found trouble on his own.

"Bring your girl," I said. "We'll have a house waiting for the two of you. Just to be clear, it's just two of you, right?"

"Yes, it's just two of us. And my animals."

"I'll make sure a fence is put up as well, or a pen at the least. You'll only have the basics for furniture, and I'll have a Prospect stock the kitchen. Just be safe, Doolittle."

"You too, Steel. I'll see you soon."

The line went dead and I headed back home. Better to tell Grizzly in person that Doolittle was coming back and might be staying a while, and that he wasn't alone. Then I'd assign Beau and Henry to make sure the place was ready. Just as soon as the Pres said which house Doolittle would get. I knew of several, but two only had two bedrooms. If Doolittle decided he was there to stay, he might want something a little bigger. The smaller homes would be fine for now, but he was so young he'd want a family someday.

If even half our Prospects patched in, we'd need more homes soon enough. I wondered if Griz had thought about it. There was a chance he'd already set up contractors, or at least had a plan in place. More homes weren't high up on the list with everything else going on. For that matter, I wasn't sure when we'd patch someone else in. Guardian was the most recent addition, but since he was in a relationship with Dagger and Zoe, he hadn't needed a house of his own.

When I got back to the compound and pulled through the gates, I immediately turned toward Grizzly's house. As much as I wanted to get back to Rachel and Coral, I had a few things to finish first. I parked my bike and hadn't even made it to the front door before the Pres stepped outside.

"What's going on with Doolittle?" he asked.

"He wasn't home, but I reached him on the phone. Some girl he met in college is in trouble. Boyfriend beat her to hell and back. He wants to bring her home, but not to his house. They want to come here."

Grizzly nodded. "Give them the blue house a few doors down from you. It's empty but a few Prospects can have it sorted by nightfall or at least by morning. Did the kid say when he was coming back?"

"He was waiting on her to be healed enough to travel. I'm guessing we'll see him by tomorrow night, possibly sooner. He's already been there a few days."

"Put whoever you want on the task of getting the house ready. Just not Harlan. He's already working on something for Demon."

I turned to go back to my bike, then hesitated. Turning to face Griz again, I asked the question I'd wondered on the way over. "We're running out of homes. What happens when we patch in more members?"

"We'll have it handled by then."

I wasn't about to question the Pres. It seemed he had a plan and I knew he'd share it when he was damn well ready. For now, I'd focus on the shit circling my family and handle it. Just needed more information, and I hoped Outlaw came up with it soon. I didn't like sitting and waiting.

I got on my Harley and drove back to the house. I didn't see Zoe's vehicle in the driveway, but her house was close enough she could have walked. As much as I liked the women my brothers had claimed, I was hoping no one was inside except Rachel and Coral. I was ready for some time with my girls, especially now they were officially mine not just on paper but by club law too.

Chapter Nine

Rachel

I'd enjoyed getting to know Zoe, and Coral had a blast with Luis. I didn't know when I'd meet the others, but I looked forward to it. Steel had come home, kissed me like he hadn't seen me in years, and hadn't said a single word about where he'd been. I hated that he'd left the way he had, but something told me it would happen somewhat often.

Coral had passed out shortly after Luis left, and she still slept soundly. It had given me some alone time with Steel, but he hadn't said much. Zoe had explained club business was exactly that, and Steel would never tell me what was going on with the Devil's Fury. I wasn't sure how I felt about it, but I could understand to some extent. Either way, I trusted Steel to keep us safe. Might be a little crazy with how little I knew about him, but my gut told me he would never hurt me.

Steel sprawled on one end of the couch, a contemplative look on his face. He spun a beer bottle in his hands, but it seemed more like an afterthought than something he did consciously. I sat next to him and placed my hand on his thigh.

"You know you can talk to me, right? I'm not here just for you to solve all my problems. I'm happy to listen if something is bothering you," I said.

He placed his hand over mine and gave it a squeeze. "Just worried about someone."

My heart kicked. Someone? He'd said he wasn't in a relationship before our rather strange marriage. Since he'd not been with a woman in a while, I'd thought that mean he didn't have anyone special in his life at all. Had I been wrong?

Steel kissed my cheek. "Calm down, Rachel. I can practically hear your thoughts. It's not a woman. There's this kid I kind of took under my wing a while back. He's now a patched member of the club, even though he hasn't been at the compound much since he left for college."

"Is he okay?" I asked.

"Doolittle is all grown up now, but he's coming here soon. Bringing a woman with him. Someone who got into a bad relationship and Doolittle ran to her rescue. I'm not sure if she's taking advantage of him, or if she's a love interest he never talked about. Either way, him being here isn't good."

"Why?" I asked.

"He's a veterinarian now. Has a nice little house in town. We've tried hard to make him keep his distance from the club. I won't lie. We don't always do legal shit around here, and I don't want that tainting Doolittle. He deserves the chance at a normal, safe life."

I cocked my head and studied him. So, he wanted Doolittle away from this life, but he wanted me and Coral here? I wasn't sure what to think. If the compound was so safe, why wouldn't he want this Doolittle person here too?

"You said he's grown up. Wouldn't it be his decision whether or not he wants to be part of the club still? Or live here?"

Steel grunted and took a swallow of his beer.

"It's okay for you to worry about him. You just can't make his decisions for him. If he's an adult, then he has to learn things the hard way. Maybe being here isn't the right move, but he won't know that for certain until he tries it, right?"

"I hate when you make sense," he muttered.

I bumped my shoulder against his. "No, you just hate not being in control of something. Time to let go and let Doolittle live his life. Doesn't mean you can't be here for him if he stumbles."

Steel finished his beer and set the bottle aside. He closed his eyes and tipped his head back, heaving a sigh. I had a feeling it was more than Doolittle weighing on him. He was trying to tackle my issue, and who knew what else. It made me wonder who was there for Steel? I knew the club had his back in times of trouble, but who did he have the rest of the time? Me. Or at least now he did, if he'd let me in. The sex between us was great, but I wanted more than good sex.

"What do you want from me, Steel?" I asked softly.

"What's that mean?" His gaze focused on me.

"We're married. Obviously, the sex is amazing. Do you want more than that out of this relationship? I feel like I'm walking through the dark and tripping over my feet. I don't know what you want from me, or what I can do to help you."

"Haven't had anyone give a shit in a while," he said. "Everyone in this club has their own issues on top of whatever we're dealing with together. We just deal with stuff in our own way. Guess my way is to bottle everything up. When it gets to be too much, I go shoot something or blow shit up."

I bit my lip so I wouldn't laugh. With some guys, that probably meant they played some macho game on the Xbox or PlayStation. With Steel, I had a feeling he meant he literally went shooting or set off explosives. He'd mentioned going to the gun range during one of our conversations. I had to admit, I wouldn't mind going to watch him sometime. I'd never personally shot a gun, and I didn't think I wanted to start now, but it might be a little hot to see him in action.

I eyed him from head to toe. It hadn't escaped my attention he owned more than one pair of camouflage pants. In fact, he seemed to prefer them over jeans. It made me wonder if that was a holdover from his military days. His black tee was tucked into his pants and he still wore his cut. Steel might not have abs for days like a lot of younger men I'd seen shirtless, but he was fit. When he held me, I felt safe and wanted. More than that. I felt desired, and everything in me warmed and craved his touch.

"Woman, you keep looking at me like that, and you'll end up bent over with your panties around your ankles."

My breath caught at the mental picture. I didn't think Coral would sleep quite long enough for him to fuck me, but that didn't mean we couldn't have a little fun. I got off the couch and stood between his legs, then knelt. His gaze was dark. Hungry. I worked his belt free, then unfastened his pants. He made me work for it, but I freed his cock and stroked him.

"Playing with fire, Rachel. Gonna get burned."

I lapped at the head of his cock. "Then burn me."

I took him into my mouth, flicking his shaft with my tongue. Steel shifted, spreading his legs more and relaxing back against the cushions. I felt the coiled tension in his thighs as I ran my hands up and down them.

"No touching," he said. "Hands behind your back."

My heart stuttered for a moment, then took off. I removed my palms from his thighs and crossed my wrists behind my back. There was a part of me that thrilled over his bossiness in the bedroom. I liked it when he ordered me to do something, or took what he wanted.

"My lovely wife going to show me how good she sucks cock?"

I hummed my agreement, my mouth too full to speak.

"Thing is, a man my age is set in his ways. Likes things done just so." He gripped my hair in his fist. "You sucked a lot of cock before, Rachel?"

I tried to shake my head, but I couldn't.

"Take a breath, little girl." I sucked air through my nose, then he forced his cock to the back of my throat. He held me there and I strained to breathe. "Swallow."

My gag reflex kicked in and I fought the urge to pull away. I finally managed to swallow and he praised me as he dragged me off his cock, only to force his way between my lips again. This time I swallowed on my own. Saliva pooled in my mouth and ran down my chin as Steel worked his cock into my mouth, using his grip on my hair to guide me. When he grunted and came, I struggled to swallow but didn't quite manage. I felt his cum leaking from the corners of my mouth.

He pulled me off and wiped my chin and mouth. "Good girl."

I squirmed, pressing my thighs together. I might have gotten him off, but now I ached even more. My nipples were so tight they hurt, and my pussy throbbed. I glanced at the doorway, and listened intently, but I didn't hear a peep from Coral. Would she possibly sleep a little longer? Long enough for Steel to make me come? Did he even want to?

I held his gaze and he reached for me, lifting me to my feet. Without a word, he yanked my pants down to my knees, panties too, then bent me over his lap. My ass was in the air and my cheeks burned, not just from embarrassment but because it also turned me on. He ran his hand over my ass, then teased the lips of my pussy.

"So wet," he said, spreading my pussy open and teasing my clit. I whimpered and squirmed on his lap. I kicked my legs, wanting to spread them more, but I couldn't.

Steel yanked my pants and panties the rest of the way off. I opened my thighs wider and bit my lip to stifle my cries. He got me off within seconds, but didn't seem satisfied. I felt his fingers stretch me as he thrust them in and out. I was getting wetter, and I knew it wouldn't be enough.

"What do you need, Rachel?" he asked. "Tell me what you want."

"I need you to fuck me. I want your cock, Steel. Please."

He pulled his fingers free and tapped my hip.

"Kneel next to me, ass facing the door." I scrambled off his lap and hurried to obey. He pressed me down until my nose practically touched his cock. "Suck it. Get me hard so I can fuck you."

I took him in my mouth again, and nearly screamed from pleasure as he shoved his fingers back into my pussy, working me hard and deep as I sucked him. I reached between his legs and cupped his balls, rolling them in my hand. I'd never done something like that before, but I'd read it in a book. If Steel's reaction was anything to go by, he enjoyed it. His cock lengthened and got thicker. I sucked him harder.

He growled and pulled his fingers free, then lifted me. It happened so fast my head spun, but he settled me on his lap facing the TV and impaled me on his cock. I moaned, not able to hold back, as he filled me. I braced my hands on his knees, my legs spread, as he gripped my hips to lift and lower me, fucking me with long, deep strokes.

"Next time I threaten to yank off your panties and fuck you, just tell me that's what you want," he said.

"Yes, Isaac."

He released one of my hips and worked his hand under my shirt. I felt him tugging at my bra until my breast popped out and he rolled my nipple between his fingers. I was so close, near to falling. I rode him harder. Faster. I felt nearly frantic with the need to come. Steel pinched my nipple and it sent me over the edge. I slammed myself down on his cock again, my orgasm tearing through me until I struggled to breathe. He released my nipple and held my hips, lifting me up enough that he could drive up into me. Steel fucked me, taking his pleasure as I floated on a cloud of bliss. When he came, I felt all warm and tingly.

He remained buried inside me while I sat on his lap. He stroked my breasts, working both of them out of my bra. I leaned back against him, my head on his shoulder. If he kept playing with me, I'd come again. I couldn't remember a time I'd ever wanted a man as badly as I wanted Steel right this moment. He could fuck me another dozen times and I wasn't sure it would be enough. Steel released one of my nipples and he slid his hand down my belly, not stopping until his fingers brushed my clit. I whimpered and pressed my breast tighter into his other hand as he worked the little bud between my legs. It didn't take much to make me come again.

"Fuck. I think you're even more responsive now than you were the first time," he said. I'd thought we'd be finished, but Steel had other ideas. I felt his cock softening inside me, but he didn't seem to care. He left me spread across his lap, my legs on either side of his thighs. He tugged my shirt up over my breasts and the cool air teased my hard nipples.

"Isaac, I... I..."

"Need more?"

I nodded. I didn't know how much time passed, but he pulled another two orgasms from me, and if I hadn't heard the thump of Coral's feet as she got out of her bed, I'd have begged him to keep going. I didn't know what the hell was wrong with me! It was like I'd become a nympho overnight. I just wanted him to make me come again and again. To stay in bed, naked, and let him play with me. I wanted to suck his cock again, feel him inside me. I shivered as I stood, his release running down my thighs. I quickly yanked my panties and pants on and hurried from the room to freshen up before I faced Coral. I heard Steel chuckling as I raced out of the room.

Good thing one of us was amused by nearly getting caught by our six-year-old. I went into the master bathroom and splashed water on my face. I smoothed my hair, fixed my bra, then used one of the baby wipes I'd stashed for emergency cleanups to wipe the cum off my pussy. By the time I'd finished, I felt a little less like a wanton slut and more like... Well, I didn't know what.

I followed the sound of voices and smiled when I saw Steel giving Coral a glass of juice at the kitchen table. His phone started ringing and he answered, cutting his gaze to me and Coral twice before he murmured something to whoever was on the phone and hung up. I didn't know what the hell that was about, but he'd tell me if I needed to know. Otherwise, I'd assume it was club business, like Zoe had said before. Something apparently the women weren't allowed to know about.

Coral finished her drink, then went outside with Victoria. I peered into the fridge to get an idea of what I'd make for dinner, then I felt Steel's hands on my hips. I looked over my shoulder, a smile curving my lips. It was nice that he couldn't keep his hands off me. Made me feel desirable. I'd been "Coral's mom" for the last six years and not felt like a sexy woman. Until Steel. Once I'd gotten over my reservations that he was up to something nefarious, it had been easy to fall for him.

Not that I was going to tell the man I was falling in love with him. We'd known each other less than a month. It was insane to even think I loved him, but somehow he'd gotten past my defenses and wormed his way into my heart. I didn't know if he'd even been trying to accomplish that or not, but he had.

"That was Zoe," he said. "Luis woke from his nap and has been chattering away about Coral. They wanted to know if she can spend the night sometime."

I'd never let Coral stay anywhere away from home before. In fact, she'd had few friends growing up. I knew she'd be inside the compound still, and since Zoe had two husbands there was no doubt she'd be well-protected. "When?"

"Whenever you say it's okay," he said. Steel rubbed his beard against my neck. "Much as I love that little girl, might be nice to have a night to ourselves."

"Can we hold off a little longer? See if the Mulligans are done? If they're still after her, then I'd feel better if she was here with me." I turned to face him. "Is that all right?"

Steel pressed a kiss against my forehead. "More than okay. Just waiting on some intel to come through, and then I'll handle those fuckers before they have a chance to hurt you. No one is taking Coral, Rachel. I won't let them."

I believed him. Or at least, I believed he'd do everything in his power to protect us. But Patrick and his family were ruthless, and I knew they'd stop at nothing to get what they wanted. If they didn't balk at killing me, I knew they wouldn't care about ending other lives. I worried for Steel. He might have been in the military, and seemed competent enough, but if they did anything to hurt him or take him from me, it would gut me.

"Promise you'll be careful," I said.

"Promise, beautiful." He kissed me softly. "I'll go check on our girl while you figure out dinner. While I'm out there, I'll let Zoe know you'll get with her later about a sleepover."

He swatted my ass, then walked out, leaving me with troubled thoughts about the Mulligans and how they could be stopped. Preferably before it was too late.

Chapter Ten

Steel

I stared at the message on my phone as Coral played with Victoria. Every muscle in my body tightened, and anger made my blood run hot. The picture on the display was of Coral, Luis, and Victoria. It was clearly taken earlier today. And it meant the Mulligans had someone watching the place. They knew where my daughter was, and were likely trying to find a way to get to her. As much as I hated to keep Coral on lockdown, there was no way I'd let her leave the compound.

Rachel, on the other hand... She seemed to like earning her own money, and I'd feel like an ass if I made her stay home. I knew those fuckers wouldn't hesitate to use her to get what they wanted. As much as I didn't want to scare her, she needed to see this, to understand they'd found her. If I kept her in the dark, she might not be as cautious as she needed to be.

"Coral, time to bring Victoria inside," I called out.

"Yes, Daddy!" She ran for me, the little pug on her heels. They scampered by and ran into the house. I scanned the area, wondering if whoever sent the picture was watching even now. I hoped they knew I'd find them, and I'd end them. No one was going to threaten my family and live to talk about it.

I went inside and pulled Rachel into a corner away from Coral. I showed her the display and she gasped, her hand flying to her mouth, her eyes wide as she stared at the image in terror. Her gaze lifted to mine and I pulled her closer.

"I won't let them get our girl, Rachel. But I need you to be careful. If you insist on working at the diner, you can't trust anyone who isn't a coworker or part of this club."

"Isaac, what are we going to do?" she asked.

"I'm going to see Outlaw. I'll let him use my phone to try and track where the image came from. It was likely a burner, but maybe the dipshit used his actual phone to send it. Don't hold dinner for me, and don't wait up. I might be late." I pressed a kiss to her cheek and headed out. I started to call Henry to see if he could watch over them, but as long as they didn't leave the compound I didn't think anyone could get to them. Not after Griz bulked up our security.

Outlaw lived on the other side of the compound, but the ride over gave me time to clear my head. As much as I wanted to charge after whoever was coming for my family, I knew it wasn't the smart thing to do. I needed a level head, a clear mind, and a plan. Right now, I was running on rage.

I parked in his driveway and walked up to the door. Elena opened it with a smile on her face. I leaned in to give her a hug, then entered the house. Outlaw was on the living room floor, with his daughter, Valeria. She was less than a year old, but cute as a button. Whatever play mat she was on seemed to fascinate her. It crinkled when she grabbed one corner, making her squeal.

Outlaw saw me lurking and got up. "If you're here without calling first, something must have happened."

I showed him my phone. His face flushed with anger and he marched down the hall. I followed him to the room hidden behind his closet, where he kept his equipment. There was a thick file sitting on the desk marked "Mulligans" and he handed it to me.

"Patrick Mulligan is their only son. When did

Rachel say the accidents started? When she first thought something was wrong?" Outlaw asked.

"She didn't say exactly, or if she did I was so pissed I didn't retain the info, but I gathered it's only been in the past year or two. Could have been less. The kid is six, but he's had no part in her life from the beginning. Why? What's the timing have to do with anything?"

Outlaw took the file from me and flipped through the papers until he found what he wanted. He handed it back and I scanned the document, my eyebrows rising with each word. Holy shit.

"So, he can't have kids after an 'unfortunate accident' which means he suddenly wants Coral? Or his parents do?" I asked.

"I think it's the parents. To an extent. Flip a few more pages," Outlaw said.

I kept turning them until I saw it. An engagement announcement between Patrick Mulligan and Maureen O'Shay. Her name wasn't familiar to me, but I knew Outlaw had a reason for showing me this. I turned another page and realized she wasn't just related to the Irish mob, she was the kingpin's niece. Fuck. My. Life.

"He needs Coral because he can't have kids," Outlaw said. "I'm betting the fiancée is pissed and doesn't want to adopt, or Coral has already been promised to someone in marriage at a later date."

"You couldn't find out?" I asked.

"No. But it's not the Mulligans or O'Shays who took that picture today. I have confirmation the lot of them are in New York for some big gala. Which means they sent hired muscle. It could be anyone."

I nodded to my phone, which he'd set down by his computer. "Keep that for a bit and see if you can trace the photo."

He shook his head. "See how grainy it is? It's clear enough to see who's in the photo, but the quality is shit. Cheap burner. I'll let Grizzly know we have a problem and need that extra security. And for fuck's sake, keep Coral inside the gates. Hell, don't even let her near the fence line."

I stared him down until I saw the slightest flinch. "I wasn't born yesterday. I know how to fucking take care of my family."

He held up his hands and I knew the matter was closed for now. I took the file with me, wanting to study it in more detail. I had no doubt Outlaw had copies of everything he'd given me. Possibly several. I shoved it into my saddlebags, but instead of going straight home, I stopped by the clubhouse. Other than walking through to head to Church, I hadn't spent much time there since bringing Rachel and Coral home with me. But right now, I needed a moment to think, and a cold beer.

I parked my bike out front and carried the file inside with me. Henry was working the bar and slid an ice-cold beer down to me. I sipped at the brew while I went through the papers, paying closer attention than the quick perusal I'd done at Outlaw's place. Whatever he'd found, I wanted to know every single detail. Needed to memorize the damn pages so I'd be prepared for whatever was coming.

The smell of cheap perfume hit me first, then I felt nails run down my bicep. I didn't even look. Only one woman would dare touch me without an invitation. The bitch was on my last nerve, but I knew my brothers liked her well enough. Or rather, they enjoyed the fact she'd let them fuck her any way they wanted and scream for more. Honestly, the only time

I'd ever fucked her, her cries had seemed fake as hell. I hadn't gone back for seconds, and regretted the fact I'd put my dick in her to begin with.

"Go the fuck away," I said as I flipped another page in the file.

"Come on, Steel. You know I can make you feel good."

I held up my left hand, ring finger and middle finger sticking up so she'd see the wedding band I'd bought, then lowered it so only the middle one remained upright. Her grip tightened, her nails biting into me harder. Should have known she'd see it as a challenge. But Dingo, Outlaw, Dragon, Dagger, and Guardian should have all proven to these sluts by now that once a Devil married or claimed a woman, that was it. He wasn't putting his dick anywhere else. The lot of us might be womanizing assholes, but not after the right woman came along.

She moved in closer, her breasts pushing against me. I had no doubt if I turned my head, I'd get a face full of barely contained cleavage. When she grabbed my junk, I reached down and squeezed her wrist, prying her loose. This time, she got my full attention.

"Don't. Touch. Me." I squeezed her wrist harder until she cried out and went to her knees. Normally, I'd be the first in line to make sure no one hurt a woman, but some of these bitches had to learn this the hard way.

Sunlight poured through the doors as they opened, and I heard a gasp that made me glance that way. Rachel stood just inside the doorway, her eyes wide as she took in the club whore at my feet. Her gaze flicked to mine and whatever she saw must have told her enough. She came closer and tipped her head to the side as she stared the woman down.

"I feel sorry for you," Rachel said.

The slut sneered. "For me? You're the one who looks like a damn kindergarten teacher. I bet you can't make a man like Steel come."

Rachel's eyebrows rose into her hairline. A slight blush tinged her cheeks, but my wife didn't cower. She held her shoulders back and looked down her nose at the bitch. "Well, apparently he likes a more wholesome look because I can assure you I can and do make him come. More than once a day. But I feel sorry for you because it must take an incredibly insecure woman to try getting into a married man's pants, especially after he's made it clear he doesn't want you."

I released Lanie and turned fully toward Rachel, reaching out for her. "Why are you here?"

She swallowed hard and her hands started to shake. Her lip trembled and she looked like she was seconds from breaking. Her eyes misted with tears. "Coral took Victoria out back, except... they aren't there."

I shot to my feet. "What the fuck does that mean?"

"They were only out about ten minutes. She worried Victoria would have an accident and might need to pee. When I went to call them inside, they were gone. The back gate stood open and they're just... not there. I called and called. Nothing." She leaned into me. It was if she couldn't hold herself upright any longer. "What if the Mulligans have our daughter?"

I ran my hand down her back and hoped she couldn't feel my heart thundering in my chest. "We'll find her."

Only a handful of brothers and Prospects were in the clubhouse at this time of day, but I knew I'd need each and every one of them. I released Rachel and got up on the bar top.

"Brothers, I need a search and rescue. Coral and Victoria disappeared from the backyard and wouldn't return when Rachel called for them. I need every hand on deck. Scour every damn inch of this fucking place." I looked over at Henry. "Call Outlaw. Tell him to pull the security footage for the compound. All of it."

I got down and took Rachel in my arms. "We'll find them."

She nodded and clung to me. "I'm so sorry. I should have gone out with them, but dinner was nearly done and I didn't want it to burn. I thought she'd be safe as long as we didn't go outside the gates."

"Not your fault, beautiful."

Wolf and Hot Shot came over, and I saw the others following. As much as I wanted to hold Rachel and assure her Coral would be fine, right now we needed to find our daughter. I wasn't going to take my bike. With Victoria and Coral both missing, I'd need one of the club trucks or SUVs. And I really needed to get Rachel a fucking car.

"Come on, wife. You're with me." I turned to look at Henry and he handed over a set of keys, not even needing to be asked. I grabbed them and led Rachel outside. Once I had her in the truck, I pulled away from the clubhouse and headed for our home. If she hadn't run across Coral on her way here, it was doubtful they'd come this way. I passed our house and kept going, but slowed to a crawl.

Rachel rolled down her window to call for Coral.

My phone lit up with Demon's name. I answered, putting the call on speaker. "I have Rachel right here with me."

"Good to know. I'll watch my mouth," the Sergeant-at-Arms said. "I'm at your place. Found a few footprints and paw prints. Looks like she wandered out the gate and walked toward the outer fence. I'm going to search around here and see what I can find. If I can get a fix on the direction she's heading, I'll call back. Got Prospects on foot and the club is on their bikes except a few who took the other vehicles at the clubhouse. We'll find her, Steel."

I heard a little sob escape Rachel and reached over to take her hand. She squeezed my fingers. After I disconnected the call, I pulled over to the side of the road. I hooked an arm around Rachel's waist and dragged her onto my lap. Her arms went around my neck, and she sniffled as the tears fell.

"Pretty girl, none of this is your fault. You hear me? Maybe they were chasing a squirrel or something. We don't know why they left the yard, but the club is searching for them. I need you to stop blaming yourself."

"But if I'd just gone out with them --" I placed a finger over her lips, silencing her. Then decided to kiss her instead. It was soft and slow. Soon, she melted against me. Even if she'd gone out back with Coral and Victoria, she couldn't have kept an eye on both every second.

"I'm a bad mom," she murmured.

"No, you're a great mom. Everything you've done the past six years has been for Coral. Do you know how many parents send their kids out back to play without watching them the entire time? Tons. And you were right. Coral should have been safe inside the compound. There was no reason for you to think she'd vanish from our backyard. Just because someone managed to take a picture, from outside the compound, didn't mean they could necessarily reach her." I kissed her again, then set her back on her seat.

"Now, let's go find our daughter."

I followed the road, circling the compound. While I saw my brothers and the Prospects, I never found Coral or Victoria. But someone did... My phone lit up again. This time it was Slash calling. When I accepted the call, I warned him he was on speaker.

"I don't have Coral, but I did find Victoria." Slash sighed. "It's bad, Steel. I think she tried to protect her little girl and failed horribly."

My stomach tightened at the news. A quick glance at Rachel was enough to tell me she was close to falling apart. She'd paled and swayed in her seat. I got Slash's location and sped up, getting to him as fast as I could.

He knelt next to the fence and I saw where someone had cut through it. Victoria lay unmoving on the ground. I got out of the truck and went to kneel next to her. She whimpered and rolled her bug eyes to watch me, but it was clear she wasn't getting up. Blood soaked her fur and it looked like someone had taken a knife to her. I removed my cut, then pulled my shirt off. I slipped the leather back over my shoulders and used the tee to wrap her. Picking her up, I carried her to the truck.

Rachel held out her arms and I settled Victoria in her lap. She stroked the dog's head and murmured to her, telling Victoria how brave she'd been. My throat tightened, but fuck if I'd ever admit I was damn close to crying over a dog. Zach hadn't shown up yet at the compound, but I knew his practice would still take care of Victoria. They might ask some questions, but I had a legitimate reason for Victoria's injuries.

"Coral's gone, isn't she?" Rachel asked softly. "They took my baby."

"Looks like it, beautiful. Once we get Victoria

dropped off, I'm going to find our daughter, and I'll make those fuckers pay." I glanced at her. "There's a few reasons they call me Steel. One of those has to do with the way I punish evil motherfuckers."

"When you find them..." She turned toward me, holding my gaze. "Make sure they can never hurt another person ever again."

"Rachel, I don't think you understand exactly what you're asking. Darlin', if I do that, it means they aren't breathing anymore. I will fuck them up, draw it out and make them suffer, and then I'll end their miserable lives."

I heard her shaky indrawn breath and wondered if I'd said too much. She'd run from the Mulligans because they were violent, and I'd just admitted I'd kill someone. Several someones. What came out of her mouth surprised the fuck out of me, and made me damn proud to call her mine. I knew, then and there, she was my equal in every way.

"I want them to hurt," she said. "*I* want to make them hurt. Promise me, Isaac. When you find them, before you kill them, I get a chance to make them pay for taking Coral."

I pulled to a stop at the vet's office and got out. I went around to her side and lifted Victoria, pausing long enough to kiss Rachel. "Promise, beautiful. As long as Demon doesn't veto me, I'll let you get a few hits in."

I carried Victoria into the clinic, gave them the information they needed, then drove Rachel home. I knew the clinic would call with any word on the little pug. Right now, we had a daughter to find and bring home.

Chapter Eleven

Rachel

I'd never wanted to harm another living being in all my life. Until now. They'd taken Coral. I knew she had to be scared, and she'd probably seen them try to kill Victoria. My poor baby! Steel had been on the phone, pacing, for the last hour. I'd caught bits and pieces of his conversation. He hadn't even tried to keep me out of the loop.

My hands shook. I'd thrown up when we got home. My stomach still churned, and bile burned the back of my throat. A knock sounded at the front door and I went to answer, knowing Steel needed to focus. I blinked in surprise at the group of women on the doorstep. Zoe waved from the back.

"We thought you could use some support right now," Zoe said.

I stepped back and let them enter. Zoe went straight to the kitchen, and I saw she had something in her hands. The others followed. I walked into the kitchen to see Zoe opening various cabinets.

"You do have a kettle, right?" she asked.

"I think so." I vaguely remembered one, but I wasn't sure where Steel kept it. He stalked past me, went to the cabinet by the fridge and pulled down a black enamel kettle. I shot him a smile as he passed me again, heading back to the living room, the phone still pressed to his ear.

"Sit and I'll make some herbal tea," Zoe said.

Two Asian women sat at the table, watching me. The younger gave me a small smile. "I'm Meiling. I belong to Dingo, and this is my mother, China."

Two Hispanic ladies sat to their right. The one on the left gave me a wave. "I'm Elena. Outlaw is mine."

Right. Outlaw. The man who had used a computer to legally -- or not so legally -- marry me and Steel. I made a mental note not to get on her bad side in case her husband took offense and did something horrible without having to leave the comfort of his home. To me, that made him scarier than all the others.

The other one snickered. "Do you say that to his face? Because I'm pretty sure he claimed your ass and not the other way around. I'm Lilian, by the way, and I'm with Dragon."

"And we've already met," said Zoe. She carried a steaming mug to the table, then shoved a chair out with her foot. "Sit. You need to drink this."

I nearly collapsed onto the chair and accepted the cup from her. I blew across the surface, trying to cool it, before I took a cautious sip. It scalded my tongue, but I didn't much care. I didn't even taste it. The fact these ladies had come, knowing I needed someone, warmed my heart. I was a stranger to them, yet they'd taken the time to come and give me comfort. I couldn't remember the last time I'd felt like I had family supporting me. I knew these ladies were part of my new family, the one I'd gotten when I married Steel.

"They'll find her," Elena said.

"When I got kidnapped, Dragon didn't stop until he had me safe in his arms again," Lilian said. "I was pregnant with our twins at the time. Trust me. The club won't rest until Coral is back home."

"Wait. You were kidnapped? I thought we were supposed to be safe here? But Coral is missing, Victoria may die, and you were kidnapped?" I asked, feeling as if I might come unraveled at any moment.

"I wasn't here when it happened," Lilian said.

Meiling snorted and poked a finger at Lilian. "Yeah, because this one thought it was an awesome idea to run away instead of her facing her daddy, and her baby-daddy."

"Um." I glanced between them. "I'm lost."

Lilian rolled her eyes. "I'm adopted. The President of the club, Grizzly? You've met him?"

I nodded, thinking of the big gruff man.

"He's my dad. He also adopted Adalia, but she offered to keep all our kids. You'll have to meet her later."

"Or more accurately, Badger heard someone broke into the compound and threatened to tie her ass to the bed if she tried to leave," said Meiling.

"Badger is her… husband?" I asked.

Meiling nodded, then frowned. "You know, I'm not honestly sure if they're married or not, but Adalia definitely belongs to Badger. The man goes psycho if he thinks anything will happen to her."

"Well, he did do time for her," Elena said.

My head was spinning and I couldn't keep up. It was all information overload. My stomach gurgled and I shot up off my chair, racing to the bathroom. I hit my knees and barely made it over the toilet before I threw up. Tears burned my eyes as I heaved until there was nothing left to come up, and even then I struggled to stop.

I felt a presence behind me. Before I could turn, Steel was kneeling next to me, his hand on my back. "Hey, beautiful. You doing okay?"

I sniffled. "Do I look like I'm okay?"

He cracked a smile. "Fair enough. You want to rinse your mouth and come sit down again? Or do you need to stay here a minute longer?"

A throat cleared and Meiling came into the room. "Not to put my nose where it doesn't belong but I'm going to assume you're like all the other men around here, which means the two of you have probably been fucking like bunnies. Any chance she's pregnant?"

Everything went still. The air thinned and I struggled to breathe a moment. Pregnant? I wasn't on birth control, and Steel hadn't used a condom any of the times we'd been together. Meiling was right about how often we'd had sex. But a baby? I tried to remember when I'd had my last period and realized I'd missed it by nearly a week. That would have meant I got pregnant possibly the very first time we had sex. If anything, past experience told me it only took once.

"Rachel." My gaze lifted to Steel's. "Darlin', could you be pregnant?"

"I-I don't know. Maybe? I didn't even think about it, but I'm late."

"Not to eavesdrop," Zoe yelled from the hallway, "but I'm totally listening and I happen to have some pregnancy tests at home. I'll get Guardian or Dagger to drop a few off if you'd like to have them. I'm sure one of my guys can be spared for a few minutes."

"Why do you have pregnancy tests?" Meiling asked. "You're already knocked up."

"You're pregnant?" I asked.

Zoe nodded. "I'm not really showing yet, plus I'm a little on the chunky side to begin with. Probably be another month or two before I have a noticeable baby bump. Well, something you can see through my clothes." She lifted the hem of her top and I saw the soft swell of her belly.

"Congratulations."

She flashed me a smile. "I'll just go make that call. I brought a few types of tea. When I get off the phone, I'll brew some peppermint. It should help settle your stomach."

I nodded and let Steel help me off the floor.

While I got cleaned up, the others left, leaving me alone with my husband. I leaned into him. He'd said he'd wanted a family, but I didn't know if he'd planned to have more kids right away. Looked like the decision was out of our hands.

He tipped my chin up, his fingers caressing my jaw. "Beautiful girl, I have no idea what's going through your mind right now."

"I want to be happy about a possible pregnancy, but then I remember Coral is out there, possibly hurt and scared. Victoria could be dying. And I just... What if we can't get her back? What if she's gone, Isaac?"

"She's not gone. They need her, Rachel. Nothing is going to happen to our daughter. I'll track the assholes down, get her back, and we'll put all this behind us."

I knew I needed to trust he'd keep his word. Steel hadn't given me a reason to doubt him. What scared me the most was him leaving to get Coral, and neither of them coming home. If Steel went to confront the Mulligans, they could hurt him. Kill him. When I'd dated Patrick I'd had no idea who his family was, or their connections. Now that I did, it scared the hell out of me. I clung to Steel, too frightened to let go.

Zoe popped her head around the doorway, then stuck out a hand. She had two boxes. "I lucked out. Guardian was already home picking up something, he dropped these off."

Steel took them from her, then shut the door. He ripped into the package and held the stick out to me. "I'm assuming you've done this before, with Coral, and don't need instructions."

My cheeks heated. "Are you going to stay here while I..."

"Pee on the stick?" he asked, a smile lurking at

the corners of her mouth. "Yeah, I'm staying here with you. I've had my mouth on your pussy, put my dick in there. You taking a pregnancy test isn't going to gross me out or chase me off. Although, maybe you should take both. Can you stop peeing mid-stream?"

I sighed and took it from him, then dropped my pants and panties. I hovered over the toilet, feeling more than a little mortified, as I took the pregnancy test. He handed me the second one after I set the first test on the counter. When I'd finished, I set it on the counter next to the other one. While I cleaned up, Steel studied the little sticks and read the fine print inside the boxes. It seemed they were different types, and didn't show results the same way.

"It says three minutes on both of them," he said. He pulled out his phone and set the timer before tugging me into his arms. "You know, if these tests come back positive, there's no fucking way I'm letting you go into a room with the Mulligans, or anything else involved with taking Coral. Your safety, and that of our child, will come first."

"That's hardly fair. And sexist."

"Really? You want to go there?"

No, I didn't. I already knew I'd lose. It wasn't that Steel didn't find me capable, but he had alpha-protector written all over him. If he thought for one minute I could get hurt, or the baby could, then he'd do whatever it took to keep me safe. It was just the sort of man he was. It hadn't taken me long to learn that about him.

The timer went off and he picked up both tests, a grin spreading across his lips. He kissed me hard and deep, making my knees go weak. I glanced at the sticks. One had two lines, the other said "positive." Looked like I was having a baby.

"You have made me the happiest man, beautiful. Go drink your tea and sit with the ladies. I'm going to find out exactly who has Coral, where they took her, then I'm getting our daughter back. She needs to know she's going to be a big sister."

I went to the kitchen and sat down again. My emotions were pinging all over the place and my mind was seconds from coming apart. It was all too much at once. I could tell they were anxious to hear the news. When I told them the tests were positive, Zoe squealed like a teenager and threw her arms around me.

"This is so exciting! Our babies will grow up together. All of ours. Elena's little Valeria is nearly a year. Same for Lilian's Ronan and Mila. Adalia's Gunner is about a year and a half, same for Meiling's Wen. And now our babies will be born close together."

"So, everyone has either recently had a baby, or is pregnant." I let that sink in a moment. "Would it be wrong to spike their beer supply with something that suppresses sperm? Is there such a thing?"

Meiling snickered. "I don't think anything could kill the super sperm the Devil's Fury seem to have."

China glanced at her daughter, warmth lighting her eyes. "And it started with you."

I didn't understand and the confusion must have shown on my face. Meiling took pity on me to explain.

"I didn't know I had parents," she said. "I went into foster care when I was a toddler. My mother was sent somewhere awful, and my dad was sent to prison for something he didn't do. I didn't find out until after I'd met Dingo that my dad was a member of this club, and both he and my mother were alive."

I glanced from one woman to another, studying each and every one. Meiling seemed to have had a tragic past. Lilian had said she was adopted, and she'd been kidnapped. It made me wonder about the others. "Did something bad happen to each of you?"

China and Meiling shared a look. It was China who spoke. "My daughter and I were both turned into prostitutes. Except she was a teenager before she suffered that fate. We're... healing. Some days are easier than others. Dingo accepted her, saw her for the jewel she is, and loves her. And Blades... there is a lot of history between us. He hasn't claimed me, but we live together here at the compound. I still struggle with all I've been forced to do and don't feel worthy of him."

My heart broke for the both of them. I looked at Elena, who gave me a sad smile.

"I'm also adopted. But not by anyone here. An evil preacher took me in, tried to marry me off to a guy who was really bad news. Outlaw kept me safe and I fell in love with him."

Lilian braced her arms on the table. "I told you I was adopted by Grizzly, but didn't say why. Another club, the Devil's Boneyard, went to Colombia to rescue one of their men. I'd been held captive, forced to service fighters who were just as much as slave as I was. The Devil's Boneyard brought me to the US and Grizzly took me into his home. I was only a teenager back then.

"I also have another adopted sister. Shella. She's not here right now. My dad sent her to the Devil's Boneyard for a bit, and she apparently took off. Her mother was a drug addict, but Shella's half-sister is the daughter of a Boneyard member. Irish kept his daughter and Grizzly brought Shella home."

I glanced at Zoe, wondering if she had a similar story. She traced a pattern on the table a moment, and when she spoke, her accent was far thicker than I'd ever heard before.

"I agreed to work in a sweatshop in order to bring Luis to the US, except the man had no intention of keeping his word. Someone overthrew him, and I was brought here with a handful of other women. Outlaw married me to Dagger, much the way he did with you and Steel. Then I fell for him and Guardian. Dagger and a few others went to Mexico to bring Luis home."

I had a feeling there was more to it than that. It was obviously these women had suffered greatly, perhaps more so than me. Yes, Coral had been taken, but I hadn't been raped, abused, or suffered in other ways. I'd run from the Mulligans so they wouldn't take my daughter, and while there had been strange accidents, I hadn't been physically hurt yet. I'd worried they'd stop at nothing to get her. Even kill me. But as I studied these strong women, I knew it could have been worse.

"I admire you. All of you," I said.

China gave me a startled look. "You... what?"

"The things you went through, the fact you're all sitting here. China, you have your daughter and Blades back in your life. You're safe. Everything that happened to you, you managed to survive and you're still standing. And your daughter obviously has that same strength."

I saw tears mist her eyes as she gazed at Meiling.

I looked at Elena, and wondered if she knew how remarkable she was. "You were open to letting Outlaw into your life, loved him, and fought to stay with him. And don't try to tell me you sat idly by while he saved you. I won't believe it. Not after your comment about claiming him."

She gave me a faint smile. My gaze landed on

Lilian, who looked seconds from crying. I reached over and took her hand, giving it a squeeze.

"I can only imagine how scared you were in Colombia. By all rights, the men who showed up that day should have scared you, but you took a chance to get on a plane with them, move to another country and start your life over. You not only overcame all that, but survived a kidnapping, and having twins! Good lord! Coral runs me ragged, especially when she was smaller. Anyone dealing with two babies at once deserves a medal."

She snickered a little and looked to Zoe. I didn't really know her well, even though we'd talked a great deal before. Still, she was the first woman in a long time that I thought of as a friend. Sometimes when you met someone, you just knew. And Zoe and I had that instant connection. As the saying went, sisters from another mister. Or something equally silly.

"And you... the love you have for Luis, the determination to give him a better life, suffering to make it happen. There's nothing greater than the dedication of a mother to her children, but I have a feeling you organized this little gathering, which means you're just as dedicated to this club and these women. I'm honored to know you, Zoe." My gaze scanned them. "All of you."

I hadn't heard Steel walk in, but he placed his hand on my shoulder and I smelled his cologne. I tipped my head back to look up at him, and he winked at me. I knew he'd heard what I said, and the look on his face clearly said he was proud of me.

"I have to go, beautiful. Might be gone a while."

I stood and faced him. "You found her?"

He nodded. "We think so. I'm leaving, along with Dagger, Demon, and Wolf. Since Coral is familiar with Matt, he's going to come too, but he'll ride in the truck. Coral will ride back with him."

I fisted his shirt and pulled him closer. "You come home to me. Understood? I want *both* of you here. In one piece."

Steel cupped the back of my neck and kissed me. "I'll always come home to you. You need anything while I'm gone, call Grizzly or Slash. You haven't met Slash yet, but he's the VP."

I frowned. "Steel, I can't call anyone. I don't have a phone right now."

His eyebrows lifted. "How were you going to get calls about potential jobs?"

"The motel room had a landline. I couldn't afford the service on my phone, and maybe I've watched too many crime shows, but I thought it could be traced. I left it behind when we came here. They found us anyway."

"I'll get Slash to stop by with a phone in a bit. He'll program some numbers in for you, including mine. And when I get back, we'll discuss the fact you needed something and didn't tell me."

I cuddled against his chest and hugged him tight. Breathing him in, I felt tears prick my eyes. I knew he needed to go, and I wanted our daughter back, but I was worried I might never see him again. I hoped I was wrong, that he'd walk through the doors without a scratch on him.

I lifted my gaze to his. "Love you, Isaac."

I said it softly so no one else would hear his name, but it seemed important to use his real name when telling him I loved him for the first time. He gave me soft smile before kissing me again, then put his lips near my ear. "Love you too, beautiful."

He pulled away and walked off. I trembled as I

sat down again. Zoe reached over and took my hand. "He'll be fine. Steel is a tough bastard. He went with Dagger to bring Luis home. Fought the Mexican cartel and freed a bunch of kids. This will be a walk in the park for him."

I hoped so. Because I didn't know how I'd live without him.

Chapter Twelve

Steel

I'd packed an overnight bag for myself, and loaded a bag of stuff for Coral, which I'd put into the truck with Matt. I didn't know what she'd need other than some clothes and maybe a few toys, but I'd wanted her to feel safe when we found her. The vet had called before I left to say Victoria made it through surgery, but she wasn't out of the woods yet. I'd have taken her with me if she hadn't been in such bad shape, knowing how much Coral loved that little dog.

What should have been a five-hour trip, roughly, took us more like three and a half. To say the lot of us were motivated was an understatement. The fact we'd picked up a few Dixie Reapers along the way, and were now flanked with three Hades Abyss and two Reckless Kings made me smile. There'd been a time my family was only my club. Now we had connections with so many other clubs, both in the south and heading out west.

Sarge, Wraith, and Grimm looked like they'd come ready for war. I saw no less than four weapons on each, and had no doubt they'd stashed more in their saddlebags. Knox, Fangs, and Dread were just as prepared, except Dread had a black bag at his feet. I didn't know much about Dread, not having been to the Hades Abyss before. I glanced at the bag, wondering if weapons were inside, or something else. He smirked and bent down to unzip it. The medical equipment inside surprised me.

"To the outside world, I'm Dr. Thomas," Dread said. "I'm sure your daughter is fine, but I thought it best to come prepared."

"I appreciate it," I said.

I glanced at Crow and Brick from the Reckless Kings. I didn't even know how they'd known about Coral, or where to meet us, but I had a feeling the Reapers were to thank. Unless... I narrowed my eyes. "Did Lilian call Beast?"

Crow smirked. "Yep."

I had no doubt Dragon would bust her ass when he found out. The fact Lilian had stayed with Beast when she'd run away was still a sore spot with him.

"What? No Devil's Boneyard?" Wraith asked. "I'll have to tell Bull his father-in-law is slipping."

I snorted. Yeah, that would go over well. Not only Bull calling Scratch his father-in-law, but taking the Devil's Boneyard VP to task. He wouldn't fucking dare unless he had a death wish.

"Wire said he had visual confirmation your daughter was inside," Sarge said, tipping his head to the dirt drive in front of us. The images I'd seen before heading this way showed a large house back in the woods. "They have four guards patrolling the outside, and from what he could see, another four inside, plus Coral and the Mulligans."

"Does this seem a little easy to anyone else?" I asked.

Sarge nodded. "I was thinking the same thing."

I looked over my shoulder, where Matt remained in the truck. I'd asked him to keep it running. The moment I was able to get Coral out of the house, I wanted her in that vehicle and heading home.

Grimm noticed the direction of my gaze. "He's taking Coral once we extract her?"

I nodded.

"I'll ride along, make sure they don't find trouble," he said. "You'll need to stay here and finish things."

Crow and Brick shared a look. The Native American gave me a nod. "We'll go with Coral too."

Wraith rubbed his hands together. "All right. The rest of us get to have some fun."

I snorted, but I knew the man wasn't kidding. He might be fucked up in the head, but Wraith was downright lethal, and I was glad to have him on our side. His family had mellowed him a little, from what I'd heard. Didn't mean I'd want to be on opposing sides or meet the bastard in a dark alley.

"Do we even have a fucking plan?" Fangs asked.

"I'm going in through the rear door," I said. "I'll take down the guard back there. My first priority is getting Coral out. Once she's safe, I want the Mulligans to suffer."

Crow held up a hand. "I'll scout and check in. Wouldn't hurt to have an open line to Wire, if he's able to see what's happening."

Sarge pulled out his phone. "On it."

While Crow surveyed the area, and Sarge spoke to Wire, I felt a nervous energy thrumming inside me. I'd never felt like this before going to war. A calmness always settled over me right before I entered enemy territory, but this was different. I wasn't taking down insurgents because the government ordered it, or rescuing random strangers. This time it was personal. Coral was my daughter.

Once the number of guards were confirmed, we made our move. We fanned out and approached the house, each of us creeping silently through the woods. I approached the rear and lurked in the shadows, waiting for my chance. Taking him out from a distance would be simpler, but I wanted this fucker's blood. I wasn't about to give him a quick and easy death. Even if he hadn't personally snatched Coral, he was part of her abduction just by being here.

He turned to pace the other direction, and I moved swiftly, staying low to the ground. I pulled the blade I kept on me at all times. Before he had a chance to even sense my presence, I came up behind him, held my hand over his mouth, and pressed the blade against his side.

"One fucking sound, and I will gut you like a fish. Understood?"

He gave a quick jerky nod.

"My daughter. Where is she?" I removed my hand and he sucked in a breath. Wire had seen her on the camera footage, but I wanted to be certain they hadn't faked it somehow, or worse, there could have been a delay in the feed.

"Second floor. Door's to the right when you get to the top of the stairs."

"You've been most helpful. Sadly, you chose the wrong child to abduct." I covered his mouth to stifle his cries as I jammed the blade into his side. I yanked it free and stabbed him in the kidney. Three quick jabs. Dropping the asshole to the ground, I hovered as he spat blood. I made a quick slice across his throat, then I stepped over him to enter the house.

Another guard was to my right, a cigarette hanging from his mouth as he tried to light it. I didn't give him time to even take a drag. I threw my knife, the blade embedding in his chest. His eyes went wide as the cigarette fell from his lips. I didn't want anyone to hear his body hit the floor, so I caught him and eased him down. Pulling the blade free from his body, I wiped the blood on his pants.

Movement caught my eye and I glanced that way, seeing Brick taking down another guard. Sick fucker was smiling as he snapped the guy's neck. I crept up the staircase. Sheathing my knife, I drew the nine-millimeter from the small of my back. I took the suppressor from my pocket and screwed it onto the custom threaded barrel. I crouched at the top, a half-wall hiding me. I spied the landing. Only one guard on this floor, and he wasn't even paying fucking attention. Trusting the others had the rest of the guards handled, I sent two shots into the bastard's chest. The look of surprise that crossed his face made me smile.

I opened the door to my right and spied Coral in the middle of the bed. Some froufrou dress I knew damn well we hadn't bought her covered her. She'd hugged her knees to her chest and stared out the window, as if she were waiting for something. Or someone?

"You ready to go home?" I asked.

She jolted, eyes wide, as she turned to face me. A smile spread across her face as she scurried off the bed and raced for me. I held up a hand, not wanting to chance I might have blood on me.

"You came, Daddy! I knew you would."

I knelt. "Of course, I did. You're my daughter, Coral. I'll always find you."

I held out my hand and she took it. Leading her downstairs, I scanned the area. I didn't see the Mulligans, but I did find Crow waiting at the front door.

"Coral, this is Crow. He's a friend." She stared up at me. "You remember Matt? He helped us the night I brought you and your mom home with me?"

She nodded.

"Matt is waiting down at the street in a truck. Go with Crow and he'll take you to Matt. I'll be behind you shortly, sweetheart, but I need to take care of something first."

Her eyes filled with tears. "They hurt Victoria."

"I know, baby. Victoria is at the animal hospital. They did surgery and I think she'll be okay, but we won't know for sure just yet. We can go see her tomorrow. Right now, I need you to be a good girl and leave with Crow. You can trust him."

She took Crow's hand and they walked out of the house. Sarge came up on my left and tipped his head to a closed door. "Have the Mulligans in there. Ballsy people didn't think they'd get caught. Rounding them up was like luring a kid with candy. Too fucking simple."

"They're connected to the Irish mob," I said. "They can't be that docile."

"I'm thinking they don't get their hands dirty much and always hire someone else to do the distasteful parts."

I nodded, thinking it made sense. I hadn't met too many rich assholes who liked to take out the trash themselves. Not saying all people with money were like that, but I'd met enough who were.

"Before you go in there, you should know we put plastic under them. Covered the floor with it. Knox found rolls of the shit down in the basement. These aren't sweet, innocent people by far. Even if they don't do the deed themselves, they still call the shots."

"What else aren't you saying?" I asked.

"Fangs is setting up the space as a kill room. Said he and Knox would hang back when you're done, take care of the cleanup."

I owed these men a debt once all this was over. I followed Sarge to where the Mulligans were being held. Someone had tied them to chairs in the middle of the room. The plastic crinkled under my boots as I walked across the floor, stopping in front of the youngest Mulligan.

"You are one stupid little shit," I said. "She loved you, until you treated her and your kid like trash, threw them away. Personally, I'm thankful. Means I get to keep them. Unlike you, I know a good thing when I see it."

Patrick didn't say a word, just stared a hole in the floor. He had those pretty boy looks so many women went nuts over, so maybe Rachel had found him attractive. I didn't see anything else remarkable about him. He was weak. Pathetic. A bully. My gaze swung to his parents, who were both glaring at me.

"And you two. Not even wanting your own grandchild until you could benefit from her existence? Ending your lives will give me great pleasure. The world will be better off without people like you. If you're even human. Far as I can tell, you're just shells filled with evil, walking and talking. You may fool others, but not me."

"You won't get away with this," the elder Mulligan said.

"Sean Mulligan." I shook my head. "You think you're big and important? Think someone will avenge your death? More than likely, someone else will move on your territory, take it over, and you'll be forgotten by tomorrow. No one gives a rat's ass about you, except for what you can do for them. Know what you can do when you're dead? Nothing."

"You'd kill an innocent woman?" Cait Mulligan asked.

"No, I wouldn't. But you're far from innocent. In fact, I'd be willing to bet you were pulling some of the strings. All those unfortunate things happening to Rachel and Coral. They were your doing, weren't they? How the fuck did you even know where they were?

Rachel left behind anything you could track."

"Not everything." Cait gave me a chilly smile. "She didn't leave Coral. You think I didn't have someone watching my granddaughter? Bitch never even knew she was followed. Should have snatched the brat sooner."

"Just kill us and be done with it," Patrick muttered. "Once a man's dick doesn't work anymore, there's not much point in living. Just end it."

I cocked my head and watched him. Yeah, it had been a hard blow when he'd discovered he couldn't fuck anyone ever again. Too bad he'd only lived with that knowledge a short while. If I didn't worry what he'd do to Coral or Rachel, I'd let him go. Death was too kind for him. I liked the idea of him suffering for another twenty or thirty years, maybe longer if he didn't piss off someone else.

"I'm thinking that fiancée of yours will thank me for ending your life. Now she won't be stuck with a man who can't satisfy her. Then again, according to Rachel, even when your dick did work, you still didn't know what to do with it." I leaned into his space. "Don't worry. I gave her plenty of screaming orgasms to make up for all she'd missed out on with you. And the baby I planted in her belly will be loved by two parents from the day they're born. That's what it means to be a real man."

Sarge, Fangs, and my brothers surrounded me. I knew they would let me seek my revenge, end the Mulligans with my own two hands, no matter how much they wanted to help. The only one of interest to me was Patrick. They could have the other two.

Demon handed me a long pipe he must have found in the basement. "Thought you might like your signature weapon."

I hefted the steel cylinder in my hands and faced Patrick. He looked a little green as he eyed it. I swung, putting all my strength into it, and slammed it into the side of his knee. He screamed like the little bitch he was, and started pleading for mercy. I didn't have any. Not for him. I broke his kneecaps, his hands, his ribs. When he was spitting up blood, and barely coherent from the pain, I dropped the pipe and pulled my knife. I sliced the material of his shirt, spreading it open.

As much satisfaction as I'd get from ramming the blade into him a few hundred times, that wasn't good enough. I made shallow cuts along his chest and abdomen before slicing off his nipples. His screams wouldn't sway me. Fucker should be glad I hadn't sliced off something else. He'd hurt my woman. Came after my kid. When I was finished, he'd never harm another person ever again. I took my time, drawing his pain and suffering out as long as I could.

"He's nearly dead, Steel," Demon murmured. "Finish it now and you can catch up to your daughter. Maybe clean up first. You look like the villain in a slasher flick."

I jammed the blade through Patrick's temple, snuffing out his pathetic life. His mother wailed and hurled curses at me, but she wasn't my problem. Not anymore. I'd let the others have her, do whatever they wanted as long as her death wasn't quick. The unholy light in Demon's eyes told me he'd see to Cait and Sean Mulligan, and probably find a great deal of pleasure in their suffering. He'd damn well earned his name.

I used the bathroom to clean as much of the blood off me as I could, enough so it wasn't noticeable and wouldn't draw attention. I walked down the long drive to my bike. Once I hit the highway, I opened her up and broke every traffic law known to man in order to catch up to Coral. It only took me fifteen minutes before I saw them ahead of me. I passed Brick and Crow, who'd taken up the rear, then slowed so I could pull up next to the truck. Little Coral was in the backseat. The moment she saw me, relief lit her features and she waved. I smiled and waved back, then remained where I was until Matt pulled off for a quick stop.

I had my daughter. The Mulligans were finished. Now it was time to get on with our lives, celebrate our little family, and make some happy memories. And I knew just where to start...

Chapter Thirteen

Rachel

Steel hadn't called or messaged me, and then I'd realized he probably didn't know the number to the phone I'd been given. Even though he'd arranged for me to have one, Slash had delivered it. There was a chance the VP of the club had texted the number to my husband, but no guarantee. My fingers shook as I pulled up his name under contacts and send a quick text. If he was busy, or in danger, I didn't want to distract him. *I hope you're safe.*

My phone chimed almost immediately with a reply.

I'm good, and so is Coral. On our way home. Right after, I received a picture of him leaning in close to Coral, both of them smiling. My little girl was safe. Steel was safe. I placed a hand over my belly. Soon, my family would be back together.

My heart soared at the news, and I couldn't help but smile. He'd gotten our daughter back! They were coming home to me. I sank onto the couch in the living room and stared at the TV. Now that I wasn't a big ball of nerves and anxiety, I could relax a little. Meiling and China had been the last to leave earlier. They'd put a romantic comedy on, claiming I needed something lighthearted. That was hours ago, but whatever app they'd used kept playing more and more movies. Even though my family was safe, I still couldn't focus on much of anything. My thoughts were racing and I had a nervous energy I couldn't shake.

I stood and paced the living room. I knew exactly what I needed to do. Coral and Steel might be hungry when they arrived. The meal I'd made before had dried out, probably from cooking it too long while I worried over Coral. I checked the kitchen and frowned when I realized I was lacking the ingredients for what I wanted to make. I didn't think cooking was an emergency, but I called Slash anyway. Making something for Steel and Coral would keep me busy, help pass the time, and they might appreciate my efforts when they got here.

"Everything okay?" he asked when he picked up.

"Steel texted me. He's on his way home with Coral."

"So you're calling because you just like the sound of my voice? Needed to share the good news? Both?" he asked, his voice tinged with humor.

"I want to cook and bake," I blurted. "I need ingredients from the store."

"Tell you what. Whatever you're baking, make extra for me and I'll go get whatever the hell you need. Make a list and I'll come get it."

"Thank you! Front door's unlocked."

He growled and I knew I'd made a mistake admitting that last part, but I'd heard several bikes drive past every hour since Steel left. I knew they were keeping an eye on me. Once the Mulligans had Coral, they had no use for me anyway. I'd just been in the way.

I hung up and raced to find a pen and paper. Once the list was made, I set it on the kitchen counter. When I'd met the VP earlier, he hadn't been quite what I'd expected, not after meeting Grizzly. I didn't know what his true hair color was, as he'd dyed it a dark blue with green tips. It seemed odd for a biker, especially one who looked like he was in his late thirties or early forties, but then I'd realized he had a good sense of humor and was a bit playful. The colored hair suited his personality from what little I'd seen so far.

Slash stepped into the kitchen. "Little girl, your man is going to paddle your ass when he finds out you left the door unlocked while all this shit is going on."

"I know you've had people watching the house. Besides, it wasn't me they wanted. Only Coral."

Slash ran a hand over his hair, disrupting the spiky strands and making them stick out like a porcupine's quills. "Got it ready?"

I handed the list over. "You don't seem like the type to be VP of a motorcycle club."

His eyebrows lifted and he studied me until I squirmed. It seemed I'd said the wrong thing. Had I insulted him?

"So, it's like this. My dad was a real asshole. Part of an outlaw club that was into heavy shit. Murder. Rape. Nothing was out of bounds with them. Had kids from a bunch of different women. He'd get them pregnant and ditch them. Thankfully, the bastard is dead now after he tried to hurt my sister, Josie. But growing up on the wrong side of town, and having that bad blood in my veins, I did some stupid shit when I was younger. Spent some time in prison."

"But you've changed?" I asked.

"Maybe a little." He held his thumb and forefinger a small space apart. "The point is this club saved me. Grizzly saved me. Gave me a spot, taught me to control my anger. When he needed a VP, he told me I was taking it. Didn't ask. Just said it was mine. I would do anything for this club, and anything for the Pres. They're my family. My life. And that now includes you."

"I get the feeling the guys here aren't as scary as I'd first thought. Grizzly included."

Slash winked. "Only nice to the pretty girls.

Unless it's Guardian and Dagger. Before they married Zoe, they were nice to the pretty boys too."

I snorted, then nearly doubled over laughing. When I was able to catch my breath, I put my arms around Slash and gave him a quick hug. He hesitated a moment before wrapping his arm around my waist and giving me a slight squeeze.

"Thank you," I said. "For everything. But especially for making me laugh. I needed it."

He held up the list. "Back in a bit."

While I waited, I tidied the house, made sure all the laundry was caught up, and I set out all the cooking utensils I'd need. I called the vet to check on Victoria. Even though she wasn't out of the woods, they seemed confident she'd be okay. I truly hoped so or my little girl was going to be heartbroken. I was starting to think she loved that dog more than me.

By the time Slash came back, I'd cleaned the house twice, taken stock of any supplies running low, and paced until I'd nearly worn a groove in the floor. He stuck around only long enough to ensure I was okay. I set out all the ingredients I'd need for the desserts first, since I'd promised Slash I'd make him some too, and put everything else away until I needed it.

I hadn't had a lot of opportunities to cook from scratch over the years, but following a recipe came easily to me, even when it involved baking. I made the pie filling, then rolled out the crust. I worked the dough around the pan and trimmed off the excess. After I smoothed the filling inside it, I rolled out more dough and cut it into strips for a lattice top. I made two apple and two cherry pies, thankful the oven was big enough to bake them all at once.

I cleaned up my mess, then pulled out the

ingredients for a lasagna. Except it seemed Slash was sneaky and hadn't bought only what I needed. No, he'd doubled it. I smiled, thinking it was likely his way of giving me a hint. It seemed he didn't just want pie, he wanted lasagna too. It made me wonder if the single men here ever got a decent home-cooked meal, unless they knew how to make one themselves.

A glance at the clock told me it wasn't too late to call my new friends. With Zoe being pregnant, I knew she might be more tired than usual. I decided to call Lilian instead. The fact she'd lived here before pairing off with Dragon might have factored into my decision a little. She didn't answer by the fifth ring and I hung up, not wanting to wake them if they were asleep already. Instead, I called Elena.

When she picked up, I heard a baby crying in the background.

"Um, bad timing?" I asked.

She laughed softly. "It's fine. Valeria is mad because her daddy put her down and she wants to be held. She'll get over it. Preferably before we go deaf."

I remembered those days. "I had a quick question. Slash ran to the store for me and asked for a pie as repayment. When I went to make a lasagna for Steel and Coral, I realized Slash had doubled the ingredients I'd asked for."

Elena snorted. "That man's about as subtle as a bull in a china shop."

"It made me think… there are a lot of single guys here. If they don't make their own meals, how often do they get home-cooked food? Not something from a box or frozen, but freshly made?"

"Never?" Elena asked. "I honestly hadn't put much thought into it. I know whenever we've had any sort of family gathering the men descend on the food like locusts."

"I realize we're all moms and exhausted on the best of days, but would you and the others be interested in doing a food rotation of sorts? Maybe twice a week we could make a few pans of something like pasta or a casserole and leave it at the clubhouse for the guys who don't have a woman at home?" I asked. "Or even just once a week. I thought it might be a nice gesture."

"Mm-hm. And would this nice gesture by any chance be an attempt at showing them how much nicer their lives would be if they settled down and stopped bringing those club whores around?"

I bit my lip. It hadn't been my intention, not consciously, but I had to admit I liked the idea of not having those women around anymore. Or at least not as often. What if Coral wandered down by the clubhouse when she got a little older and saw those women? I wasn't ready for those sorts of questions, not until she was at least fifteen or sixteen. I knew it was doubtful I'd be able to keep her blinded that long, but I could hope.

"I'll talk to the others," Elena said. "I have a feeling they won't mind. We could even pair up. With there being six of us now, seven counting China, if two of us made something complementary and took it over once a week, we not only wouldn't have to make so much by ourselves each time, but every few weeks the guys would get a different type of food. Although, I'm not sure how much cooking China does. I don't want to leave her out, though, assuming she wants to do this with us."

"Just let me know and we can set up a rotation or something. I think it would be fun, and I'm betting the club would love it."

"Maybe you should have married Slash instead," Elena said. "You'd be great as an old lady for the VP or Pres."

"I think Steel is all I can handle."

After I hung up, I got to work on the two lasagnas, thankful Steel had two pans I could use. If I'd known Slash wanted one too, I'd have asked him to get a disposable one at the store. The last thing I wanted to do was track him down to get a dish back. I pulled the pies from the oven and set them aside to cool, then finished layering the lasagnas and slid them into the oven.

The sound of a motorcycle pulling up out front had me racing for the door. They shouldn't be here already, should they? My heart pounded as I yanked the door open and tears pricked my eyes as I watched Steel get off his bike. I ran for him, but he held up his hands before I could throw myself into his arms.

"Easy, beautiful. I'm a little messy even though I cleaned up a bit before I headed home. Let me shower and change. Matt isn't far behind me with Coral."

My gaze skimmed over him, and I didn't notice it at first. Gradually, the darker spots on his cut came into focus, and when he shifted, I saw droplets of blood on his shirt. "Steel... is that..."

"Blood? Yeah, darlin'. It is. Not mine, and not Coral's."

My shoulders sagged in relief. "Good."

He kissed my cheek as he walked past me into the house. I hurried to catch up and started the shower for him while he undressed. I eyed the clothes on the floor and the cut he'd set on the counter. I had no idea how to get blood out of leather. The shirt would come clean easy enough with some stain remover.

Steel tapped on the glass of the shower door.

"Just leave it. I'll handle all that when I get out. Don't want that asshole's blood touching you."

"He's... dead?" I asked.

"You really want to know?"

I gave a quick nod.

"Made sure he won't hurt anyone else. Demon and the others remained behind to handle Cait and Sean Mulligan, and clean the place up when they're done. No one is coming for Coral, or you. If there's any backlash from them disappearing, we'll deal with it."

"Oh, God. I hadn't even thought... can they trace their deaths back here?" I asked.

"Not after Wire and Outlaw are finished. They're erasing any footage from the security feeds, setting off a virus to wipe out any systems that had access to it, and are going to make it look like the Mulligans left the country."

I started to ask if they could really do all that, but then I remembered how easily Outlaw had married us. It made me grateful he used his powers for good and not evil. Steel stepped out of the shower and I handed him a towel, biting down on my lips as I watched the water droplets run down his body. His cock twitched and started to grow. My breath caught and I took an involuntary step closer.

Steel chuckled and covered himself with the towel. "Much as I love that look on your face, and want to do whatever just crossed your mind, Coral will be here any minute. We don't have time, beautiful. But later? That's a different story."

He pulled me to him, kissing me breathless. The front door slammed, breaking us apart, and I staggered away from him, feeling drunk and entirely too warm. My lips tingled and I knew my nipples were hard. I tried to get myself back together by the time I reached the front entry. Matt was leaning against the wall, but I didn't see Coral.

"She's looking for Victoria," he said softly.

My heart ached. "I'll go find her and explain."

"Think Steel already did, but..." He shrugged.

I found Coral in her room, holding the toy she'd picked out for Victoria. Tears fell down her cheeks as she looked up at me. "It's my fault she's not here."

"Oh, sweetheart. No! It's not your fault, not even a little." I knelt in front of her, taking her into my arms. "She wanted to protect you because of how much she loved you. I spoke with the vet just a little bit ago and they said she's doing well. I bet we can go see her tomorrow even if she can't come home yet."

"That's what Daddy said, but I hoped he was wrong and she was home waiting on me."

I felt Steel's presence before he stepped into the room. He hugged Coral and kissed the top of her head. "Your mom is right. We can go visit tomorrow, and you can tell her how much you miss her and love her. I'm sure that's just what she needs to hear in order to get better faster."

"Are the two of you hungry? I have a lasagna in the oven and made some pie for dessert."

At the word "pie," Steel smirked at me, making my cheeks heat.

"I'd love some pie," he said.

His shoulder shook with silent laughter as Coral broke free and raced toward the kitchen. I leaned in closer to him. "That was terrible! One day she's going to know what you mean."

"But that's not today, beautiful. We have a little more time before I have to find creative ways to get you all hot and bothered when the kids are around."

My eyes went wide and I placed a hand on my

belly. "Did you tell her?"

"Figured you'd want to do that together. Come on, before that little monkey climbs the counter and eats all the dessert."

"She better not. Two of those are for Slash since he went to get the ingredients for me."

We found Coral peering over the counter at the pies. Before we ate, I decided it was time she found out about the baby growing inside me. It had just been us for so long, and she'd only had a daddy for such a short time, I worried she wouldn't be all that happy about the news.

"Coral, you know how you used to ask for a little brother or sister?" I asked.

"Yeah. I used to ask for a daddy too, but now I have one." Her eyes went wide. "Am I getting a sister too?"

I glanced at Steel, who was fighting not to smile. "Well, I don't know if it will be a brother or sister, but there's a baby growing in mommy's tummy, just like you did. You'll have to teach them how to do all the important stuff only a big sister knows how to do."

Coral squealed, jumped out of her seat, and ran three laps around the kitchen table. Steel lost his battle and burst out laughing as I watched my daughter. It had gone better than expected. I only hoped she was this excited after the baby arrived and took up so much of our time.

Epilogue

Steel -- One Month Later

Dropping my daughter off at school still filled me with a joy I'd thought to never experience, even though I'd been doing it for a few weeks now. She always kissed my cheek before she got out of the SUV I'd bought for Rachel, then waved as she entered the school building. Despite her trouble making friends in the past, she'd made several at her new school. My girl was happy and thriving. She was going to be over the moon excited when she found out I'd already made plans for her summer break. One that included a trip to a certain location managed by a great big mouse. Rachel had confessed Coral had asked to go several times, but she'd never been able to afford it. While my wife was skeptical about going when our other kid would only be a few months old, I knew we'd be fine.

I made a few stops on the way back home, intending to surprise my sweet woman. She'd run herself ragged since Coral had come home, and it made my gut twist every time I caught her scanning her surroundings. I didn't know how long it would take for her to feel safe again. Even when I'd taken her to the doctor to confirm her pregnancy, her gaze had darted around as we'd walked into the building. If Patrick Mulligan wasn't already roasting in hell, I'd kill the fucker all over again for what he'd done to Rachel and Coral.

I found a parking spot partway down the main strip in town and pulled in. All my stops were along this road, and there was no point in re-parking every other block. I'd just haul it all with me and leave the car here. The maternity shop was the closest so I ran in there first. Rachel wasn't showing yet, but I'd caught her wistful expression as we'd passed this store the other day. To say I looked out of place was an understatement, and the woman behind the register looked ready to bolt at any moment.

Browsing through the racks, I selected two tops and two pairs of pants I thought my wife might like. It was the dress in the window I most wanted. I found it on the back wall and dug through until I found Rachel's size. The day would come when suddenly nothing fit right, and I wanted to make sure she was at least a little prepared. The woman had given me the greatest gift in the world and I was damn sure going to keep her as comfortable as possible.

I lay the purchases on the counter and the blonde tucked her hair behind her ear, her fingers shaking so hard she looked like an addict in need of a fix. After over thirty years in the Devil's Fury, I'd gotten used to the way people reacted to us. It was either flirtatious smiles, or fear.

"Relax. I'm just shopping for my wife. You're not in any danger," I said in what I hoped was a soothing tone. I'd sooner cut off my nuts than hurt a woman, but she didn't know that.

"Wife?" she asked, her gaze darting to my left hand. I held it up for her to see the ring. Hoping to set her more at ease, I showed her the screensaver on my phone -- Rachel and Coral. "Your daughter is cute."

"Thanks." I smiled. "Can't wait to find out if this one is a girl or boy. I think my daughter is hoping she'll get a sister."

She gave me a smile, and the tension in her body eased a little. I paid for the items and walked out. My next stop didn't require me to carry any packages. Meiling had told me the spa in town had a special for pregnant women. I booked an appointment for Rachel and paid in advance. All she'd have to do was show up. It was the last shop that was the most important.

Sweet Treats was bustling as always, but I'd placed my order in advance. I walked over to the pickup counter and gave the girl my name. She lifted the lid on the box so I could inspect my purchase before leaving. Everything was perfect.

I was careful going home, so I wouldn't toss the bakery box on the floor. I'd barely cleared the gates before a woman ran in front of me with Doolittle chasing after her. The kid had taken the house Griz offered and had decided to stay for the time being. The girl he'd rescued, however, was another matter. I hoped he got wise and shook loose of her sooner rather than later. There was something that wasn't adding up about her story, and I'd started to wonder if maybe a boyfriend hadn't abused her at all. If she'd made that shit up, I was going to personally escort her ass out of here. Too many women were in trouble out there for a bitch to lie about being in the same circumstances just to get her way.

Putting them out of my mind for the moment, I drove the rest of the way home. At one time, my house had been a refuge of sorts, but it had been empty. As I pulled into the driveway, I smiled at the changes Rachel and Coral had brought to my life and home. Flowers flanked the porch. A rocking chair sat to the left of the door. Coral had left her hoop and ball in the grass, and it looked like Victoria's rope toy was there too.

As if merely thinking of her had conjured my woman, she stepped outside. I got out and hadn't even closed my door before her arms were around me.

"I wasn't gone that long," I teased.

She gripped my beard and tugged me down

closer, her voice lowering. "Isaac, I'm pregnant and a raging mass of hormones. When my clit starts throbbing and I get all hot and wet, I need your cock. Not in an hour, right that very moment."

I had to admit, it was a perk of her pregnancy I'd enjoyed quite a bit. Except for the times she was insatiable. I'd gotten creative on ways to get her off after my dick decided he was done for the day.

"Is that right?" I asked. I slid my hand up her bare thigh and under the hem of her dress. "Should I just bend you over the car and take you right here and now?"

Her eyes dilated and her lips parted. The pulse in her throat raced. I didn't think she'd ever actually want to be fucked in public, but the idea of it certainly turned her on. Her gaze scanned the area but I laughed and smacked her ass.

"Inside, beautiful. I got a few things I need to carry into the house, then I'll take care of that little problem you're having."

"I-I..." She looked around again, and I wondered if maybe she'd become more adventurous than I'd thought.

"Unless you need me to take the edge off right now?" I asked.

She swallowed hard and nodded. Well, fuck me sideways. I slipped my hand back under her dress, the hood of the SUV hiding us from the waist down. I groaned when I realized the little vixen wasn't wearing panties.

"Such a naughty girl. No panties?" I brushed my fingers over her slit. Yeah, she was fucking soaked. "Did you play with this pussy while I was gone?"

She shook her head so hard I thought her neck might crack. "No. I didn't. I swear."

"Spread your legs, Rachel. Let me in."

Her thighs parted more and I was able to work my fingers inside her. She moaned and her eyes slid shut as her head tipped back. The move made her breasts thrust out, and her hard little nipples taunted me through the top of her dress.

"Isaac…"

"How far you willing to go, beautiful? No one's looking right now, but you know damn well that could change any moment."

"Anything. I'll do anything, just make me come. I need it. Need you. I hurt, Isaac."

"Unbutton the top of your dress. Let me see those pretty tits." She gasped but quickly worked at the buttons. The material gaped and I saw the creamy mounds of her breasts spilling out of her bra. "Show me."

She tugged her bra down and I lowered my head, taking one of her nipples into my mouth. I sucked on it hard, giving it a slight nip as I drove my fingers into her deeper. Rachel cried out, her pussy gripping me as she came. I yanked my fingers free with a growl and lifted her into my arms. Fuck the shit in the car.

I stalked up the porch steps and into the house, kicking the door closed behind me. I set Rachel down and spun her to face the wooden door. She grabbed at her dress, pulling it up over her hips. I couldn't remember a time I'd ever pulled out my cock as fast as I was now, but within seconds I was buried balls deep inside her, thrusting hard. I held onto her breasts, locking her in place as I fucked her.

A second orgasm hit her, pulling me under as well. I grunted as my balls emptied, my cum filling her up. Panting for breath, I leaned my forehead on her shoulder. "Fucking hell, Rachel. You're going to kill an old man."

She giggled and her pussy squeezed me.

"Think that's funny? You come out there teasing me like that again and I may damn well fuck you right out there in front of everyone."

"Sorry, Isaac. I'm just so…" Yeah, I knew exactly what she was. A horny pregnant woman who got cranky if I didn't get her off when she needed it. "It wasn't like this before. It's your fault."

"How do you figure?" I pulled out of her, but held her dress up so I could watch our mingled release slide down her thigh. Hottest thing ever.

"You're the one who showed me how great sex was, how amazing you could make me feel. Is it any wonder I want to experience that all the time now?" She turned to face me, reaching up to cup my cheek.

"No, beautiful. I like you wanting my dick that badly. Just not always a good time and place."

She bit her lip. "Isaac."

"You still need to come, don't you?"

She nodded. I couldn't help but laugh a little. In the last few weeks, her sex drive had kicked in and now the greedy little thing wasn't satisfied without five or six orgasms. I'd created a monster, but the best kind.

"Go get naked. I really do need to get that stuff from the truck."

I smacked her ass as she ran off, then I zipped up my pants and brought in her gifts. I put the bakery box on the kitchen counter and left the maternity clothes on the table. When I got to the bedroom, she'd stripped down and lay in the center of the bed -- starfished. Her hungry gaze landed on me, and I knew I'd give her anything she wanted, whenever she wanted. If it sent me to an early grave, at least my headstone would have something interesting to say.

I removed my clothes and got onto the bed, caging her between my arms. She was so fucking beautiful, so sweet. And until I'd showed her how amazing sex was, she'd been pretty damn innocent. Now she was pulling her tits out in the driveway and begging me to fuck her.

"You're amazing," I said softly. "Beautiful. Passionate. A great mother. Kind-hearted and thoughtful. You're the whole package, darlin', and I'm damn lucky to call you mine."

"Love you, Isaac."

I kissed her soft and slow. "Love you too, beautiful."

If someone had told me a few months ago I'd be lying here with my naked wife, I'd have laughed in their faces. I didn't know what or who put Rachel in my path that day, but I owed them one. Or a few hundred. She was everything I'd always wanted and thought I'd never have, and I'd spend the rest of my life making sure she never regretted choosing me. Her, Coral, and our unborn child were my world, and I'd die to keep them safe, just as I knew my brothers would protect them if anything ever happened to me.

She was mine, and I was never letting her go, even if I had to march straight into hell to keep her by my side.

Harley Wylde

Harley Wylde is the International Bestselling Author of the Dixie Reapers MC, Devil's Boneyard MC, and Hades Abyss MC series.

When Harley's writing, her motto is the hotter the better -- off the charts sex, commanding men, and the women who can't deny them. If you want men who talk dirty, are sexy as hell, and take what they want, then you've come to the right place. She doesn't shy away from the dangers and nastiness in the world, bringing those realities to the pages of her books, but always gives her characters a happily-ever-after and makes sure the bad guys get what they deserve.

The times Harley isn't writing, she's thinking up naughty things to do to her husband, drinking copious amounts of Starbucks, and reading. She loves to read and devours a book a day, sometimes more. She's also fond of TV shows and movies from the 1980s, as well as paranormal shows from the 1990s to today, even though she'd much rather be reading or writing.

Harley at Changeling: changelingpress.com/harley-wylde-a-196

Changeling Press E-Books

More Sci-Fi, Fantasy, Paranormal, and BDSM adventures available in e-book format for immediate download at ChangelingPress.com -- Werewolves, Vampires, Dragons, Shapeshifters and more -- Erotic Tales from the edge of your imagination.

What are E-Books?

E-books, or electronic books, are books designed to be read in digital format -- on your desktop or laptop computer, notebook, tablet, Smart Phone, or any electronic e-book reader.

Where can I get Changeling Press E-Books?

Changeling Press e-books are available at ChangelingPress.com, Amazon, Apple Books, Barnes & Noble, and Kobo/Walmart.

ChangelingPress.com

Printed in Great Britain
by Amazon